THE HERALD OF DAY

THE HERALD OF DAY

BOOK 1 OF THE BOAR KING'S HONOR TRILOGY

NANCY NORTHCOTT

Charlotte, NC

FALSTAFF
BOOKS

WWW.FALSTAFFBOOKS.COM

This is for Gerri Russell, a loyal, generous friend and a brilliant writer who always believed in this book.

CHAPTER 1

Dover, England
September 1674

Most of Dover's folk turned out for the witch's hanging. Merchants in fine silk and linen mingled with farmers and laborers in stained homespun. Shoulders hunched against the damp salt air, they chatted while they waited.

To see justice done. Or so they thought.

Miranda Willoughby knew better. Although she hid her own powers, they would alert her to anyone else's gifts, and she'd never caught a whiff of magic around old Mistress Smith. But saying so wouldn't save the woman. It would only win Miranda a hanging of her own.

"Black Bess, now," said a short woman, "she danced like a hen on a hot slate b'fore she died."

Her burly, male companion shook his head. "That don't compare to Jack Dawes, the highwayman—took near half an hour dyin'."

Their anticipation rasped across Miranda's magical senses as harshly as rough surf scraped the shore. Standing by a small cart in the midst of the crowd, selling hot bread from the inn where she worked, she steeled herself against the callous talk.

She'd known how people would react and so had pushed to be the maid chosen for this duty. While her limited magical skills could do little

1

to ease the doomed woman's passing, Agnes Smith would at least have one person in the crowd who recognized the injustice of her death.

"I seen a double hangin' in Canterbury," the inn's driver said from the cart seat. "Pair o' thieves danced a merry jig."

Standing by the front wheel, his friend nodded and grinned.

Miranda gritted her teeth. If only she could stop this. But Mother had died before she'd had the chance to teach Miranda more than summoning and glamours, and they were no use here.

She and the inn's driver had arrived early to secure a spot near the hanging tree, a stout oak. The noose dangled from a thick limb above the crowd's heads. Swaying in the moist ocean breeze, it taunted her with her lack of power.

To her right, a narrow, rutted dirt lane ran toward the town. The sheriff would bring the doomed woman that way.

The pie-seller's stand to Miranda's left did brisk business, and a juggler near the road collected coins in his upturned hat. Shrieking, laughing children chased each other through the fringes of the crowd.

A sturdy, blond man in rough woolen garb stopped beside her. "A hot cross bun, mistress."

He barely glanced at her, which was no surprise. Men didn't favor plain women, and she'd used her magic to become so. Her dark brown hair appeared thin and limp, her form scrawny, and her face pox-marked. In homeliness lay safety that was well worth its cost to her in other ways.

She uncovered one of the three pails in the back of the cart, where warm bricks kept the buns hot. A sweet, yeasty scent rose from the pail. Reaching in, she said, "That'll be a farthing, if you please, sir."

He passed her the coin and accepted his bread.

As he turned away, a shout rose from the crowd. They surged as one toward the road. Their bodies obscured her view of the approaching wagon, but its lone passenger, her aged face twisted with fear, stood high enough for Miranda to see.

People stooped, picking up rocks and dirt clods. Threw them at that helpless woman.

Miranda gripped the edge of her cart, the weather-worn wood biting into her palms. What use was power if you didn't know enough about it to help someone in need?

The sheriff's wagon rattled its way toward the tree. The crowd followed, gleeful over the woman's helplessness. A stone flew through the air and hit her shoulder. With her hands tied behind her, she couldn't deflect the missile. She cringed, turning into the path of a dirt clod that struck her temple.

Shuddering, Miranda swallowed against nausea. If she lost her breakfast, she'd draw attention she couldn't afford.

The wagon stopped under the tree, and the sheriff's men pulled the old woman out. They pushed her up onto a ladder below the noose and put the rope around her neck.

The sheriff stood in the wagon to read the sentence. The wind kept his words from carrying clearly, but Miranda caught some phrases. "For the crime of witchcraft ... Squire Mason's cows ... "

Miranda frowned. *Cows, hah!* This had more to do with Squire Mason's desire for the old woman's land. Everyone knew he'd tried to buy her little plot at an absurdly low price, which the widow had resented. That resentment had opened the way for the witchcraft accusation. As had the old woman's eccentric ways and homely, pox-scarred features.

Miranda's hand rose to the pox scar illusions on her cheek. Her disguise could have liabilities she hadn't expected.

"Hanged by the neck until dead," the sheriff finished. He rolled his parchment with a flourish and jumped from the wagon.

"I'm innocent. I done nothing!"

The crowd's derisive shouts drowned the old woman's screech. "Nothing anymore," a man yelled, and everyone laughed.

Sickened by the cruelty, Miranda stepped on the hub of one of the cart's wheels, boosting herself above everyone's heads. Her eyes sought the condemned woman's in the probably vain hope of making her last sight a kindly one.

"Now," the sheriff yelled.

Someone kicked the ladder away. Mistress Smith's body dropped, pulling the rope taut. She thrashed wildly in the air. In her reddening face, her eyes bulged. Her desperate, pleading gaze met Miranda's.

Miranda's stomach lurched, and she tasted bile. Swallowing frantically, she murmured, "Ease," and tried to push power into the words. "Stop the pain. Stop."

It wasn't working. Desperately, she whispered, "Stop!"

Nothing changed. Oh, if only she could do something. Anything!

Wrenching pain lanced through her head, and the crowd vanished. Purple-gray mists swept around her, swallowing the shouting, hooting voices.

Beneath her feet lay solid shadow, and the nasty odor of rotten eggs pervaded the dank, foggy twilight. Her neck and arms tingled with magic. With cold foreboding.

The fog receded, revealing a white boar—with blue eyes, not small, black, piggy ones—lying on a carpet of deep blue bordered in mulberry. It struggled to rise, its eyes dark with pain and mute appeal that wrenched her heart.

Above it loomed a red dragon bugling in triumph. White and green striations shimmered on the undersides of its spread wings. Blood dripped from its talons and flowed from gouges in the boar's side. She'd always loved tales of dragons, but this one's joy stabbed into her with the certainty that the creature was evil.

Summon the boar's knight, said a voice in her head.

Knight?

As she backed away from the gory tableau, the reeking fog closed around the images. A man's face flashed into her mind, his strong, stern features framed by a knight's helm. Clad in gleaming, silver armor, he galloped a black charger through the swirling vapors to confront the dragon.

On his left arm, he bore a shield emblazoned with twin stripes of mulberry and blue down the middle and a white rose backed by the rays of a sunburst in the center. Etched boars and sunburst roses covered his armor.

Beneath straight, dark brows, his blue eyes narrowed as he eyed the dragon and its prey.

If he opposed the dragon, did that mean he was a force for good? Her instincts said yes, but how could she know?

The dragon roared, a ground-shaking threat, and the knight's expression hardened. He slammed his visor shut, drew his broadsword, and spurred his mount to charge. The dragon belched flame.

No! He'd be killed.

The fog closed over the scene, then cleared.

Miranda found herself sitting on the ground by the cart, surrounded by half a dozen anxious townsfolk and the inn's driver. The vision, or whatever it was, was over. Gasping in relief, she clutched the arm supporting her.

Its owner was the last man who'd bought a bun. "Did you hit your head, mistress? Are y'all right?"

They were watching her—all looking at her face. Staring. Oh, no—

4

were her glamours—? But she could feel her power still shrouding her, holding them in place.

Shaky with relief, she scrambled upright. "I'm quite well. I thank you. I must have lost my balance."

Of course she had. That had felt like a true magical vision, as unexpected as it was disturbing. Until today, though, she hadn't used her magic for anything other than her glamours in years. Not since coming to the inn. Why would such a vision come to her now?

And why would a man fight a dragon for a boar?

She could worry about that later. Now she couldn't afford to draw so much notice. "I'm all right. Truly."

"Been hexed, more like," said an elderly woman in stern tones. "No tellin' what a witch'll do at the end."

If only the explanation were that simple, but Mistress Smith's limp body dangled at the edge of Miranda's vision. The old woman had passed beyond caring what anyone thought, God rest her soul.

Miranda mustered a weak smile. "I thank you, all of you. I'm quite well now."

"You missed the show," a man said. "Glad you're well, mistress."

Nodding her thanks, Miranda let the driver help her into the cart. The sooner she escaped all this attention, the better.

Wind rattled the window panes of the inn's empty common room, whispering of change and danger and warning. The glass blocked most of the chill, but Miranda shivered. Her hands tightened on the broom. The shadows the firelight cast over the familiar plaster walls and beamed ceiling felt ominous. Threatening.

There'd been no eerie wind the night Mother died, thirteen years ago, but Miranda had felt just as unsettled and anxious, on top of her heartbreak and grief. She'd been only nine then, but she'd never forgotten those feelings.

She set her jaw against the old pain. Perhaps she was imagining things, overwrought about today's injustice.

The hours since this morning's hanging had been too busy for pondering strange events. Now that she had time and quiet, she should puzzle out the strange vision, not chide herself over what she couldn't help.

As though summoned by her thought, the purple-gray fog blotted out sight and sound and scent. She stumbled. Caught herself on a bench.

The fog swirled aside to reveal a bedchamber. A young man, brown-haired and sturdy, writhed in pain on the floor. He was dying, and before his time, she somehow knew. From somewhere near, triumph poured over her like flood waters.

Miranda shuddered. Who could glory in that?

Skeletal creatures rushed, shrieking, out of the mists, and a cry choked in her throat.

"Miranda?" A familiar voice broke into the torrent, ending the horrible visions. Short, blonde Lucy, the friendliest of the other maids, hurried into the room.

"Are you ill?" Lucy picked up the broom.

Miranda didn't remember dropping it. "I'm all right," she managed. At least her glamours had remained steady.

"You're gray as an old sheet. I'll do this."

Miranda pushed herself to her feet. "My thanks, but I'm almost finished." Perhaps Lucy's calm presence would help keep at bay the warnings that seemed to hover in the air.

Lucy reluctantly surrendered the broom, and Miranda turned back to her task. The dying fire gave off little light and less warmth. Even with her unusually keen sight, she could barely see the worn, oak floorboards. She had once swept up a shilling, but tonight the broom caught only the usual rubbish, bits of tobacco, scraps of food, and too much tracked-in dirt.

Lucy settled onto a bench. "I can't believe we've had a witch so near. Why, she came in here from time to time. With her potions." She shuddered.

Miranda's fingers clenched on the broom. "Those potions were once well received." She couldn't stop the words, unwise though they were.

What would Lucy say if she knew how close she sat to a true witch?

"Well, we're safe now, anyway." Lucy paused, eyeing Miranda. "Ned says some of the farm lads would show an interest if you'd talk sweet to them now and again."

"And if I looked more fetching." Miranda forced a smile to push away the twinge of longing. Lucy and Ned would probably wed soon and then start a family. They didn't realize how fortunate they were, sharing an honest, open love.

Not having to keep secrets.

Lucy sighed. "If you didn't wear dresses what make you look like a stick—a crime, as well as you sew—or scurry away as though the lads had the plague, they'd overlook a few scars."

"I am as I am," Miranda replied. She pushed the last bit of dirt to the door. "I've no money for new dresses."

"Oh, Miranda." Lucy shook her head.

Miranda shrugged. Of course she wanted beautiful dresses and flattery, but safety lay in avoiding attention. Peace of mind lay in shunning, as her mother had not, ties to a man who couldn't know what she was. "Would you open the door, if you please?"

Lucy pushed aside the heavy latch, and Miranda whisked the dirt out before the shrieking wind could fling it back in their faces. A chill that owed naught to cold ran down her back.

"I'll bank the fire." Lucy knelt by the hearth.

"My thanks." Miranda set the broom in its corner, then threw the bolt on the door. Lucy meant to be a friend, but Miranda couldn't risk becoming close to anyone.

She swallowed a sigh. Loneliness, however bleak, was necessary. And safe.

The two women climbed to the garret together. Lucy chattered softly about Ned, but Miranda barely listened.

Without the distraction of chores, she couldn't ignore the wind's keening. Prickles of dread ran down her neck and along her arms.

The window at the end of the loft admitted a generous draft but only a narrow rectangle of moonlight. The other two maids, April and Sarah, already slept in the cold, darkened room. Miranda and Lucy undressed and dived into their beds.

Miranda pulled the thin coverlet over her ears. The wind's moan mocked her uneasiness.

Perhaps today's visions meant she knew—or could know—more than she thought. She closed her eyes, trying to remember what Mother had said.

Purple fog that reeked of rotten eggs swirled around her. The red dragon's roar mingled with the sound of a horse's galloping feet and an animal's squeal of pain.

Heart pounding, Miranda jolted awake.

In the next bed, April grumbled and turned over. No one else stirred. Miranda clenched her icy hands on the coverlet.

Mother had said foresight could come as visions or dreams, and she'd warned against ignoring such things. *Dire events will come to pass if you do,* she'd said.

If only Mother had lived long enough to teach her more about understanding what she Saw.

Still, thanks to the old tales Grandmother had told, Miranda did know dragons were symbols of power. The legends Grandmother loved said they were also beings of great wisdom.

Yet the one in the vision stood for evil—she'd felt that unmistakably—but what sort? What did the white boar symbolize?

Who was the knight the vision wanted her to summon? Armored knights were the stuff of legend, symbols of times long past.

She couldn't interpret the dream, but she knew summoning. It drew on the same illusion skills she used to create her disguising glamours. She could summon the knight or whatever he represented in the real world. If she dared.

Discovery would mean death.

She shivered. No. She couldn't do it. Wouldn't.

Others with Gifts, better trained, could deal in arcane visions. She couldn't risk it.

"**M**iranda? Miranda, I say!" Master Warren, the innkeeper, squeezed his thin frame between the common room's crowded tables. "That fellow by the hearth says he's tried right well to tell you he needs more stew, yet you seem not to hear him."

Miranda blinked. The bustle of the noon meal surrounded her. No vapory shadowland. No dragon or boar, but she'd been almost asleep on her feet.

She gritted her teeth in frustration. The troubling wind had died away after a day, but the strange visions and dreams continued to plague her. For the past three nights, she'd been unable to sleep because of them.

"I beg pardon, Master Warren. I'll fetch it at once."

"See that you do. You've been half asleep these past days, and you'd best awaken to your duties right now."

"Aye. I know, sir." The implied threat turned her insides to ice, for she had nowhere else to go.

Warren turned away, and Miranda rushed down the narrow, dark corridor to the kitchen. Plague take that dream! Having it torment her sleep was bad enough without it ruining her work or making her draw scrutiny.

She'd first created her glamours shortly before Father died, when men began looking at her in ways that made her skin crawl. She'd gradually made more changes before coming here. She knew what a serving maid's life was like, and she had no desire to draw attention from lecherous customers. As time passed, she'd realized the glamours also prevented anyone from looking closely enough to notice anything odd about her.

Until now.

In the hot, busy kitchen, Flora, the cook, and her two helpers sliced bread and meat and stirred kettles. A scrawny lad by the hearth turned the meat jack with one hand while wiping sweat from his brow with the other. Tiny, red-haired Sarah, one of other maids, waited by the long table in the room's center, tapping one foot impatiently while a cook sliced venison for her.

For once, Owen, the cheerful scullery lad, stood at his post near the door, so Miranda didn't have to wait. He dished up the hot stew and handed it to her on a tray.

She spun toward the door, but the opening was closer than she thought. Her shoulder banged into the door frame. Stew sloshed over her thumb, and scalding pain flashed up her arm. She choked back a cry but managed to stagger sideways, bracing the tray against the wall lest she drop it. Another mistake, and Warren might dismiss her.

Owen grabbed the tray. "I'll clean and refill it. Good thing only a bit spilled."

"Aye. My thanks." She blinked against the sting of tears. Spilling as much as half would've sent her to bed without supper tonight to make up the cost of the spilled food, even if she didn't lose her job. She wiped her throbbing hand on her apron.

The burn wasn't as bad as she'd feared but raw enough to hurt. She sucked the spot to ease it. If she weren't so weary, she wouldn't have made the mistake. Somehow, she had to manage a full night of uninterrupted sleep.

Owen brought the tray to her, and she hurried back to the common room.

She set the platter of stew and bread in front of her customer, a heavyset man whose suit of fine, green wool with simple lace at his wrists and throat marked him as gentry or a prosperous merchant. He thanked her with a grunt.

Turning, she almost collided with Lucy, who caught her arm to steady her. "Flora told me what happened. Are you hurt?"

"Not much." Miranda forced a shaky smile, shifting her gaze aside. A framed linen square over the hearth caught her eye. "Where did that sampler come from?"

It looked ordinary enough, a man and woman flanking a tree with a meticulously embroidered alphabet below them, but it hadn't been there yesterday. Or this morning.

Lucy's round face twisted in a frown. "You're lost more sleep than I thought. That's been here longer'n we have, made by Master Warren's wife before she died."

A chill ran down Miranda's spine. "Died when?"

Lucy frowned. "Seven years or so ago, I think. Miranda—"

"I was merely confused. I've customers, Lucy." She broke free and hurried between the tables. But she wasn't confused. Despite its weathered colors, that sampler was new, and Master Warren had never married.

What was happening? Was she going mad? Lucy had no reason to lie, so she must believe what she said. But how could that be true? Miranda scrubbed her hand over her bleary eyes.

Dire events will occur, Mother had warned. Was this the sort of thing she'd meant?

Summon the knight, the dream voice had ordered. If she did as the voice commanded, perhaps the visions would end.

B efore dawn the next day, Miranda crept into the woods behind the inn. Her heart beat fast, and her hands felt chilly, but not from the cold. She hadn't tried a major working in years. Despite the risk, excitement over the challenge hummed through her.

Shadows concealed the hollows in the landscape. The cold autumn air bit through her clothes and turned her breath to fog, but she had left her cloak in the garret. Anyone who saw her return to the inn mustn't suspect she had been out long enough to need it.

She had to hurry. Starting her duties late would anger Master Warren. But she also had to take care that no one saw her.

She reached a wide, level clearing as the stars began to fade. Half a mile into the woods, it was her favorite place for spending time alone.

Dropping her protective glamours, she opened her senses. Birds and small animals stirred in the forest. An owl returned to its nest after a night's hunt.

Despite all the movement around her, the back of Miranda's neck remained free of the tingle of awareness that signaled a human presence.

Good. She hurried to the center of the clearing. The hard ground lay under a colorful blanket of frost-tinged autumn leaves. On her knees, she scraped away leaves and twigs to bare a circle of earth about six feet across.

She took a slow breath to calm herself. Summoning required creating an illusion creature to go and find the one she needed, then deliver her message or else lead the one summoned to her. This time, sending a message seemed better. The creature might have to travel far away before it found the knight. If so, the magic sustaining it might fade away before it led him here.

She had never tried to form anything larger than a bird. A bird would do for this, but would a knight pay attention to something so small?

A dragon would be much harder to ignore, and the evil one in the vision hadn't changed her fondness for them.

Her hands shook as she untied the small bag at her waist and dumped its contents into her lap. The needle shone in its scrap of green felt as she pulled it free.

Drawing on her power, she pricked her left fourth finger. A droplet of blood fell into the center of the bare patch. Atop it, she placed a dried, green poplar leaf, a robin's feather, and the paring from one of her fingernails.

She held her left hand out so more blood dripped onto the little pile. "Nail for scaling, earth for might, leaf for color and feather for flight."

Before the blood could dry, she struck flint to catch a sliver of tinder, then laid it on the bloody spot with an oak twig. The twig smoldered, then caught.

Quickly, she chanted, "Oak for endurance, day and night, fire and blood to give vision life. Go, my dragon, and find the knight." She closed her eyes, the better to channel will into words and the vision into being, and slid backward.

Magic flowed through her like liquid sunlight, warming and strengthening her. Behind her eyelids, she could almost see her small fire become a looming, indistinct shadow. Rustling movements nearby told of birds

11

and small creatures scurrying for cover. Then came sudden silence as they found it.

Her creation took on form and substance. Sprouted wings and a snout. Became a dragon. The woodland creatures' fear of it brushed over her skin like a cold breeze.

The air heated. Something flapped with a leathery sound. A great gust of wind pressed her clothes against her body.

The flow of power within her ebbed. Died.

With a sigh, she opened her eyes. The small fire had gone out, and no sign of her workings remained.

But the center of the clearing bore two sets of three deep slashes as long as her forearm, like the marks of giant talons.

A grin tugged at her mouth. She lifted her head.

High above, a dragon's graceful silhouette glinted emerald in the faint pre-dawn light. Great wings pushed downward against the air, and she could almost feel the movement in her shoulders. Her spirit soared with the dragon. For one moment, she felt its freedom and strength.

Then it wheeled westward and vanished. Because of its limited substance, it wouldn't become visible to anyone else until—unless—it found the one it sought.

Her smile faded. Summoning had always come easily to her, but there were so many other skills she'd never had the chance to learn.

If only she could safely find a Gifted teacher. She wouldn't have to conceal herself all the time, and simply being with someone who also had Gifts would be a joy.

But there was no use wishing for the impossible. People like her didn't announce their skills, not with the gallows waiting for them. Nor could she go seeking such a one.

Rising, she brushed off her skirt. She'd enjoyed more luck than many people did. After her parents' deaths, a cousin had helped her find this position at the inn so she wouldn't starve. Or have to marry out of desperation. She managed to make time now and again to earn extra money with her needlework. Even embroidered mythical beasts like dragons for customers once in a while.

A wise woman would count her blessings, not long for more. Part of counting her blessings was keeping her job. Perhaps now she could do it in peace. Miranda hurried toward the inn.

She was halfway there when a sulfur reek stung her nose. Fog obliterated her sight, then rolled back to reveal the knight sitting upright in the saddle, blocking the red dragon's path to the wounded boar and a bloody stag. He still bore his shield, now marred by black scorch marks, and his sword gleamed silver in his steel-gloved fist.

Stretching its neck, the dragon roared, the sound frustrated and impotent now.

Your time is done. The knight's deep voice rang in her mind with the clarion power of unearthly trumpets. *The untruths and evils you nurtured shall not prevail but pass away. They are but the shades of night, and I am the herald of day.*

The vision faded, leaving her standing in the wood. Blast it, she'd hoped her summons would banish the visions. Would buy her peace.

Did this new twist, the knight's speech, portend that she'd done what was needed to solve whatever problem triggered the vision?

Or that she hadn't?

CHAPTER 2

Ordinary folk would see no cause for concern in today's dreary weather. But Richard Mainwaring was not ordinary, and the day was not merely dreary.

Cold, muddy water stood in the road's deep ruts. Brisk gusts caught red and gold leaves sodden from the day's rain, snapping them from their stems. All that was normal for late September. The taint on the wind, however, was not.

It grated on Richard's Gifted senses. The worst of the ill wind had died five days ago, but an almost imperceptible wrongness lingered in the air and roiled in the gusts.

"Shoot him and have done," Richard's companion, Captain Cabot Winfield of the Royal Navy, advised.

"What?" Richard blinked at his friend. They and their mounts were alone on the muddy road.

Cabot grinned at him, gray eyes alight in his square, tanned face. "When you're preoccupied, there are only two explanations. I guessed you were considering the George problem."

Richard grimaced. "If shooting him would straighten out his wayward wits, I might do it." He could always heal his wastrel cousin, who unfortunately was also his heir, afterward. So long as the wound wasn't instantly mortal.

Unfortunately, he and George shared only the Mainwaring blue eyes. The height, the black hair, and the steadying traits had missed George.

"That wasn't what I was thinking, though," Richard added. "I don't like that wrongness in the air."

Cabot frowned up at the leaden sky. "If I were at sea, I'd set my course away from it with all speed. I wonder how far that ill wind blew."

"Reports are probably coming into London." The city was the head-quarters of the realm's Gifted, known as the Conclave, and their governing Council. "The Council will likely need to meet sooner than we'd planned because of it."

"What a joyous event that will be." Cabot shook his head. "Better you than me, wrangling with that lot. You'll be lucky if you can make the rest of them decide anything."

"They do love to argue." After two years on the Council, Richard knew any issue would be chewed into rags before the group made a decision.

A sudden gust blew a lock of sun-streaked, brown hair into Cabot's face. Frowning, he shoved it back.

The cool air brushed Richard's neck with an unearthly chill. He turned up the collar of his cloak. Occasional drizzles might recur, but his wide-brimmed beaver hat and oiled leather cloak shed them well enough.

"There's another solution to your problem with George. Besides murder." Cabot kept his gaze on the road ahead.

With good reason. That *solution*, marriage and the heir it could produce, had too many drawbacks, ones Richard hated discussing. He raised an eyebrow at Cabot. "Impressment into the navy?"

"God help any ship cursed with him as a sailor." Scowling, Cabot added, "You know what I meant."

"Yes. Leave it."

Zeus pranced through the muddy ruts with no hesitation. Richard tugged the reins to avoid a puddle that was probably deeper than it looked.

The roads needed work, but the king had little interest in harassing the parishes about upkeep. After Oliver Cromwell deposed and killed King Charles I, Charles II had spent years in hiding, poverty-stricken and dependent on the charity of European royalty. Upon his restoration to the throne in 1660, he'd thrown off the puritanical shackles imposed by Cromwell's protectorate. The king had led the nation in seeking pleasure ever since. Road repairs, unfortunately, were not a pleasure.

Cabot said, "Thanks for going to Portsmouth with me to oversee the

Rose's refit. It was good to have the company even though we're done and headed home sooner than I expected."

Richard grinned. "I'd had enough of court, so I was glad to go." Especially with Cabot, who was rarely in England because he spent most of the year patrolling the West Indies.

"I'd rather face a pirate fleet—or even the bloody-minded, encroaching Dutch—alone than endure an evening at court." Cabot steered Neptune around a wide puddle. Staring into the distance, he added, "George's choices are not your fault."

"Leave it, I said—"

They rounded a bend, and a flash of green dropped from the clouds. Arrowing toward them, a dragon glittered in the weak light. Huge wings spanned the road as the creature landed.

"Cabot," Richard snapped in warning. That couldn't be a real dragon, but some illusions could harm. He drew rein.

The horses reared, hooves pawing at the air, and whinnied. What the—?

Horses usually couldn't see illusions. Perhaps they felt the magic crackling like invisible flame in the air around this one. Shifting his balance forward, he sent a tendril of power into Zeus's mind to restore both calm and control.

The stallion trembled but obeyed the commands Richard gave him through reins and knees. Cabot also had Neptune under control again.

"Where in Hell's fields did that come from?" Richard demanded.

"I was about to ask you." Cabot's face reflected Richard's shock.

The dragon settled onto its haunches. A yard taller than they were on horseback, it blocked the road even with its wings folded. Its scales glowed deep emerald, and its eyes glinted a fiery gold.

Another tendril of power, this time directed at the apparition, revealed its limited substance. Richard could dispel it, but only a fool would do so without learning why it sought them out.

Folding his hands over the pommel of his saddle, he eyed the creature coolly. "There are no dragons in England anymore."

The beast's voice rasped in his mind. *I seek the boar's knight, and I have found you.*

Richard straightened. "Why do you seek this knight?"

If you would right a wrong, Sir Knight, see the serving maid at the Golden Swan Inn on the Folkestone road, outside Dover. Tell her a dragon called you the herald of day.

"I've no trust in riddles," Richard replied. Nor did he trust apparitions, but his pulse quickened. Had this creature sought him out because of his family curse? Or for some less obvious reason?

Stretching its glistening wings out and up, above the hedgerows, the creature leaped skyward. He could have sworn it vanished before it reached the heavy clouds. Only then did he realize any inn near a busy port like Dover would have several maids. How could he know the right one?

After a moment, he smiled. One Gifted person, as any maid sending such a summons must be, would stand out soon enough in a crowd of ordinary folk. If she had the power to create such an illusion, she should know him on sight.

"'Od's fish," Cabot said. "To create a beast out of myth, someone must badly want to see you."

"So you heard it, too." Richard stared at the spot where the dragon had stood. "But why go to such lengths?" The power required for such summoning had led most people to abandon the art long ago.

He kneed Zeus to a walk. "Strange, that the dragon should carry a message so well suited to me."

Of course, no one else had as much reason as he did to care about the dead king who'd used a white boar as his emblem, Richard III. Perhaps this was, at last, a chance to lift the family curse.

Unless it was a trap.

He set his jaw against a rush of hope. Grasping at straws, such as this likely was, could distract him from learning what the summons truly portended.

On Neptune, Cabot kept pace with him. "Coming on the heels of that wind, the dragon's summons must be related, and that means danger."

"Regardless, I'm going to Dover."

Richard's ancestor Edmund Mainwaring had unwittingly helped his liege lord murder the late King Edward IV's sons, who'd become known as the Princes in the Tower. Horrified by what he had done, Edmund had thrown himself on the mercy of King Richard III.

The king had ordered Edmund to keep silent because of the political situation. Then King Richard had died at Bosworth Field, and the Tudors who followed him had blamed him for the boys' deaths and anything else they could lay at his feet.

Plagued by guilt, Edmund had sworn that neither he nor his heirs would rest in life or death until they cleared the king's name.

In a dry voice, Cabot said, "Odd, how this brings de Vere to mind. Or Lord Wyndon, as he is now. He could create such a manifestation as easily as either of us could, and he would know how to intrigue you with its message."

"Be that as it may, I've exhausted every lead. I've no more idea how to clear King Richard's name than I did when I began. I can't ignore this summons."

Not with the Mainwaring heirs doomed to a shadowy realm between life and death, unable to pass through the portal to final judgment until someone proved the truth about the royal boys' deaths. The curse also caused high rates of obsession, madness, and suicide among the doomed Mainwarings.

Cabot frowned, then shook his head. "I don't like it, Richard. The only thing Wyndon would prefer to dancing at your deathbed is driving you to it, regardless of the rules of engagement. Remember that."

"I'm not likely to forget." Those rules forbade the Gifted from using magic to mislead or harm one another. The penalties ranged from a rebuke to death, but it would be just like Wyndon to assume no one would catch on to what he'd done.

Shooting Cabot a wry glance, Richard said, "You know I can't ignore any chance, however slim, to discharge my blood debt."

Only doing so would allow him, finally, to marry, perhaps even to beget a responsible heir. He was two and thirty years old, overdue by anyone's standards.

"I can reach Dover in a couple of days," he said. "If Wyndon created the beast as a trap, he has violated the Code and given me cause to challenge him that even the Conclave cannot deny. If it's not Wyndon, perhaps I'll find an explanation for that unearthly wind."

A frown still creased Cabot's face. "If I didn't have to report to the Admiralty in London, I'd come along. Since I can't, you watch your back."

"Count on that." Richard rubbed his chin with one gloved hand. The Earl of Hawkstowe would draw too much attention, so which of his many aliases should he use?

Aloud, he mused, "A merchant could stay at an inn without undue notice, so perhaps 'Ralph Wyatt' will pay this girl a call." He'd used that identity often during the struggle to end Oliver Cromwell's protectorate and restore the monarchy.

Cabot nodded. "Farewell, then, 'Master Wyatt.'"

"I may not return in time for the White Rose dinner on the second."

He welcomed an honorable excuse for missing that annual gathering in Richard III's honor. "Explain my delay to my grandmother, will you?"

"Of course. Don't tarry overlong, or I'll come after you." Despite Cabot's light tone, worry lurked in his eyes. "Godspeed."

"To you also." Richard turned Zeus. He'd have to backtrack to reach the Dover road.

Riddle or no, this adventure at least promised a further reprieve from the grinding, shallow gaiety of attendance at court. As for what else it might offer, it was best not to hope too much. He'd watch his back, certainly, and all the possible angles.

~

Two days later, in the late afternoon, Richard reached the outskirts of Dover. Big, fluffy clouds hovered over the English Channel to the south, and a faint hint of brine rode the breeze.

The Golden Swan inn stood alone opposite a farm lane. The passage of years had given the rambling, two-story structure's half-timbered walls a slight outward tilt, but barren rose bushes clung tenaciously to the weathered stucco. The setting sun cast a golden glow over the white-washed walls.

Such an unprepossessing place looked unlikely to harbor great secrets. Of course, that might make it perfect for such.

He rode through a boxy passageway and into a big, square yard. Men and women in homespun lingered in the yard, chatting. Some also stood on the galleries that fronted the upper story on all four sides of the yard.

A similar passage across the way revealed a rear yard that held a well and a rough, wooden building that might be a stable.

In a roped-off area at one corner of the main yard, brightly costumed men loaded props into a wagon. They must be the acting troupe he'd heard of on the road. From the look of them, they'd just finished a performance. Good. This crowd they'd drawn would let him locate and observe the mysterious serving maid without attracting notice.

A deep breath, a shake of his head, and the Ralph Wyatt identity settled into his mind. Wyatt would seem less imposing to this girl than an earl. Of course, someone with the power to send such a summons might not prove easily intimidated, but best to take no chances.

The odors of horses and dung pervaded the air. Opposite the yard entrance, a door on the ground floor stood partly open. Voices coming from it signaled the public room's location.

The yard could have accommodated half a dozen coaches and teams easily, but it held only the players' cart and a large wagon with no horses hitched to it. Its driver must mean to stay the night. Big, wooden casks filled the wagon and emitted the pungent aroma of tobacco, probably imported from the Virginia colony.

A man in rough wool and homespun loped through the passage across the yard and waved to Richard. "I'll take 'im, good sir."

Dismounting, Richard nodded. "I'll stay the night."

The ostler touched his cap. Richard slipped him a penny to ensure good food for Zeus, who snorted as though he would prefer to spend the night in a better hostelry. Richard patted his neck before turning toward the public room.

The two of them had stayed in worse places. The heavy, thatched roof and leaded glass windows spoke of regular maintenance. Perhaps someone occasionally aired the sheets.

Linens, however, mattered little next to the larger problem of the reason for this summons. While suspecting Wyndon came naturally, there were other unscrupulous wizards. Some allied themselves to the forces of darkness. Richard would take this wench's measure before choosing his course.

He made his way into the common room, ducking beneath the low entry. Light from the front windows didn't penetrate far into the long, gloomy chamber. Lanterns mounted on the walls provided little illumination, but he could see better than most men. Curse or no curse, being Gifted had its advantages.

A table in the rear stood vacant. He edged through the crowd to claim it. The scents of pipe smoke, hot meat and bread, and unwashed bodies hung in the air. Conversation and occasional raucous laughter created an amiable din.

He seated himself and glanced over the crowd. A sturdy, brown-haired maid rushed out of a passage opposite the door. Carrying a tray laden with wooden plates and leather tankards, she moved with brisk efficiency that belied her dour expression. Behind her came a petite, red-haired girl. Neither seemed remarkable.

He let his gaze drift over the room. In the far corner stood a tall, lanky girl, dark-haired and pox-scarred. Judging by her apron and that of the thin, tired-looking man facing her, she was a maid and he, the innkeeper. Behind them, a sturdy, smiling blonde hoisted a tray of empty plates.

His attention swung back to the pox-scarred girl. She seemed unremarkable, and yet ...

He summoned power, narrowing his eyes, and her face became translucent, like a reflection in a window pane. Under the concealing glamour lay smooth skin, thick, glossy dark brown hair, and a fine-boned, elegant face. Even more appealing were the intelligence in her light blue eyes and the self-possession in her expression.

The Gifted one did, indeed, stand out.

~

"You've done well of late," Master Warren muttered. "See that it continues."

"Yes, sir. Thank you, sir." Miranda had had no more dreams or visions in the four days since dispatching her dragon. Mayhap she'd truly bought herself peace.

"Now see to that gentleman in the far corner."

"Aye, sir." Looking for the newcomer, she turned.

An instant later, she met the level, confident gaze of the man she sought. His shoulder-length, black hair framed the strong planes of his face and jaw. Across her vision flashed an image of him facing the red dragon.

The helm had hidden most of his strong, chiseled features, a face that would make any woman's heart beat faster. He wore the stylish coat and long vest of a prosperous gentleman, with lace at his throat and the coat's broad cuffs.

"Miranda. Don't go daydreaming again." Warren's voice cut into her daze. "See to the man."

"Aye, sir." The image faded, but the man's alert yet relaxed posture spoke of power that would awake in an instant. The air of danger he'd worn in the vision still swirled about him. He made her painfully aware of her homely appearance, faded, worn garments and work-roughened hands.

She shrugged off the awareness. A prosperous man such as he would take no honorable personal interest in a serving maid, regardless of either of their appearances.

21

Swallowing hard, she sidled through the crowd. She knew him, but surely he didn't know her. He couldn't.

He smiled, a slight, knowing twitch of his lips. Excitement mixed with sudden dread of what he might bring, sending a chill rippling through her. Some part of her hadn't believed anyone would answer the summons. Now that he had, the danger of the whole situation pressed in on her again.

She reached his table. He lifted an eyebrow at her, and his stern eyes made the gesture both question and command.

"What will you have, sir?" Her voice sounded thin but steady. She swallowed and tried again. "We've mutton stew today."

"The stew will do." In a low voice that wouldn't carry in the noisy public room, he added, "Along with an explanation of your summons." The note of authority in his deep voice boded ill for delay even as it sent a thrill of recognition through her.

But there was more than his voice to that sensation. He seemed familiar in an eerie, unsettling way that owed naught to her visions.

"I cannot stop to talk now. I'll have time to myself after supper service, in an hour or so."

His gaze stayed level. Confident. "Of course. Later, then."

Relieved to escape, she hurried toward the kitchen. He knew her. How, she couldn't fathom, but he did. Her chest felt tight, and her hands shook.

She drew a steadying breath. Once she told this man of the visions, they would be his problem. The sooner she could manage that, the better.

CHAPTER 3

Supper service was drawing to a close. As it did, so did Miranda's ability to avoid thinking of what lay ahead. Taking the next step, explaining to the man, carried risks, too.

At least he'd gone to his room, or somewhere, and wasn't hanging about or watching her. She was nervous enough without that.

She carried her last tray of dishes into the kitchen. Even hotter than the common room and busy with the washing up, the room seemed too close. She needed air. Stumbling backward, she mumbled something about the privy and fled through the rear door.

Flora, the cook, called, "Bring some water when y'come back in." Miranda flapped a hand at her without pausing.

The well stood in the rear yard, about halfway between the kitchen and the stable. Turning the windlass to pull up the bucket forced her hands to stop shaking.

The man seemed so self-assured, even arrogant, but mayhap she worried too much. This mystery knight could be as brave and noble and capable as the legendary Sir Lancelot. Surely he would know what to do once she told him of the visions. Why else would she have been directed to summon him? Soon she would be free of the whole business.

The bucket rose into view. She held the windlass to keep it steady and reached for the bucket.

"Allow me," said a deep, firm, too-familiar voice.

Startled, she spun to face the stranger.

He eyed her closely as he bowed. "Your dragon called me the herald of day. I'm at your service, mistress."

"Uh, I can manage the water, but I thank you, sir." The windlass slipped. She tightened her grip on it.

"Nevertheless." He caught the rope and swung the bucket neatly onto the side of the well.

Guests didn't extend such courtesies to servants. Was he naturally kind or merely seeking to put her at ease?

Miranda stepped back. "I still have duties, and this is not a good place to talk at the moment. People walk through here until they settle in for the night. Later would be better."

"For now, at least, we're alone," he noted. "Pray explain why you summoned me."

Miranda squared her shoulders. "Who are you, sir?"

"Ralph Wyatt. I'm a merchant. Despite urgent business in London, I've ridden hard to answer your summons. And you are?"

"Miranda Willoughby." Annoying as it was for him to accost her while she still had duties, nothing about him raised the prickly chills over her skin that warned of danger. Yet there was that strange sense of recognition again. Without the table between them, he seemed even more imposing, and she couldn't help noticing his broad shoulders and tall, straight frame.

Miranda hesitated.

"Let's not waste time." He raised an eyebrow. "You ply your glamours well, but they won't serve against me. I know full well what you are."

Knew and accepted.

The realization gave her an unexpected rush of pleasure. Still, revealing herself after so many years in hiding didn't come easily. If he knew about the summons, though, she must be meant to trust him despite her fears.

She took a deep, slow breath. "I've had strange visions, a disturbing dream. About a boar and a dragon. There was a stag, too, and a knight." His face showed only intent interest, and she added, "The knight could be your twin. The visions came in fragments, but they directed me to summon the boar's knight."

Something flashed in the depths of his eyes, but she couldn't interpret it. Still, she felt certain the reference to the knight meant something to him.

"How many times have you had these visions," he asked, "and were they always the same?"

Shaking her head, Miranda said, "Never exactly the same, and I had them several times a day until I sent the dragon."

His brows knitted in a thoughtful frown, but he said nothing.

"My mother always said one should heed a dream of power," she continued. If only heeding this one didn't turn out to be a mistake. "Do you know what it means?"

"It could mean a number of things," he answered slowly.

"Miranda!" Flora stood in the doorway, her stout frame spattered with flour and her habitual frown deeper than usual. "I need that water, girl. Quick, or you'll rue it." She stomped back inside.

Miranda untied the bucket from its rope. As she stepped back from the well, a sudden, chilling awareness rippled across her neck. She wheeled. "What was that?"

"What do you mean?" Frowning, Wyatt stepped up beside her.

"That chill, there, like someone watching. What—"

His raised hand signaled her to wait as he took a sudden step forward. He pivoted, staring hard at the spot he'd crossed. "There's something here, a coldness in the air."

"Perhaps it's just a draft." She didn't believe that, though, much as she wanted to. Not after that tingle, like power, that'd run over her skin.

"It's no draft," he stated. "As you well know." He stepped back over the spot. "It's gone."

He gazed at her, his expression unreadable. What could she say? He was right, but dismissing her reactions to anything unseen had become second nature. A matter of survival.

"We must talk more," he said at last. "I'll escort you to church on the morrow, at St. Mary's on the castle headland."

The Church of England. "My thanks, but I must decline." Her father had despised the Anglican Church's Popish rites, so she usually attended a chapel that, while Anglican, as mandated by the law, held a simpler service.

"I must insist." His stern expression brooked no refusal. "I haven't pledged you my aid, nor will I until after church."

How overbearing. "Why church?"

The ice in his eyes could have frozen the sea in summer. "Because, pretty dragon maid, not only the decent have power. I'll aid a Gifted woman to my dying breath, but I'll stir not a step for an agent of darkness."

Fury ignited in her heart and shot down her right arm like lightning, but unless he attacked her physically, she dared not slap a paying guest.

Her hands balled into fists. Through taut lips, she said, "My father was a man of God."

He'd been a Dissenter, officially disapproved of by the Church of England, but he'd lived a devout life.

"Nevertheless, those are my terms. We can be sure of each other after church. If you are what you claim to be, if you've cause for that blazing outrage, you should see that this course protects you also."

She hadn't thought of that. His experience in magical matters obviously far outstripped hers. She'd never cared much that others had more wealth than she did, but the disparity between his magical education and hers burned. As did his condescending manner.

"Very well." Pig swill would taste better than this galling concession, but she had to see the matter through. "I'll go with you."

"Tomorrow, then." He bowed and turned away.

She scowled at his departing back. Unlike the chivalrous knights of legend, this man displayed arrogance that would do justice to a spoiled nobleman. How disappointing. Ah, well, she would attend church to convince him of her integrity and then be done with him.

Except ...

He was not only Gifted but trained. He must be. He'd somehow known she was the one who sent the dragon. Had seen through her glamours. If she asked, would he show her one or two simple things?

The memory of Mistress Smith's limp body flashed into her mind, and she shivered. No. Far better to tend to her job, hauling in this water and placating Flora.

She hoisted the water bucket to carry it inside, but the dangerous thought persisted. Surely he could teach her something that wasn't a risk. If he would.

Instead of scowling as Miranda expected, the cook greeted her with a smile. "Wyatt, that merchant, he said you was giving him directions. Begged my pardon most prettily for delaying you, he did. You run along, Miranda. Help April with the sweeping up."

Baffled, Miranda hurried toward the common room. What had Wyatt done to Flora, to charm her so?

Charm her. He must've done exactly that.

A chill ran down Miranda's spine. Wyatt was more dangerous than she'd realized.

~

An apparition invaded Richard's sleep, jolting him awake. In the chair by the window sat a middle-aged man dressed in tunic, hose, and boots, garb fashionable two centuries earlier. Faint traces of gray streaked his black hair. At his side hung an empty scabbard. The chair and window frame showed through the man's body.

The ghost's faint glow wavered at the edges like a candle flame and blurred its features, but Richard didn't need a clear view to recognize this specter. He swallowed an oath. The last thing this situation needed was interference from the man who'd started the Mainwaring curse.

"Go haunt someone else," Richard said. He turned over, presenting his back to the unwanted visitor, though he knew that wouldn't discourage the family ghost.

"You're thinking of the quest. You must be, if I could break through your mind's defenses." The apparition's voice had the hollow, grating quality he remembered. "You have erected formidable barriers." The ghost now sounded wistful.

"Did you need something, Edmund?"

"'Grandsire Edmund' would suit me, even if 'tis a bit short for the number of generations between us."

God's teeth. Sleep had flown, so Richard sat up. "You surely did not interrupt my slumber to discuss names."

Edmund sighed, the sound like a creaking windlass. "You think me an old fool, so you've barred your mind to me for a decade."

"I meant to bar it yet." Patiently, because he knew Edmund felt guilty, Richard added, "Going over and over your reasons for cursing all your direct heirs achieves nothing. The situation is unresolvable, and I'll live with it as I choose."

"So you remain determined not to wed." The ghostly eyes darkened with reproach. "Hawkstowe needs a better heir than your cousin George."

"Every family produces an unreliable heir at some point." Shooting Edmund a disgusted look, Richard ran a hand through his disordered hair. "I won't permit your curse to poison another marriage or condemn future generations."

27

His mother's resentment over the doom his bloodline imposed on Richard had turned his parents' marriage bitter and distant.

His own desires aside, though, George's rising debts and deteriorating character made finding some solution imperative.

"The girl's vision offers hope, do you not see?"

Hellfire. He shouldn't be surprised Edmund knew about her, but that would complicate matters.

"I told you not to spy on me." Though he'd suspected at the time that the warning was futile. "How do you even know about this girl, anyway?"

"I was wandering the London house when young Winfield came to see your grandmother. After he told her about the dragon, I came here posthaste. Heard the last of what the maid told you." Edmund shrugged. "I kept my distance so as not to bother you."

That must explain the sensation Richard had felt by the well earlier. Edmund had been careless.

"We both sensed you in the yard, but even if we hadn't, eavesdropping will avail you nothing. My conversation with Miranda Willoughby won't change either of our fates."

The ghost frowned, then shook his head. "You seemed unsettled by a cold patch in the yard earlier, but that had naught to do with me. I was farther away from you."

Edmund's face held no trace of deceit. But if not Edmund, what had caused the cold spot in the yard? "Did you see anyone or anything else watching us?"

Edmund shook his head. "I was alone. Whatever caused it, that's over and done, Richard. Her vision is far more important. It could be the key to everything."

"Or not," Richard said, his voice dry. "What she's said about it thus far is so vague as to mean little without refining it. Which she apparently lacks the training to do. She's abysmally ignorant about the need to be certain one is dealing with Gifted who follow the light and not the darkness."

"She created the dragon and has a certain proficiency with glamours, as her disguise proves," Edmund responded. "If she spoke truly tonight, she could be a powerful seer, whether or not she knows it."

That was true, and it might mean she had the power to help in Richard's quest regardless of whatever value her dragon visions held. But he knew too well the bitterness of false hope.

Richard said, "Her skill level and inherent power will take time to determine."

"I'll watch over you." Edmund beamed at him.

"No. Begone, Edmund."

"As soon as you hear me out."

Richard shook his head. "I know your sorry tale too well. What I've never understood is why you felt the need to curse us all."

Edmund had the grace to look ashamed. "I went too far. I know that, but 'tis done now." He sighed. "At least the boys' poor bodies were finally discovered this summer, when that staircase at the Tower was demolished. I suppose King Charles plans an elaborate tomb."

"So he says. Now, go away. I need to sleep."

"Richard, I pray you, understand I meant no ill. I kept silent only at King Richard's behest. I never dreamed that green, craven Henry Tudor would defeat him at Bosworth, nor blame him for the boys' deaths. I dared not speak while the Tudors reigned, but I had to see justice done. I owed them that, the king and the lads. Can you not see?"

Edmund's eyes took on a pleading look. "We need you, Richard, you and the children you could have." The ghost's sigh rippled through the air like a sudden draft. Edmund glided toward the bed. "Do you think I never regret all this? I left a confession, you know. Had it not burned ere your grandfather could—"

"Let's not plow that ground yet again." Richard kept his voice even with an effort. He'd barred his mind to Edmund precisely to avoid endless repeated justifications. "I won't do to any woman what my father did to my mother." Or what his grandfather had done to his grandmother. "Now, begone."

Edmund stood, scowling. "Someday, grandson, you will hear me out in full." He vanished.

No oath Richard knew could vent his frustration. He kicked back the covers and sprang out of bed.

Pacing in the chilly predawn air cooled his temper. He opened the window to take a deep breath.

In truth, he had some sympathy for Edmund. Anyone, even a wizard, could be cozened into trusting a dishonest master. Unfortunately, Edmund had compounded his mistake by damning his entire line until they cleared King Richard III's name.

Richard frowned. The girl's vision likely did have some connection to the family curse, and as Cabot pointed out, the timing of the dragon's appearance implied it was also related to the ominous wind. Richard would pursue deciphering her vision, but carefully.

Her face flashed into his mind, those intelligent eyes focused and damnably wary. She was an attractive woman, the more so because she seemed unaware that she was. Nor had she tried to bargain, he realized, his frown deepening. Many of her station would have tried to sell their information, either for coin or for advancement. Yet she hadn't.

Which made her even more appealing, blast it. But she was not for him, and he knew better than to let a woman distract him. Even if her power proved true, and not dark-spawned, she could still be allied with Wyndon.

He straightened his shoulders. "Hear me, Edmund, if you yet remain. I will not warp the meaning of her vision to suit your purposes. What comes of it will come, naught else."

He waited a moment to let his words sink in before softly adding, "I swear on the sword of Hawkstowe, by the blood of Morgan, and into the dawn. So shall it be."

CHAPTER 4

The service would end soon. Then this Master Wyatt would depart to do whatever dream knights did. At least he would leave Miranda in peace while he dealt with whatever her visions meant.

Even better, her life would return to normal. Last night's unsettling dream—which at least had not involved dragons or boars or danger, only a strange book—would be the last, and he and this troubling awareness of him would be a memory.

She sat at his side in a worn, oak pew in St. Mary's Church. All through the service, she'd been conscious of him beside her, of his strong profile, of his large, clean hands on the prayer book. He was a well-favored man, and hers weren't the only eyes drawn to him.

The sanctuary looked faintly dilapidated, but its stained glass windows muted the sunlight and cast jeweled patterns onto Miranda's best gown, a pink one she rarely wore. Candlelight gave a gentle glow to black-and-white vestments while voices raised in song echoed from the thick stone walls. The Anglican service had a grandeur her father's Dissenter services couldn't match, though admitting it felt disloyal to Father's memory.

At last, the rector delivered the benediction. Ushers opened the doors. The congregation, some townsfolk and a number of soldiers from the castle garrison, filed out. Miranda sighed in relief and let Wyatt escort her outside.

A crisp, salty breeze from the sea stirred the musty scent of fallen leaves. It rippled the grass around the church's tiny yard and dropped bright autumn leaves from the trees. Wispy white clouds scudded across a sky of bright blue.

The fine day would've lifted her spirits if she hadn't been so torn between what she knew was best, sending Wyatt on his way, and the temptation to ask him more about magic.

To ask him anything to draw his attention.

When had she become so foolish?

Behind the little gray church was an ancient tower of matching stone. The Roman lighthouse, now used as a powder magazine, stood like a sentinel watching the clouds pass. Kings had come and gone while the lighthouse stood here. It would likely outlast whatever her dream betokened.

Farther inland, the great keep of Dover Castle loomed. The civil war of the 1640s had damaged other great castles, but not Dover. It still guarded the English Channel and the bustling port at the foot of the white cliffs.

Wyatt followed her glance. "Dover wears its years well."

"Aye, it does." The thick walls radiated strength and certainty.

Parishioners gathered in the church yard. Miranda strolled with Master Wyatt away from the chatting throng, toward the low earthwork at the cliff's edge. From there, the ground dropped toward the Channel in a long, steep slope.

"I compliment you, mistress, on your knowledge of the service," Wyatt said. "Reluctant or no, you seemed at home."

"My grandmother made certain I knew the litany she considered proper. Along with many other things."

"What sort of things?"

Miranda shrugged. "Old tales. Traditions."

Legends of knights in armor, of sacrifice in the cause of right. Of valor and magic and honor. All those had brought sparkle to a life made lonely by the need to hide her magic, but he would probably laugh if she told him.

Glancing at him, she said, "I trust I've satisfied you as to the source of my power."

The breeze whipped her cloak and skirts about her legs and brushed her face with tendrils of hair that had escaped its braid. She held her cloak tighter at the waist.

"We can trust each other on that point," he agreed.

There was something about this place. Something different that tingled at the nape of her neck and bubbled deep within her. "This isn't just another church, is it?"

"No." He nodded, as though in salute. "The Saxons built the first church here on a place infused with great power. That power, rather than the liturgy, is why I brought you here today."

His level, assessing gaze locked on her face. Suddenly she'd had enough of his suspicions.

Before she could say so, he continued, "This was Morgan Le Fay's stronghold in southern England. The Gifted used it for centuries, until the growing power of Christianity drove us into hiding. This headland is a stronghold of the light, and those who serve the dark have never been able to endure it."

Miranda frowned. The sorceress in the tales of King Arthur had not been a force for good, but there was no point debating that with him. "So being here proves we're both of the light? If you're telling me the truth."

"Quite. Very good. Your doubts show you're learning to think defensively. But I am telling you the truth." He paused, eyeing her thoughtfully. "All this frightens you, doesn't it?"

Surprised by his kind tone, she answered him honestly. "I can deal with fear, but you treat me as though I've done something to you. Mayhap I have, but not apurpose. There's no need for you to be so suspicious."

"Mistress, the Gifted, as a group, are no more honorable than anyone else. If I've treated you with suspicion, there are others who would treat you as a lamb to the slaughter."

Slowly, as though just realizing it himself, he said, "But I've treated you less well than I might have. I beg your pardon. The symbols of your dream touch on matters private to my family. Will you hear me out?"

He seemed sincere, so she turned to face him.

Wyatt glanced toward the distant coast of France. "I traveled under a false name to avoid notice, but you've earned the truth. I'm a Knight of the Garter and a knight in fact. Sir Richard Mainwaring, Earl of Hawkstowe, at your service." He made her a bow fit for Queen Catherine.

He couldn't be serious. This was like falling into one of Grandmother's stories. If these claims were true.

She narrowed her eyes at him. "Why didn't you say so all along?"

"Wisdom demands caution in dealing with Gifted strangers."

A lesson she should heed. "How do I know you've told me the truth now?" His clothing, while fine, lacked the elaborate lace and jewels worn by the few noblemen she'd seen.

"You must trust your instincts." He met her probing gaze without flinching.

"As Flora trusted hers?"

"Flora? Ah, the harpy who rules the inn's kitchen." He shrugged. "She hasn't your instincts. I merely tweaked her mood a bit. I did her no harm and made no lasting change."

Flora had seemed as snappish as usual since then, so perhaps that was true. But what if he was doing the same thing now? She shouldn't just accept his word without question. "How can you be a knight, though? That is—you do mean you're a knight like the ones in the old tales?"

When he nodded confirmation, she said, "You say you're telling me the truth, but there're no knights anymore, save for honorary ones like those of the Garter."

He smiled, humor suddenly dancing in his eyes. "Nor are there dragons."

That smile made her heart beat faster, but she couldn't let him dodge the question. Raising her chin, she held his gaze.

"If you must know," he said, "I grew up on a great deal of nonsense about chivalry. I asked the king to knight me because I was young and mush-brained enough to honor that imaginary tradition. Because he was young but had seen his youth fly away, he humored me."

What he said made sense, and he seemed earnest. For now, at least, she would take him at his word. She looked away, toward the castle's great keep. Discussing these strange events with someone else, even someone she didn't entirely trust, felt strangely daring and yet liberating, too.

"Is there anything you haven't told me?" he asked.

"A couple of things," she said. "The first is that a sampler suddenly appeared in the inn. When I asked about it, another maid told me the landlord's wife made it about seven years ago. But he never wed, and I know the sampler wasn't there until four or five days ago."

He frowned. "You didn't simply stop noticing it, out of habit? Or mistake the landlord's history?"

"No. Do you know how such a thing could be?"

He shook his head slowly, as though considering. "Have you seen anything else odd?"

"There's a wrongness in the wind. Not so much as there was, but still ... disturbing."

"Aye. When did you first notice it?"

"A few days before the sampler appeared. I tried to ignore the strangeness of it, the dread in it, but if you noticed it, too, then it's not just my uneasiness over all this."

"It's not." Grim-faced, he asked, "Have you had any other visions?"

"Some." Miranda frowned. "Nothing was clear, mostly just impressions, one a vision of a man and a place I didn't recognize—that flashed by before I truly knew what they were." She told him about the hanging and what she'd seen during and after it.

"They were all very strong," she said. "Most of them came only once, but the one with the dragon and boar kept coming back, blotting out the world. I couldn't see or hear what was around me, so I made mistakes. Missed things I should have attended to."

"I'm sorry." Although he spoke quietly, his gaze remained keen. "Go on."

"The dragon visions were the most complete, save the one I had last night, the other thing I wanted to mention. I dreamed about the pages of a book changing while I watched."

"Do you read, or did you simply see the shapes of letters change?"

Her cheeks warmed, but it was a fair question. Most servants could neither read nor write. "My father was a clergyman," she said, "and he saw to it that my brother and I could read."

"Could you tell what the book was?"

When she shook her head, he asked, "Where are your father and brother now? Have you discussed these visions with them?"

Miranda drew a painful breath. "They died eight years ago, in the Great Fire." The blaze had destroyed vast parts of London. While the tally of the dead was small, that didn't matter if people you loved were among them.

The loss still hurt, but she was used to it. "As I was saying, the dreams were briefer, but they ... felt the same, for lack of a better word. They felt true. Magical."

His face remained gravely attentive, not mocking or doubtful, and she found the courage to add, "My mother said I had the seer gift, but ... mayhap I imagined these things. Because I was distressed by the hanging."

"That seems doubtful, all things considered," he said, frowning.

"Mistress Agnes Smith was innocent," Miranda stated. "I know she was." As Mother had been.

"Of course she was. Our kind can charm our way out of such fixes. Usually."

Our kind. She hadn't been among her own kind since her mother's death.

"My mother was hanged as a witch," Miranda blurted. The pain she'd been trying to ignore surged into her throat. "She couldn't charm her way out of it, but she wasn't evil. She wasn't." The words nearly choked her, and she turned to the water, seeking composure. "She was a healer."

Saying so triggered another memory, and with it, the pain of loss. Miranda had hoped to be a healer, too. Someday. But that hope was gone.

Quietly, Hawkstowe said, "I'm sorry. Have you other family?"

"Only distant cousins who were glad to see the back of me." She managed a shrug to downplay the pain in that and turned to face him again.

After Mother's death, Miranda and her father and brother had gone to live in London, where Mother had said there were many Gifted. But Father didn't even know they existed, so Miranda hadn't been able to seek aid from them. Then he and Johnny had died in the fire, and she'd been alone.

"Did your father train you?" Hawkstowe asked.

"Oh, no. No, he was unGifted. Mother trained me until she died. Then no one did."

His gaze sharpened. "Mistress Willoughby, many strongly Gifted wizards couldn't form a creature of illusion such as the dragon you sent for me."

"Wizards?" She frowned. "I don't know that word. Is it like witches?"

"It's more or less the same, but we tend to use wizard more. As I was saying, someone must've trained you, at least in summoning. Who?"

Not more suspicion. Miranda squared her shoulders. "I've had a knack for glamours and summoning since I was very young. I know that's unusually early, but that's what happened. My mother trained me in those skills. But she died when I was nine, before I began to show any other Gifts."

"And now you have visions," he murmured, frowning out at the Channel.

"Yes. And I would rather not."

Yet magic could be useful. He knew how to charm ill-tempered folk like Flora, the cook. "My lord, could you have saved Mistress Smith?"

"No." The word fell from his lips like an oak chip from an ax, and his expression hardened. "If the unGifted choose to kill one another, it's not our affair."

"But an innocent person—surely—"

"What would you have had me do? Blast the gaol apart and sweep her away? Then what, having shown my power to a woman it surely would terrify, who would see me as evil, who would tell every soul she knew?" Frustration rang in his words.

"But can't you make people forget or something?"

"I'm a Gifted mortal, Mistress Willoughby, not God Almighty." He scowled at her. "If there's nothing else—"

"No, but those other things—blasting the gaol apart and such—you could truly do all that?" Were such things really possible?

His chest rose and fell in a long, deep breath as the anger faded from his face. "I could," he said quietly. "For that matter, so might you if you had enough training and skill, however inadvisable the doing."

Having such power, though—if she could learn to use it in subtle, undetectable ways—would be a great boon. She could help people.

"Perhaps you know more than you think," he said. "Your visions might help the Gifted's Conclave Council, in London, understand these unsettling omens. You should come to London with me."

"Go to London?" With him? Surely she hadn't heard him aright.

"I'll house you in safety, give you a sum of money to start a new life, and see that you have proper magical training, which is long overdue."

"In London." She remembered little about the city. Going would take her from everything she knew and the only home she had.

But he knew so much more about magic than she did. Staying would cost her what might be her last chance to learn about her Gifts.

He offered what she'd long yearned for. If she could trust him. He hadn't shown any improper interest, but ... "What would you expect me to do for this money?"

"You think I have lustful designs on you, mistress?" he asked gently. The warmth in his eyes offered understanding rather than mockery.

She couldn't help liking that he understood, but that changed nothing. "I dare not simply assume you have only good intentions."

He raised an eyebrow. "If you're fearing I want to spirit you away to prey on you, be aware I don't need to lure you to London for that."

Although he didn't move, power swirled out from him like a crisp breeze. The skin of her face tingled, and magic crackled in the air around her. Miranda's knees trembled.

Gazing at the sky, he said, "Take a step."

She couldn't. Her heart hammered in sudden fear, and she strained against the invisible grip that held her immobile.

"Let me go," she gasped. Desperate, she flung up a glamour that made her appear to vanish.

"Clever," he said, frowning, and the sense of his power died away. As though to reassure her, he gave her a wry smile. She wanted to run, but he could stop her easily if he chose. She'd never met someone so adroit. So dangerous.

"I beg pardon if I frightened you," he said. "I meant only to prove my point."

"Of course." He had done both, but he hadn't pressed his advantage. Could she trust him or not?

"Don't do that again," she said.

"I won't." His level gaze seemed sincere. "I've a problem your visions might help solve in addition to aiding the Gifted Conclave Council, whose duty it is to investigate strange magical occurrences. My grandmother, who lives with me, will lend you countenance."

"What is the Gifted Conclave Council?"

"The leaders of our kind."

He'd frightened her, but nothing about him felt threatening. She took a deep, slow breath and opened herself to instincts she barely understood, the ones that had kept her out of danger so often before.

Nothing changed. No warning tingle slid along her arms. Regardless of his earlier pretense, he was dealing honestly with her now. "I've no other home. If I leave, especially with a man, Master Warren will never take me back."

"I'll find you a better situation, likely an easier one. With training, which I'll help you obtain, you could make a place for yourself among the Gifted."

He paused, studying her. "Power untrained is dangerous. So is isolation. There are many Gifted in London. You wouldn't be alone, as you seem to be here, nor would you need to hide your appearance or your talent. You should come with me."

Their eyes met, his dark with understanding. Going with him would bring her into company where she could openly learn the skills she'd dreamed of possessing. Could lead to a better, safer life.

If she dared leave this familiar, comparatively safe place.

"During Cromwell's Protectorate, when I was but fourteen years old," he said quietly, "I sneaked back to England alone from our refuge in France. I had magical skills, wealth and connections, but none of that kept fear at bay."

He did understand, and he offered a kind of paradise—being with people who knew the dangers she faced. Living among her own kind.

But she would be utterly dependent upon him. Away from anyone who knew her or expected to see her or cared even a little about her.

"The risk feels overwhelming," she confessed.

He nodded. "It's a difficult choice, and I wouldn't presume to dictate to you. I can only suggest that you look beyond this day and make the choice that will be right a year hence."

Torn, she bit her lip.

"Think on it overnight," he said. "I return to London in the morning."

All her instincts screamed for her to go with him, to take this chance. But if she did, she would be alone and friendless in the city. At his mercy.

Was the chance to learn worth that risk?

Yes.

Miranda raised her chin. "I've decided. I'll come to London and do what I can to help you."

CHAPTER 5

Hawkstowe had not returned to London. The information gnawed at Henry de Vere's brain, muting the sounds of street vendors, horses, and cart wheels as his carriage clattered over the cobblestones. Cabot Winfield had returned, but alone. That meant something important had detained Hawkstowe.

The change Henry had created in the timeline already rippled forward, shifting the world's fabric. The shift would gradually become a wrinkle, then a tear, and then, in no more than a month if he'd calculated correctly, a new and stronger weave in which the Gifted ruled England.

Oliver Cromwell had been succeeded as Lord Protector by his inept son, whose bungling had opened the way for Charles II's return from exile and the restoration of the monarchy. But that wouldn't happen now. Henry had gone back in time and slain the inept Richard Cromwell before his father's death. Henry's younger self was busily ingratiating himself with those in power. He, not that hapless fool, would succeed Cromwell as Lord Protector, and he would rule with a fist of magic-forged steel.

If nothing went wrong.

Once the changes began to manifest, his old nemesis, Hawkstowe, would be quick to suspect him. As a member of the Gifted Conclave's Council, the young earl could make trouble if he had the least ammunition.

By scrying, Henry had seen him with Cabot Winfield on the road, but Winfield had returned alone. Hawkstowe's delay could mean nothing to Henry's ultimate plans, but it could also signal trouble. Alas, but scrying did not convey sound, so Henry hadn't been able to determine what they discussed.

Best to investigate further without delay.

The carriage turned in between the gateposts of his new house in Holborn. As soon as the coach passed through, the gatekeepers would shut the wrought-iron gates and lock them against the unwelcome. What use was the wealth of an earldom if one couldn't secure privacy?

What use was magic if it didn't secure power?

Henry scowled. Hawkstowe and his ilk, with all their puling about honor and decency and the obligations of power, missed a critical point. The powerful should not have to hide from their inferiors.

Soon, if Henry's plans succeeded, the days of concealment would end. His family's honor would be vindicated, their longtime goal attained at last.

He would choose his time with care, though.

His *time*.

He smiled. Indeed it would be. Meanwhile, he must use discretion.

The carriage slowed, rattling to a stop before his steps. The coachman set the coach steps in place and opened the door.

Henry stepped out and climbed the front stairway. Built of brick and stone after the Great Fire destroyed his house near the Strand, his new London home provided an elegant seat for the earldom of Wyndon. Sunlight sparkled off the new windows, which were fitted with sashes instead of the old leaded casements. The new Wyndon House was a fitting place from which to launch a dynasty.

Unless Hawkstowe or some other Gifted meddler miraculously found a way to interfere.

Scowling, Henry reached the front door. It opened to reveal his well-trained porter, who bowed obsequiously. Henry favored the man with a nod. Ordinary, or unGifted, mortals did have their uses.

The footman, also unGifted, sprang forward to take his gloves, cloak, and plumed beaver hat. The exchange took only the few moments Henry deemed proper. He stalked across the elegant parquet flooring and upstairs to the first floor.

He strode into his parlor. The fire kept burning on the hearth ensured a warm haven from the afternoon chill. The setting sun cast a golden glow into the room, gilding the carved wood of the armchairs and table and brightening the maroons and blues of the Turkey-work upholstery. Henry noted it all with a glance. Fine as the room was, it could be finer. Would be, if not for the Mainwarings of Hawkstowe and their infernal meddling.

The old wrongs, however, served only to fuel his family's resolve. Soon enough, he would have his revenge.

Some two hundred years past, the Mainwarings had revealed his ancestor's scheme to use the chaos of the Wars of the Roses to seize control and elevate the Gifted to rule. Roland de Vere had been put to death, thanks to the Gifted Conclave Council, and the family prohibited from ever sitting on the Council.

Well, he would soon put an end to the Council and their idiotic blathering about protecting the unGifted.

He'd hoped he was done with the shadowland, the cold, wraith-ridden realm between the worlds of the quick and the dead, but it offered the most effective way to prevent trouble. He could even travel back in time, if need be, to see what Hawkstowe had been doing.

He chose a pebble from the basket of river rocks beside the hearth, an eccentricity his servants knew better than to notice. Returning to the living world required a sturdy, natural anchor, an object not shaped or altered by man.

Taking a deep breath to steel himself, he drew power from within him and focused it on the door to his dressing room. The silvery current, barely visible to his Gifted eyes, flowed toward and around the doorway. It limned the frame, then filled the opening. Thanks to long practice, he no longer needed a framed opening to form a portal, but having one made the transition easier.

He strode forward, mentally reaching for the sensation he'd had when communing with the wraith in the shadowy afterworld. He'd needed that link the first few times he'd breached the place. Since then, however, he'd developed the skill to dispense with it.

The deluded creature had thought Henry offered it salvation, but the remnant of its soul hadn't survived the drain of passing on its knowledge.

It had been no great loss. The wraith had been damned anyway, trapped between the living world and eternity. Creating a better England would cost men and women with purer souls their lives, but the result would be worth a few deaths.

He reached the glowing doorway. His power now bridged the worlds.

The shadowland occupied the same space as the living world, like a ghost realm. Only by creating such a portal could the living reach it, and only he knew how to do so.

He stepped into the glow. As he passed through, he drew the power around his body, forming a silvery aura as a shield against the perils ahead.

An instant of icy chill, and the world winked out. In its place swirled purple-gray mist that reeked of rotten eggs and thrummed with invisible power. He drew more of the power into himself, strengthening the nimbus of his shield with a burst of crackling, purple magic.

The dead rushed toward him, their doomed faces ghastly with gaping wounds or flesh-bare, skeletal mockeries of their living countenances. Soul-tearing shrieks pierced the fog.

The creatures swooped around him, their hatred pouring over his shielded form in waves. He grinned, knowing it angered them, and savored their renewed howls of rage. So long as he maintained the cloak of magic, they couldn't touch him.

He could vanquish them easily, thanks to the sway the quick held over the dead here, but their frustration provided some amusement. That and their fury over their fates made them restless and easily bored anyway. They would leave soon enough.

As he expected, the shrieking and howling slowly diminished. The trapped souls peeled away, one by one, in search of other prey. Legend said they often found it among the living, in those susceptible to visions and eerie imaginings. They might well. If visionaries couldn't control their power, they didn't deserve it.

He wandered through the fog, his mind fixed on Hawkstowe. Movement always helped find a person or place.

The fog thinned, settling around his ankles, and a scene came clear. An inn, somewhat south of Canterbury, drew him. He followed the impulse into the building, to a modest parlor. Hawkstowe leaned one hand on a simple, unpainted wooden mantel and stared into the flames below it. Judging by his brooding look, his journey hadn't gone well.

Good.

A closed door in the far corner signaled a second room. Henry drifted toward, then through, the plain, unfinished oak panel and into a bedchamber. No candles burned, and the setting sun outside cast little light through the curtains. His eyes needed a few moments to adjust.

As his vision sharpened, he realized the lump on the bed was a wench.

The dim light made her features hard to discern, but she seemed comely enough. Thick, dark hair in a straggly braid trailed across the pillow. A worn cloak covered her.

Had she caused Hawkstowe's discomfiture? One might always hope.

Who was she, though? If she were Hawkstowe's mistress, surely she would be in the parlor, catering to his comfort. So who was she?

Judging by the cloak and the crude, unfashionable braid of her hair, she was not only common but poor. Henry's lip curled. Perhaps she was some sort of charity case Hawkstowe meant to help.

Rubbing his jaw, Henry scowled. London held an abundance of poverty-stricken wenches if Hawkstowe or his tiresome grandmother wanted to indulge their charitable leanings. What made this one special?

Focusing on the earl's first meeting with the girl, Henry walked forward. When the mists cleared again, he was looking at an inn yard, the two of them standing by a well. He drifted closer to listen.

So the wench had visions, eh? If they were prophetic—

The girl grabbed the bucket from the well and stepped back, through his invisible form. "What was that?" she demanded.

"What do you mean?" Hawkstowe narrowed his eyes.

"That chill, there, like someone watching. What—"

Hawkstowe's raised hand signaled her to wait as he took a sudden step forward and through Henry. He wouldn't know what he'd sensed, though. The fool knew the afterworld waited for him, but neither he nor any other Gifted knew the living could travel it.

Henry smirked. Even if Hawkstowe learned what Henry was doing, he would have no idea how to stop it. Oh, it really was a shame that gloating openly would draw the wrong sort of attention. Playing with the young idiot would have to do.

But first, Henry would spy on whatever conversation they had after church and find out whether these visions of hers had the potential for trouble. While no one living had the skill to undo what he'd done, especially since he'd stolen the scroll that contained information on summoning and trapping wraiths, he'd rather not deal with the meddlesome councilors who ruled the Gifted Conclave. Not until he was ready.

So ... Dover after church. Focusing, he set off through the mist.

B ending over the basin, Miranda splashed water on her face. As she wiped it dry, Lord Hawkstowe called, "Mistress? Supper's here."

"Coming," she called. He probably expected her to set out the meal. She should hurry.

Miranda hastily tied her worn shoes and hurried into the parlor between their bedchambers. She'd expected to be housed with the inn's servants, not to have a guest chamber.

Lord Hawkstowe stood before a table that had been set up near the hearth. He directed a keen gaze at her. "Are you feeling better?"

"Yes. Thank you, milord. The sleep helped."

"Good." He turned to pull out one of the two chairs by the table, and she saw that the meal had already been set out. Why didn't he sit in the chair he'd pulled back? What was he waiting for?

With a slight smile that made her pulse kick, he asked, "Would you rather sit on the other side?"

Heat rushed to her cheeks. He'd pulled out the chair for her. No one had ever done that. Foolishly flattered even though she knew he was merely being courteous, she shook her head and hurried to sit.

At least her "thank you" came out clearly.

He took the folded linen napkin beside her spoon, shook it out, and laid it neatly across her lap. Taking his seat, he gestured to the food. "You must be hungry. Help yourself."

Unsettled by the jouncing coach he'd hired, she hadn't eaten all day. She was about to insist he go first, but his wry smile stopped her.

"You slept well?" he asked as she laid a slice of beef on her pewter plate.

When she nodded, he continued, "Earlier, I had a feeling similar to the one in the inn yard, that I was being watched." Reaching across, he poured ale from a pewter pitcher into a leather tankard.

"Any more cold patches?" She tore a chunk of bread from the round loaf on the table as delicately as she could.

"No." Helping himself to meat, he said, "Yet it was unsettling."

She frowned at her food, and he said, "I can mix an herb posset to help settle your stomach for tomorrow's journey, though mine won't be as good as some others could make. You should eat your fill while you can."

It was sound advice, so she took it. Throughout the meal, he refilled her ale and made sure she had enough food. Nothing in his demeanor

45

implied anything but courtesy. Indeed, he performed the small tasks almost absently. Yet they unsettled her.

Without her familiar glamours, which he'd convinced her to shed in the coach as part of the new life she meant to build, she already felt exposed. Having him serve her only added to her sense of being out of place.

He offered her more bread, and she shook her head. "Thank you, no." Carefully, she said, "You're kind to look out for me so, Lord Hawkstowe, but I can manage."

To her relief, he didn't take that amiss. Instead, he smiled, in such a friendly way that relief vanished in irrational warmth and a senseless impulse to touch.

Miranda took a firm grip on her napkin.

"You're my guest," he said simply. "I see to my guests' needs."

"That's good of you, but I'm not used to it. I can do for myself."

"You'd best become accustomed," he warned. "I've a house full of servants who'll be offended if you don't let them do their jobs."

That didn't make any sense. She frowned at him. "I thought I was to work for you, too. You said you would give me money."

"As a boon from one Gifted to another, and in appreciation for your time and help. You'll need to spend more time with my grandmother and me than any servant would, so you'll be our guest. As I said."

That still seemed strange. So did having him look directly at her when he spoke. She was accustomed to people looking at her when they spoke, of course. What she was not accustomed to, after so many years of relying on her disguising glamours, was having anyone actually *see* her. Yet Lord Hawkstowe did, glamours or no.

"Did you have enough to eat?" he asked. When she nodded, he continued, "You said you knew summoning and glamours. What of scrying?"

Miranda frowned again. "What's that?"

Surprise flickered in his eyes. "Let's have these dishes cleared, and I'll show you."

Henry walked out of the shadowland and into his own parlor. He gripped the stone in his pocket, his anchor to the real world, and reached for the fire's warmth. The chill faded, the slight veil obscuring the room vanished, and he was home.

Not before time, either. Any trip through the shadowland was tiring, in part because of the need to maintain shielding. One lapse, and the wraiths would tear him apart. Today, he'd spent long enough in their realm to be nearly drained.

"Bloody bitch," he muttered.

"Father?"

Henry wheeled. His son, William, Viscount Canby, stood in the doorway. Sturdy and fair, with the narrow, straight de Vere nose, he was clearly Henry's son. His long, curled wig and elegant attire marked him as a man of rank. His appearance did his family credit.

"Who's the bloody bitch?" William asked.

"Hawkstowe has taken up with a serving wench from Dover." Henry quickly told William what he'd seen, then continued, "The visions she described hint that she possesses the seer gift. If so, she might be of very great consequence indeed. That could be why Hawkstowe travels with her."

"What are you going to do?" Frowning, William seated himself by the hearth.

Henry shrugged. "I must determine whether she's his mistress or merely his tool. Either way, perhaps she can be persuaded to be useful."

"If you would teach me to travel as you do, I could help you."

"No. It's too dangerous." Especially in light of William's ambitions. He wouldn't hesitate to push Henry aside and claim the power in England for himself if he could. Only a fool would give him the means to do so. "Ring for some food, William."

Complying, his son shot him a sullen look. "If it's that dangerous, you should have someone with you."

Henry poured himself a brandy and sat by the fire. "I prefer to protect you." And himself.

"Stealing that old monastic chronicle will pay off doubly now," William said. "I could help you guard it."

Before Henry could answer, someone tapped on the door.

"Enter," he called. This had best be the food. And it was. His mouth watered at the succulent beef aroma.

When the footman left, Henry jabbed a fork into a slice of beef. "The book is well hidden."

He couldn't risk anyone finding the chronicle from Croyland Abbey and its description of time travel, least of all his ambitious son. That the monastic record also contained material supporting Richard III's claim to the throne of England in 1483 was an added benefit. The loss of that material would surely distract Hawkstowe if he became suspicious.

That was why Henry'd stolen it at a point in time when the theft would ensure that Sir George Buck didn't find it and include it in his defense of Richard III. Because that chronicle was the only record of the parliamentary act that removed King Richard's motive for murdering his nephews, it was vital to anyone defending the king's reputation.

Anyone such as Hawkstowe, for example.

William smirked at him. "You want Hawkstowe to realize it's missing."

"Of course. I'm counting on it. Because of his family curse, he'll be too worried about Richard III's reputation to bother about anything else changing until it's too late."

Henry smiled. "I'll enjoy watching him scramble about, hunting for it, while the changes in time roll forward and our family rules England."

William raised his glass to his father as Henry added, "When we shape our new England, Hawkstowe's will be one of the first heads rotting on the end of a pike."

Though it wouldn't actually be the de Vere family ruling England, just Henry as Lord Protector. Best not to let his power-hungry son know that, however, until it was done.

"Still," Henry added, clinking his glass against William's, "it's best to keep an eye on Hawkstowe. You're around the same age as his irresponsible and perpetually debt-ridden heir. I want you to befriend George Mainwaring. See what you can learn."

With a nod and a smirk, William said, "We'll soon know all about this wench and her connection to Hawkstowe."

"Try again." Richard kept his voice steady despite his impatience. "Reach out to the fire with your magic until you can feel the way the flames move."

Biting her lip, Mistress Willoughby nodded and stared at the hearth in their parlor at the inn.

Nothing appeared in the flames. His brows knitted. How could she create something as sophisticated as her dragon and yet know nothing about a simple skill like scrying? Yet he could feel her magic. She was trying.

Or else she was a brilliant actress.

Her shoulders slumped. "I'm sorry, but there's naught."

"Like all else, this takes practice." He passed her a plate of bread and cheese he'd kept from supper. "You've expended a great deal of energy, so you should eat something."

With a weary nod, she chose a wedge of creamy, yellow cheese. "May I ask you something?"

"I'm your teacher. I'm here to answer questions."

She hesitated before looking up at him. "This may sound foolish, but you seem ... almost familiar. In a way that has naught to do with my visions. When I'm close to you, it's almost a feeling of, well, recognition. Have we met before?"

"No. What you're describing is what one Gifted person feels in the presence of another. If you have that feeling in a stranger's presence, then that person is Gifted."

The light of understanding dawned in her eyes, and he fought the urge to cup her smooth cheek and assure her that all would be well. But he didn't yet know he could trust her.

Her expression thoughtful, she stared into the fire. "You'll see anything I raise. I saw what you raised to show me earlier. If there were anyone else here, would they see it?"

"Only if they were Gifted," he said. "This chamber could be filled with unGifted and they would see nothing."

She nodded, her gaze still on the flames.

Perhaps now, while her guard was down, was the best time to probe. Watching her face, Richard asked, "Had you ever heard my true name before I told you who I am in Dover?"

"No." She answered simply, her gaze direct and slightly puzzled. "How would I have?"

"Someone might have mentioned it to you." Watching her closely, he asked, "The Earl of Wyndon, perhaps."

"I don't move amongst titled folk, milord," she said quietly. He wanted to believe her, but Wyndon could've hidden his true identity. Better to retain a bit of suspicion than to trust too readily.

He noted, "You're an odd mix of skills, mistress, able to create something as complex as that dragon and yet not able to perform so simple a task as scrying."

Her eyes narrowed. "Are you suggesting that someone else created the dragon?"

"I'm asking."

Hurt flashed in her eyes, spurring a jab of guilt he ruthlessly quashed, before her face went stony. She stood and moved to the kindling box at the hearth's corner.

Kneeling by it, she raised an eyebrow. "With your lordship's permission?"

He nearly winced at the hurt radiating from her, but he had to know. His dealings with her would be much simpler if he didn't have to be on guard against her.

And if he weren't so drawn to her, but that was a separate problem.

She drew out a piece of kindling about as long as his forearm and as big around as his index finger. "I can make this more elaborate if you'll wait while I fetch a needle to prick my finger."

"We need not go to that length. A simple demonstration will suffice."

She broke the stick into pieces and laid them on the hearth with one in the middle and four slightly shorter ones at right angles to it, two on each side. At one end, she placed a piece no longer than her thumb. A single hair plucked from her head and laid along the central stick gave it a bit of color.

She took another long piece of kindling in one hand and held her other one, palm down, over her little figure. Magic crackled in the air around her fingers.

"Sticks for bones hard as stones," she intoned, reaching into the fireplace to light the tip of the kindling she held. "Hair for a coat against the cold." She touched the lit stick to its mates on the hearth, and the fire danced along the sticks.

Tossing the extra piece into the hearth, she added, "Fire alone to give vision life. Go, my kitten. Find the lord and prove my word."

Magic swirled with fire in a tiny whirlwind that obscured her creation. When the whirlwind died, a small kitten with a coat the same dark brown as Miranda Willoughby's hair stood on the hearth. It shook itself, glanced around the room, and pranced toward Richard.

So you see, a tiny voice in his head said.

He looked beyond the little construct to its maker. "My apologies."

"Accepted, of course."

A wave of her hand, and the kitten became sticks again. Gathering them up, she said, "But I haven't proved anything else to you. I can't prove that my skill isn't greater than I admit, and I can't prove no one put me up to summoning you. I can only give you my word that I've dealt with you in good faith."

He studied her. Her shoulders slumped just enough to be noticeable. In the firelight, she looked tired and dejected. Hurt lurked in the backs of her eyes, shadowing the pale blue, and he hated knowing he'd put it there. Especially since all his instincts said she was telling the truth.

Of course, he wanted very badly to believe her, and that wanting could influence his perceptions.

But he'd always trusted his instincts. For now, he would accept her word and see where that led them.

CHAPTER 6

An unusually large crowd filled Southwark's Borough High Street, blocking the way to London Bridge. Richard frowned at the throng. He'd never seen its like.

Perched in front of him on Zeus, Mistress Willoughby said, "I seldom traveled the bridge, but I don't remember hearing of crowds like that. They seem to be milling about, not going in."

"That's exactly what they're doing," he replied, surveyeing the mass of people.

Rather than take the hired coach home through the press of London traffic and send it back, he'd turned it in at the Tabard, one of the many inns lining the street. Mistress Willoughby had seemed glad to leave the carriage despite some nervousness when he first boosted her into the saddle.

She was a tall woman, and her soft hair brushed his cheek, enticing him, making him even more conscious of her warmth pressed against his chest and her body in his arms. She tempted him to flirt, and that wouldn't help either of them.

The sooner they reached his house, the better.

As they neared the bridge's gateway, the crowd grew denser. Carts, wagons, travelers on foot and herders with various sorts of livestock jammed the road between the half-timbered shops and inns. The throng even spilled into the yard of St. Saviour's church on the left.

Angry muttering about delays came from all sides. Beside the road, a lad tried in vain to corral a dozen geese he must've brought to market. "It's no use," the boy cried. "We've stood here too long."

"My lord," Mistress Willoughby said, just loudly enough for him to hear over the din, "do you feel the taint in the wind?"

"The wrongness." Grimly, he responded, "I do."

It wasn't evil, but an unearthly power in it raised the hair on the back of his neck. The air had been free of eerie taints for days. Why had the wrongness returned?

Above the crowd's heads, a line of halberds bristled in front of the bridge gate. Soldiers must be keeping order.

"Let's see what the problem is," he said. Richard urged Zeus through a narrow gap between the mass of people and the buildings lining the road.

The soldiers blocking the bridge wore steel helmets and breastplates over red tunics with blue trim, but he could see enough to recognize them as grenadiers, part of the foot guard. They usually protected the royal palaces. Odd. But the face at the front was familiar.

"Sergeant Mathers," Richard called. "Good day. What's the delay here?"

The burly, stony-faced man stepped forward and touched his helmet's front brim. "G'day milord. Bunch o' folk went through this morning, got in a quarrel and someone's pipe landed in a barrel. Afore anyone could blink, two houses caught fire."

The passage across the bridge was only ten feet wide in places, so one quarrelsome person could block traffic for a time, even without causing a fire.

As Mistress Willoughby murmured, "How awful," the soldier stepped closer.

"Fights in the city, too," he said softly, "so we're letting folk through a score at once from either end. The king's orders." With a sideways glance, he added, "If you want to go ahead, milord, you bein' His Majesty's friend, I can slip you in."

Mistress Willoughby said nothing, but her body tensed. At the thought of trading on social privilege?

Surveying the crowd, Richard thought others would have a more violent response.

"Hey, no shovin'," a man's deep voice rumbled.

"Outta my way," someone else yelled.

Curses filled the air. The crowd lurched back and forth. They might've been dodging a fight or seeking one. In the press, discerning

53

which was impossible. The soldiers rushed forward, halberds ready, to impose order.

Richard leaned down to Mathers. "My thanks, Sergeant, but I'll wait my turn."

"Thankee, milord." Mathers touched his helmet brim. Flinging a dark look at the crowd, he marched back to his station.

"My lord," Mistress Willoughby murmured. "Could the strange wind be why folk're on edge?"

"I don't know, but they seem too aggravated for a mere delay to cause."

"Make way," Mathers bellowed. "Folk comin' out. Make room, and then some o'you can go. Count off a score. You lot, form a queue! No shoving!"

Richard frowned. Adding people in such ugly moods to London's dense traffic could well lead to a riot.

"It's too bad there's no other bridge," Mistress Willoughby said softly.

"Yes, but we'll brave the chaos. Anything else would take longer." Riding down to Lambeth to take the horse ferry across with Zeus or, instead, stabling him at one of the inns nearby, taking a boat across, and then finding a hackney to reach home, all so he could send a stable boy back for the stallion, would be far more trouble than waiting their turn here.

In a dry voice, she said, "I'd forgotten some of London's inconveniences. The crowds were bad enough before this odd weather struck."

"I can't argue with that." Too much felt wrong of late. The Conclave should already be at work on at least some of it, preferably without endless dithering.

At last, Lord Hawkstowe rode through the cramped, dirty confines of London Bridge and crossed Thames Street. Miranda drew her worn cloak tighter against the cold wind blowing off the river.

Pushed back against him by the horse's motion, she couldn't help noticing the solid strength in his chest. And the way his deep voice rumbled against her back when he spoke. With his arms around her, she felt safe. Even wanted to curl closer, but that made no sense. She barely knew him. He'd been kind when they stopped for the night and was patient in his lessons, but what did that truly tell her about him?

More important was whether he would keep his promises.

Overhead as they rode up Bishopsgate, where he'd said his house was, a pall of brown wood smoke blended with the lowering clouds. Rank smells rose from the open sewage in the gutters. Coaches, carts, and horsemen crammed the narrow streets. Peddlers and liveried servants added to the congestion. She'd forgotten how chaotic the city was.

Tension crackled in the air, like the calm before a storm. Most folk dealt with London's usual crowding as a necessary ill, the jostling and squeezing unavoidable. Now they seemed as likely to shove and punch. At least she and the earl hadn't seen anything more worrisome than that.

Without her disguising glamours, she still felt exposed. Vulnerable. But no one looked twice at her.

Miranda stretched her neck. At least the ache in her shoulders would remind her to keep them straight when she met the Dowager Countess of Hawkstowe. Knowing how to serve people's food was a far cry from knowing how to talk to a woman who had never churned butter nor carried water for someone else's bath. Miranda had to manage, though, as Hawkstowe had warned she'd be spending time with both him and his grandmother.

He turned the horse off Bishopsgate Street and into a stone archway blocked by an iron-banded, wooden double gate. Mullioned windows sparkled on the front of the two stories above, but the gray stone wall had no windows at street level. Beside the gate hung a bell. He leaned over to tap it.

Someone opened a small hatch in one gate and peered out. "A moment, milord," a man's voice said.

The hatch shut, and the gate swung back to reveal a passage through the wall. Beyond lay a wide courtyard and walls of gray stone. The gate-keeper, a tall, sturdy man with grizzled brown hair and beard, held the gate as they passed through.

"Welcome home, milord." The man tugged his forelock as he spoke. Then he pushed the thick panel shut and swung the bar into place.

"Thank you, Morton," Hawkstowe said. He introduced the man to Miranda, adding, "His family have the kept the gates at Hawkstowe properties since the reign of Edward IV."

Something like two hundred years, then. Miranda smiled as Morton puffed up with pride. "It's a pleasure to meet you."

"Welcome, mistress."

Hawkstowe clucked to the horse. It lurched forward once again, passing onto the packed earth of a courtyard surrounded by stone walls rising to a height of four stories. Tall, narrow windows overlooked the yard. The rooftops bristled with chimneys, each subject to the two-shilling hearth tax.

If Hawkstowe could afford to pay it, he was wealthy beyond any of her imagining. Miranda swallowed against a rush of dismay. She didn't know how to behave with such people. Or in such a place.

In the center of the wall to the left, a grand, stone stairway led to a wide landing. At the top, a wide, eight-paneled door with brass fittings was clearly the main entrance. Other, less grand doors opened into the courtyard on all sides.

A dark-haired youth in blue wool breeches and jerkin and a white linen shirt ran forward from the gate area. He reached the wide stairway just as Hawkstowe stopped beside it.

The earl tossed his reins to the young man. "How are you, Robin?"

"Right as can be, milord." The lad tugged his forelock. "Welcome home."

"Thank you." Hawkstowe swung his right leg over and dropped to the ground. "Rub him down well. He's had a long journey."

"Aye, milord, you can depend on it."

The earl presented the stable boy to her, and the lad tugged his forelock again as he grasped the horse's reins.

Hawkstowe held out his arms to Miranda. When she put her hands on his shoulders, he grasped her waist to lift her down.

Her legs were unsteady, but he caught her before she could fall. "Easy," he murmured and held her in the curve of his arm.

Her cheeks heated. The temptation to linger there and the knowledge that it was foolish had her shifting away as soon as she could.

He didn't seem to mind. "All right now?" he asked.

"Yes, thank you, but I should bring my bundle," she said as they mounted the stairs.

"It'll be taken to your chamber."

Not since her childhood had anyone carried her burdens. It was a small thing, but a daunting vista of other small things, other customs she didn't know, loomed ahead. She knew how to be a servant, not a guest. Was all this courtesy some sort of ruse? Or was he just odd?

They reached the doors. A short, stocky, middle-aged man in a simple blue suit opened one of them.

"Good afternoon, Enderby," Hawkstowe said.

He ushered Miranda into an elegant foyer with salmon hangings, oak walls, and a gleaming parquet floor. Someone must spend a great deal of time keeping that wood so clean and shiny. The whole of it made her feel even more out of place.

The man bowed. "Welcome home, milord. Good day, mistress."

Nodding, Hawkstowe thanked him. "This is our guest, Mistress Willoughby. Order her things taken to the yellow bedchamber and have someone ask my grandmother to join us there. I'll kindle the fire myself."

The servant said, "At once, milord."

Miranda scarcely heard him. She would have a fireplace of her own, a warm room. It sounded too grand to believe.

Enderby had the same air of familiarity as Lord Hawkstowe. He, too, must be Gifted.

A man in blue livery, a footman, she guessed, came forward. Hawkstowe surrendered his cloak and hat and assisted Miranda in removing her cloak. Its shabbiness made her want to wince, but the footman didn't seem to notice as he walked away.

"My lord," Enderby said, his expression troubled, "if I might have a moment."

An unreadable look passed between the two men. Hawkstowe said, "Of course. Have John escort Mistress Willoughby to her chamber and send Patience up to her."

"Of course, milord." The man beckoned, and the same footman came forward again.

Miranda followed him and tried not to gawk along the way. This place was so grand, and she was so plain. If she didn't live up to their expectations, would they cast her out?

❧

G od's wounds, Richard thought as his guest followed John up the stairs. *More problems.*

When the pair were out of earshot, Richard cocked an eyebrow at his porter. "Well, Enderby?"

His face expressionless, Enderby said, "Master Mainwaring has been in residence for the last sennight."

Richard frowned. If George was here, he needed something, likely money. George had no self-discipline, and he'd been trading on his status as heir presumptive to cause problems at Hawkstowe. He seemed unlikely ever to straighten himself out.

"I'd best see him straight away, then." Conducting magic lessons with his unGifted cousin in the house, even though George spent much of his time out gambling, whoring, or drinking, would require some care.

"I believe," Enderby said coolly, "your lordship's cousin is still abed."

Richard acknowledged the information with a nod and stalked toward the wide, oak stairs. His cousin would soon be very much out of bed.

Richard strode to the first floor and turned right. The rush matting on the corridor's parquet flooring muffled his footsteps, but George wouldn't hear them anyway unless he'd drunk far less than usual.

The tall windows overlooking the back garden admitted weak afternoon sunlight. The trees in the orchard seemed to droop, as though they hadn't had enough rain. He'd have to ask Grandmère how long the eerie wind had blown here.

He reached the room his cousin usually occupied and entered without knocking. Curtains of pale blue damask blocked the courtyard windows on the room's far side. From behind the matching bed curtains came loud snoring.

"Damnation," Richard muttered.

A flick of his hand magically opened the window curtains, a move he wouldn't have used if George could've seen it. Light poured into the room as he stalked around the bed, to the window side. When he yanked open the bed curtains, their rings rattled and clanked. Light poured over the mound under the covers, which obscured all of George except his tousled, brown hair.

The snoring stopped. Burrowing into the pillows, George turned his back to the window and jerked the coverlet over his head.

Richard grasped the coverlet's edge to yank it free. "Up, George." Richard flung the coverlet to the foot of the bed.

George dived sleepily for it.

Slamming a hand onto the crumpled folds, Richard said, "Get out of the bed before I toss you out."

"I say." George squinted at him. "'Tis early, Richard."

"It's midafternoon. Get up." Richard gripped the edge of the mattress. The enhanced strength of the Gifted didn't compare to that of mythical giants, but that and a bit of magic would allow him to pull the feather mattress out from under his cousin.

"A'right, a'right." George slipped through the curtains on the bed's far side. His bare footsteps plodded toward the hearth.

Richard strode to meet him. "No wine. You've had enough."

Hand on the fine Venetian glass decanter, George scowled. His face looked pasty in the sunlight, bloated from too much drink and too little sleep. His hair, cut short to make wearing a wig easier, stuck out from his head in spikes. The stain on his nightshirt looked old.

"I need a drink to wake up," he said.

"You need a clear head. Sit down."

George glared but had the sense not to bring the decanter as he shuffled toward one of the chairs by the hearth. He seated himself slowly.

Settling into the opposite chair, Richard caught a whiff of heavy, floral perfume. "If you brought a woman in here—"

George shook his head, then winced, rubbing his brow. "Grandmère'd kill me before you could. I had a lusty wench, indeed, but at Little Nell's, down by the docks." He smiled. "You should try Nell's girls. You need to have some fun, Richard."

"I needn't bother. You have enough for an army. What have you done now, George?"

"Done?" George opened his eyes wide.

"You look about as innocent as one of Nell's girls. How much do you need?"

George shrugged, his glance drifting to the cold hearth. "Not so much. Fifty or sixty pounds."

"Last month, it was twenty. How did you run up such a debt?" Richard directed a cold look at him.

"I really think that's my affair, Richard." George drew himself up in the chair.

"My money, my affair. That sum would pay the Hawkstowe steward for two years or all the footmen in this house for a year."

God's wounds, but the tenants of Hawkstowe deserved far better than George's negligent, self-indulgent care. Yet Richard couldn't marry or beget heirs unless he lifted the curse.

George fidgeted, a sulky expression on his face.

"Well?" Richard prodded.

George stared down at the rush matting. His gaze drifted to the gold-and-brown Turkey-work carpet draped over the table by the wall.

"As you wish." Richard stood. "I trust you'll find Fleet prison comfortable when your creditors have you arrested for debt. You've an hour to leave the house."

"You can't mean that!" George shot to his feet. "'Od's fish, I'm your heir."

Richard stared hard at him. "You have expectations, George, no more. I'll no longer tolerate your meddling at Hawkstowe—"

"I didn't, I merely—"

"I trust my steward. You manhandled the smith's daughter. I won't stand for that, nor will I pay for your drunken follies. We're done." Richard wheeled and marched toward the door.

"Wait," George cried.

Richard turned slowly.

George prodded the rush matting with a bare toe. "I was gambling."

"Losing sixty pounds requires a great deal of gambling."

George shrugged.

Inwardly, Richard groaned. A stay in a cell would do George good, but it would distress Grandmère, even though she'd agree he deserved it. "I'll pay your debts. This time."

George looked sidelong at him.

"I'll also pay for a room somewhere in the city until the spring, but that's all. Truly all. Ever." Perhaps the shock of being ejected would help George decide to straighten up.

"You won't need to help me again, Richard."

He always said that. But he never meant it, and only a fool would believe this time would be different.

"Good, because this is your last chance." Richard waited until his cousin met his gaze. "You're going out to Jamaica to work with my steward there, whose commands you will obey."

"Jamaica," George yelped. "I can't go to Jamaica!"

"You can't stay here, either, without making a mess for yourself."

Jamaica was far enough away that George would land in debtor's prison before he could appeal to Richard, but Grandmère wouldn't have to know it. Or have people comment upon it. If George turned himself around and did well, they could discuss a larger role for him in managing the family properties. But saying so now would only bring forth promises Richard dared not trust.

"You'll sail with the supply ship in the spring. If you run into debt again before then, I'll hand you over to a press gang and let the Royal Navy pound the nonsense out of you."

"You—you—that's kidnapping," George sputtered.

"No, it's impressment. Meanwhile, I'll disinherit you."

Crossing his arms, George smirked. "That, you can't do."

Richard raised an eyebrow. "Only the title and Hawkstowe itself, where you're none too beloved just now, are entailed. The rest of the estate is mine to do with as I will."

George's eyes narrowed. "You've no other kin to leave it to."

"I can find someone," Richard ground out. "Or else tie it up in trusts you'll never break. I warn you, George, don't try me."

They glared at each other. George's face slowly reddened.

Light footsteps sounded in the corridor. Behind Richard, Grandmère's low, firm voice said, "Well. Another bout of familial affection, I see."

Richard turned to greet her. "Good day, Grandmère."

"Welcome home, Richard." She kissed his cheek. Her glance raked upward from George's bare feet to his irate face.

"For goodness' sake, George, put on some clothes. Richard, Cabot Winfield asked that you join him and his brother for supper as soon as you returned." Despite her casual tone, her green eyes held a knowing look.

Of course Cabot would be aware that he'd returned. By scrying in a fire, he could monitor any parts of the journey conducted outside warded buildings or chambers.

"And I want to hear about Dover," Grandmère said.

For George's benefit, Richard smiled. He slid her arm through his. "Dover was interesting."

With a glance back at George, he said, "I meant what I said." In answer to Grandmère's questioning look. Richard added, in a flat tone that closed the subject, "George will be leaving us."

As they walked down the corridor, he told her about their guest and her visions. Grandmère listened in thoughtful silence.

She must've stayed in today, for she wore a simple gown of rich green wool that bore no elaborate decoration, only frills of lace bordering the square neckline and elbow-length sleeves. The fringe of silvery hair over her brow and the clusters of curls at the sides of her head framed a face that looked younger than her sixty-three years.

"This girl doesn't sound like the sort of tool Wyndon would use," she murmured when he finished. "Though of course that would make her ideal, from his viewpoint."

"Exactly. So I didn't accord her the use of my given name."

Grandmère's brows rose. Such use was so common among England's Gifted that they considered it the merest courtesy.

Frowning, he said, "I don't think she knows the custom." He told his grandmother about his talks with their guest on the road. "See if you can win some confidences from her. If she is as she seems to be—and I think she is—dealing with her will be much simpler."

They reached the yellow bedchamber. Through the open doorway, he could see Miranda Willoughby perched gingerly on the edge of the bed, her fingers tightly clenched.

His pulse kicked, and his eyes clung to the smooth curve of her cheek, so different from her disguise. His fingers itched to touch, but that was beyond unwise. He clenched them into a fist.

When he knocked on the door jamb, she leaped to her feet. She looked relieved to see him, and he had no call to preen over that.

Grandmère said, "You are our guest, mistress. No need to stand on ceremony."

Richard introduced the two women. The girl made a quick dipping movement that might've begun a curtsey but stopped it abruptly.

"You have a beautiful home," she said.

He smiled acknowledgment. "It will be warmer once I have the fire going."

Striding to the hearth, he realized the yellow damask hangings at the windows and halfway down the pale oak walls and the blue-and-white Delft tiles on the firebox surround were likely finer than anything she had ever known. Yet she had the breeding or the sense not to gush about them.

"You look done in, my dear," his grandmother said behind him. "Was the journey rough?"

"I fear I don't do well in coaches, milady."

"Many people don't," Grandmère replied.

Envisioning fire, Richard waved his hand above the wood in the firebox, letting magic bring his intention to life. A spark caught in the stacked kindling, and he fanned it.

"Mistress Willoughby," Grandmère said, "you must want a bath to wash off the road dirt. Come sit by the fire while I send for water. We can become acquainted while we wait for it."

"Thank you, milady."

His grandmother added, "Richard, you likely want a bath yourself and clean clothes for supper."

"Indeed." Besides, their guest might confide more in his grandmother if it were just the two of them.

~

P ondering his guest, Richard started down the stairs an hour later. A young woman alone in the world had to guard herself. A Gifted young woman had to take even more care, lest she fall under the control of someone who would abuse her Gifts.

Mistress Willoughby could have found someone to keep her in far greater ease if she had shown her true form, yet she had taken the harder path. He had to respect that.

Travel by coach was uncomfortable at best, and he'd set a punishing pace because of his concern about what her visions might mean. Yet she had never complained. Did her stoic endurance signify backbone?

Acceptance of a hard lot in life?

Or determination to see a scheme to its end? He thought—even hoped —not, but niggling doubts remained.

Grandmère met him at the foot of the stairs. "Our guest fell asleep, wearier than she knew from the journey. She's an interesting girl and seems well brought up, for all her straitened circumstances."

Richard said, "I trust she told you of her family's deaths?"

"Yes, poor thing, though I had to pry the details out of her. It's no wonder she has such a guarded look in her eyes. Her life cannot have been easy."

"No, and it left her woefully untrained. She didn't even know what scrying was until we tried it at an inn on the way here. We tried for quite a while, but she couldn't manage even a simple image."

Grandmère raised her eyebrows. "Truly?"

"I don't think she was feigning her inability, though the strain of travel may have left her too weary for the attempt. I promised her magical training before we left Dover."

"I'll help if you wish."

"I hoped you would. Unless she's a good actress, she has excellent perceptions but little training except in glamours and such." He paused. "I want to trust her, Grandmère, but I'm not yet certain I can."

His grandmother nodded her understanding. "Before you go, I must warn you. Frances Vale is a dreadful gossip, but she does glean useful information at times. Wyndon has returned to London. According to Frances, he seemed very pleased about something, said it had to do with old grievances but wouldn't explain."

"No sane man would tell Lady Vale anything he didn't want all over the city. Wyndon is likely so pleased over the discovery of the princes' bones at the Tower last summer. His pleasure will pass in time."

Richard extended his senses to make certain they were alone. "Yet all these events so close in time strain coincidence. Naturally, I suspect Wyndon. I scried last night while Mistress Willoughby slept and could find no trace of her with him in the recent past."

His grandmother looked thoughtful. "She has a sweetness about her that wouldn't survive any dealing with him. We're so accustomed to plots and intrigue from our time at court. Perhaps too accustomed. While we need not trust her fully until we know her better, we should give her the benefit of the doubt. Unless we discover a reason not to."

"On that, Grandmère, I bow to your judgment."

She chuckled. "As well you should, my lad. I think your instinct to treat her as a guest is a good one, but we'll need to have the dressmaker and the cobbler come in."

"I agree. What clothing she has looks well made but old and worn. Since she's not only our guest but our Gifted kindred, we should remedy that."

"I'll see to it." Grandmère patted his arm. "At least all of this gave you an excuse for missing the annual White Rose banquet. I'm sure your friends will give you a full report."

As he grimaced, she said, "Enjoy your evening. I know you'll like seeing Cabot and the others."

He thanked her and beckoned to Enderby.

The porter brought Richard's cloak, then departed with a bow. Richard swung the dark blue velvet garment around his shoulders.

Grandmère adjusted the set of the collar. Frailty suddenly appeared in the determined lift of her chin, a gesture that dared time to do its worst. "You look very like your father, you know. You could be my Robert come again."

"Yes, Grandmère, I know." She'd lost her son too soon and so, he suspected, doubly cherished her grandson. Richard leaned down to kiss her cheek.

Enderby opened the door for him. Richard nodded thanks and loped down the courtyard stairs to his waiting coach.

As the coach pulled out into Bishopsgate Street, his mind drifted to his hazy memories of his father—the sound of laughter, the scent of pipe tobacco, snatches of whistled melody. Only impressions, save for three or four exchanges he could recall.

Most of the time, his father had been in England, working for the king's restoration. Such work left little time for a boy too young to help. So Richard had been sent with Grandmère to safety in France.

His last conversation with his father remained clearest in his mind. On the eve of going to war, Robert Mainwaring spoke solemnly to him. "Son, never forget you are an Englishman, and only the restoration of the true king can bring order and peace to England. Remember, too, that our family owes blood debt to King Richard III and the house of York."

Richard had promised. His father had embraced him, kissed Grandmère's cheek, and departed in a swirl of velvet cloak. He had died a few weeks later in King Charles II's defense at the useless battle of Worcester.

The memory burned like a hot coal in Richard's mind. With it came the old doubts about whether his father's death had been a natural result of battle or a consequence of obsession and distraction due to the family curse. Grandfather had taken his own life in a fit of madness after years of fruitlessly trying to lift the curse. Grandfather'd had Grandmère's love and support, while Mother gave Father only bitterness and resentment. Would that make a man snap sooner?

Richard sighed. He hated the annual gathering of the League of the White Rose because it threw the family curse in his face. But it was a link to his father, who had never missed the dinner if he could be in London for it.

Descendants of Richard III's supporters, the league's members gathered each year on October second, the dead king's birthday, to honor the man whose motto had been *Loyalty binds me*. Out of loyalty, they preserved the true story of his life in defiance of the slanderous tale perpetuated by the Tudors and their pet playwright, Shakespeare.

Richard's studies had given him a reluctant appreciation for the king whose name he bore, the last of the Yorkist line. If not for Edmund's damning vow, he might have found some pleasure in the dinner, despite its tedious traditions. At least this year, he could hear about anything important from his friends without having to endure the gathering.

Cabot and the others would doubtless have much to say. Then perhaps they could help untangle his current puzzle.

CHAPTER 7

"This year's White Rose banquet wasn't as tedious as they usually are," Cabot said. He led Richard and the others into the library of Aysgarth House, the Winfield family's London home. "We've a mystery to solve, and I don't mean the ill wind and tension in the City."

"Then we have two," Richard said. "I brought one back with me."

His favorite chamber here, the library smelled of beeswax candles and leather bindings. The Great Fire had swept through this part of the city, destroying the medieval house, but the family and their servants had managed to save many of the books and paintings.

A cheery blaze crackling on the hearth banished the autumn chill. Richard turned to wait for Cabot, who was locking the door. With the evening meal finished and no servants likely to disturb them, they could speak freely.

Cabot's brother, Jeremy, dropped onto a straight-backed chair by the hearth. "The evening was tedious enough," he said, grimacing. "If one more man had said, 'The fact that those bones in the Tower were found where Thomas More said they'd be doesn't mean they belong to the Princes,' I might've bolted from the room."

Thomas More, Henry VIII's rebellious chancellor, had written a damning biography of Richard III. His account was widely believed though More had been only seven when the king died. Much had been made of the bones under the stairs in the Tower of London's White

Tower as evidence of the boys' deaths and their uncle's guilt. Only Richard and his friends—and Wyndon, who doubtless found the whole thing amusing—knew the blame belonged elsewhere.

Pouring madeira into goblets of Venetian glass marked with delicate tracery, Cabot said, "An aide to the Archbishop of Canterbury bolting from dinner? Undignified, Jeremy. What would the archbishop think?"

"Since he isn't a member of the group, I doubt he would ever hear of it." Accepting the wine Cabot handed him, Jeremy shook his head. "Whenever I come up to London, the archbishop expects me to stay at Lambeth Palace. He then embroils me in some sort of church political strife. Every year, I vow I'm not coming up from Canterbury for this. Yet every year, here I am."

"Because you're loyal," Richard said quietly, taking the glass Cabot offered. "King Richard valued loyalty, too."

And had inspired it in others, as demonstrated by the annual gathering in his honor. While the Tudors reigned, the group had met discreetly, doing so openly only after the Stuart James I succeeded to the throne.

Jeremy raised his goblet in salute.

Like Cabot, he stood over six feet tall and had their father's high cheekbones and aquiline nose and their mother's wide, generous mouth and intelligent gray gaze. Jeremy, however, was slimmer of build and paler, with hair of darker brown. He spent his days indoors reading scripture and dealing with church politics instead of outdoors rigging sails. His was a quieter but equally imposing presence.

The fourth member of the party, Christopher "Kit" Grayson, Earl of Havelock, in Northumberland, ran a hand through his dark hair and smiled at Richard. "It's only natural that everyone would talk of those bones, what with their just having turned up this summer, but the talk grew tiresome."

Richard nodded at him. "I'm certain it did. But let's share our mysteries. What happened at the banquet?"

Cabot quirked a brow at him. "You first. Tell us about Dover."

Possibilities whirling in Richard's brain made him too restless to sit still. He paced the room while he told them of Miranda Willoughby and her strange visions.

Standing by the hearth, he concluded, "Add to that, Wyndon was out of London all the latter part of the summer. According to Lady Vale, who may rattle like a coach on a country lane but generally speaks the truth, he returned very pleased with himself over 'old grievances.' As far as I know, he has no grievance older than the one against the Main-warings."

"As far as you know." Jeremy frowned. "What of this maidservant? Do you think she has some connection to him?"

Her face rose in Richard's mind, her clear eyes troubled as she stared out at the Channel in indecision. He liked her, he realized.

At last, he shook his head. "My instincts, and Grandmère's, say no. I think she may be just what she seems."

Or so he hoped.

Cabot rose to refill his own glass. "Talking of old grievances reminds me of our news and of what Brackenbury said at the White Rose gathering. About his copy of Buck, do you remember?" He glanced at Kit and Jeremy, who nodded.

Sir George Buck had written his *History of King Richard III*, the first defense of the late king, during the reign of James I, some one hundred and thirty years after Richard III's death. Every man in the room owned a copy.

"He said it didn't read aright," Kit recalled.

Cabot nodded. "It doesn't. I skimmed over my copy this afternoon to check it. Brackenbury isn't Gifted, which may explain his inability to spot the difference, but a big part of it's gone missing."

"What do you mean?" Richard asked as his gut tensed.

"It seems to have all its pages, but all references to the *Croyland Chronicle* are gone." Cabot rubbed a hand over his jaw. "I put away the problem to deal with later, but given the boar, stag, and dragon symbols in the vision you describe, it's doubly worrisome."

The *Croyland Chronicle*, a record of events in England kept by monks at Croyland Abbey, had formed the basis for Buck's defense of King Richard's actions in assuming the throne. In the *Chronicle*, Buck had found and reported the text of the *Titulus Regius*, the act of Parliament setting forth the reasons why Parliament considered Richard III, and not his brother's son, the rightful heir to the throne. With Parliament supporting his claim, King Richard had had no reason to murder his nephews.

Slowly, Kit said, "But the only way to do that, to change all the books, would be by magic. And even then, there must be hundreds of copies out there. Buck's *History* has been in print for decades. It would be impossible to change them all, singly or as a group."

"Not if you could splice time," Richard said. A chill spiked into the back of his neck. "If you spliced from now back to a point before Buck found the *Chronicle*, then destroyed it—"

"It wouldn't—couldn't—be in the text," a pale-faced Jeremy finished. "I read Buck last year before the banquet. The references were there."

"No one at the gathering commented specifically on the difference in Buck's book," Cabot noted. "If you're right and someone tampered with the *Chronicle* magically, perhaps only the Gifted can remember what things were before."

"Mistress Willoughby dreamed of a book's pages changing before her eyes," Richard said, his concern deepening. "And now this." Memory stirred, and he added, "She also saw a sampler that suddenly appeared on a wall, stitched by the wife of a man who'd never wed."

Kit frowned. "You went to Pendragon to study splicing last summer, Richard. I remember you said you didn't find any clues to lifting the family curse. Did you learn anything that could explain how all this could happen?"

Pendragon manor, deep in the Cumberland hills, was the secret stronghold and homestead of England's Gifted. The manor and its library were open to any of them who cared to visit.

"I found references to splicing across time," Richard replied, "as well as across distance. One scroll said an event that touches one time as well as another can weaken the barriers between the two and help create a splice."

"And the boys' bones were found this past July, tying 1674 to 1483, the year they died, and linking all the years they lay buried," Jeremy said. "I don't like the coincidence."

"If what we suspect is true," Richard said, "someone out there is dangerous. If you can go back in time, why not change the source of whatever you dislike?"

If he could travel back in time, he could undo the murders of Richard III's nephews. Prevent the family curse.

But that would violate natural law. Surely there would be consequences—such as the recent eerie wind, perhaps? Or something worse?

Cabot said, "Mere dislike doesn't seem reason enough to try something that must involve considerable risk. The princes, their bones, and King Richard's reputation would be motives for some of us. Personal advantage is an understandable desire. But where's the benefit in changing the text of a comparatively obscure book?"

"Perhaps more to the point," Kit added, "who benefits?"

"While I'm always ready to suspect Wyndon," Richard said, "I don't see what changing that small detail gains for him. Besides, many people have browsed through the old scrolls and books at Pendragon at one time or another. All of us did and never saw anything specifically saying how to travel time."

Kit rose to pace before the hearth. "Yes, but the library's generally a disordered jumble. Whoever did this might have found something amidst the mess. Or elsewhere. And hidden the source. The library's supposedly warded so nothing can be removed, but any ward can be broken or evaded if one applies enough power."

"Good point," Cabot acknowledged. "Are we really considering that someone has changed time? Doing so would be a violation of natural law and thus forbidden, no matter how much anyone might speculate about it."

The four exchanged grim looks. "It seems the only explanation," Richard muttered.

"Didn't you say, Richard," Kit asked, "that everything you found was theoretical? That nothing was practical?"

Richard studied the flames. "I found vague, confusing references to methods in some of the oldest scrolls. The writing had faded beyond even magical recall in some places. In others, the terms made little sense. They refer to taking Death's path with a foot in life on either side. One said something about walking through the wraiths. It's obvious this would be dangerous, even potentially lethal, but the material isn't specific enough to be of any use."

"Aye." Cabot rubbed his jaw. "But why the *Croyland Chronicle*? Aside from the men at the banquet and their families, there can't be above two-score people in England who care about claims to the throne in 1483."

"Perhaps as a test, to see if it was possible," Kit said.

"Or as bait," Richard added. "For that or a distraction, such a deed would catch my attention more than anyone's once it came to light. Which again argues for Wyndon's guilt. The Conclave Council punished the de Veres for Roland's magical sins, but he was also convicted of treason and attainted under King Edward IV, costing the family lands."

"Regardless," Jeremy said, "we're discussing the power to alter reality. If you can destroy a document, why not a life? Why not go back and kill Oliver Cromwell and win the civil war? Why not, if you serve Rome, kill Martin Luther before he even conceived his theses?"

"If you have that power," Kit suggested, "why not use it boldly? Yet the change, as far as we know, is merely this one book."

Cabot shook his head, frowning. "For that reason, I agree with Richard. This smells of bait laid for us, particularly for him, though we shouldn't rule out the possibility that this was done for some other reason we can't fathom. Perhaps it was merely practice for something bigger. Who can say whether other changes have been made, ones we haven't yet noticed?"

Kit said, "The *Chronicle* covers more than the reigns of Richard III and Edward IV. It could've been taken because of something else it contains. Or by someone who subscribes, as many yet do, to the idea of Richard III as a monster and detests the fact that Parliament supported his claim to the throne. The loss of that information bolsters the Tudors at King Richard's expense."

"As the Tudor dragon threatened King Richard's boar in Mistress Willoughby's vision," Richard noted.

Cabot stood to pace. "Someone who had the power to change history would want to eliminate anyone who could combat him. Or her. Some of the Gifted lack the raw power, but those of us who spring from Morgan's and Merlin's lines are much stronger."

They all nodded. Morgan le Fay and her twin, Merlin, had stood at King Arthur's side, wielding astonishing power in his service. Joining their magic made them more than doubly stronger. Until they quarreled over the role of magic in the realm and everything started falling apart.

Richard wrenched his mind back to the present as Cabot added, "In fact, I think only someone of that lineage would have the power to cause such a change or combat one who created it."

Kit rubbed the back of his neck as though it ached. "Wyndon springs of those lines, but so do we four. And many others. So we can't consider him our only suspect. I wonder whether there's still a copy of the *Chronicle* in the library where Buck found it. And if not, then what?"

"I wonder," Richard said, gazing unseeing at the night, "assuming it's gone, whether Mistress Willoughby's dream comes as a warning of that. Or, as we said, as bait."

"Well, we've enough problems for the moment," Jeremy noted. "You seem to be at the center of this, Richard, based on the girl's vision. Have you a suggestion?"

"If we can determine what changed first," Richard said, "it will tell us when the alterations began, and perhaps how." He glanced at Jeremy. "Can

71

you search the Church's records and see whether anything else seems amiss?"

Jeremy stared down into his wine. "I can put my clerks to work writing summaries of parliamentary acts, starting with last year and working backwards to the Restoration. I'll also have them rework the same periods each fortnight or so. If the summaries change, history has. That could help us trace the changes back in time."

Nodding approval, Kit added, "I'll see what I can find among the private libraries of the Gifted. People are used to having me poke around when I'm in London. Maybe they have something about time travel."

"We can hope," Richard said. "I'll work with Mistress Willoughby on her dreams until I know for certain what they mean." He cast a grim look at the fire.

Jeremy nodded. "We shouldn't discount the chance that this girl actually had a dream of power. If the *Chronicle* is gone, her visions might be our best chance of finding it."

~

Miranda struggled against the dream. Hidden in the bushes, a bear tracked the knight, Hawkstowe, as he rode down a forest track. The beast exuded malice. She had to warn him. She tried to call, then to scream, her throat working frantically, but no sound came out.

Suddenly, the dream changed. The forest trees dissolved into shadow. When the shadows cleared, she stood on a ladder above a crowd, her throat tight with terror, her eyes on the cross atop a distant church's steeple.

Help would not come. If only she'd had the chance, just once to—

With a gasp, she broke free and opened her eyes. She lay in a bed with a canopy. With curtains, even.

At Lord Hawkstowe's house. Safe.

She hadn't dreamed of Mother's death in years. Mayhap all the uncertainty she felt had triggered the vivid images, taking her back to the day that shattered her family's soul. She hadn't actually been there when Mother died, of course. Father had forbidden it. But he had gone, lingering on the outskirts of the crowd, and had hardly spoken for days after.

Wiping sweat from her upper lip with her sleeve, she peeked through the bed curtains. The banked fire left the room dim and chilly. In the far corner, Patience, the young, square-faced maid who'd been assigned to her, slept on a truckle bed. She was not Gifted, but Miranda still felt as though she had more in common with Patience than with the house's owners.

She shook her head. For all she knew, this also was a dream. A maid assigned to her. This beautiful chamber with its damask hangings and ornate mantel carved with cherubs and flowers. She'd never slept under a plaster ceiling or known anyone who did.

She rubbed her eyes. The room didn't vanish, but she was definitely awake now. She should do as Lady Hawkstowe had asked and write down her dreams while they were fresh.

The beautiful, green satin dressing gown Lady Hawkstowe had loaned her lay across the corner of the bed. Miranda slipped into it.

Carefully she lit a candle with flint and tinder and placed it on the delicate table by the window. The beeswax gave off a sweet scent and a steady glow, unlike the rush lights, wicks dipped in fat, they'd used at the Golden Swan.

Patience sighed, burrowing into her covers, but didn't rouse. Miranda uncapped the inkwell on the desk and drew paper and a quill pen from the lone drawer.

All this was so confusing. Why had her gift awakened now, and with such insistence?

Regardless, she had to learn to control the visions. Making her gift useful was the best way to convince Lord Hawkstowe to value her. To earn enough of his regard and his grandmother's that they would help her find a new situation. Going back to the inn from a place like this would be even harder than enduring it before had been.

CHAPTER 8

As Richard made his way through his quiet house, he mulled over the changes to Buck's book. How did Miranda Willoughby's dream tie into them? How could he and his friends determine that?

Faint light, as though from a single candle, showed under the door of the yellow bedchamber. Bait, or a guest in need of aid?

His duty as her host overrode his vague suspicions. He tapped softly on the door. "Mistress Willoughby?"

Footsteps approached, so quietly that a man with normal hearing wouldn't have caught the sound. "Lord Hawkstowe?"

"Yes. Is anything amiss?"

She opened the door a crack to peer at him around it. "No, I thank you," she whispered, likely to avoid awakening her maid. "Your grandmother told me to write down my dreams, and I had one, and so I've written it down. I was just finishing when you knocked."

Beneath her nightcap, her hair had strayed from its loose braid. Her eyes looked too large in her pale face.

"The dream disturbed you?" he asked.

"I . . . some." Her chin rose as though to ward off pity. "I dreamed of my mother's death."

"Of course. I understand."

"Well, then. Thank you, my lord, for inquiring."

She started to shut the door, but his question stopped her. "Can you sleep?"

"Soon enough, I should imagine. Your lordship need not trouble yourself over me." Her cheeks flushed as though he had asked her something personal.

"'Tis no bother. I was going to my library for a drink. Would you like one?"

She clutched her dressing gown tighter at her throat. "I dislike strong spirits, my lord."

"Even my grandmother has a sip of brandy when she cannot sleep. Come, I thought we agreed that you would trust me." Even though he yet harbored tiny doubts about her.

"If you're certain 'tis not improper."

"At this hour, who would care? The servants long ago sought their beds." With a slight smile, acknowledging that she knew how such matters were treated, he added, "Besides, they notice only what I wish them to see."

"I suppose you're right. After all, you hire only the best servants, do you not?" A twinkle flitted through her eyes.

Smiling, he replied, "Only the best."

"Then I thank you, my lord. I confess, I didn't look forward to trying to sleep."

When she stepped into the hallway, he recognized the garment she clutched around her as one of his grandmother's dressing gowns. He touched her elbow to steer her toward the library, and his blood stirred at the contact.

Ignoring his reaction, he asked, "You said you've had this dream before?"

"Not quite like this, and it—it felt like the recent ones."

"A dream of power, you mean."

"Yes, but it came immediately after another vision, and I was … " She hesitated. "Thinking of Mother's death always distresses me."

"That's understandable." He opened the library door and stood back for her to enter first. Stirring the banked fire magically took only a moment.

She waited in the center of the room, looking at the tall bookshelves. His library might not have the elegance of the one at Aysgarth House, but it must look magnificent to someone from her background.

"Pray be seated," he said. "You'll be warmer near the fire."

75

She chose a low stool by the fireplace, settling onto it so that the full skirts of her shift and dressing gown flowed over her bare feet.

The subtle gesture proclaimed an innate dignity that survived her reduced circumstances. He had to admire that composure, but mentioning it would be rude. Richard poured brandy into fine silver goblets, taking care not to put much in hers.

When he turned, his breath caught in his throat. Firelight cast golden highlights over her face and the tendrils of hair that had escaped her braid. The loose, modest dressing gown and shift conformed to her shape instead of forcing it to theirs. Thus draped, the curves of her hips and breasts had a seductive power of which she seemed unaware.

Or was she?

Oddly, she looked as though she belonged here. Or could. He gave himself a mental shake and handed her the goblet.

She accepted it with a word of thanks. "You look very elegant, my lord. You must have had a fine evening."

"You and my valet would find yourselves in agreement. But yes, seeing my friends is always a pleasure." He settled into the chair across the hearth from her.

"Do you want to talk about your dream?" he asked. "It might help you sleep."

"It might." Her face lost the color the firelight had restored. She turned her gaze back to the flames.

If she'd dreamed of anything useful, he would do better to attend to that than to her beguiling looks.

After a moment, she said, "I remember only a fragment. I stood somewhere high, looking down on a jeering crowd, and I was so afraid. I looked aside and saw a cross on a steeple. And I knew nothing could save me—as she must have known—and I regretted something—"

"What was it?" he asked, more to break the chain of parallels that haunted her than to learn the answer.

"I don't know. Then I awoke." Her hands shook, forcing her to use them both instead of one to lift the goblet.

Richard peered at her. She couldn't sleep in such a state, and he hadn't given her nearly enough brandy, even for someone unaccustomed to it, to blot out those memories.

Perhaps confronting the memory would help. He gentled his voice. "What brought your mother to that point?"

She stared at the flames. "Mother attended the ailing son of a local

Royalist."

Richard could guess what was coming, and he hated it. The Royalists, supporters of the newly returned Charles II, had been intent on taking back the lands and authority they'd lost when parliamentary forces, advocating for government without a monarch, killed the prior king. While King Charles had urged tolerance, keeping a certain restraint at court, the struggle had taken some ugly turns out in the country.

"After the Restoration," she continued, "as you must know, dissenting clergy like my father lost their places. Father's was the living on this man's land. Land a Parliamentarian had taken over during the civil war but had to give back at the Restoration."

"The boy died," Richard said, not needing Sight to guess.

"Yes. The man said Mother had—that she'd killed his son because we'd lost our home. Father said the man coveted Mother, and she was so beautiful, so generous and kind, that perhaps he did, but nothing swayed him. She ... " Mistress Willoughby scrubbed at her eyes. "I miss her so much."

"Of course you do." That, at least, was genuine grief. If she was feigning it, she belonged onstage at Drury Lane.

"So you came to London," he prompted.

With a nod, she said, "We had to leave, Father, my brother, and I. Father was distraught, and there was no work for him. He took what he could get, a position in his brother's bakeshop. He never liked the work. Really, he was never the same after Mother died."

She raised her gaze to Richard's, and the pain there stabbed into his soul. He clenched his fist to keep from offering a comforting touch that might be misconstrued.

"Father used to read with me," she told him, "and with Johnny, my brother. After she died, he so rarely wanted to."

She gulped her brandy. The coughing that followed, although it seemed to embarrass her, gave her a chance to recover her composure along with her breath. She mustered a weak smile. "I do beg your pardon, my lord. I don't usually go on like this."

"So I've observed. I asked you, remember."

She sipped brandy, staring into the fire, and he fought the tug of sympathy. After a moment, he asked, "What else did you dream?"

"Of you," she answered slowly. "I saw you riding through a forest. You looked ... sad." She shot him a glance, then looked down at the hearth. "Then I saw a dark shape in the bushes. It was pacing you. Stalking you, almost."

77

"What shape?"

"At one point, I saw it clearly. It was a bear."

The Wyndon crest included a bear. Careful to keep his voice neutral, he asked, "Is that all?"

She nodded. "Then the dream changed to the other."

Richard nodded. Was this a genuine warning, or was she trying to beguile him by warning him of an enemy he already knew he had?

"You saw nothing besides the bear?"

"No." Her brow furrowed, and she added, "But I could feel that it meant you ill."

"I know who the bear is, an earl whose crest is the bear and portcullis."

She looked relieved. "What does it—he—want?"

"Nothing good." He studied her in the flickering light. "I mentioned the Earl of Wyndon to you on our way back from Dover. That's his crest."

"The man you asked me if I knew." Her expression tightened, but her gaze didn't waver. "My lord, I know there are things about me that seem strange to you, but still you've given me a chance to change my life. You've been kind to me. I wouldn't bring trouble to your door."

Her eyes held only an earnest plea, no trace of calculation or deceit.

He believed her. Whether he should or not. "You trusted my word when you came here," he said at last, "so I'll trust yours now."

"Thank you." She smiled at him, and his blood stirred again.

He stared into his goblet. "As for trouble, you're not the one bringing it, so we'd best hope your lessons progress quickly. You may need them."

"That's a frightening idea." Looking wary, she picked up her goblet. "Why might I suddenly need to use magic?"

Watching the firelight play over her face, he replied, "For good or ill, you're caught up in this, and great matters may be in motion. You've a role to play, and there's no certainty it's limited to visions."

"I'm a clergyman's daughter. A serving maid." She raised startled eyes to his, and they were dark with fear. "I'm no one."

"Dreams of power don't come to *no one*." He studied her for a moment. "If you aren't sleepy, let's have a lesson."

He took the goblet gently from her fingers and set it with his on the small table beside him.

"Now, look into the fire. Imagine someone or something you'd like to see."

"It would be good to see Lucy, from the inn. What do I do?"

"Hold the image and extend your power to the fire until you can feel it flicker. Then look for what you seek there."

A crease formed on her smooth brow. Her magic brushed his, so he knew she was trying, but the fire crackled merrily, producing no images.

Perhaps they should start with something more basic. "Do you know how to open your senses and see if you're alone?"

When she nodded, he said, "Do that. Good. I feel your power in the room. Now I'll do the same. Tell me what you feel."

"It's a light touch. Whispery. On my neck. It tingles."

"Good. That's my magic and yours mingling. Now I'm going to scry in the fire."

An image formed, his grandmother seated at a table in an elegant bedchamber.

"Do you see it?" he asked. When she nodded, he said, "Turn your perceptions toward the fire and away from me. Aim them that way, if you will."

"All right."

"Do you feel the way the flame flickers, the way it crackles around the logs?" When Miranda nodded, he added, "Hold that feeling and think of the image you seek replacing that one."

"I would like to see Lucy. I miss her."

The vision in the fire wavered. Flickered away. Died.

Nothing replaced it.

His guest bit her lip and blew out a breath, her face frustrated. "I don't feel it anymore."

"It takes practice. Let's try again."

An hour later, she was slumped with fatigue, but she couldn't achieve even a faint image. It was time to stop.

"We can try again when you're not so weary," he told her. "Don't worry. Controlling magic takes time and practice."

She nodded but didn't look reassured.

"The control will come," he told her. "We've had a long journey the last few days, harder on you than on me. It's no wonder you're tired. Do you think you can rest now?"

"Yes. My lord, thank you for your kindness."

"You're welcome. We can try again tomorrow. My grandmother taught me and may be able to offer suggestions I cannot."

He smiled at her and opened the library door. "I'll walk down with you."

She looked surprised but didn't protest. They walked back to her room in silence. Before she closed the door, she gave him a solemn look. "You've been very kind. I'm in your debt, my lord. A good night to you."

"To you as well." Richard turned back toward the library. Despite what he had let her believe, he had too much on his mind to sleep for a good while yet.

He poured himself another drink and settled into his favorite chair by the hearth. His glance fell on the footstool where she'd sat.

I'm in your debt, she'd said. If she could help him end the family curse, he would owe her a debt far greater than she could imagine.

Miranda walked toward the library the next morning with a sense of anticipation. As a treat, Lady Hawkstowe had ordered chocolate for Miranda with the morning meal—taken in her bedchamber, as though she were a real lady. Patience had served the sweet, expensive drink as casually as though it were water.

Now Miranda and Lord Hawkstowe and his grandmother would discuss her vision. Mayhap her dreams as well. She had her written account in hand. Better to think of that than of seeing his lordship again.

He'd given her a gift last night, one he probably didn't recognize as such. She'd been honest with him about her dreams and about her family. Not since Mother's death had she been able to speak so candidly. He'd been kind and understanding, signs of a warm heart under his stern demeanor.

During the last several days, she'd come to like him. Even to admire him. His rare smiles warmed her. When they'd met, he'd called her *pretty dragon maid*. Even if he'd said it sarcastically, he wouldn't have used *pretty* unless he thought her so.

Where was the harm in appreciating all that? Especially so long as she kept the gap in their stations in mind.

When she entered, the room looked welcoming. Rain drummed on the library windows, but even the grayish light couldn't dim the rich maroon, gold, and blue tones in the lush carpet draped across the table. The carpet, the leather-bound books, and the embroidered chair cushions proclaimed this family's wealth.

What did it say about her, that she was not so wide-eyed at its lavishness as she'd been just last night?

Lord Hawkstowe stood by the hearth, one elbow on the mantel. His pleasant but impersonal nod of greeting, a contrast to the sympathetic interest of last night, jabbed her with disappointment. She shouldn't be surprised, though. Last night, he'd been offering comfort. Today, he'd returned to the business at hand.

"Good morning, my lord."

"Mistress Willoughby. We'll wait for my grandmother, but pray be seated."

Miranda settled herself onto the stool again. The fire's hearty warmth still seemed like such a luxury.

Lady Hawkstowe entered, waving at Miranda to remain seated. She took the armchair across the hearth from her grandson but looked at Miranda, who pushed down the disquieting sensation born of having someone's attention on her without her glamours. She would grow accustomed in time, of course, but it still felt strange.

The older woman asked, "How are you today, my dear?"

"Well enough, my lady. I had two dreams last night and recorded them as you asked." She handed the papers to the older woman, who glanced over them before setting them aside.

"Richard mentioned that you had a difficult night and told me a bit about your dreams. I'll look these over more thoroughly later."

Frowning, Lady Hawkstowe leaned forward in her chair. "The meaning of these dreams may tie into the one that led you to summon Richard. Did they seem connected? Or give you any insight into the earlier vision?"

"Not that I could see, milady, but I've scant knowledge of heraldry."

"Richard, what do you think?"

"As yet, I see no connection between last night's dreams and the dragon vision, though the one about the bear may indicate Wyndon's involvement."

He stared into the fire crackling on the library hearth. She smoothed the worn skirt of her pink gown, once again feeling out of place. At least the angle of her body hid the beer stain near her hip so it wasn't visible to the others.

Finally, he said, "Assuming we can trust the obvious interpretation, the red dragon, the Welsh symbol, represents the Welsh King Henry Tudor, and the boar, King Richard III. The stag would be Sir George Buck, one of the first to write a book defending King Richard."

"But how can that be?" Miranda asked. "In the dream, the dragon is evil, not the boar. But everyone knows King Richard was the monster, not

King Henry. He was two years within his mother's womb and was born with long teeth, a wicked, withered hunchback, as befits one of such evil intent. Why, King Richard slew his own nephews to gain the crown. He—"

"Enough!" The word snapped from Hawkstowe's lips as sharply as the crack of a wagoner's whip.

Shock stopped the words on Miranda's lips, and she recoiled.

"Richard," Lady Hawkstowe said sternly.

His eyes sparked with irritation and something else Miranda couldn't read. The look between them held while the heat in his eyes slowly died.

At last, he said, "I beg your pardon. I shouldn't have taken such a tone with you."

"I meant no offense, my lord." At least her voice held steady.

His chest rose in a deep breath. "Of course not. However, I suggest you not rely in this matter on what *everyone knows*, lest you find yourself led astray."

"I don't understand."

"What everyone thinks they know about King Richard," he told her, his voice flat, "amounts to no more than a pack of lies concocted to prop up Henry Tudor's shaky claim, through a bastard line, to the throne of England."

"But how can that be? Surely a king wouldn't do such a thing!" She looked to Lady Hawkstowe for support but found the dowager countess smiling at her indulgently.

"In fact," the older woman said, "kings from time immemorial have often done just that to one degree or another while assuring themselves they merely did God's will."

Hawkstowe added, "In fact, King Richard was a well-favored man born after the usual time in the womb. He administered almost half of England for his royal brother in a just and honest manner. As a battle commander, notwithstanding his insane final charge, he had few peers."

"Perhaps," Miranda conceded hesitantly, "but what about his nephews, the princes in the Tower?"

"Bastards, the result of a bigamous marriage, not princes. They weren't murdered on his account or by his wish." He sounded so definite.

"How do you know that?"

The ice of winter hardened his eyes. "Because my ancestor unwittingly helped the true murderer and so incurred a blood debt I am sworn to avenge. Not only in your dream but in truth, I am the boar's knight."

His talk of blood oaths and knightly quests sounded like something from an old tale, but she couldn't dismiss it, not after her haunting vision or in the face of his certainty. The ice in his eyes looked not so solid now. Behind it, something that might have been pain roiled.

Softly, Lady Hawkstowe said, "Very dramatic, Richard."

The ice dissolved, giving way to frustration. He shot his grandmother a sour look.

"As it happens," he said to Miranda, "I learned something last night that reminded me of one of your early visions. One of King Richard III's defenders wrote a history of his life that contradicted the traditional account. The history drew on a monastic chronicle that contained the only known version of the parliamentary act settling the crown on Richard III instead of his nephew."

"Parliament did that? I never knew of it."

"Likely because Henry Tudor ordered all existing copies burned unread." Raising an eyebrow, he added, "Not precisely the act of a man who had confidence in his own claim."

"When did someone notice the change in the book?" Lady Hawkstowe asked, frowning.

"The day of the White Rose banquet." To Miranda, he added, "That's an annual gathering in honor of Richard III's memory."

Grimly, he continued. "Everything connected to that monastic chronicle has disappeared from the printed text, leaving no gaps or obvious omissions. As though by magic. Only the Gifted remember how the book read before."

"And I had a dream about the pages of a book changing." Miranda looked directly at him. "You didn't mention this last night."

He shrugged. "It could wait until this morning, and you had enough on your mind."

"Speaking of books," his grandmother said, "I've lost a spell primer, the one that appears to unGifted eyes to be a volume of poetry."

"Didn't you lend it to Lady Parkhurst?"

"Yes, but she returned it a fortnight ago. I thought we might need it for Miranda's lessons."

Frowning, Hawkstowe replied, "I'd say it must be here somewhere, but too much odd has happened of late. We'd hoped the changing book was an isolated incident, but if your book is truly gone, then there are likely others."

"Since we cannot solve that problem at the moment," Lady Hawkstowe said, "Miranda, let's consider your visions, by which I also mean your visionary dreams, further."

Miranda nodded in acknowledgment, and the older woman continued. "What Richard said about the symbols does fit the vision. I know little of these matters, yet I wonder whether such a thing would have so clear a meaning."

The earl turned to his grandmother. The older woman looked thoughtful.

At last, she said, "Richard has told you the truth about Richard III and Henry VII, regardless of what you may have been told to the contrary. Given that you do believe to the contrary, however, I wonder whether we've read the dream aright. Perhaps the correct interpretation would fit more with something you've always believed."

Hawkstowe said, "How could it? We cannot reverse the symbols."

"No, Richard, but perhaps they have nothing to do with kings and princes long dead. Perhaps they refer instead to something more current. Perhaps something in Mistress Willoughby's life?"

Naught in her restricted life could evoke such images. Miranda shook her head.

Thoughtfully, Lady Hawkstowe continued, "A magical vision rarely flies in the face of a seer's beliefs, and Mistress Willoughby has always accepted the unfortunate, traditional view of King Richard. A vision must include something the one it touches can believe, else the seer may refuse to acknowledge it."

Miranda's cheeks warmed. She looked down at her worn shoes. "The knight in the dream serves good. I've always believed in the noble goodness of knights."

"Then you are worse educated than I thought," Hawkstowe said dryly.

How dare he belittle her? She looked up, but his smile softened his words. He'd meant only to lighten the moment. She smiled in return and the warmth in his eyes made her breath catch.

He means naught by it, she reminded herself.

"Well, then," Lady Hawkstowe said, "that might have sufficed. In any event, you must pursue this dream. We must make certain of its meaning."

"Yes, milady." Perhaps that pursuit would involve more lessons in magic.

Again, Hawkstowe and his grandmother exchanged a look. Miranda gathered her courage. "Have I said something wrong?"

CHAPTER 9

A gain, a look passed between the earl and his grandmother. He said quietly, "It's nothing to do with you. Your visions offer hope of solving the unsolvable, and I distrust that hope."

Knowing the pain of false hope, Miranda could understand that.

"In the meantime," he added, "there's a custom we've neglected. Among ourselves, England's Gifted use one another's given names."

That was a staggering notion. Miranda frowned. Had she heard him correctly?

He explained, "It's an acknowledgement of kinship, and I should have broached it sooner. I would like you to call me Richard and allow me to call you Miranda."

"And I am Arabella," his grandmother said.

Were they were having a joke at her expense? Their solemn faces made that unlikely.

"As you wish," she said, though the custom was astonishing.

The older woman smiled. "Good. Let's return to the business that brings us all here. Richard, what are you doing about the *Chronicle's* disappearance?

"Jeremy's looking into that." To Miranda, he said, "Jeremy is a friend, and the *Chronicle* is the monastic record I mentioned earlier. For several centuries, the monks of Croyland Abbey compiled reports of events in

England. The particular volume that relates to the symbols of your dream has gone missing."

His grandmother directed a speculative look at him. "Without subsequent visions, which may or may not come, to clarify this one, Morgan's pool offers our best hope of refining it."

The earl nodded agreement. When Miranda gave him a puzzled look, he added, "The pool has properties that may help us explore your dream."

"What does it do?"

Lady Hawkstowe—Arabella—said, "It will put the two of you into a vision that matches yours, possibly even show you related events. You could do this alone, but since Richard has more training and appeared in your vision, his help may be essential."

Blood debts and magic pools. She had fallen into a realm of legends made real.

"Is it dangerous?" she asked.

Arabella said solemnly, "Blood magic is always dangerous."

A chill ran down Miranda's spine. She'd used blood to make her dragon, never dreaming she ran a risk. Had she simply been lucky, or were some uses less dangerous than others?

"The pool is in Cumberland," Hawkstowe—Richard!—stated, "at a place called Pendragon Manor. We can leave tomorrow."

Traveling. A horse. Or worse, a coach that would make her ill. *Oh, pray, no.* Miranda groped for an excuse to delay.

"Ah, but you cannot," his grandmother said. "Have you forgotten the masque at Whitehall on Monday next?"

"I would as soon forget it," he said.

"Richard, the queen expects us. If you mean to beg off, you'll need a better excuse than the reputation of a king two centuries dead. Besides, I've already sent to the palace to ask if we may bring our young cousin, who has lately joined our household."

The dowager countess smiled at Miranda, who gazed back in bewilderment. She had met no cousin.

"You cannot be serious." Wonder tinged Richard's voice. "Those hyenas will do to her what the lions meant to do to Daniel."

Realization dawned, but ... Surely not. "You mean me?" Miranda gulped, trying to settle her voice. "Why would you do such a thing?"

Arabella replied, "It will give you a chance to meet the Gifted nobility, who might be useful in finding you a new place. As for the courtiers, Richard, who are any of them to question a kinship we claim? We can scarcely leave our guest here alone while we jaunt off to court. Besides, every good Englishman or Englishwoman should see the king at least once, don't you think?"

"Still, Grandmère—"

"I beg pardon," Miranda managed at last. "With respect, my lady, I cannot go to court. I appreciate your kindness, but I wouldn't like anyone, especially yourselves, to think I had forgotten my place."

"Your place. I see." He studied her.

"I wonder if you do, my lord." He'd no business looking at her in that curious way.

"Ah, but I do. And my name is Richard." Glancing at the mantel clock, he said, "At the moment, though, we have a decision to make. Miranda, do you remember discussing the Gifted Conclave Council when we were in Dover?"

"Yes, mil—um, Richard. You said they were the leaders of our kind."

"The Conclave is what we call gatherings of all the Gifted in London. There's a meeting this afternoon to discuss this odd weather and the events surrounding it."

"All the Gifted? How many is that?" What would it be like to look around and see only those who knew what you were?

"There are about three hundred in the city proper, more who move in and out. Usually around a hundred turn up."

He flicked a look at his grandmother. "You have a right to go, Miranda, but we ask that you not do so this time. Lord Wyndon, the man your bear dream most likely represents, will be there, and he'll notice you if you come in with us. I'd rather not call his attention to you yet."

"Especially," the older woman added, her nose wrinkling in distaste, "in a setting where you cannot warn him off."

"Why not?" Miranda asked.

"Because of the kinship our Gifts create. In that setting, aside from debating questions, extraordinary courtesy rules. One cannot snub or rebuff anyone there."

Richard added, "Exactly. Miranda, we'll take you if you wish to go, but I'm sure Grandmère can put the time to good use if you stay."

"With magic lessons." Arabella smiled. "And dressmakers and whatever else comes to mind."

Dressmakers? Why?

Before Miranda could ask, Richard turned to her. "What will you have? The Conclave or a quieter afternoon?"

"The quiet." If they thought going to this Conclave would bring her to the attention of the man she'd sensed was evil, she would happily miss the gathering.

"A wise choice." He smiled at her and rose. "Grandmère, I leave this to you. When I return, I'll send to Morgan's handmaidens here in London and see if they have a vial of the pool's water we can use. Waiting until after this masque four days hence to set out for Pendragon and the pool itself is too much of a delay."

"I agree," his grandmother said.

Richard smiled. "I'll see you both at supper." He kissed his grandmother's cheek, bowed to Miranda, and left.

Miranda gulped, her mind reeling once again. In the space of a few minutes, she'd been told she had rights she'd never imagined, would participate in blood magic, and might meet more of the Gifted. It was a great deal to take in.

The door shut behind Richard, and his grandmother smiled. "We'll dine, and I'll send to the dressmakers and the cobbler. If you're to be our cousin while you're here, you must be dressed for the role."

"Milady—Arabella, I mean—I cannot pay—"

"Nor shall you. I haven't had a young woman to order clothes for in years. I'll enjoy it. Besides, if you're to find a new station when we've unraveled these mysteries, you should appear not to be in great need of one. I'll send my letters before we eat. Afterward, we'll resume your lessons and I'll explain why you not only may go to court but should."

Richard scarcely heard the rain pelting down on the roof of his coach. The Conclave faced grave issues. Could they put aside their usual tendency to talk everything to shreds and actually solve this problem? Given the strange events occurring—samplers appearing, books disappearing and changing—it seemed unlikely.

With harness jingling, the carriage turned into Walbrook Street and slowed to a halt before the Green Bull tavern. It had closed early for the Conclave.

They'd left the unGifted footmen at home for secrecy's sake, so Richard flung open the coach door and jumped down into the storm. Rain pelted him. Wind swirled his oiled leather cloak around him and threatened to snatch his hat.

He looked up at his coachman through the downpour. "Remember the door off the alley, Thomas. It's a shorter path."

"Aye, Richard," the stocky man said, hunching against the storm. "Soon as I have 'em under a roof." He shook the reins. Heads lowered against the weather, the horses hurried forward.

Richard ran into the tap room. The stout door muffled the sound of the wind, but gusts rattled the windowpanes. Lanterns cast a dim light in the low, boxy common room, and the scents of tobacco and mutton from the day's business hung in the air.

The room's lone occupant, a stout, middle-aged man with a kind face, stood by the rear door. Beaming, he strode forward to greet Richard. "Welcome, cousin," he said in the customary greeting of one Gifted to another. "'Tis a vile day out, but we've food and drink, o'course."

"Thank you, Daniel." Richard nodded. "You do well by us."

"They pay me right nice for it." Daniel grinned. "Between that and the fee for early closing, I'm having a good day."

"As you should." Richard clapped him on the shoulder and strode through the door at the rear of the chamber. He turned into a doorway on the left side, then descended a flight of rickety stairs lit by candles in sconces.

Luck had favored Daniel in that his tavern sat atop the ancient Roman temple to Mithras. The power infused in the ground by two hundred years of faithful worship during the Roman rule of Britain made it a welcoming place for the Conclave.

The stairs ended in a low-ceilinged cellar stacked with large casks containing beer or ale. The scents of damp earth and wood filled the air. At the bottom, Richard turned into a narrow, low passage that was warded so only the Gifted could see or enter it. Light and the pleasant din of conversation spilled from the doorway ahead.

The passage ended in a wide, brightly lit room full of people. Carved from several cellars in buildings Conclave members owned, it offered ample space for the gathering. The appetizing scents of roast meat and warm bread mingled with the sweet one of beeswax candles and the jumble of musk and sandalwood and floral perfumes worn by some in attendance.

Nobles or gentry clad in fine wool or velvet with copious lace at collars and cuffs mingled with more common folk clad in homespun linen and rougher wool.

And there was Henry de Vere, Earl of Wyndon, across the room by the hearth with his libertine son, Viscount Canby. At least Wyndon's daughter, Lucretia, who was reputed to have a poisonous temperament, was not here.

"There you are, Richard!" Kit emerged from the crowd to join him. Softly, he added, "I see Wyndon and Canby are here."

"Wyndon never misses a gathering," Richard murmured.

They worked their way toward the tables of food in the back of the chamber, near where Wyndon and Canby stood.

Kit stopped to greet the Council head, Lucius Balfour, a tall, slightly stooped man with silvery hair and a weathered face. "Good day, cousin."

Lucius smiled. "Kit. Richard. How good to see you."

"And you," Richard said. Because Lucius was a tanner, their familiarity would appear strange outside this chamber. Inside it, though, magic made them kindred.

"We'll need the Council to stay after," Lucius said. "A smaller group sometimes makes more headway. If you want to send Thomas home, Richard, I'll take you back when we finish."

Richard thanked him, and Lucius continued quietly, "Nuisance though the rain is, it makes travel safer because it drives people off the streets. Folk are more quarrelsome than they were. They take offense at naught. There's something in the air. The Council will discuss it."

"I noticed it," Richard said.

"Anyone with even a bit of magic should." Lucius grimaced. "Pray excuse me. We must begin, or we'll be here all night." He shouldered his way through the crowd, heading for the hearth at the end of the room.

They might be here that long anyway, but saying so wouldn't help. Richard frowned. "I'll fetch ale for Thomas," he told Kit. "Do you want anything?"

When Kit shook his head, Richard worked his way through the press to the table by the alley door. Set next to a large barrel with a tap at the bottom, it held rows of leather tankards. He grabbed one and filled it for his coachman.

Lucius stepped onto a box set before the hearth. "Good afternoon. Let us begin."

He didn't shout, but his voice carried throughout the crowded chamber. "We are met to discuss the recent eerie wind and unnatural weather. As you know, London's folk are more on edge than at any time since the execution of our late King Charles I, of blessed memory."

As though to underscore his words, muted thunder rumbled outside.

His expression turned wry. "Does anyone have anything to report about this situation?"

The tension in the room seemed to mute even the fire's crackling. At last, a short, dark-haired man with a grizzled beard pushed forward to stand by Lucius.

Beside Richard, the alley door opened, admitting a gust of wind and blown rain. Thomas stepped inside and shut the door quickly. Water dripped from his leather cloak and wide-brimmed hat. Richard handed him the tankard, and Thomas nodded his thanks.

"Peter Gregson," the bearded man at the front said by way of greeting. He cast an apologetic glance at Lucius. "It may be naught, o'course, but my father's candle molds've disappeared. They're good ones, made of iron by my uncle just before the Restoration. I'd like 'em back, and I can't scry any sign of anyone stealin' 'em. I left 'em by the hearth, same as always, two nights ago. Next morn—" he shrugged "—an empty spot."

"I found something that oughtn't be there," a deep voice said from the back of the room. Sir Robert Welmore, a baronet from Hampshire, squeezed through to the front. "My quarterly accounts now show income from a small farm in Sussex, but we lost that farm years back."

A sturdy, grim-faced man in homespun stepped forward. "Josiah Wortham," he said. "That wind blew away the rye and wheat I'd sown—crops we needed for the winter."

"Same at our farm," a woman called.

Men and women came forward in a steady flow to announce that things had appeared or disappeared mysteriously. Richard reported Grandmère's primer missing. More farmers complained of wind and torrential rain destroying their fall plantings.

Richard's eyes met Lucius's across the room. The loss of those crops would be grievous, come winter.

Kit murmured, "That litany's alarming. We're not dealing only with one changed book and a mysterious sampler."

"No," Richard replied, "and matters seem to be getting worse, not better. For everyone here who reports a change, there must be unGifted who've experienced one and don't remember it. God's teeth, how widespread is this problem?"

At last, Lucius stepped forward again. "We can reach only one conclusion from all this. Someone, cousins, has changed the past and thus, the present."

The room erupted. "Impossible!" someone shouted.

Richard's gut knotted. What he and his friends had hoped was a relatively narrow problem was appallingly widespread. But why was this happening? How?

At least there would now be more Gifted working on answering those questions, though the discussion could alert whoever'd made the change to those efforts.

"Can't be done" and a chorus of similar opinions roared through the air. Through them all ran a current of entirely reasonable fear.

Richard spotted Cabot and Jeremy standing by the corridor door. He and Kit made their way through the crowd to the brothers. Their grim faces and the worried looks they shot him signaled their shared dismay that the time shift was more drastic than they'd realized.

Not mentioning the changes to Buck's defense of Richard III had seemed tactically wise before. Now it seemed imperative. Whoever was responsible for these widespread changes had to be in this room or connected to someone who was. Keeping that person ignorant of their suspicions was the best move, at least for now.

A sound like a thunderclap, but closer and sharper, broke through the din. Richard wheeled to see Lucius lower his hands.

"Cousins," Lucius said in that carrying voice, "we must try to determine when the course of events changed. Those of you adept at scrying the past—"

A rumble of dissent rose, and he flung up a hand to stop it. "I know the present limits on scrying the past, but we must attempt it. Those who can do so, come forward, and the rest depart, save for the Council. We'll send word of what we learn."

Richard turned to Kit. "What did he mean, *limits*?"

"All this moaning helps nothing." Wyndon's deep, harsh voice cut through the silence. He stepped forward and swept the room with a contemptuous look. "If the past is, indeed, changing, chasing a cause we don't understand is a waste of effort. Scarce resources and mysterious weather lead to fear and then to anger, an urge to lash out at whoever is handy. Only we Gifted can impose order for everyone's benefit. We should do so without delay."

"Folly!" a woman's voice shouted. "That would mean war."

"Dangerous lunacy," a man agreed. "Remember how magical conflict back in Morgan and Merlin's day pushed England into the Dark Ages."

Merlin and his twin sister, Morgan, had initially supported King Arthur while keeping most of their magic hidden. As the Saxons pushed into England, the twins had quarreled over Merlin's decision to interfere in Britain by using his magic openly. The dispute, known among the Gifted as the Chaos Age, had spread, setting the Gifted against each other and the land aflame, sowing fear of magic that yet endured.

Scowling, Richard raised his voice to carry. "Wyndon, you know the history of the Chaos Age as well as anyone. Do you discount it? Or do you know something the rest of us don't?"

Wyndon stared hard at him. "These strange events may signal great changes ahead. A chance for our people to stop hiding. I'd make peace even with you, Hawkstowe, to seize that moment."

"Which would ultimately lead to fighting among ourselves," Richard replied, "as well as battling the army, and possibly topple the unGifted governments of Europe. No. We've no right."

"Perhaps they deserve to be toppled. Think about it." Wyndon shifted his balance. "You're ever quick to accuse me, but I seek the best fate for our kind."

"Did you engineer this?" Richard demanded.

Wyndon rolled his eyes. "By what means? Change what has already happened? That would take more than magic. If you've uncovered the secret to traveling time, pray, share it with us all."

That wasn't exactly a denial. Richard narrowed his eyes.

Lucius stated, "Alteration of events in the past violates natural law. It's forbidden."

"Mayhap Henry's right." A stocky man in a suit of fine brown wool pushed through to join Wyndon.

Other voices rose, taking sides. Lucius clapped his hands again, but the dispute grew louder. More heated.

Richard frowned. Wyndon looked strangely satisfied with the discord, as though peace were not to his advantage. As though he knew more than he revealed. But Richard had no proof. Wyndon had enough allies to prevent further accusations based on mere suspicion.

"Order," Lucius bellowed with intensity that rang in Richard's ears. "We will have order, cousins." He glared around the room. "The scryers will stay and work. The Council and those who wish to debate Henry's proposal will also remain."

Richard swore silently. There went any hope of an effective Council meeting.

A few people exchanged uncertain glances. Talking in disgruntled tones, most of the crowd drifted toward the stairs.

"What in Hell's bailey was that about scrying limits?" Cabot asked.

"Scrying more than a few months back is now impossible, though we could do it several days ago," Kit explained, his tone grim. "I figured it out this morning when I tried to scry backward for the *Chronicle.*"

"What's next?" Richard demanded. "People appearing and disappearing?"

"I fear so," Kit answered.

"God's feet," Cabot muttered.

Richard glanced over his shoulder. The Council was gathering by the hearth, along with others who would argue for Wyndon's view or for Richard's. His friends would stay to back him, of course.

"As to the scrying," Kit said, "I hope it's only because time and events are in flux, but I fear it means the changes are happening too quickly for even magic to track."

~

L uncheon started a whirl of activity Miranda could scarcely believe. Salmon, beef with parsnips, a salad, and a blancmange offered more than she could eat. There was even a refined wheat bread instead of the coarse bread she was used to. She hadn't known anyone ate so luxuriously.

Even the utensils looked odd, silver instead of the pewter or tin the inn in Dover had used. And the fork had three tines instead of the usual two.

After luncheon, the dressmakers and cobbler arrived, and time passed in a flurry of beautiful fabrics and quick measurements. All of it felt as though she were receiving a reward she hadn't earned. If they were going to all this trouble and expense, though, that probably meant they didn't intend to send her packing anytime soon, even if her visions weren't proving useful.

Not until mid-afternoon did Miranda and Arabella return to the library. A small table by the hearth held a plate of gingerbread squares. With the plate sat a wooden box of crushed leaves, a small, ornate silver bowl of lumpy sugar already snipped off the loaf, two even smaller, delicate white bowls decorated with blue flowers, a wide, shallow, silver bowl, and a silver pitcher with steam drifting from its spout.

"Have you ever had tea?" Arabella asked.

"No, never." The cost was far too dear for all but the very wealthy. The same held for sugar. At the inn, Master Warren allowed its use only rarely and kept the precious loaf locked in his chamber the rest of the time.

Arabella scooped leaves into the shallow bowl. "I'll pour hot water over the leaves, and then we'll let them steep a bit. Then we'll drink from the porcelain ones. They come from China, as did the tea."

Miranda watched, rapt, as Arabella prepared the brew.

Finally, the older woman sat back. "While the tea steeps, let's deal with this question of the masque first. Our claim of kinship has some truth to it. We Mainwarings come of the old blood, the powers native to this land, as does your seer gift. Your proficiency with glamours belongs to the newer powers, from folk who arrived about the time the Romans left Britain. The two lines have intermarried from time to time. Somewhere, however distant the point, our family trees entwine."

"My lady, Arabella, all your kindness cannot change my common birth. Serving maids don't mingle with the nobility, let alone royalty." She mustn't let the lure of being treated as though she belonged with such grand people seduce her from the truth she knew.

"Apparently I haven't explained very well." Arabella pursed her lips. "Let's leave that for a moment. Tell me about your training thus far."

"Most of what I know relates to glamours," Miranda began. "My mother taught me the basic skills of creating those. I figured out summoning on my own when I was very small, and my mother refined that gift."

"'Tis a pity she didn't have a chance to teach you more."

"Yes, it is." The regret had stopped feeling sharp and bitter, but it would never entirely leave her. She had nothing of her mother's save memories of the secret they'd shared.

"Your father was not Gifted, Richard said?"

"No, nor did he know my mother was. The need to hide the lessons from him made finding time for them even more difficult."

"While such pairings are not unusual, one rarely finds unGifted clergy in one," Arabella commented.

"They were both kind and generous," Miranda said simply, "and drawn together by affection."

That she was already conceived when her parents wed was no one else's business, but she sometimes thought her mother might've chosen a different man if not for that.

"Lord—I mean Richard has tried to teach me scrying but with no success."

"Hmm. Have you ever done anything else outside the realm of glamours or summoning? Or perhaps, tried and not been certain whether you succeeded?"

Hesitantly, she told the older woman about the hanging. "Nothing seemed to happen before I had the vision. When it ended, Mistress Smith was dead. Limp, a mercy at last, but I don't think I helped her at all."

"I see." Arabella frowned.

After a moment, she said, "Perhaps we should start with what you already know. Show me the glamours you devised for yourself."

Summoning the image still came easily, in the blink of an eye. "This is it."

"Quite different. Stand up." Arabella circled her slowly, her gaze intent. "Effective, as well. Can you summon any other appearance?"

"I could when I was learning from my mother, but I haven't tried since."

If she meant to try now, she should choose someone she knew. She'd spent plenty of time watching the cook, Flora. Miranda closed her eyes, calling Flora's image to mind, feeling the bulk of her form and the scowl on her brow. Shaping the magic. She opened her eyes. "How's this?"

"Excellent." Arabella gave her a measuring look. "Now show me what it would be like if no one were there. Conceal yourself altogether. If you can."

Miranda closed her eyes. *Not here*, she thought. *No one here.*

"Very good," her teacher said, pouring tea into the porcelain bowls. "You've made a promising beginning. Come, sit down again."

A candle in an ornate silver stand adorned the sideboard, its flickering light doing little to banish the rainy gloom. Arabella walked over and snuffed it magically. Then she brought it to the table where the tea tray sat.

She set it carefully in the table's center. "Do you know how to light it?"

When Miranda shook her head, the dowager countess said, "Extend your power outward, to the candle, and order flame."

Miranda drew a deep breath. "I know how to open or extend my senses but not my magic."

"Extend your magic the way you do your senses. Envision the candle burning."

Miranda tried for several minutes, but the candle remained unlit. "I can see it burning in my mind," she said, swallowing frustration.

"Hmm." The older woman passed her one of the delicate bowls and saucers. "Have some tea before we begin."

Arabella picked up her bowl and held it with her thumb on the bottom and her fingertips at the rim. Delicately, she sipped.

Miranda tried to do the same. The hot brew was unexpectedly bitter, not quite the treat she'd expected, but she smiled to be polite.

"It's an acquired taste," the older woman admitted. "Let's add some sugar."

She set her tea bowl down and used a spoon to scoop a little sugar from its bowl on the tray. Tipping it into Miranda's cup, she said, "You're starting from farther behind than I expected. We generally start the candle exercise with children."

Miranda's cheeks heated, but there was no point feeling defensive. "My mother did the best she could."

"I don't doubt it," Arabella said kindly, "and circumstances can provide great obstacles. I fear the years you spent in hiding are also inhibiting you. You've built walls around yourself. For good reason, but walls can trap as well as protect. Let me think a moment."

The idea made sense, that blocking the power all those years could make it harder to summon now. But if she couldn't sense these walls, how could she find her way past them?

"Let's try something new." Arabella set her cup on the table. With a flick of one finger, she lit the candle again.

Miranda longed to do such things with the same ease and confidence.

The older woman said, "Summon your glamours—yes, very good. Now, widen your awareness. Take in more of the room, until you touch the candle."

Miranda tried, but nothing changed. "I've never done anything like this. I don't know what to do."

Arabella's eyes suddenly brightened. "Let's try to build on something you know. Put a glamour around the candle. Make it a rose. Move nearer to it if need be."

Glamours, Miranda understood. She summoned the image, the memory of the petals and the thorn, and looked at the candle.

Its flame burned steadily.

"Try harder," the older woman prompted. "Think of wrapping the candle in the rose."

Red petals replaced the flame. The wax became a green, thorny stem.

Miranda gasped. "I did it!" The rose vanished, leaving a candle in its place. "Oh, no."

"Oh, yes. Very good, my dear. You lost focus only because you were excited. Now try it again."

The second time came more easily, and the third. On the fourth attempt, Arabella said, "Hold the rose glamour in place. Now imagine there is no flame."

"But if I'm making a rose, how can I change it another way at the same time?"

"You aren't. You see the flame behind the rose in your mind, do you not?" When Miranda nodded, Arabella added, "Now, see the candle with no flame."

The glamour flickered, flame shining through.

"There is no flame," the older woman repeated softly. "A rose, but no flame." She drew a slow, audible breath. "Now, no rose."

Miranda dropped the glamour. Where the flower had been, the charred wick curled over the wax, a thin plume of smoke drifting upward. Miranda gaped at it. Her gaze shot to Arabella's face.

The dowager countess smiled. "Very good. Very good indeed. We ordinarily start with lighting a candle, but unmaking is ever easier than making. I want you to practice this tonight."

"Yes, mil—Arabella." Surely no bird could soar higher than her spirits were rising. She had done it!

"Eat something, too. Magic comes from within, and it burns the body's own power for its fuel."

Miranda helped herself to a piece of gingerbread, the surface dusted with precious cinnamon. Its flavors burst over her tongue, and her eyes widened. At the inn, Flora rarely used spices other than salt.

"Magic also heightens the senses," Arabella said. "It gives, even as it takes. You must never forget to eat after using it."

Miranda swallowed. "My mother said magic's a divine gift. It does feel heavenly just now."

"Early success can be intoxicating." The older woman's smile faded. "Your mother was right, though some of our Gifted kin say it comes from the goddess." She shrugged. "If the source is divine, male or female matters not. What matters is how one uses the power."

Father would have called that heresy, but it seemed reasonable enough. Miranda took a sip of tea. The sugar made a great difference. The taste was now exquisite.

98

Solemnly, Arabella said, "Magic is like any other gift. It can serve evil as well as good, and many use it for fell purposes. That's one reason those of us who serve good consider power a great leveler. When evil marches through the world, we cannot afford such petty distinctions as rank."

I'll stir not a step for an agent of darkness, Hawkstowe had said in Dover. "Lord Hawkstowe—Richard, I mean—warned me that not all who have power use it for good ends."

"They don't. We judge one another by how we use power, not by the ranks of our births."

Cautiously, Miranda noted, "Yet your family has rank in the peerage. I don't understand."

"We don't disdain birth rank." With a smile, Arabella added, "I'd be a fool to do so."

"Then what do you mean?"

Looking thoughtful, the dowager countess sipped tea. "This brings us back to what I tried to tell you earlier."

She set the tea dish down, looking squarely at Miranda. "If Richard took the field with other Gifted men and women, some of them would defer to him because he has an inherent grasp of strategy and deployment, not because of his rank. By the same token, he would defer to a cobbler, for example, who knew uses of magic he didn't."

The words went against everything Miranda had ever observed or heard about the nobility. "But why?"

"Magic levels the field. You're a serving maid, or you were. You're also a Gifted woman and therefore, so much more. Many Gifted men, some of noble birth, would value your bloodline and the Gifts you carry more than the wealth of an earldom."

The assurance in Arabella's voice opened vistas of freedom and security such as Miranda had never allowed herself to imagine.

She looked down at her chapped, work-reddened hands. No lady's hands. "I know of no such men."

"I dare say you don't. How would you meet them, when you had to live every day concealing what you are?"

Miranda's pulse leaped. Looking up, she found comprehension in the dowager countess's bright eyes.

"Come with us to Whitehall," Arabella said. "Enjoy the music and the gaiety and the admiration you'll surely garner. I would love to order a gown for you. Your manners are pretty enough already, and I can teach you the little more you would need to know. You should enjoy your youth while you have it, my dear. I did, and I regret not a moment."

"I can't imagine you doing anything to regret, my lady."

The older woman's eyes twinkled. "Not for lack of thinking about it, I assure you. You'll come, then?"

"You advised me to stay away from the Conclave lest I draw your enemy's attention. Would going to a gathering at the palace not also attract notice?"

"It would. Considering the connections you could make there, however, and the fact that Richard can, as your kinsman, keep anyone he chooses from approaching you, the benefit outweighs the risk. If he warned off a wizard at the Conclave, he would be thought abrupt and uncivil. At court, alas, such actions are acceptable. Come to the masque, Miranda."

A precipice lay before her. If she stepped off it, she would open the way for dangerous hopes, possibly even expectations. Yet the unknown future glowed with bright possibility the familiar past had lost years ago.

Miranda took a deep breath and jumped. "I'll come."

CHAPTER 10

Miranda slept poorly. Richard's report of the Conclave meeting had been very disturbing and had underlined the need to make sense of her visions. Yet naught she'd tried thus far had made any difference.

She had to do something. But what use were glamours or summoning against changes in history?

On her way to the library, she eyed the portraits on the wall. Her glance fell on a painting of a dark-haired man clad in short, puffy breeches and a doublet with a lacy ruff around his neck. A globe stood beside him. He looked remarkably like Richard, with the same black hair, straight nose and strong chin.

"Good morning, mistress," Richard said, emerging from a chamber down the corridor.

She blinked at the formality before realizing there might be unGifted servants about. "Good morning, my lord. That portrait resembles you closely."

He gave her a wry grin. "I fear all the Mainwaring men look much alike. That particular one is Miles, one of Queen Elizabeth's vaunted captains. We lost our title and most of our lands over the little matter of Henry VIII's divorce. Miles impressed Elizabeth so much that she restored them."

"How fascinating." And worrisome, no doubt. There were advantages to living in obscurity.

Movement from the stairway caught her eye. She glanced toward it. A footman led a tall, kind-faced young man toward them.

"Thank you, Colin," Richard said.

The footman bowed and hurried back down the stairs. The visitor strolled toward them, a polite smile on his face.

Richard nodded at him. "Reverend Dr. Jeremy Winfield, allow me to present our cousin, Mistress Miranda Willoughby."

"A pleasure, cousin." The young man bowed to her. "Miranda, if I may? And I'm Jeremy."

"I would be honored." Because he'd bowed, Miranda curtsied. She had the same feeling of familiarity, almost recognition, with him that she'd experienced when she'd met Richard. "I'm pleased to meet you, Jeremy."

"You'll be in my grandmother's parlor this morning, Miranda," Richard said. "Fourth door on the left."

All the doors were on the left because of the gallery that ran along the side of the house, but Miranda nodded.

She walked to the indicated door and found it ajar.

The dowager countess stood by the hearth, and her grave expression renewed Miranda's frustration. Surely there was a way to master her Gifts faster. They were no use if she couldn't wield them properly.

"Come in, Miranda, and sit down."

"Is something amiss, Arabella?" Miranda seated herself carefully in an armchair near the fireplace. Using the dowager countess's given name still felt odd, but not as much as it had.

Arabella sat in the chair opposite Miranda's. "Last night, I scried the hanging you described to me. Although that was just a fortnight ago, I had difficulty holding the scrying and so am not entirely certain I saw clearly. Your lips seemed to move, though just barely, as though you were trying to help."

"I barely whispered. If anyone had heard—"

"I doubt you made much of a sound, and everyone was watching that poor woman. Word magic has long been used by those just coming into their skills. Those who are fully trained no longer need it, but the earliest use of magic relied on words, in spells. An incantation, carefully used, carries great power."

"My mother said that magic was the will and the power. She taught me naught of spells, save the basic ones for summoning and glamours."

Miranda shook her head slowly. "If I used a word spell, my lady, I did it unknowingly."

"That, I do not doubt because of the result." Again, she hesitated. "My dear, I cannot be certain, but I think there's an excellent chance that you killed Mistress Smith."

"Killed?" Miranda shot to her feet, fists clenched. "But I didn't mean—I couldn't have! I wouldn't."

"No, I don't believe you would deliberately do so," Arabella said gently.

Miranda's knees wobbled. She dropped back into her chair.

"Nevertheless," the older woman continued, "I believe you have the power to do so, and that you likely did."

"No," Miranda choked, shaking her head.

"I watched you. You seemed to say 'stop.' You did it again, and then a third time, and Mistress Smith stopped thrashing."

"But people do. They die, I mean. And stop." Under her teacher's steady, compassionate gaze, her cheeks heated. "I meant to give her ease, to stop the pain. Only that."

"Of course, but you directed your thought at Mistress Smith, who must have wished to escape the torment, if she could still think at all." Sympathy darkened the older woman's eyes as she added, "Your command could have empowered her wish. Or else, without any wish of hers, quenched a spark already nearly extinguished."

"Killing is wrong. So is helping suicide." Her father's words sprang to Miranda's lips. Suddenly cold, she rubbed her hands over her arms.

"So we believe. Yet there is also the ancient tradition of the *coup de grâce*, the killing blow administered in mercy to end a wounded warrior's suffering."

Miranda swallowed against nausea. If she'd killed Mistress Smith by accident, what other havoc might she wreak?

"My dear," Arabella said quietly, "those who do not die instantly on the gallows have a slow and agonized passing. That woman was suffering, and wrongly. Do you not think she would have wished for a quick, merciful end?"

Of course she must have. Miranda couldn't deny that, but killing her was still wrong. "I didn't mean to kill her," she said, her voice shaking.

"I know. I feared this possibility might distress you. Remember, I'm not certain that you slew her. Your creation of the dragon illusion, however, proves you have sufficient magical power to do so, and the circumstances indicate a strong probability that you did. One who possesses such power cannot be allowed to walk about in ignorance of it."

Ignorance sounded wonderful. Mute, Miranda shook her head.

A rustle of silken skirts, then the scent of lavender, and Arabella knelt beside her. The older woman put an arm around her. "Weep if you like, child. I know you grieve her death."

This shock stabbed too deeply for tears. If she accepted Arabella's offer of comfort, was she accepting the power to kill? Miranda sat rigid.

"I wanted—I hoped to become a healer," she managed. "Like my mother."

"You still can be." The older woman squeezed her arm lightly and rose. "You see now why we must bring your skills under control without delay. Come, let's try a scrying. Something that's happening now would be easiest to summon."

Miranda's hands shook. She locked them together in her lap. Dully, she stared at the fire.

"Miranda." Arabella's firm tone broke into her daze. "Reach out to the fire and summon an image."

Miranda turned to the flames. *Lucy*, she thought, struggling against the cloud of guilt on her soul. Nothing happened.

"Try harder. I can't feel your power."

Miranda took a deep breath and tried again, pushing magic toward the flames. Still nothing.

"Better," Arabella said. "Again."

They tried for almost an hour, but Miranda failed to summon anything in the flames, even with Arabella's help. Through her mind, again and again, ran the image of Mistress Smith's limp form.

At last, the dowager countess said, "We'll stop for a while. I think the news has disturbed you even more than I feared. Rest for a bit. We'll try again before supper."

Miranda nodded wearily and rose. "Yes, Arabella." She rose and started for the door.

She had nearly reached it when Arabella said, "It may help you, Miranda, to see what you may have done as good for Mistress Smith even if it's troublesome for you. While you rest, consider the good someone with your power might do."

~

Miranda could only pick at her food during the noon meal, which Patience had brought to her in her chamber. Afterward, she sat by the fire, watching the flames without seeing them. Despite having donned her cloak, she couldn't seem to get warm.

As it had for hours, her mind turned around and around the same thought like a spinning wheel on its hub. She might have killed an innocent woman. Arabella had presented the information as possibility, not as certainty, but it seemed more likely to be true than not.

If she had, it would have been a mercy. Must have been. But still murder.

Could any number of healings make up for that? Assuming she mastered the skill one day?

Someone tapped on her door. She jumped but didn't answer. Perhaps whoever it was would assume she slept.

The knock sounded again, harder. "Miranda," Arabella's voice said.

She took a deep breath that did nothing to steady her. "Come in."

The older woman opened the door and stepped inside. Silhouetted against the lights in the corridor, she looked even more imposing than usual.

"Why are you sitting in the dark, child?"

In the dark? Outside, thunder rumbled, and the churning clouds blocked the daylight. "I didn't notice that it was dark."

"I imagine not." Her teacher shut the door and, with a wave of her hand, lit the candles in the sconces. "Your feelings do you credit, Miranda, but you mustn't let them overwhelm you." She seated herself on the opposite side of the hearth.

"How can I not?"

"You were desperate to help that woman somehow. At such times, one does what one must. What one can."

"Even if it's wrong?"

"Would it have been, to grant a dying, tormented woman a merciful end? Is that wrong?"

"My father would've said so." Miranda hesitated. "Milady—Arabella—what would you have done?"

The older woman shook her head. "I can't say. It's possible, with skill, to induce a sort of unconsciousness in another person though few of us possess that knack."

With a sigh, she added, "I might have tried to do that. If I couldn't, I don't know whether I would have slain her. I've never faced that choice. I do know that power such as yours must have the restraints that come with training. So we're going to continue your lessons."

"I'd really rather not, just yet."

"Of course you don't want to try again, for now you fear your magic. All the more reason to control it. Come, Miranda. Sit up, look at the fire, and face your destiny."

The argument made too much sense to ignore. Miranda squared her shoulders. "What shall I do?"

"I think you held back your power earlier." After a moment, Arabella said, "Let's try a new exercise. Move your chair closer to mine, so you're facing the hearth."

When Miranda had done so, the older woman said, "Take my hand."

Miranda complied, and Arabella said, "Now I'll summon an image, and I want you to feel what I do." An image appeared in the flames, Richard and Jeremy sitting in the library.

"What do you feel?" Arabella asked.

"Nothing, I'm afraid."

Patiently, Arabella said, "Extend your perceptions until you can feel mine. Open your senses and then try to reach farther. Close your eyes if it helps."

Miranda shut her eyes and opened her mind. The ticking of the mantel clock and the crackling of the fire grew sharper. She reached outward, and her power brushed someone else's. As it had when she'd tried with Richard, it created a tingling at the nape of her neck.

"Very good," Arabella murmured. "Now trace my power and align yours with it."

Miranda tried, but the tingle vanished.

"Don't try so hard. Let the magic flow."

Flow? Trace? There was something ... like that?

"That's it," her teacher breathed. "Hold your power there and open your eyes."

Miranda obeyed. The image in the flame showed clearly. Richard and Jeremy sat in chairs by the library hearth, talking. Sipping ale.

The tingle faded. The image flickered.

"No," Arabella snapped. "Hold it steady."

The sense of other power faded, yet the image in the flame held. Miranda caught her breath. Was she doing that?

The older woman released her hand. "Now think of what you'd like to see."

The image wavered. Faded. *Lucy*, Miranda thought, straining. Nothing happened.

"I'll help you," Arabella murmured. "Joining my magic with yours will more than double what each of us wields, but I'll withdraw mine as soon as you summon an image. The only way to learn control is on one's own."

The tingle on the back of Miranda's neck grew stronger, as though someone were prodding her there. Her friend's face appeared in the flame. Lucy smiled, chatting with the scullery lad.

The tightness in Miranda's chest eased. This was a small step, nothing that could hurt anyone. Mayhap her fears of doing accidental damage had been exaggerated. As Arabella had said, she'd been desperate at the hanging.

Miranda glanced at the older woman. "That's Lucy, my friend."

"Good. Now hold it steady."

The prodding sensation faded. Miranda reached for the image.

"Steady, child. You're losing it."

The image died. No!

Miranda reached, throwing her perceptions outward. The image flickered. Turned nightmarish purple-gray with swirling mists. Her heart leaped into her throat.

"Hold," Arabella urged her. "Stay with it."

The mists thinned. A dark-haired man lay crumpled on the ground, his sweat-damp shirt clinging to his shoulders. Around him darted ghostly shapes with ghostly faces, some with gaping wounds and others with no flesh.

He curled his arms over his head, as though to fend them off, but they rushed toward him. Their claws raked his back, opening bloody welts. His body jerked as though in pain.

The man was Richard. Miranda couldn't have said how she knew, but she was certain, even though his arms covered his face.

Her chair crashed backward as she shot to her feet. "I can't—can't stop it."

"Let it go." Arabella stepped in front of her. "Miranda. Look at me."

She couldn't. Power surged through her, a link from somewhere else to her head and then to the fire.

"Make it stop," she panted, heart pounding.

Arabella yanked the bell pull, then rushed into the corridor. "Fetch

Lord Hawkstowe at once," she ordered someone, her voice sharp with command. She hurried back into the room.

Power surged against the vision. Miranda scarcely felt it. In the flames, the horrifying torment continued. Richard writhed, helpless against it.

Then he stood before her, his face real and solid. "Look at me," he ordered.

"I am." But she couldn't shut the vision from her mind. It lay over his face like thin, colored glass.

His hands wrapped around both of hers. "Grandmère, stand with me. Jeremy, douse it."

His grandmother stood beside him, an arm around Miranda's shoulders. Power surged into Miranda's mind, a wall inching up between her and the hearth. In her mind, silver flickered against the fire, smothering it. As the sense of it ebbed, so did the strength in her knees.

Supporting her with one arm, Richard righted her chair. She sank into it, suddenly cold and queasy.

He stripped off his coat and wrapped it around her. "Breathe slowly. Deeply," he ordered. He knelt by her chair and drew her against him. Over his shoulder, he said, "Jeremy, you know what to mix?"

"I'll raid your grandmother's herbs, if I may."

Minutes dragged by. Shivering, Miranda huddled in Richard's embrace while he rubbed her arm steadily. The warmth of his body and the faint bay leaf scent of his garments were comforting.

"You can't—" Her teeth chattered. "You—I didn't mean for that to happen."

"Don't worry about it now. Just breathe." Gently, he brushed her hair off her brow.

"But—I think—you might be in—in danger." Her teeth clacked together so hard that they hurt.

"The flames do not lie." Arabella spoke quietly, though worry shadowed her eyes. "Still, future scrying shows only possibility, not certainty. Richard—"

"Later for that," he insisted. "Ah, Jeremy."

Holding a goblet, Jeremy's hand moved into her vision. "Drink it down," he ordered. "Quickly, so as not to taste it."

Her shaking hands banged the goblet against her teeth. Richard cupped his hand around hers and guided it to her mouth.

"Quickly," he repeated. "Jeremy believes in nasty medicine."

He truly did. The bitter, acrid taste made her stomach churn, but she would drink anything to stop the shivering.

Fighting the urge to gag, she passed the cup back.

Richard stroked her hair again, the touch soothing. "That's it. Breathe."

Slowly the shivering subsided, and she fought the temptation to burrow into his hold.

"What was that drink?" she asked, straightening.

Richard released her but remained kneeling by her chair, his face grave.

"Herbs and magic," Jeremy said. "Your power escaped your control. Unpaced, it drained you and trapped you in the vision. The herbs will let you rest and recover."

"Thank you," she said.

"Of course."

The earl still knelt beside her. "Jeremy brought interesting news. We'll share it with you, and then you should sleep for a while." He glanced at his friend.

"But we should talk about that vision." Miranda insisted. "It was awful, and it was about you."

His eyes wintry, he said, "It can wait."

Jeremy knelt to face her. "A friend of ours went to the Cottonian library, where Buck found the copy of the *Croyland Chronicle* he used. They had a number of monastic chronicles, but none from Croyland."

"So it's gone."

"Yes," Richard confirmed, grim-faced. "Now we must discover what became of it."

❧

Miranda awoke in her bed. Its yellow damask curtains hung open. Blinking, she stared at the matching canopy. She'd been in the chair by the fire. How—?

Fabric rustled in the corner, and Patience hurried to the bed. "How're you feeling, mistress?"

"Better." Tired, but not deathly ill. Or shivering, as she had been earlier.

"Milady said you might come down for supper if you like. The reverend is staying. Or y'can eat here."

"I'll go down." The coverlet lay over her. Beneath it, she wore only her shift. "Who undressed me?"

"Milady and me. Are you sure you're feelin' well, mistress?"

"Yes. Thank you." How mortifying to have caused so much trouble. "I'll dress for dinner."

"His lordship said you fainted. I'm glad you're better."

"So am I. Thank you." *His lordship?* That could only mean Richard, but it made sense. Arabella couldn't have carried her to the bed. And they'd given the UnGifted maid, who couldn't know the truth, a logical explanation.

Patience dressed her and tidied her hair. Miranda wiped her own face, and the cold water revived her a bit.

She opened the door to go downstairs. When Patience followed, Miranda said, "I'll be fine, Patience, I assure you."

"I'm glad to hear it." Richard stepped into view, as though he'd been waiting against the wall near the door. "I'll escort you to dinner."

A polite nod dismissed Patience.

Such thoughtfulness was part of the reason she liked him far too much. "That's kind, but I don't want to trouble you further."

"It's no trouble."

They walked a few paces in silence. "You were very brave today," he said.

"I didn't feel brave. I fell asleep in the chair."

He smiled. "Yes, but you did it without hysterics. Which I do appreciate. How do you feel?"

Though his smile made her pulse skip, she summoned a casual tone. "Much better, thank you. I apologize for all this fuss."

"Pray, don't. Everyone hits a rough patch in training."

"If that was a rough patch, I'd hate to see a serious problem." She hesitated. "Richard, about that vision—"

"We won't discuss it."

"But if you're in danger, we must."

He stopped, staring into her eyes. "I know what it portends," he said, his face grim, "and talking about it won't help. Besides, it may not come to pass."

Reluctantly, she nodded. "As you wish." If he knew, he'd been warned, and he likely wouldn't welcome her prying.

His expression softened into one of concern. "On another point, you must let me know if you feel any loss of focus or if you have another vision you cannot control. They're dangerous. It's better to cause a *fuss* by asking for help than to combat them alone."

"I believe you, but I don't like asking for help. I cling to what my father called arrogant pride."

Richard's eyes met hers steadily. "Sometimes only arrogant pride, a stubborn refusal to give up, keeps us standing."

He was talking about more than magic. The depths of his eyes held pained understanding of the desperation that made hope a mean joke and stubbornness a lifeline. Oh, she knew that feeling.

Softly, she replied, "Very true, my lord."

He held her gaze a moment longer before he said, "Let's go to dinner, then."

The impersonal mask dropped over his face again and remained there while they walked through the house. Still, Miranda found herself unable to forget those few seconds when she and he had shared perfect understanding.

That moment owed nothing to magic and all to who the two of them were. Thus it became doubly precious.

When the time came, leaving here would be very difficult, but necessary. No matter what his grandmother said about magic compensating for rank, no earl could develop a serious interest in a serving maid.

"Grandmère told me of your discussion about the hanging and of your lesson before that final vision. I understand why you're distressed. I'm sorry for the shock it gave you."

"Thank you. Do you have any advice for me?"

"I can add nothing to what she told you, but we agreed that you should have lessons in magical healing. She has a teacher in mind for that, and when Jeremy has time, he'll instruct you in the magical use of herbs. No one knows more about that than he does."

"I'm grateful. That's kind of him." Especially since he scarcely knew her. And such lessons would take her closer to her dream of being a healer like Mother.

At the dining parlor doorway, the earl paused. "One warning. Once tapped, power such as you displayed today grows ever stronger. It can be lethal, so learning to control it is imperative, but don't practice scrying alone. An incident such as today's, if you had no help, could kill you."

CHAPTER 11

"**R**ichard. I know you can hear me, lad."

The spectral voice grated in Richard's ears. For once, though, Edmund might prove useful. Awakening, Richard sat up. The ghost had seated himself on the bed, leaning back against one of the foot posts. Its ornate scrollwork was visible through him.

"Sitting on the bed's a bit encroaching, Edmund." Richard raised a hand to forestall the ghost's reply. "You've studied in the Pendragon library. Do you know how to splice time or whether someone living could do it? Can the dead?"

"So far as I know, no one can do it, though I can commune across time with our kinsmen." Frowning, the ghost rubbed his chin. "Each of them resides in the years that made up his life. While I can't go to them, when I think of them, or they of me, we see spectral images of each other in the fog. I suppose that's a way of splicing time, though rather limited."

"So you never actually meet with them?"

"Alas, no," Edmund said. "Those whose lives overlapped, however, can find each other, though 'tis difficult.

That was disappointing. Richard had always thought of his father as having all his kinsmen, at least, for company. He would likely have no one but Grandfather. And someday, Richard.

"Yet you can come to this time and speak to me. How?"

Edmund shrugged. "Perhaps because I started the curse. Whatever the reason, I'm drawn to the living Mainwaring heirs. The curse and shared blood both bind us. But I cannot travel backward in time, even to see my beloved Margery."

What a lonely existence. Not knowing what to say, Richard started, "Edmund, I—"

The ghost talked over him, any pity obviously unwelcome. "As far as splicing time, though, if I read the old scrolls aright, it involves passing through here. This is the path of death, with life before and after—for most men."

Richard frowned. "I thought that place was merely a path to the portal of judgment."

"'Tis that, yes, but also much more. This nasty realm touches all the world. All times past, or so the lore claims."

"So you studied it."

"Aye, for the same reason I imagine you did, looking for clues to find the proof we need to clear the king's name. From experience I know one can cross vast distances with great speed. Even breach walls as though they weren't there, unless they're warded. I can breach Mainwaring wards because they're made by my kin, but only those."

Richard sat straighter.

Had Wyndon gone there to change the past? To spy on Richard and Miranda? There'd been those freakish cold spots, that sense of being watched. But how could a living man cross into the shadowland to do such things?

One thing Edmund said niggled at him. "Breach walls without being detected?" Richard asked.

"Aye. Remember, this place lies around and alongside the world of the quick, like its ghost. That's what ghosts are—folk here, talking to their descendants or, in rare cases of grave injustice, seeking redress or comfort."

"A cheery thought." It explained, though, why people most often saw family spirits. "So someone living who managed to reach that place could go anywhere, to any time?"

Even back to the Tower of London in 1483 to stop two murders that shouldn't have happened?

"If my guess is right, the living can do things here the dead cannot. Only if that were true could anyone splice time. The dead cannot, after all."

Richard nodded absently. What would be the consequences of saving the boys in the Tower? Could such a thing be done without wreaking the kind of chaos occurring now?

He would worry about that later. If Wyndon or someone like him had learned to travel the afterworld, then someone on the side of right must master it as well.

"If this is possible, I need to learn it," Richard said. "Can you teach me?"

Scowling, Edmund crossed his arms. "I've no idea and refuse to try. This place is dangerous. There're wraiths all over, perpetually damned souls looking to prey on the newly dead. What they could do to a living body doesn't bear thinking about."

Richard hated the idea of that shadowland, but he couldn't spurn a skill that might hold the key to restoring whatever had been altered in the past. "Coming there could enable me to set everything right, Edmund."

"Or it could kill you, you young fool. Then where will all the rest of us be?"

"No worse off than you are now," Richard shot back.

Edmund shook his head.

"Those who can help," Richard said, "have a duty to. You've tainted my life, Edmund. God's feet, you owe me your help."

"To destroy yourself? To end the Mainwaring line and leave us all trapped here forever? No."

"To keep the world from destroying itself in all this upheaval. To see that matters are put right."

Edmund opened his mouth, then shut it abruptly. "Do those matters include the murder of the boys in the Tower?"

"If that can be done without more upheaval, yes." Unlikely though that seemed. But Richard needed Edmund's help. If he had to stretch the truth to get it, he would. Too much was at stake for mincing around the hard choices.

"I'm not certain I can teach you," Edmund said slowly, "but I studied those old texts, too. I can make some guesses, though you must realize there are dangers aplenty here. First, though, I've news for you from Hawkstowe. I was concerned about this unnatural weather, so I drifted there to see how the folk fared."

"You still care?"

Edmund raised an eyebrow in a gesture much like Richard's habitual one. "I held the title and lands longer than you yet have. They're my folk, too. Anyway, Richard, they've worse problems than the weather. The livestock are sickening, as though whatever's making all these changes has affected their feed. The folk are much on edge."

"Yet people aren't ill."

"Eventually, they may be. Animals are more sensitive to the natural world than men."

"My thanks, Edmund." Richard blew out a frustrated breath. "I'll send advice to my steward. At least he's Gifted, which gives him better skills than most for coping with errant weather, magical or not."

They couldn't just alter the weather, though. First, because change in one place usually created changes in others. Second, and more important, was the fact that the weather was the symptom of a bigger problem, not the cause. That might be why the Conclave's weather wizards had thus far been unable to affect the unseasonable climate.

"If you can learn to travel here," Edmund said, "assuming that's truly possible, you could arrive at Hawkstowe much faster than you could through the realm of the quick. With the roads so boggy, the journey would take far longer than usual. Roads will wash out if this keeps up."

Not a pretty picture, country folk starving and their lords unable to reach them. "We'd better set about it, then."

"The old lore says you need something to anchor you to the real world so you can return there from here. Something not shaped nor altered by human hands."

Richard frowned. He had nothing of the sort, at least not indoors. "I'll find a pebble in the garden." He grabbed his breeches, stepped into them, and hurried outside. The cold weather shocked him fully awake, but he had no difficulty finding a suitable stone. Gray and irregularly shaped, it was about the size of a robin's egg.

When he returned to his bedchamber, he found Edmund pacing. "I hope we won't regret this, lad," the ghost muttered.

"Let's get on with it, Edmund."

With a sigh, Edmund said, "Hold the stone in your hand. Now, think of how this feels, talking to me. Reach for me with your mind."

Richard tried.

"Are you reaching?" Edmund stood beside the bed.

"Aye. If you've never taught this before, how do you know what I should do?"

"I'm guessing, mostly based on a scroll on necromancy I read once and on odd things one of my old Oxford dons, a fellow spectacularly Gifted but rather impractical, used to say. Reach for me and pour your power into a doorway. An open one is better. You're making a ghost door, not going through the real one, but you don't want to walk into the door if you fail."

Richard drew power from within him and let it flow toward the doorway to his dressing room. The frame turned silver. Its glow spread to fill the portal's outline.

With Edmund pacing beside him, Richard walked toward it. Kept walking. A cold current pushed against him.

He passed through the doorway, out of the chill, and into the dark dressing room. "Stop," Edmund said. "Are you keeping your mind on me?"

"Reluctantly. I feel like a fool." Richard glared at him.

"Well, that can't help." Scowling in turn, Edmund demanded, "Did you feel anything else?"

"Icy cold, but it ended when I passed the threshold."

"According to the scroll I read all those years back, that's a good sign. Try again."

Richard frowned at him. "I don't remember a scroll about that at Pendragon. I looked at everything I could find."

"There was one. About the length of a man's forearm, fist-thick. Very ornate ends and bindings. Bound with a red cord, as all those touching on dangerous matters are, with the dragon rampant seal on each end. Mayhap it crumbled, or mayhap it's lost in the disorder at Pendragon. Try again."

They tried several times without success. At last, Edmund said, "I don't think you want it badly enough, my boy."

Richard didn't want it at all. He dreaded the shadowland, especially after Miranda's vision of it, but he'd tried his best. He sat on the edge of the bed. "Do you know of anyone living who can do this? Have you ever seen Henry de Vere there?"

Drifting back to the bed, Edmund said, "You mean, walking about? Egad, no. How would he learn?"

"That's what I'd like to know. Any ideas?"

Edmund pursed his lips. "He might have figured it out. Someone once did, or there'd have been no scrolls for me or anyone else to read."

Cheerful thought. "Do you know who?"

"Only God is omniscient, boy." Edmund hesitated for a moment. "You know, Richard ... I never meant—"

"I know. Good night, Edmund."

The ghost vanished. Richard stared at the bed's canopy. Someone must've learned how to travel the afterworld. And from there, learned to manipulate the past. No other explanation made sense. Therefore, Richard also could do these things. He would simply have to keep trying.

Stifling a yawn, he glanced at the ornate, silver clock on the mantel. Six in the morning, so he'd best haul himself out of bed. He was to meet the king at seven to go fishing in St. James's Park.

Court gossip now seemed even more trivial compared to the pressing issue of time change, but he'd given his word to his sovereign. At least fishing didn't involve much chatter and so would give him time to think.

~

Miranda hoped the dread she felt didn't show in her face when she greeted Arabella in the library after breakfast. Learning about magic had not been the joy she'd expected. She had what she'd always wanted, only to find that it made her dangerous in ways that were difficult to accept. Perhaps she should go back to the Golden Swan, where she knew what she was doing and couldn't possibly hurt anyone.

Or perhaps she should stop sniveling and learn to use her Gifts in a way that would help people. Miranda steeled her spine.

"Yesterday," the older woman said, "was painful for you. I salute you for being here and not trying to avoid this."

It had been difficult for Arabella, too, especially that horrible vision in the fire. The dowager countess's face looked grave, and shadows lurked in her eyes. Yet her cool, composed manner did not invite comment.

"Avoiding this will only make it worse," Miranda said. "I realize that."

"Indeed." Pouring tea into ceramic dishes, Arabella said, "The dragon, the incident at the hanging, the visions you've had, the dreams, and now a scrying you could neither direct nor break. You are very powerful, my dear."

"Yet I've never felt powerful." Especially not now, when nothing she tried seemed to yield a useful result.

"Sometimes one who's very adept at some tasks may not have the same skill at others. Nonetheless, you created that dragon, which requires a great deal of power. The simple magics, such as basic scrying, extended senses, weather manipulation, or glamours, are easier, coupling power and will, but the combination of scrying with vision, as happened last night, takes prodigious magical strength."

"Then what I saw was real? Or could be?" When Arabella nodded,

117

Miranda said, "I don't want that to happen to Richard, but he won't talk about it."

His grandmother shrugged. "He is a man. But even if your vision was a foretelling, Miranda, that does not mean it must come to pass. It may be only a possibility, especially now that events are so dreadfully in flux."

"I hope so." Miranda hesitated, but she, too, worried for Richard. "I would hate to have that particular vision come to pass."

For an instant, Arabella's fear for her grandson shone stark in her eyes. Then she drew a breath, straightened her shoulders, and composed her face. "Let us hope so."

Briskly, she added, "Now, let us see what you can do this morning. Look into the fire and summon an image, but think of something safe, perhaps your bedchamber."

Again, the older woman's power joined with Miranda's, nudging gently. Miranda tried, but nothing appeared in the flames.

"Keep trying," Arabella prompted.

Miranda pushed her power at the fire and tried to think of the lovely, yellow chamber. But nothing happened.

Long minutes slid past before Arabella gently touched her arm. "That's enough for now. We'll try again after you eat a bit."

She passed Miranda a plate piled with knot biscuits, palm-sized bread looped over itself as though in a knot. "Do you need to rest?"

"No, thank you." Miranda helped herself to a biscuit and savored the rich flavor. "This is wonderful."

"The recipe uses mace and aniseed, among others." Arabella smiled. "Have another."

Miranda did. She would likely never stop noticing the glory spices could give ordinary food.

They were about to begin again when Arabella's head rose in a listening posture. "Wait."

A moment later, Miranda heard rapid footsteps approaching, muffled by the walls and door. The door swung open to admit a brown-haired man of middling height and amiable countenance.

"Grandmère—oh. Ah. I beg pardon."

"I'm sure Enderby told you I was occupied," the dowager countess said coolly. The glance she flicked at Miranda held a warning. "George, come and make your bow to your cousin Miranda Willoughby."

His brows rose. "Cousin?"

Miranda fought the impulse to rise. A cousin would not, though she had no blood claim to being any such thing.

"On Richard's mother's side," Arabella replied. "Miranda, this is your cousin George Mainwaring."

"Richard's heir," the man added. Eyeing Miranda appraisingly, he sauntered into the room. "Grandmère, can you spare a cup of tea? The weather's rotten."

"Not at the moment, George. We're rather busy. Miranda and I have much to discuss about her stay with us."

"Do you indeed?" Speculation gleamed in his eyes.

Miranda set her tea dish down carefully. If she didn't handle it well, he'd know she didn't belong here.

"George, you must await Richard elsewhere." Sternly, his grandmother stared at him. "Miranda and I have much to do."

"I came to see you, Grandmère, not Richard." His smile didn't warm his eyes. "Now that I've met our lovely cousin, I'd like to further our acquaintance." He stopped before the low, red velvet sofa.

"Another time," Arabella insisted.

"Oh, very well." His petulant expression matched his voice. "Grandmère, cousin Miranda, good day to you."

"Good day, si—George," Miranda said.

"Yes, good day," Arabella said.

He strolled out of the room, leaving the door ajar. Miranda hurried to close it.

"Thank you, Miranda." Arabella waited for her to sit down again. "George is not Gifted, and he is sadly irresponsible. Should you encounter him again, you must take care what you say."

"I will. Thank you for warning me."

The older woman nodded. "I don't wish to press you, but I fear time is not on our side, and I think your visions are very important. If you cannot control them, we must seek some other means to bring them to the fore."

"What other means?" Why did Arabella look so grave?

"Magical means. Which are not without risk. Come, let us try again."

Before they could, someone tapped on the door. A footman opened it a moment later and stepped in. "Your visitors are here, my lady. Enderby asked me not to show them up while Master Mainwaring was here."

"Quite right. Show them in, Colin."

Miranda rose. "I can practice in my chamber while your guests are here."

"You could, but you needn't. They came to meet you."

"Me? Why?"

The dowager countess smiled. "Your mother was a healer, and you wish to be one. Perhaps you have a gift in that area."

Three women of varying ages walked through the door Colin held open. The first was of medium height, with brown hair in fashionable clusters of curls and shot with gray. The smooth wool and minimal lace trim of her dark pink gown and the simple, silver locket at her throat marked her as from the merchant or gentry class.

The other two were more simply clad, in homespun and with their hair in coiled braids at their napes. One was blonde and appeared to be a bit younger than Miranda, and the other looked to be past her first youth though her hair was still dark brown.

Again a sense of recognition tingled at the nape of Miranda's neck. She was growing accustomed to it now, to being among her own kind. She would never take that for granted.

Colin bowed himself out.

Arabella didn't rise but said, "Cousins, let me make you known to each other. This is Miranda Willoughby, newly come from Kent to join our household."

Indicating the first woman, she added, "Miranda, this is Elspeth Taylor."

Miranda and Elspeth exchanged greetings, and Arabella nodded to the blonde woman. "Anne Wilfleet and her mother, Sarah. Elspeth is a mercer's wife, and the Wilfleets are fishmongers."

As they greeted each other and the newcomers found seats, Arabella said, "Sarah is a healer, and Elspeth can sometimes help breach magical barriers. They're part of my Gifted circle here in London. Anne came along because she wanted to meet you. She's very good with defensive magic as well as the more aggressive sort."

"If you need a wall blown out," Anne said, grinning, "I'll gladly have a go." Her smile was so friendly that she didn't seem to be bragging. Miranda smiled back.

"We work together on magical problems," Elspeth added.

Arabella explained, "That's what a magic circle does. Now. Let's see how you handle a healing spell."

She walked to the cabinet across the room and removed a dagger in a tooled leather sheath. "We'll use this in our lessons today."

Sarah held out a hand, and Arabella offered her the weapon, hilt first. Sarah drew the dagger, a simple one with a leather-wrapped hilt and a sleek steel blade.

"I'll cut my palm," Sarah said. "Elspeth will heal it and show you how it's done."

Miranda's fists clenched in the folds of her skirt. "I saw a girl cut her hand in the kitchen once. Carving meat from a spit. It putrefied, and she —lost the hand. And left the inn."

Sarah waited until Miranda lifted her gaze from the blade to Sarah's face. "We'll teach you how to stop that from happening," she said. Pressing her lips together, she drew the blade over the heel of her hand.

When a thin, red line welled behind it. Miranda swallowed hard. Anne took the blade, wiped it, and magically cleaned it. "This purifies it as well," she noted.

Supporting Sarah's hand in one of hers, Elspeth beckoned to Miranda. "Come stand by me so you can see. You'll touch a finger beside one end of the cut, only one finger, as I'm doing now. Then envision it closing as you trace its line, feeding magic to the image."

As Elspeth's finger moved, Miranda could feel the flow of healing magic over Sarah's skin, the strands of it weaving across the wound like a shuttle through the strands of a loom. The wound on Sarah's hand closed as though it had never been there.

Sarah smiled at Miranda. "Now Elspeth will cut her hand, and you'll try to heal it."

As Elspeth made the cut, Miranda's stomach still felt jittery. She couldn't seem to make the power flow.

"Steady," Elspeth murmured, smiling. "Call the power. Don't try to yank it."

"May I use words?"

"If you must, but it's better if you don't."

Miranda closed her eyes, the better to focus on the magic flowing within her. It should flow down her arm. To her hand. Yes. Now her finger tingled with it.

She traced the cut, and it closed.

"Well," Arabella said, "you seem to have inherited your mother's knack. I believe your success calls for celebratory tea. Ring for it, Miranda, will you?"

The celebration was short-lived. The next lesson, scrying, produced no improvement.

Unfortunately, that was the skill she needed most.

~

Easy to feel superior, George decided, nursing his coffee, when one had great wealth. What was the harm in his staying at Hawkstowe House? It was his future home, after all. Now Richard had shunted him off to a mean little room above a tavern in the Strand. Ridiculous!

The bustle of people going in and out of the coffeehouse at mid-day, the voices of patrons, and the rich smell of tobacco surrounded him, yet here he sat with nothing but coffee, and the penny and a half for it feeling rather dear. At least he had the long table, one of a dozen in the place, to himself for the moment.

The rough plaster walls and beamed ceiling might've seemed cozy, but the place was altogether too busy with people who were no concern of his. As was the inn where Richard had booked him a room. Really, the place was full of tradesmen!

But he couldn't afford better with the paltry sum Richard allowed him.

As heir to the Hawkstowe titles, he should have a larger allowance. Especially if he were to attract a wealthy wife to bring in fresh funds. Yet Richard, instead of seeing reason, acted as though he had a poker up his arse. He'd be furious when he discovered George had taken a silver tray today.

Not that the money from selling it would last long. He'd intended to ask Grandmère for a loan, if she hadn't been so busy.

Frowning, he sipped coffee. Who the devil was that girl, anyway? He'd never heard of any Willoughby kindred.

George sniffed. The girl didn't matter. Nor did Richard. The tray came from his own chamber. He was entitled to it. Besides, he needed the money.

Richard didn't understand what losing a wife and child could do to man. If he did, he'd have come to Kendal Manor when Mary Rose and James had been so ill. Perhaps even brought one of his fancy London doctors. Who knew how they might've helped?

"May I join you?" A harsh voice broke into George's reverie.

Squinting through tobacco smoke, George saw the newcomer's burgundy velvet suit, thick lace foaming at the wrists and throat, and then the man's face. It was square and amiable but with a hard set to the mouth. A long, light brown wig framed his face in curls.

"Do I know you?" George asked.

"By reputation, I imagine, and not a good one in your family. You're George Mainwaring, aren't you?" At George's nod, the man seated himself on the opposite bench. "I'm Canby."

Canby. Lesser title of ... Wyndon. "You're a de Vere." George shrugged. "I've no quarrel with you."

"I'm pleased to hear it. I'm here to have coffee and read the newspapers. May I order coffee for you?"

"You'd buy for an enemy's kinsman?"

"As you said, we've no quarrel, have we?"

Something felt amiss, but most men didn't court one so down on his luck as George. Who was he to spurn a kind gesture? "I thank you," he replied.

"It's the least I can do." Canby beckoned to a serving wench. When she reached their table, he ordered more coffee for George and a dish for himself.

George nodded gratefully. "What brings you to share a table with me?"

Canby leaned forward. "In truth, Mainwaring, I need your help. Your cousin Richard has seduced away a young woman from my father's lands in Kent, a former serving maid. He refuses to allow Father to meet with her, to be certain she is well. I want you to help arrange such a meeting."

Nothing. Nothing and more nothing despite an afternoon of trying. Seated in the library, Miranda bit her lip in frustration.

Arabella said, "Let me help you. I'll scry, and I want you to feel what I do. As we did before."

An image appeared in the flames, the staff working in the kitchen. "Extend your perceptions again. Reach outward with your magic," the older woman said. "Close your eyes if it helps."

Miranda shut her eyes and opened her mind, reaching for her magic. Her power brushed Arabella's, creating a familiar tingle at the nape of her neck. Blending with someone else's power came more easily now.

"Very good," Arabella murmured.

"Hold your power steady and open your eyes."

Miranda obeyed. The image died.

No! She reached, throwing her magic at the flames in frustration. The image flickered. Died, then surged into one of a great city. London. The eastern part, she somehow knew. where she had once lived with Father and Johnny and Uncle Peter.

But the buildings were different, brick or stone, not the wood and stucco she remembered from before the fire. These streets were not bustling but nearly empty. House doors were marked with the red X of the plague.

Men with cloths over their lower faces stood guard outside. Stooped men, also covering their mouths and noses with cloths, pushed carts laden with corpses. Ahead and behind walked men carrying cylindrical, long-handled bells. Plague bells.

A man seized a cat. Raised a knife—

"No!" She sprang to her feet, and the vision winked out. Heart pounding, she turned to her teacher. "How can that be? There's no plague now."

The older woman looked grave. "If you have the seer gift, you perhaps could scry the past, the plague of 1665, but aside from the fact that's now impossible, the buildings are wrong."

"But—" Miranda swallowed hard. "Was that ... the future?" Pray, no.

"We must look again to find out."

Miranda drew a steadying breath. "Of course."

Men had killed stray animals during the plague, fearing them as carriers. Had sealed afflicted families into their homes to die. If she had even a slim chance to prevent that, nothing excused failing to try.

"If plague is coming," Arabella said, "the Gifted must lose no time preparing for it. Lives will depend on how many healers we have ready."

CHAPTER 12

Spending an evening on frivolous pursuits seemed odd to Miranda
when the weather was unpredictable, the farmers were suffering,
and plague might break out. But as Arabella had replied when
Miranda questioned her earlier, staying home would change none of that.

"Besides," the older woman had pointed out as they entered the Hawkstowe carriage, "staying in the good graces of the king and queen is never
a waste of time."

So they'd come to Whitehall Palace. Their coach deposited them near
a three-story gateway of flint and stone in a checkerboard pattern. It had
two eight-sided turrets, and terra cotta medallions adorned them and the
face of the gate. Despite her best efforts, Miranda found herself gawking.

From the gateway, their group made their way to the Great Hall, on
the far side of the palace. Richard had led the way without ever needing
to ask a footman to direct him. He must have come here often.

In the ornate Great Hall, they watched a play, with dancing, about the
need for a monarchy. The king had even danced with the players. Then
the Master of Revels had announced dancing in the banqueting house.

The banqueting house was magnificent, with gilding on the ornate
ceiling that outstripped anything Miranda had ever imagined. The
chamber was ablaze with sweet-smelling beeswax candles set in sconces
and crystal chandeliers lighting the ceiling murals. In the center of the

floor, the bejeweled peerage of England bobbed and stepped in time to the music.

For this one evening, she could mingle with these titled, wellborn guests, but she could only pretend to belong among them.

"I'm still not certain I should have come," she whispered to Arabella.

"Nonsense, my dear. I told you, none will gainsay our honest claim of kinship." The older woman smiled. "Besides, you shouldn't pass up the chance to see the king and queen."

Seeing them was all very well. Meeting them, if Miranda was lucky, would not happen. Despite Arabella's careful instruction, her throat seemed more likely to close in the royal presence than to push out the proper words.

She peered around the lovely room. Father disapproved of the frolicking court, but it didn't seem as bad as he'd said gossip painted it. The men and women behaved perhaps too familiarly, touching each other's faces and bodies, but not to the point of licentiousness.

Among the women, only she and Arabella wore necklines with any claim to modesty, and hers pushed her breasts up rather more than she was used to. Clad in emerald satin with cream lace petticoats, part of her new wardrobe, Miranda had trouble believing she could look so fine. Her new shoes, her first with heels, still felt teetery, but she'd avoided accidents so far.

Harder to accept was her hair, now pulled into a bun at the back of her head and gathered into two fashionable clusters of curls on the sides with a fringe across her brow. She felt very unlike herself.

Richard smiled down at her, making her pulse skip. "Do you dance, cousin?"

In genuine regret, she shook her head. Dancing with him would be such a pleasure. "I never learned. My father thought it sinful."

How polite of him to look disappointed. Clad in blue satin with a smallsword at his side and with his dark hair not covered by a wig, he cut a dashing figure. He could likely have any woman here as his partner.

The candles' heat and scent mingled with the various floral and musky perfumes worn by the guests crowding the chamber. The air felt more oppressive than a July midday in the heart of London.

"Excuse me," Richard said. "Cabot's over there. I'll invite him to join us."

Arabella tugged Miranda's elbow gently. "The queen wishes to meet you."

"The queen? But why?"

"She meets all the young ladies who come to court." The older woman leaned closer. "To see if they're potential rivals."

"How could someone compete with the queen?"

"By becoming the king's mistress."

If half the rumors were true, many women had done that. How awful that the queen had to deal with rivals under her very nose.

Arabella led the way to one end of the long chamber. On a low dais, the queen sat with brightly dressed women around her. Small and dark, she had prominent teeth and a long nose.

"The king once described Her Majesty as having excellent eyes and an agreeable face," Arabella whispered. "She shows to better advantage since giving up the heavy use of cosmetics." She drew Miranda to a halt some half a dozen feet from the queen's party.

A bewigged man in an ornate suit of pale green satin, with frothy lace billowing at his cuffs and throat, stepped forward. "Your Majesty, here are the Dowager Countess of Hawkstowe and her cousin, Mistress Willoughby."

Arabella sank into a deep curtsey, and Miranda followed suit. All that practice walking in her new shoes was serving her well.

"You may rise," the queen said.

Arabella led Miranda forward. "Good evening, Your Majesty."

"Good evening, milady." Queen Catherine's dark eyes flicked over Miranda. "Mistress, how do you like our court?" The elongated vowels of her Portuguese accent gave her speech a charming lilt.

"It's beautiful, Your Majesty. But overwhelming." Miranda smiled apologetically. "Rather grand for the likes of me."

Arabella leaned forward and quietly said, "Mistress Willoughby is of modest parentage, Majesty. And modest virtues."

Comprehension flickered in the queen's eyes. She smiled slightly. "Welcome to London, mistress."

"Thank you, Your Majesty."

"A good evening to you both." Queen Catherine nodded, ending the interview.

Arabella curtsied again. Miranda followed suit. Rising, they backed away. As they blended into the throng again, Miranda said, "She seemed very pleasant."

"Because she now knows you won't try to bed the king." Arabella frowned. "He's the most amiable of men, but really! No man should flaunt his mistresses and their bastards before his wife. And while a man should certainly support his get, giving them all titles is a bit much."

Miranda blinked. "He gives them all titles?"

"Yes. Here comes Lord Trentford," Arabella said softly. "He's not only Gifted but reliable, a good connection for you to form."

A broad-shouldered man of medium height broke out of the crowd. His long, brown wig framed a genial, fortyish face. Smiling, he greeted Arabella as the now familiar feeling of recognition tingled at Miranda's nape.

"This is Mistress Willoughby, our cousin," Arabella told him, stressing the last word.

Comprehension flickered in his eyes, and his smile became warm instead of merely polite. "Cousin," he said, inclining his head to Miranda as she curtsied.

"How do you like London?"

"Well enough, my lord. I was modestly reared, so this is all very different from what I've known."

"Your origins don't matter nearly so much, cousin, as where your Gifts can take you. Will you be staying in London long?"

"That depends, my lord."

"We're exploring possibilities," Arabella said, smiling.

Trentford nodded. "I expect you will find many doors open. Call upon me if I can be of service. Good evening to you both."

He turned away, and Arabella squeezed Miranda's arm. "Excellent, my dear. Trentford is unfailingly courteous but not particularly inclined to extend himself. I believe you've caught his interest."

Miranda's cheeks heated. "That seems unlikely to me."

"Then we must see that you meet more of the right people. That will convince you more effectively than anything I can say."

Frowning, the older woman added, "Alas that trying to straighten out all these changes is consuming so much time. We've little to spare until that's put right again."

"By undoing whatever was done," Miranda said. When Arabella nodded, Miranda added, "If all is undone, though, none of this will matter anyway. I likely won't even know you."

Or her grandson. The realization hurt more than it should've. Dismayed, Miranda looked for him in the crowd.

Richard stood across the room with a tall, broad-shouldered man who had his back to her. What were they discussing, that the earl scowled so?

~

Richard glared as the Earl of Greenhold approached Grandmère and Miranda. "Od's fish, must Grandmère present her to every lecher in the room? And where's the king? If he'll only make his entrance, I can present her, as Grandmère insists, and we can go home."

"You'd spoil her grand evening?" Above the rim of his goblet, Cabot's gray eyes gleamed. "You'll regret this 'cousin' tale your grandmother devised. Even if the lass looked like a sow, every unwed man in the room would still angle for a dowry from the Hawkstowe fortune. Not to mention the additional motives of the Gifted ones."

"I knew this was a bad idea." A damnable one. Now he would have to fend off suitors, a distraction from the more important issue of the time change. All six of the Gifted peers in sight had wangled introductions, as had several unGifted.

She deserved better than any of them.

Cabot smiled, clearly enjoying Richard's irritation. "Not to make matters worse for you, but I heard Castlemaine went in to see the king a short time ago. She wants something, rumor has it, so they'll be a while."

"How pleasant for them," Richard muttered. Lady Castlemaine was one of the royal mistresses, a prime favorite, and known for wheedling whatever she wanted out of the king. No matter how costly. Unfortunately, her wheedling tended toward the carnal and thus consumed a great deal of time.

"Did you speak to the Duke of York?" Richard asked. The king's brother took an interest in naval affairs. He'd been Lord High Admiral of England until the Test Act, requiring all officeholders to swear allegiance to the Church of England, went into effect the previous year. Then his adherence to Catholicism had forced him out of the office.

"Briefly." Cabot grimaced. "He made me no promises but did agree to speak to the king about getting the sailors' back pay released."

Richard cocked an eyebrow. "So why are you still here? I thought you hated these affairs."

"I'm enjoying the stir Miranda has created." Saluting Richard with his glass, Cabot added, "And seeing you deal with it."

"Then you may as well be useful. Come along. You can help me guard the lady's virtue." An odd phrase to use about a serving maid, but he would wager his fortune that it fit Miranda.

He and Cabot shouldered their way through the throng, skirting the dancers. As they broke through the last of the crowd, his eyes met Miranda's. Her pleasant smile seemed to brighten, but he shouldn't care if it did.

Richard smiled in return. She did look beautiful, not least because her evident pleasure contrasted with the boredom many women at court affected. "Miranda, allow me to present Captain Cabot Winfield of His Majesty's Royal Navy. He's Jeremy's brother."

"A pleasure, cousin." Cabot bowed.

She curtsied, her eyes shining. "I'm pleased to meet you, captain. Are you enjoying yourself?"

"Aye, and we can see that you are. You're the talk of the evening, you know. In a good way."

"Thank you, captain." Pink flooded her cheekbones in a blush that made Richard's hand itch to stroke it as she added lightly, "These people must live shallow lives, to consider me worthy of such notice."

"Not at all. You're not only new and well connected but young and comely."

Her blush deepened, and her gaze dropped to the floor.

Smoothly, Cabot added, "The combination is intriguing."

Richard stifled a surge of annoyance. Cabot didn't usually display such gallantry.

Cabot frowned at something behind the women. "Speaking of talk, there's Denning, from the Admiralty. I must speak to him. There must be some aid he can offer my struggling sailors while they await their pay. Richard, ladies." With a hasty bow, he stepped past them.

Richard forced his face to stay pleasant. He shouldn't resent Cabot for telling the girl the truth. She deserved to know of her appeal. Her surprising concern over that damnable vision showed what a kind heart she had, as well as the resolve to make the best of her lonely life at the inn. If she could find a suitor, she should. He had naught to offer her, and she needed to make a place in the world. In that, she could do far worse than Cabot.

"Come, my dear." Grandmère drew her aside. "I'll introduce you to the Comte de St. Michel."

Richard fell in behind them as their escort. As they crossed the room, one man after another nodded to Grandmère, only to shift his gaze, raking Miranda's bosom. Richard's jaw tightened. Some of those men wouldn't stop with a look, and he would not allow them to embarrass her.

Suddenly, George stepped into his path. "Good evening, Richard."

"George." The tray he'd stolen wouldn't cover the cost of the new gray, brocaded satin he wore, which thus signaled deepening debt. Well, George could pay for it himself or go to prison. Richard was done. "You're lucky I haven't had you arrested for theft."

"Grandmère wouldn't approve." George smiled. "Do you like my new tailor's handiwork?"

"Enjoy it while you can. You'll lose him when he realizes you can't pay him."

George's expression turned mutinous. "If you would make me a more generous allowance, Richard, we wouldn't be so at odds." He paused. "I rather miss the days we were friends."

"So do I." For the sake of that memory, he repeated something he'd said several times before. "George, I would've come if your message had reached me in time. I'd have brought a physician." A Gifted one, who might've made all the difference.

"Well, you didn't." George's lips tightened, then relaxed. "You don't know what it's like in Kendal, Richard. How quiet it is. Let me stay with you, learn the estate."

"You've had several chances at that," Richard said bluntly. "You can't manage it, George, not while you're drinking so heavily, and now you've stolen from the house."

"It'll all be mine one day, anyway. This is your last chance, Richard. Give me my due."

"Or what?" Richard raised an eyebrow at him. "You'll slander me all over London? I'll chance it."

"We're done, then." Glaring, George stalked away.

Richard watched him go. What the devil had that been about? Probably just drunken blathering. George could imbibe a great deal without showing the effects.

Yet something about the exchange felt wrong. Richard looked for George, but he'd vanished in the crowd.

Grandmère and Miranda weren't in sight, either. They must have gone to the privy. He accepted a glass of wine from a passing footman and leaned against the wall to wait for them. What could go wrong in a retiring room?

～

M iranda had heard of such retiring rooms but had never seen one. To visit the privy, the ladies repaired to a large, paneled chamber down a corridor. Each of its curtained areas contained an odd chair called a close stool, something she'd first seen at Hawkstowe House. One lifted one's skirts, sat on the chair, and relieved oneself into a basin beneath the chair. Servants changed the basins promptly.

What a miserable job that would be. At least the slop jars at the inn had lids.

She and Arabella paused by a large, gilt mirror to straighten their gowns. Miranda had convinced the older woman to let her avoid both powder and rouge. Although she had an unfashionably natural complexion as a result, she didn't have to worry about ceruse cream hardening into a gray mask on her face, nor did she have sweat streaks to retouch in powder.

"You've done well, my dear," Arabella murmured.

Around them, the ladies of King Charles's court laughed and chattered. So many had come to the retiring room, in fact, that the air had become as close as that in the banqueting house. Miranda longed for a breeze. She inhaled cautiously. To her relief, her bosom stayed in the gown. Barely.

"There you are, Arabella," a woman's light voice said. Miranda turned with Arabella to greet a small, spare woman who was on her way out. The woman's bright brown eyes darted to and fro as though assessing the crowd. Four large diamond rings adorned her age-gnarled hands.

"Good evening, Frances. Lady Vale, allow me to present Mistress Willoughby, our cousin. Miranda, this is Lady Vale."

Miranda sketched a curtsey.

Lady Vale gave her a quick smile and nod of acknowledgment. "Good evening, child. You're the talk of the gathering, did you know? Not that anyone talks of anything for more than a moment or two. I vow, Arabella, the crowd in there grows worse each time. You'd think His Majesty would object. Of course, he may like the crowd. His Majesty does enjoy having a good time, eh?

"Not that half of those here are much more than hangers-on. I'd hate to have to bear them, myself, but I suppose they have their uses, as do the rich and titled gentlemen here. Just the type one wants one's maiden cousins to meet. And of course, the type one doesn't. You'd best watch out for them, not that I have to tell you that, knowing as I do—"

"Frances." Although she smiled, Arabella spoke firmly. "You must excuse us. We're returning to the dancing."

"How fortunate! I'll walk with you."

They'd reached the door when someone shrieked in the room behind them. They turned in time to see an older woman in pale blue satin sag to the floor.

"She's fainted!" someone yelped.

"We can see that," Arabella snapped. "Stand you back and let her breathe. Oh, bother! Frances, will you deliver Miranda to Richard?"

"Of course, Arabella. Come along, my dear."

Miranda turned back toward the confusion. "But I—"

"Go with Lady Vale. I'll join you presently." Arabella marched toward the flock of women surrounding the one on the floor. To a servant, she said, "Fetch a basin with water, quickly!"

Miranda looked from her to Lady Vale, who started down the corridor. "Come along, dear. Such a crowd, 'tis a wonder more people aren't fainting away. You'd never know 'twas October from the heat in there. I vow, it grows worse each time. Where did you say you were reared?"

Arabella still leaned over the fallen woman. Miranda hurried to overtake Lady Vale, who was waiting for her.

"I beg pardon, milady. I was distracted."

"No wonder, child. Such a to-do! You'd think the silly females had never seen anyone faint. Anyway, my dear, I asked where you were from."

Cautiously, hoping the answer wouldn't lead to more questions, Miranda said, "I grew up in London mostly but lived in Dover of late."

"Never cared much for Dover. Smells of fish, you know?"

"I suppose the docks—"

"Still, my late husband—quite a sailor, he was, too!—always swore he found the salt air bracing." Frowning, she added, "Too much fresh air ruins the complexion. I preferred to get my bracing from him."

Heat flared anew in Miranda's cheeks. "Of course, milady."

Lady Vale cast a keen eye at her. "Oh, you'll know all about that soon enough, my dear. With looks like yours and the Hawkstowe fortune, you'll find yourself wed in a trice. Plenty of eligible young lords here tonight, and they've noticed you right enough. Just have Richard pick one."

He couldn't possibly take such an interest, and Miranda didn't want him to. Nor did she have a stake in the Hawkstowe fortune, however great it might be, but she couldn't say that to Lady Vale.

"He'll be cautious of course, but he's a practical man, always was," Lady Vale continued, "and you want your husband to know you've kinsmen behind you. Keeps them honest."

"You don't say," Miranda managed. The banqueting house door loomed ahead, offering escape from this embarrassing conversation. Miranda picked up her pace.

"Oh, and I do. Take my word on it. I've buried three of them. Husbands, that is. And here we are," Lady Vale said. She craned her neck to see over the dancers. "Now where can Richard have taken himself off to? Men are so seldom by when you need them. Oh, there he is, over by the windows."

Richard stood with his back to them. He faced Cabot Winfield, who smiled broadly.

"Frances!" A tall woman wearing bright yellow satin and a cartload of pearls hurried toward Lady Vale. Her round lips were pursed, and she lowered her voice to a whisper. "You'll never believe what I've just heard."

"Excuse me a moment, my dear," Lady Vale said.

"I can find my cousin, milady. I've no wish to delay you."

"Only be a moment, child."

Miranda sketched a curtsey to the newcomer. Lady Vale and her friend conversed, apparently absorbed. Surely Miranda needn't wait. What could happen in such a crowded place?

She excused herself to Lady Vale, who absently nodded.

Miranda started around the room. To avoid unwanted attentions, she took care not to look anyone in the eye.

Dodging a footman with a tray, she found George Mainwaring in her path. "Good evening, George," Miranda said.

"Cousin. A word, if you please."

"I'm sorry, but I'm to find Richard."

"Must you rush away? After all, we're newly met kin." He smiled.

Was that calculation in his eyes?

He continued, "Surely you can spare a moment to become acquainted."

The dance ended. With people crowding around the edges of the floor, Miranda had no room to evade him.

"Pray excuse me, George, but I really must go."

He raised his brows. "If you insist, but if we hurry, we can avert the crisis before Grandmère returns. It would distress her greatly."

"What crisis?" Miranda glanced toward Richard.

Cabot had left him. The earl bowed to a young woman dressed in green and bedecked in pearls. Miranda tried to catch his eye but failed.

At her elbow, George said, "If you don't care that gossip about your low origins will embarrass them, so be it."

She barely swallowed a gasp. "What?"

"Surely you knew Richard had enemies. For the sake of our kinship, I'd not have him or Grandmère fall prey to their gossip, but perhaps you don't care. I suppose one should expect ingratitude from a common serving wench."

Miranda's heart pounded. "I don't know what you mean." Despite her efforts to hold her voice steady, it quivered.

"I can't explain here. Too many ears. Come or do not, but choose quickly, before Richard sees us."

No one will gainsay us, Arabella had said. It appeared someone would. "I wouldn't want anyone to make trouble with some—some ludicrous tale."

"Of course not." He smiled, but his eyes darted to the side, as though he watched for someone. "Come. We must hurry."

"Wait. Why don't you tell Richard or your grandmother?"

"They don't approve of me, but they'd listen to you."

"Yet you would help them?" Something about this business wasn't right.

He shrugged. "We're family, and I'm Richard's heir." His face took on a pleading look. "Would it hurt to hear what I have to tell you?"

"I suppose not."

"Then come along. Hurry."

He led the way out into a corridor behind the banqueting house. With a last look toward Richard, who was still conversing with the young woman, Miranda followed. They went down a short flight of stairs and turned into a paneled corridor. Soon, they turned again. He seemed to be heading toward the river.

The farther they went into the warren of corridors, the more suspicious this seemed. "George, this is far enough."

"Only a bit ahead lies a parlor where we can be private."

She would likely have explanations to make anyway. She might as well learn something. "A little longer, then."

They turned into another corridor, and he opened a paneled door. "In here."

Miranda followed him into a small, paneled room hung with tapestries of hunting scenes. Candles in wall sconces cast a soft light, and a fire blazed on the hearth. Armchairs of dark wood with cushions of crimson damask sat at intervals around the wall.

In the center of the room stood a long table with elaborately carved legs. Two silver goblets, a silver tray laden with bread and cheese, and a silver pitcher sat atop it.

He walked to the table and stopped. His mouth curved in a mocking smile that sent a chill of alarm through her.

"What did you want to say?" she demanded, edging toward the door.

He glanced beyond her. "It's really Lord Wyndon who wants a word."

CHAPTER 13

Cold flashed up the back of Miranda's neck and down her arms. Heart pounding, she whirled.

"My thanks, Mainwaring." Just inside the doorway stood a stocky man in blue satin and an elaborately curled brown wig.

As George stalked out of the chamber, the man said, "There are some things you need to understand about your situation, girl."

"You must excuse me, milord," Miranda said, silently cursing George for leaving her with this man. "I cannot stay here with you. We haven't been properly presented."

"Lord Hawkstowe's obliging cousin presented us, or weren't you listening?"

"I must return to Lady Hawkstowe."

She stepped sideways. He moved into her path.

"My lord, I must insist." Twisting to the left, she sprang forward. Lord Wyndon caught her arm in hard grip and pushed her back against the table. Her heart surged into her throat.

"No, I insist." He leaned forward until his face hovered inches above her own. "You're no more the Mainwarings' cousin than I am. I know every bump on every twig of their family tree, none of them you."

Icy fear rolled through her. Would Richard and his grandmother miss her? If they did, how could they find her?

She fought to steady her voice. "Perhaps you're not as well informed as you believe, my lord."

"And perhaps you're in some scheme with Hawkstowe and the old hag." His fingers tightened until she gasped. "Either way, you'll tell me what I want to know."

"You've an active imagination, my lord." The pain in her arm made her voice sharp. "I hope you consider it worth my cousin's anger."

Cold, condescending amusement lit his eyes. "The day I fear that calfling, I'll dispatch myself."

"Nevertheless, I must go."

"When I'm finished with you." He traced the line of her jaw with one finger. "Tell me what I want to know, serving wench, and I'll pay you twice what he's offering."

Although his touch made her skin crawl, she refused to flinch. She could scream, if there was anyone by to hear her. She doubted the king would thank her for disrupting his evening, nor would Richard like her to draw such attention. Nor would her word prevail against a lord's if it came to that.

Lord Wyndon smiled confidently. His hand wandered lower, stroking her neck. "If we come to an arrangement, I can ensure your comfort in addition to paying you."

Miranda shuddered. The light in his eyes was calculation, not desire, but she couldn't trust that to stop him if he decided to assault her. He probably shared the common assumption that all women who served in taverns and inns could be bought.

Her gaze fell on the tray of bread and cheese. Perhaps she could save herself. She inched one hand toward the tray.

"Now," he said, "tell me why Hawkstowe pulled you out of that inn. What have you done for him in London?"

"Nothing." Her fingertips touched the ornate handle. Slid forward until she gripped it. "Let me go."

"I think not." His hand tightened on her arm. "One way or another, you common bitch, you'll answer me."

Over by the window, silvery light shimmered in the corner of her eye, but she scarcely noticed. She caught the tray's edge and heaved upward. Cheese, bread and knife flew off the table. Lord Wyndon dodged but not in time. The heavy oval banged into his brow.

His grip relaxed. She broke free and ran.

"You trollop," he roared.

A man sprang past her—Richard! Oh, thank goodness!

She spun in time to see him plant himself between her and Lord Wyndon. Miranda's knees nearly buckled from relief.

"Hold, Wyndon," Richard ordered in a hard, flat voice.

Lord Wyndon's lip curled. "I wondered whether she was yours. Now I know."

"She's my cousin and my guest, and so under my protection. Stand away."

"Or what, lordling?"

The air between the two men suddenly crackled with invisible power. Miranda sidled closer, at an angle so she could see Richard's face.

His smile had a dangerous edge. "Do you truly want to find out?"

"You wouldn't dare, especially not here."

The coiled tension of a cat at a mouse hole thrummed in the lines of Richard's body. His left hand lightly touched the smallsword at his side.

"You attacked this woman, so the rules of engagement don't bar me. As for the place, shall we see who has better credit with His Majesty?"

Wyndon flushed. Miranda drew breath to speak, to offer a sop to his pride, but a tiny shake of Richard's head stopped her. Although she pressed her lips together and stayed silent, she couldn't bear the idea that he might be injured in a duel. Especially not one over her.

Suddenly, Wyndon straightened. "Another time, stripling."

"I look forward to it." Richard extended his arm to Miranda. "Cousin, let us return to the banqueting house."

She laid her fingers on his outstretched forearm and fell into step with him. Judging from the set of his jaw, he had a great deal more to say.

She didn't care. Even if he was angry at her for mistakenly trusting George, she had never been so glad to see anyone. "Thank you," she said, "though that doesn't begin to suffice."

In the corridor, they met Cabot, his face hard. "I've handled George," he said. "I was ready to back you, Richard, if you needed it."

"I counted on that." With a glance at Miranda, he said, "Cabot, will you tell Grandmère where we've gone? Miranda and I must talk."

The captain nodded and strode toward the banqueting house. Richard led Miranda down a different corridor. He stalked along with a stony face and taut shoulders.

"This should do." He stopped and jerked open a door, then stood aside for her.

A wave of his hand lit the candles in the sconces. Small and scantily furnished with two writing tables and chairs, the room looked like some sort of clerk's office.

She marched inside. Surely he wasn't fool enough to think she'd wanted to meet that frightening man.

He shut the door. "Are you all right?" Peering into her face, he touched her arm gently.

"I think so." Miranda let out a shaky breath. "I was only frightened, not injured."

"What happened? Why did you leave the dancing?"

"Your cousin said he knew about me, about my being from the inn. That other people knew and would tell. I didn't want you to have trouble over me."

"Hellfire." He pinched the bridge of his nose. "Unfortunately, George's upbringing made him a self-centered, overindulged wastrel, something he has no desire to change."

"Then I've confirmed what was probably a guess. I'm very sorry, Richard."

He shook his head. "Had I told you more about George, I doubt you would have left with him. You would have been on your guard." He paused. "Which brings us to Henry de Vere, Lord Wyndon. My family and his branch of the de Veres have had a deadly feud going since the Wars of the Roses. He'll pass up no chance to do me an injury, and he has the scruples of a viper. I should have told you more about him after your dream about the bear stalking me, but I didn't think it was something you needed to know."

With a nod, she accepted that. "How did you find me?"

"Cabot saw you leave with George and fetched me. I beg your pardon for not being candid with you about him." He shook his head. "I'm perhaps too accustomed to keeping my own counsel."

"In fairness, Richard, if I had known, I might still have walked into trouble. I didn't know Lord Wyndon would be there, you see."

"I do see, and I don't blame you. I didn't know George and Wyndon had formed an alliance, nor did I expect either of them to approach you. Even so, I'd have thought Grandmère and I, between us, could protect you from the likes of them."

"You would have, if someone hadn't fainted in the retiring room."

"What's this?" His brows drew together.

"As your grandmother and I left the room, someone fainted. It was nearly as close in there as in the banqueting house. The heat could easily trigger a fainting spell, especially in someone laced too tightly."

"It could. Still, she fainted at a very convenient time."

Her eyes widened. "You're not suggesting that was a ruse?"

"I neglected to mention something important about Wyndon. He's not only unscrupulous but Gifted. And not above using bribery or threats to get what he wants."

The idea that he'd arranged that fainting scene made sense, too much to ignore. What else had he done? What was that glimmer she'd scarcely noticed?

She told Richard about it, and his face hardened. "How well did you see it?" he asked. "Could you determine its shape?"

Miranda shook her head. "I didn't really look at it. I was more concerned with escaping."

"That was clearly the right choice, and you did well." Solemnly, he added, "You know what has been happening and how much is at stake. Your visions may hold the key to solving the problem. The fact that he's so interested in you makes me doubly suspicious of him."

"But it doesn't prove anything, does it?" she asked.

Richard shook his head. "It isn't enough to lay charges, not with all the allies he has on the Conclave Council. But that glimmer could be important. We must scry it, get a better look at it, as soon as we can."

The Hawkstowe carriage bounced over the cobblestones and up White Hall toward the City of London. Although Richard sat in a relaxed posture across from the two women, anger hung in the air around him.

He glanced at his grandmother. "It's time she learned defensive uses of magic, Grandmère."

"I agree."

The exchange reminded her of the way he'd used power at Dover, the things he'd said about blasting open the gaol. Miranda shook her head. "I can't even hold a vision steady in a fire, and you want me to learn to defend myself with magic?"

"One's qualms," Arabella said, "tend to vanish when one's safety is at stake."

"I suppose that's true," Miranda replied. They could discuss her reservations later.

"I shouldn't have sent her back with someone so prone to distraction as Lady Vale," Arabella said. Sorrow darkened her eyes. "Richard, about George—"

"We're done. He has pushed me too far." He rubbed a hand over his jaw. "I've had no reply from Morgan's handmaidens. I'll send to them again. We must explore Miranda's visions."

"Who are Morgan's handmaidens?" Miranda asked. "I meant to ask you the first time you mentioned them, but I became distracted by other topics."

Richard smiled. "That was a busy day. Morgan's handmaidens are keepers of her pool. As Morgan lay dying, she streamed all her remaining power into a pool at Pendragon, a manor all the Gifted share in Cumberland. The water heightens magical power, but it also compels truth. With my knowledge and your vision, we'll see in full the omens you've glimpsed in fragments."

His grandmother responded, "I'll send to them. You've other things to attend to."

She lifted the window curtain. "Richard. Miranda. It's snowing," she said in wonder.

Big, fat flakes drifted down to settle like lace on the cobblestones. In London, in October.

◞◟

I t was past midnight when they climbed out of the coach and walked up the stairs to the door in weary silence. Miranda's excitement had faded. Her bones throbbed with exhaustion, but sleep seemed unlikely.

In the foyer, they surrendered their cloaks to the footman. He bustled away, leaving them alone. Arabella turned to her grandson. "I imagine you young people won't retire yet. Richard, perhaps you could give Miranda a lesson if you aren't too weary."

A lesson. A possible foray into lethal danger. Miranda shot him an uneasy look.

His gaze held hers. "We'll see, Grandmère. Good night." His arm swept toward the stairs, inviting Miranda to precede him. "Miranda, shall we repair to the library?"

She gathered her skirts. "Are you sure that's such a good idea?"

"We cannot leave it forever, as I explained. Besides, we have much to discuss."

"While my last vision stopped when I wanted it to, it took three of you to free me from the one before it. If we've only you and me, is that wise?" She sneaked a glance over her shoulder.

"I'm confident of rising to any challenge. The changing weather is a bad omen. We shouldn't delay any longer."

He was right. Miranda nodded and tried to pretend she wasn't nervous.

They climbed the stairs to the first floor and walked down the corridor. The rush matting underfoot muffled the sounds of their footsteps.

Richard opened the library door. A fire burned low on the hearth. He knelt to add more wood. "Pray be seated, Miranda. By the hearth, if you will."

She settled into a carved chair by the fireplace. "Do you always do that?" When he glanced at her in question, she nodded toward the fire he was stoking. "You could summon a footman."

"I could, but most of them are abed, and it takes only a moment."

What an odd nobleman he was. Perhaps because of what his grandmother had said about not esteeming rank as much as magic.

"First," he suggested, "let's scry that glimmer you thought you saw. Scrying oneself is difficult, so I'll handle that."

"I keep meaning to ask your grandmother, and I forget. What keeps people from scrying each other's private business?"

Richard's mouth crooked up in a wry grin. "Well, there's the *do unto others* principle, which might also be called fear of retaliation, and most of us ward our houses against scrying. The Mainwarings always have."

"But the unGifted can't do that."

"No, but most of the Gifted don't concern themselves with folk who are no threat to them. And because scrying doesn't carry sound, eavesdropping on business decisions isn't possible."

"That isn't a very reassuring response."

"It's all I have, alas." He turned back to the fire.

In moments, an image formed, Wyndon pressing her back against the table. Her throat tightened with the echo of her fear then. The image of her groped for the tray, and a silvery glimmer appeared around the window frame.

"There," she said. "Did you see it?"

The tray slammed into Wyndon's brow, and the glimmer vanished.

"I did." Richard started the scrying anew. As it progressed, his frown deepened.

"Do you know what that is?" she asked.

"Not for certain. But he may have been trying to form a passage, to escape without being seen."

Miranda frowned. "I don't understand."

His face closed over. She thought he wouldn't answer, but he said, "There is a way to move unseen from one place to another, by moving outside of time, so to speak."

"Do you think that's what someone has done, making all these changes?"

With a nod, he said, "I now suspect Wyndon more than ever, but I've no proof I can offer that this is possible, and he didn't actually form a portal."

"What about the water from Morgan's pool? You said it could compel truth. If you drank it and he drank it, wouldn't that settle the matter?"

"It that were possible, yes, but Wyndon has allies on the Council. They won't vote to compel him without a reason that's beyond doubt. In addition, some members know of the long dispute between his family and mine and are inclined to look askance at my suspicions of him."

"But you're certain he has something to do with it," she said quietly.

"Doubly so now, but certainty doesn't matter nearly so much as proof." Frowning, Richard asked, "Did Wyndon say anything that might indicate knowledge of how events began to change?"

She shook her head. "He asked me questions. You said his family and yours had been enemies for generations. Do you think he took this book, this chronicle you mentioned?"

"He would do it just to spite me. Thanks to an ancestor who drank too much, he knows of my family's interest in Richard III. On top of that, one of my ancestors exposed a magical plot by one of his to rule England during the Wars of the Roses."

His voice dry, he added, "Then, as now, the argument was that we Gifted should take advantage of the upheaval and seize power. If the plot had succeeded, England would likely have found itself in another Chaos Age."

"Chaos Age?"

"The magical conflicts that led to the fall of Camelot and to what we like to call the Dark Ages. Wyndon's ancestor was executed for misuse of magic against the unGifted, but the Council of that era found a way to prosecute him among the unGifted as well, for treason. The death warrant was signed by King Edward IV and carried out by the Constable of England, Richard, Duke of Gloucester, later Richard III. They didn't know they had assistance from the Conclave Council, who bound de Vere's powers so he couldn't use them."

"So Lord Wyndon has reason, or reason enough for him, to resent King Richard."

"And he does." With a grimace, Richard added, "The enmity became personal between him and me over a chambermaid at Whitehall palace. He used her shamefully and then denied it. I brought the matter to the king's attention."

He knew the king well enough to do that? Miranda gaped.

The earl didn't seem to notice. "Wyndon had to pay her a substantial sum and lost a lucrative office." With a shrug, he added, "The king feels strongly that a man should support his bastards."

"Admirable, I suppose," Miranda said. "If you think Wyndon has this book, can you scry in his house for it?"

"Not past his wards. Even if I could, that might not help. Time is changing so much and so quickly that scrying into the past now only allows us to see a few days back. A fortnight would be difficult, farther back than that impossible. I've been thinking, too, of how we sensed a presence when we talked at the Golden Swan."

His eyes narrowed, turning to her. "Think carefully. Did his presence seem in any way familiar?"

"No." Frowning, she shook her head. "I was too frightened to notice whether he had the same familiar sense other Gifted do, but I'm sure I've never seen him in a dream. At the inn, we both walked through the cold spot. How could someone be standing there?"

"That would be the question," Richard told her. "The answer might also explain the sensation of being watched I felt at the inn near Canterbury."

Slowly, thinking through the jumble of visions and changes, Miranda suggested, "If he dislikes you so, perhaps he destroyed this book anyway. And what are wards? I think my mother may have used that word, but not in a lesson."

"Wards are magical energy barriers the Gifted erect. They repel most forms of magical intrusion."

Standing to pace, the earl continued, "As for the *Chronicle*, if he took the book, he likely still has it. That family would rather keep than destroy whatever anyone else values. Once something is destroyed, it cannot be used to taunt or torment."

He paused, as though struck by an idea, then shrugged. "My grandmother is correct. You must learn defensive magic. We'll start with using words and gradually move to not speaking."

When she nodded, he stood and stepped aside. "Push my chair magically. Tell it to move away, envision what you want, and feed magic into the command."

That sounded much easier than scrying or manipulating candles. Miranda stared hard at the chair and imagine it moving. "Away," she said, and fed power into the image.

To her amazement, the chair slid back a foot. A triumphant smile tugged at her mouth.

"Oh, well done!" Richard grinned at her.

Their gazes locked. His eyes warmed, and his grin faded. Miranda's heart beat hard. She licked her lips, and heat flashed in his eyes.

He took a step toward her.

Muffled footsteps sounded in the hall, approaching the library quickly. Richard's gaze met hers. "I know that tread," he said, frowning. "Cabot."

At this hour? Her glance shot to the tiny clock on the mantel, which read one o'clock.

Richard hurried to the door and yanked it open. Still clad in his finery, Cabot Winfield hurried through the door.

"Richard—" His eyes met hers, and he checked. "I beg pardon. I didn't think, this late, you'd be occupied."

"We were having a lesson," Richard said. "Miranda, pray excuse us."

"Of course." She rose to leave.

"No," Cabot said, "Miranda, stay. My news is no secret."

"Then spit it out," Richard said.

Grimly, the captain told them, "First, I saw James Beauchamp's father walking into their house in the Strand on my way here."

Richard tensed. To Miranda, he said, "James's father died more than a decade ago."

A chill ran down her spine. "So now the dead walk."

"As though that weren't enough," Cabot added, "I've bad news. George is betrothed to Wyndon's daughter Lucretia. Word began circulating at the palace shortly after you left."

146

"Well," Richard said after a moment. "Now I know how he gained my heir's assistance."

Cabot said, "I'd wager he expects to get more than tonight's meeting with Miranda in exchange for his daughter's hand. But what?"

"Perhaps it's time for a closer look at my old nemesis," Richard suggested.

CHAPTER 14

The next night, Richard and Cabot watched from the mews behind Wyndon House as its lights began to go out. Many of the neighboring houses had already gone dark.

Into the far end of the mews rumbled a coach. The horses' breath made puffy clouds in the cold night air. As grooms unhitched them, Richard and Cabot drew deeper into the shadows. They waited in silence until quiet again settled upon the other end of the lane.

The night was much colder than usual, but the snow had stopped that morning and had mostly melted in the afternoon sun. There would be no footprints to betray their visit to Wyndon's property.

"It's a slim chance of finding anything," Richard admitted. "Still, we can't ignore any lead." Wyndon was out of the city tonight, taking George and Canby with him, and there might not be another such chance for days. "What better place for him to hide a stolen document than in his own secure, warded home?"

"True enough."

Although Richard couldn't scry into the house because of its wards, nothing prevented them from searching it manually. If they could find a way to enter undetected.

The wards would either bar magical intrusion or respond to it by raising some sort of alarm. They could be used anywhere, but no one warded against ordinary housebreaking. Doing so would raise an alarm whenever someone opened a window or door and thus required removing the wards daily to allow normal traffic and replacing them nightly.

Most people considered such arrangements more troublesome than useful. The houses of the Gifted thus enjoyed little more protection against ordinary crimes than those of their unGifted neighbors.

Thanks to serving the Crown in a covert capacity, Richard happened to have some experience as a housebreaker. The pouch of lock picks hanging from his belt had seen a good bit of use, though not lately.

"If he did take the *Chronicle*, what makes you think he didn't destroy it?" Cabot asked. "I would, in his place."

"When Kit scried for it, he couldn't locate it or learn what happened to it, which means either it's in a warded place or it ceased to exist before the time we can still scry backward. I prefer to assume the former. Besides, you don't have his family's love of power. The more someone else wants a thing, the more they yearn to have it. If they destroy it, they don't have it either."

Given the de Veres' desire to hold what others needed, Edmund's confession might still exist. Perhaps it only appeared to have been destroyed in a fire at Hawkstowe. Was that possible?

Before he could explore the idea further, Cabot touched his arm. "The cellar and garret are dark."

"We'll wait a few minutes."

In the street beyond, the watchman passed. When the sound of his footsteps faded, Richard stepped away from the stable wall. "Remember," he told Cabot, "no magic unless we meet someone. We don't want to trip a ward by mistake."

They hurried across the street to the tall garden gate. Its lock yielded easily to the first pick Richard tried. He and Cabot stole along the hedges to the rear of the house and slipped up the short flight of stairs to the kitchen door. Cabot turned to keep watch.

Richard stood still, waiting for the barks that would signal a dog in the kitchen. None came. One less obstacle to fear.

Bands of iron reinforced the heavy wooden door. When he touched the lock, it tingled with the faint residue of a ward. He took a deep breath and inserted a pick. The warding tingle remained steady, as he had hoped. Wyndon had set it against magical intrusion only.

Of course, he had a very good lock to protect him from housebreakers.

Richard returned the pick to his belt pouch and tried a second. A tumbler clicked. Another, however, remained in place. He swallowed an oath. Holding the first tumbler open, he chose another pick.

The second tumbler moved. He pressed to keep it open. "Lift the latch," he whispered.

Cabot reached across him to open the door. They stepped into the silent kitchen and eased the door shut. The tantalizing scents of mutton and onion still hung in the air, a reminder of the night's supper.

The two men stood still while their eyes adjusted to the dimness. Shadows filled the long, high-ceilinged room. A wide table dominated the center of the chamber. Moonlight glinted dully on the curves of iron kettles.

To the left of the door, lost in shadow that would have hidden them from ordinary men, narrow stairs wound upward. A steep flight led downward, likely to the cellar.

"One room at a time," Richard breathed. "We'll search the library together, then the other rooms down here and meet at the front stairs."

"Aye."

Like a ghost, Cabot slipped through the door that led to the front of the house. Richard followed.

The library held an impressive collection of books ranged on three walls. "Oh, hellfire," Richard muttered.

"Too bad we can't use magic," Cabot commented. "This could take a while."

"Yes, but feel that tingle?" It barely flicked the edge of his awareness, a subtle but unmistakable warning. "As we thought, he's warded the room."

Richard turned to the nearest shelf and examined the books. "I'll try opening my senses. That will make my touch more acute but shouldn't cause trouble if I don't reach out with my own magic."

"Don't use enhanced sight, hearing, or smell."

Richard nodded. Those senses could extend perception and might trigger the wards. Careful not to reach out, he opened his mind to perceive more subtle energies. The warding tingle grew stronger, but nothing else changed.

Cabot let out a slow, relieved breath. He turned to the nearest shelf and grasped the first book. Richard moved to the other end of the room to begin his own search.

~

S earching the library took nearly two hours. They found nothing there, nor in the dining room, nor in the parlor. Frustration gnawed at Richard. He'd had hopes, admittedly slim, of finding the *Chronicle* here.

The guest rooms on the second floor also held nothing of interest. He and Cabot went down the long gallery at the back of the house, heading for Wyndon's chambers.

A quick check of the master suite revealed that it comprised three rooms, a sitting room, a bedchamber and a tiny withdrawing room, or closet. Cabot chose the sitting room. Richard started in the bedchamber.

Jutting out from one wall, a high, ornately carved bed with a canopy proclaimed its owner's wealth. Gilt angels similar to those in the king's rooms at Whitehall held back the damask bed curtains. Marble faced the hearth, and rush matting protected the parquet floor. Tapestries of hunt scenes hung over the mantel and on one wall.

He opened his senses, again taking care not to extend them and thus trigger the wards, and ran his fingertips carefully over the carved panels. He finished the first wall, by the door, without finding anything. The portrait over the hearth concealed nothing.

Running his fingers along the edge of the marble fireplace, he noticed a slight movement, as though the carved angel concealed a latch. His breath hitched in sudden hope as he pressed against the cherub's inner side.

The stone figure slid silently to the right, toward the edge of the mantel. Behind it lay a space the size of Richard's fist, housing a marble knob that just fit within it.

He slid his hand toward the space. No warding tingle brushed his skin. Slowly, hoping he wasn't about to trigger a concealed ward, he twisted the knob.

Something popped on the far side of the hearth. He jumped back, but no ward exploded. The bottom panel on that side had sprung open. He knelt in front of it and found himself staring into a cubbyhole about a foot square.

Before he reached inside, lest Wyndon had put a special ward on the space, he closed down his senses again. He also took care to note the positions of the objects within.

The secret cabinet held a pouch of jewels, a box of deeds, and a purse filled with gold. Biting back disappointment, he reminded himself that such a hidey-hole might well serve as a blind for a more important one behind it.

He pressed firmly on each edge of the left panel. Nothing happened. The rear, bottom, and right panels also yielded nothing. So much for slim hopes.

As he replaced the deed box, a sudden hunch struck him. He pressed the edges of the top panel. Something gave, barely, but nothing moved. His heart jumped.

He pushed hard in the center of the top panel. Something popped softly behind the wall to his left. The panel above the hidden cabinet sprang forward and struck him in the shoulder. Inside lay a scroll about the length of his forearm and as thick as his fist. A red cord bound it, and the end of the dowel he could see bore a red, dragon-rampant crest.

This document had come from the Pendragon manor library.

But how?

Heart hammering, Richard noted the scroll's position before lifting it out of the cabinet. Beneath it lay a scrap of parchment that read *CroylChr 16 Feb 1463*.

Surely that meant the Croyland Chronicle. But was February 1463 the date of an entry in the *Chronicle*, or was it a date Wyndon had sought through time?

Mulling that, he carried the scroll to the window and carefully unrolled the parchment. The ink on it had faded, but he could make it out if he squinted. One word seemed to leap out at him, *Necromancy*. As in magic involving the dead.

Could this be the scroll Edmund had mentioned? It fit his description.

Richard skimmed rapidly, his blood chilling as his eyes ran across phrases like *the dead land* and *binding of the dead*.

But he saw nothing about splicing time.

If only he dared take this with him. He needed to read it more carefully. The fact that Wyndon had it here, concealed, showed how much he feared having anyone else discover its contents. If he had this, could there be something else concealed here, something that dealt with splicing time?

Cabot came silently though the door from the adjoining chamber. "Nothing there," he whispered.

"Look at this." Richard extended the scroll to his friend. "The key to traveling the shadowland may lie in this treatise."

"Unfortunately, we dare not take it." Cabot skimmed as Richard had. "Wyndon would scry and find out who took it."

"Indeed," Richard agreed, biting back a curse. "With his many friends in the Conclave and on the Council, his having this, even though he shouldn't, isn't a clear enough tie to the changes to be damning."

"Even though it deals with binding the dead for magic? And belongs in the Pendragon library?"

"There's no proof he did anything with it, nothing to tie it to the time changes." Richard ran a hand through his hair. "He can always claim to have found it."

"And the magic worked into the air and ground at Pendragon repels scrying." Cabot shook his head. "God's feet, Richard. He must feel damned secure, to keep that thing."

"Perhaps he thought he might need it again."

Before they replaced the scroll in its cupboard, Richard showed Cabot the scrap of parchment. Cabot let out a soft whistle. "Very interesting," he muttered, "but also not proof of anything."

"No," Richard agreed, "Nor do we have enough circumstantial clues to bring the Council around."

To make certain they didn't miss anything, they searched the rest of the chamber and the tiny closet beyond. They found no more hidden spaces and nothing indicating that Wyndon could splice from one place to another.

Cabot cast an inquiring glance at Richard, who nodded. Time to go, while their luck held.

$\sim$

Miranda jerked upright with a scream locked in her throat. Before it burst free, she recognized her chamber at Hawkstowe House. She took a deep breath, trying to still her pounding heart.

The dream had seemed so real. She dared not assume that it wasn't, not the way her dreams had run lately. "Please, no," she whispered.

As her initial fright faded, a new tension took its place, a strange certainty. Richard was in danger.

Her heartbeat gathered speed again. Now that she was accustomed to the house, Patience had taken to sleeping in the garret again, so there was no need to be quiet.

Miranda slid out of bed to pour herself a cup of water from the pitcher on her washstand. The pitcher trembled in her grasp. She set it down hastily.

"This is ridiculous," she muttered. "I'll wager he came home and went to bed hours ago."

Flinging the green dressing gown over her shift, she hurried into the corridor. Richard's chamber lay a few doors down from her own, nearer the stairs. The house was silent around her. Everyone else had long since gone to bed.

His door stood open. Neither sound nor light came from within.

She took a deep breath. He had not come home. The dark, empty room implied that his servants did not expect him tonight. Had he sought out a woman, as so many men did?

She had no right to care if he had. Still, she doubted it. The tension she sensed remained too strong to dismiss.

The dream's foreboding seeped back into her. Cold rose in her throat and danced down her neck and arms. She couldn't sleep until this dread eased. Neither could she hover outside his door like a worried parent.

Nor could she rest until he was safely home.

The library was around the corner. She'd read while she waited.

R ichard and Cabot made their way through Wyndon's house as quickly as they dared. As they reached the ground floor, Richard heard a faint thump. He and Cabot froze at the same time.

Someone giggled in the kitchen. Its door stood ajar. Had it when they entered?

They couldn't go out the front. Not only would Richard have to pick the lock, but they'd risk being seen by the watch. If they used magic to avoid that danger, they would trigger the door wards.

"Oh, Ormsby, yer too wicked, you are," a woman's voice said.

"For a taste o' them hot teats, I'll show you wicked," a man chuckled. A loud sucking sound, accompanied by gasping and moaning, followed.

Finally, a muffled shriek came from the kitchen. A hoarse groan followed.

"Hsst!" the woman said. "What was that?"

Richard swallowed a curse.

The woman's companion said, "I didn't hear nothing."

Richard glanced at Cabot, who jerked his head toward the dining parlor behind them. They backed toward it.

"Come from belowstairs, it did," the woman snapped. "I'll wager that little tart, Marian, means to meet up with that new footman what's been eyeing her."

"Jamie, that'd be."

Richard exchanged a look of relief with Cabot. They stood still, listening.

"Aye. Come along wi' you, Ormsby. Let's put a stop to it now. His lordship don't like the little trollops spreading theirselves for nobody but him, you know."

"That he don't."

Fabric rustled in the kitchen. "Where's me slipper? Ah, there 'tis."

The sounds of more heavy breathing and muffled groans ensued. Richard rolled his eyes at Cabot, who scowled.

The woman sighed. "I'll have to put the mutton joint away again. Go on, lovey. See to Jamie, and I'll take care of the silly girl."

"G'night, then, lovey."

Richard and Cabot stole closer to the kitchen. Footsteps went up the rear stairs. Cabinets opened and closed. Muttering, someone went down toward the cellar.

"Come on," Cabot breathed.

Needing no urging, Richard followed him out the door and through the garden. They reached the mews and hurried to the street.

～

Miranda huddled on the library sofa. The crackling fire seemed to give off no warmth. *Paradise Lost*, having failed to divert her, lay forgotten on the floor.

At least the feeling that Richard was in danger had faded. She wouldn't rest easily, though, until he returned. Fretting, she fell into an uneasy doze.

A latch clicked. The sound of footsteps on the rush matting tugged her toward awareness as someone sat beside her and brushed her hair off her temple.

"Miranda?"

She opened her eyes and saw Richard bending over her, his face furrowed with concern.

A gasp of relief ripped out of her. Sitting up, she flung her arms around him.

He caught her against his chest and held her there, his face pressed against her hair. "Are you all right, sweet?"

Into his neck, she gasped, "I'm so glad you're safe!"

His arms tightened. He raised his head. Only then did she realize what he'd called her and notice the firm, solid feel of his body against hers. Their gazes locked, and the intensity of his stole her breath.

Carefully, hardly daring to do it, she touched his cheek. He caught her hand, closed his eyes, and pressed a kiss to her knuckles. Heat shot up her arm and into her heart, and then lower.

He made a sound like a strangled groan. When he opened his eyes, they were bland. The warmth within her faded to disappointment, but truly, she should've expected naught else.

Gently, he set her away from him and shifted to the chair by the hearth. The firelight gilded the strong planes of his face and flickered in the blue of his eyes. Her heart yearned.

But social ranks aside, he'd shown no personal interest in her. Whatever feelings that hand kiss and the look in his eye betokened, he didn't mean to act on them.

"That was presuming," she said, her face heating. "I shouldn't have. I was afraid for you."

"I appreciate your concern, but what has you worried? Why are you still awake?"

"I had another dream, a terrible dream."

"Tell me about it." His eyes narrowed in concentration.

She bit her lip and looked away, avoiding the newly precious sight of him. "I dreamed about you."

Her heart twisted. How could she say this to him? Somehow, she must.

She took a deep breath and faced him. "In the dream—Lord Wyndon accused you of breaking into his house. The two of you fought a duel. With swords, but he attacked you magically, and … Richard, you died."

CHAPTER 15

The next day, Richard met Kit, Cabot, and Jeremy in Kit's London rooms. When Kit had poured ale for them all, Richard dropped onto the wooden settle by the hearth and told them about Miranda Willoughby's latest dream.

"What are you going to do?" Kit asked, passing the ale around. A lock of dark hair fell into his face, and he shoved it back impatiently.

"Try not to fight a duel with Wyndon, obviously." Richard answered in a dry voice.

Kit added, "I heard about George's betrothal. God's feet, Richard, you cannot let that stand."

"I cannot stop it." Richard took a long draught of the bitter brew. "George is of age, and he's living in Wyndon's pocket."

The unseasonable snow had given way to biting cold that suited Richard's mood. So did the Spartan surroundings, leased chambers in a formerly grand palace in the Strand. Some of its neighbors had already been pulled down, while others, like this former home of the Duke of Wayland, had been divided into tenements.

Using these rooms only once or twice a year, Kit saw no reason for elaborate furnishings. Of course, that would likely change when he married his Alice.

Into the grim silence, Kit said, "I found something that may be a clue. Back when I first started reading about Richard III, when I was at Oxford,

I talked to one of the dons about the *Chronicle*. He'd read that entire fifteenth-century bit, not only the parts about King Richard. I went through my notes last night and found something I'd forgotten. He said there was an account in the early part about a heresy trial, someone who claimed to have traveled through, and tinkered with, time."

Richard's pulse kicked. "How could you forget that?"

"I thought it was nonsense." Kit shrugged. "But when you mentioned that bit about walking the path of death with a foot in life on either side, I knew I'd heard it before, just couldn't recall where. It's in my old notes."

"What else is in there?" Cabot asked, leaning forward in his seat.

"Not much, alas. There was a bit about currents in time being like branches of a river, but who knows what that means?" Shaking his head, Kit added, "My old don was Gifted, so he'd thought that was worth noting, but he also thought it was nonsensical. We touched on it only briefly, in passing."

Richard asked, "Is he still teaching? Could you—"

"Afraid not," Kit answered. "He was rather old when I studied under him, and he died a few years back." Frowning, he added, "Supposedly."

"That," Jeremy said, "is worth looking into. It may be that the *Chronicle* wasn't taken because of its material about King Richard at all."

"I'll make inquiries among the old fellow's friends," Kit offered.

Richard thanked him and turned to Jeremy, who occupied one of the chairs flanking the hearth. "What news from your archives?"

"No changes spotted yet, and they're back to 1667." Jeremy shrugged. "I hope that means we haven't yet looked far enough back to find the critical moment. I'm tempted to tell them to skip so the task goes faster, but if we do, we might miss something important."

Kit slid down in his chair, his feet thrust out toward the fire. "Has Miranda offered you anything helpful?"

"Not much," Richard answered, "though she has made substantial progress in using her powers."

Jeremy asked, "Have you learned any more about her?"

Richard shrugged. "Only a bit. She's well enough educated, though she has little to say."

"She may feel badly out of place," Kit said. "Do you see much of her?"

"Only for lessons and at meals. She seems sincere and, for a woman who worked in an inn and public house, somewhat naïve."

Richard stared out the window. Instead of the rain-wet street below, he saw her troubled blue eyes when he'd arrived home last night. He'd

THE HERALD OF DAY

managed to avoid thinking of her in his arms, holding him close with her breasts pressed into his chest and his arms locked around her warm body. Kit's question, though, brought the memory roaring back. Letting her go last night, doing the honorable thing, had been painful.

"She has steel at her core," he said softly.

"I expect she needed it," Jeremy commented.

Silence fell, broken only by the sounds of the rain on the windows and the hiss of drops falling into the fire. Richard rubbed his tense neck. He should be thinking of this puzzle, but Miranda haunted him.

"She's an odd creature," he mused, "a shy woman with inner resolve, a lower-class girl who doesn't curry favor or seek to take advantage, a Gifted woman who fears her Gifts."

Softly, he added, "An independent creature who asks for little."

"All of that draws you," Cabot said quietly.

The words broke over Richard like a blow to the forehead, and he realized he'd spoken aloud. He rubbed a hand over his face. "It doesn't matter. It can't, because nothing about any of this promises a way to lift the family curse."

A wary light came into Jeremy's eyes. Slowly, he said, "All this digging in the archives has turned up something of interest, Richard. Apparently deeds of great courage and daring can sometimes expiate a blood curse."

Hating the sudden stab of hope, Richard said, "Deeds like slaying a dragon, swimming a moat wearing mail, rescuing a fair maiden? Those sorts of deeds?"

"I was thinking," Jeremy replied, his gaze level, "of correcting an altered timestream."

"Don't." Richard's sharp tone cut off Kit, who abruptly closed his mouth.

Taking a deep breath, Richard softened his tone. "Jeremy, I know you mean well. I'm grateful you care. But you all know what the curse did to my parents. What it could do to me. Hope is the devil's poison when it comes in vain. I won't indulge it."

No one spoke. Richard watched the fire burn. His mother had never forgiven his father for the oath that had doomed Richard, their only son. How could any woman? The madness that often came upon the doomed earls, with no rhyme or reason as to which ones suffered it, only made matters worse.

"You won't go mad," Cabot stated. "We won't allow it."

Richard had to smile at that. Their loyalty would always be beyond question, even if those words were likely hollow. Not even magic could stop madness.

"You know," Kit said quietly, "none of us can put himself in your place when it comes to this family curse. I wouldn't presume to tell you how to feel about it."

"But you're about to?" Richard guessed.

Kit shook his head. "I understand why you feel a duty to spare those unborn, even if that means they never come to be." He looked down at his ale, turning his goblet between his hands. "Yet you must know anything George inherits, Wyndon or his heir will control. What will it mean for the folk of Hawkstowe if your lands fall into their hands?"

What of your duty to them? he meant.

Richard stared at him. Of his close friends, only Kit also held a title. Only he had been trained to consider those responsibilities.

"I've been trying not to think of that," Richard admitted. "Or of the disaster George will be as an earl." Thinking of that, truly facing it, might force him down a path he'd forsworn.

Which carried more weight—his duty to generations yet unborn or his family's duty to the people on their lands? He feared it was the latter, but saving his people led down a road fraught with other troubles.

Slowly, Richard said, "If we can restore the true stream of history, that betrothal will likely come undone."

"Or not," Cabot said. "We've no way to know which events are the result of the alterations in history and which are not."

"There's no denying that." Richard frowned. "Perhaps Morgan's pool will give us an answer. Morgan's handmaidens have consented to let us use its waters tomorrow night to explore Miranda's visions."

"Took them long enough," Jeremy commented.

"They won't allow anyone to use it," Richard told him, "even at Pendragon, unless one of them is by. Tomorrow is the first night a handmaiden was available."

"A dangerous move," Jeremy said, "using blood magic."

"Life is full of danger," Richard replied. "Hiding from it never helps."

Kit's faced paled. Doubling, he gripped his stomach.

"Kit?" Richard sprang toward him as Jeremy rushed around the table.

Reality collapsed, twisting in on itself. Darkness blotted out the world, then gave way to rolling, stinking purple-gray fog. Off-balance, Richard reached out for support. Into nothingness.

A heartbeat later, the fog cleared. He staggered into a table and clutched it. Across it, Jeremy's figure blurred, then became clear, as he grabbed for the table and missed. Jeremy crashed to the floor.

The room spun. Richard shook his head and cleared his vision except for fuzziness at the edges. Steadying himself against the table, he lurched around it.

"Jeremy?" The name emerged as a croak.

He dropped to his knees beside his friend. "Jeremy!"

Jeremy winced. Rising on an elbow, he said, "I hit my head on the table's edge." He pressed the heel of his other hand to his temple.

"Let me see." Richard brushed Jeremy's brown hair aside carefully. "You've a knot coming up already but no blood."

"That's a boon. Room's not spinning anymore." Jeremy pushed himself upright, blinking. "But it's the wrong room. And where's Kit?"

Bracing Jeremy with one hand, Richard glanced around them. Kit's parlor had become a paneled chamber hung with maroon damask, its corner bedstead covered and curtained in the same fabric. "This looks like the room you use when you're at Lambeth."

"Because it is." Jeremy's lips set in a line. He hauled himself to his feet. "So what are we doing here?"

Time shifts changed life and death—"Kit always comes to London this time of year. We should be in his rooms."

"Unless something happened to him," Jeremy said. "I imagine Cabot's at our house, but I'll send someone to see."

"We must see about Kit. Can you travel as far as the Strand?"

They raced to the stables, saddled mounts themselves, and rushed to the waterside. The horse ferry ride across the Thames seemed to last an age.

The ride through Westminster and past Whitehall Palace seemed interminable. Richard and Jeremy pushed their mounts through the crowds on the Strand until they reached Wayland House. Ahead loomed Temple Bar, Christopher Wren's elaborate, Portland stone gateway to the City of London. Statues of the king and his father still flanked the window above the arch. So the order of kingship, at least, had not changed.

Wayland House, where they'd just been, lay ahead on their right, past Middle and Inner Temple Lanes. The two streets were lined with lawyers' chambers and led to the river.

Richard drew rein and stared at the house. The gray stone front wall looked tightly mortared and well kept. The gate itself, a double one like

Richard's, looked new, not worn and rain-bleached as it had been a short time ago.

Richard turned to Jeremy, who was looking at him with fear stark in his eyes. Richard said, "I'll ask."

They drew their mounts to the side, out of traffic. Richard dismounted, passed Jeremy his reins, and strode to the doorway beside the big gate.

He knocked, and a man opened a panel in the door. Richard said, "I'm here to see Lord Havelock."

The man frowned. "This is Lord Wayland's house," he said. Richard's heart plummeted, and the man added, "There's no Lord Havelock here."

Damn. Richard said softly, "My mistake."

Shaking his head, he walked back to Jeremy and mounted.

Jeremy said, "I feared this from the look of the house. Since it was divided into rooms to let, it hasn't been as well maintained."

"Perhaps Kit's merely not in London," Richard said. But fear gnawed at his throat. Because of the White Rose dinner, Kit always came to the city in October.

"If he's in London, we should have word by the time we return to Lambeth. We should go there and consult the archives. We're holding peerage records for the College of Arms until their new building is finished."

The old building had been destroyed in the Great Fire, but many of the records had been saved. Some were stored at Westminster and others at Lambeth Palace.

They returned to Lambeth Palace and were relieved to meet Cabot there, waiting for them just inside the main gate. He'd found himself at home in Aysgarth House.

"We went looking for Kit," Jeremy told his brother.

"And?" Cabot asked carefully.

Jeremy shook his head, and fear flashed in Cabot's eyes. His face tightened.

"We've come to check the archive from the College of Arms," Jeremy said. "Perhaps Kit is still alive but not in London."

Cabot nodded. "Then lead on."

Fearing any hope was in vain, Richard held fast to it anyway as they walked his and Jeremy's mounts to the stable and turned them over to grooms.

A grim-faced Jeremy led the way across the hall courtyard, up a flight of stairs, and into the upper cloister and the library. The low-ceilinged chamber had narrow windows with bookshelves lining all the space in between. Below the carved ceiling, a row of small windows added light in the central area, over a table. The place smelled of old leather and parchment.

"The peerage records are over here," Jeremy said, hurrying to a shelf on the room's left side. He scanned it for a moment and then reached for a thick, leather-bound volume.

"This covers the last half-century and Kit's succession to the title." He laid it on the table and flipped it open. "Hamely ... " He turned several pages. "Hatfield ... "

Jeremy turned another page. Cabot leaned closer. Richard skimmed the text, and his neck tightened with foreboding.

"Havelock." Jeremy turned ashen. "Oh, God."

Lapsed. The word jumped off the page at Richard. He glanced hastily over the text, looking for descendants. His eyes locked onto Kit's name, *Christopher Stephen Edward Grayson.* Information followed—the names of his parents and sisters, and then—

Richard's chest went tight. He stared at the page. It couldn't be true. It mustn't.

But he knew it was.

The last line of the entry read, *Killed in a coaching accident, eighteenth September in the year of our Lord 1659.*

Kit had been dead for 15 years.

~

Despairing, Richard stared around the Council table in the Green Bull's cellar that afternoon. No one had any suggestions for stopping the wrenching changes rolling forward daily. Kit's wasn't the only life wrongly cut short. And without him, they'd no idea which Oxford don he'd consulted about the *Chronicle* or who that man's friends might've been.

"People are disappearing and coming back to life," Richard said for the fourth time, haunted by Kit's pained face in the moment before he vanished. "We've a duty to question anyone who might know anything about how to fix this."

"Fair enough," stout, balding Hugh Bentham, a draper, said, "but you've given us no reason to assume Lord Wyndon does."

Richard gritted his teeth. If he had to admit to his search of Wyndon's home, Hugh and others would cling to that and refuse to hear anything else he said.

"Wyndon has always been the loudest voice among us for coming out of hiding," Richard insisted, "and he argued that we should turn this change to our advantage."

"He wasn't the only one," Hugh pointed out reasonably.

"He was the most insistent," Richard countered. "And he studied necromancy at Pendragon last year. And his family was part of an ancient plot to seize power for our kind."

Hugh replied, "That's not on him. And even if it were, he'd not likely admit it."

"If he drinks the water from Morgan's pool," Richard shot back, "he'll have to tell the truth." If Richard could only convince them to order that test. "We must question him. With the weather changes growing even worse, and people appearing and disappearing, we can't just do nothing and hope things improve."

Three of the other six members, including Lucius, listened attentively. Eliza Harper sat forward, frowning, her thin frame tense. Bentham toyed with the bread on his plate.

"You don't know Wyndon's done anything," Thomas Surry said. An excellent carpenter, he believed in what he could see. "So what if he studied necromancy? Many of us have dabbled with it. 'Tisn't forbidden. And I don't see how it changes time."

Richard hesitated. Could he frame this in a way they would not only grasp but believe? "There is a theory that the world of the dead is all around us, that someone who knows how can pass from here to there. And the world of the dead touches all places and times."

The men and women at the table traded bemused glances. Only Lucius seemed ready to listen.

The Council head said, "That's an interesting theory, Richard. Where did you see it?"

"I heard it from an ancient scholar." Surely Edmund qualified as that after all this time. "Besides, after what Wyndon said in the Conclave the other day, you must see that he's the most likely person to have tampered with the timeline."

"I asked him what he meant about seizing the moment," Bentham told them, frowning. "He said he merely wanted the best for the Gifted out of this upheaval."

"So he'll doubtless maintain," Lucilda Denby said. The blonde woman, a mercer's spoiled wife, looking bored, readjusted her green wool skirts. "Besides, Richard, liking the result doesn't mean he brought it about. Unless you can show us Henry knows how to travel time, we have no grounds to question him. We can't scry the truth with everything in such upheaval, so it's your word against his, with bad blood between your families for two hundred years."

Most of the councilors, other than Lucius, nodded. Eldred Carstairs, an elderly baronet, appeared to be dozing. Poking him, Lucius nodded to Richard to continue.

"Heard there was a near riot in Smithfield Market yesterday," Eldred said suddenly. "Not enough bread to go round."

"If this continues, we can expect more of that." Sarah Marling, a wiry, keen-eyed tavern owner, leaned forward. "Before we accuse, let alone question, someone with so many friends, we need proof."

"I would give it to you if I had it," Richard admitted. Even the necromancy scroll wouldn't prove Wyndon could splice time.

Frustration and loss welled into Richard's throat. *Kit*, he thought, and then forced himself to steady.

Richard swept the table with a gaze as earnest as he could make it. "Cousins, our messengers' reports show we're moving toward a famine once current food stores begin to run out. The wind and rain damaged barns and blew away many of the winter crops. The forage and hay are rotting—unduly fast, even considering the heavy rain. Add to that, people's lives are in upheaval. We've a duty to act."

"Yes, but we must act in a way that's effective," Sarah said, "and we don't yet know of one."

Hugh noted, "The Thames is frozen a foot thick. Folk are already setting up a frost fair on the ice. They'd best take their pleasure while they can, for the cold will likely freeze what little remains in the fields."

"Add to that," Lucius said, "Animals are mysteriously sickening. For all we know, people will be next."

"I read something about mystery sicknesses at Pendragon once." Surry frowned as though searching his memory. "Could be, all this is nature's way of dealing with change."

Bentham shook his head. "Dreadful. Simply dreadful. We should organize relief plans. If we can repair the roads enough to reach affected areas, some of the Gifted could help dry out that food."

"Not when it's already rotted." Richard could barely keep from shouting. People were dying, the dead were walking, and they wanted to prattle on about frost fairs and relief schemes.

"If not," Bentham said, "Henry de Vere has offered to help procure supplies from France."

Lucius shot a warning glance at Richard. Given the widespread knowledge of his quarrel with Wyndon, Richard had to be careful in pressing his suspicions.

Lucius said, "We're talking about rather a lot of grain and hay. How will Henry pay for that?"

Bentham shrugged. "Not my problem. Good of him to do it."

"Yes," Lucilda. "Very good."

"Indeed," Sarah said sharply, "but come back to the point. If time is changing, that violates the natural order. Which may well explain this freakish weather and the resulting problems. Including people dying before their times or living past them."

"We'll vote," Lucius said. "Who favors questioning Henry?"

Richard raised his hand. Nodding, Sarah did the same. Hugh, Eliza, and Lucilda folded their hands on the table. Lucius looked to Eldred.

"I don't like Henry." The baronet cast a pointed look at Richard. "I abstain."

Richard set his jaw. With three votes against and two for, Lucius voting only in a tie, nothing would happen. He needed to prove Wyndon's involvement.

CHAPTER 16

Beneath the wide brim of Richard's plumed beaver hat, his face looked drawn and tired. Miranda doubted he even noticed the coach's rattling, bouncing progress over the cobblestones.

Of course, he'd lost one of his closest friends to the time shifts. He must be frantic to put things right. So he was on his way to meet secretly with the head of the Conclave Council.

There'd been no more snow, but the Thames had supposedly frozen solid, something Miranda would believe when she saw it. Despite the heated bricks beneath their feet, their breath made puffs of fog in the chilly air. No man as clearly weary as he was needed to be out in the cold.

"Richard," she said tentatively, "I understand why you want to meet this man outside the Council chamber, but I don't see why you wanted me to come."

His gaze shifted back to her, sharpening into an intent stare. "I want to share your visions with Lucius, and it's best if you describe them to him. Perhaps tomorrow, after we explore your visions tonight, would be better, but I feel as though we've no time to waste."

By exploring them, he meant using the water from Morgan's pool. The visions were frightening enough in snatches. The thought of plunging fully into one sent shivers down Miranda's spine.

Seeking a distraction, she peered out the coach window and tried to see the river. "It's hard to believe people play on the ice. Especially now, with the weather so harsh and food becoming scarce."

"Food is scarce every time the weather turns so harsh. In 1649, the year the king's father was executed, the weather was as harsh as this, with crops failing and the civil war still raging. Yet there was a fair on the Thames, as there is today, though it was later in the winter."

"Amazing."

He smiled. "Folk will rarely pass up the chance to make extra coin, especially if doing so diverts them from their troubles."

Miranda quirked up one corner of her mouth. "Let me guess. Everything costs more on the ice."

"But of course." Though he smiled, the weariness in his eyes remained. "The crowds give me a chance to talk with Lucius and not be remarked, as we would be at either of our homes. Your presence also makes this seem more like a social outing."

The coach slowed, harness jingling, and stopped. A footman opened the door. Folding down the steps, he said, "Have a care, milord, mistress. It's slick underfoot, it is."

"Thank you, Harry," Richard said. "You and Thomas can wait at the Twisted Cockerel. We'll meet you there."

Richard climbed down and held his hand out for her. "This is Middle Temple Lane. From here, we'll walk down to the ice."

His firm grip on her elbow steadied her as she stepped onto the slick cobblestones. "Hold onto me," he said.

She took one gloved hand from the soft, sable muff his grandmother had loaned her and laid it on his arm. Carefully, they picked their way over the icy cobblestones. On either side, tall buildings of red brick with names painted over the arched entries lined the cobblestoned passage. Several of them had stuccoed overhangs, and each floor jutted out slightly farther than the one below it.

"Those are barristers' chambers," Richard said.

Glancing ahead, she caught her breath. Beyond a winter-brown orchard at the bottom of the hill on the left, the Thames sparkled icy white. A village of tents covered its surface, with throngs of people going to and fro.

Staring at the scene, she said, "I confess that I thought you were joking at first, but there truly is a fair out there. On the Thames, of all places."

"It happens from time to time," he replied. "Usually in January or February, occasionally in December. Never in October." He shook his head. "The hard freeze runs from London Bridge down almost to Westminster."

Walking through the withered orchard at the bottom of the street, they had a wide view of the river.

A row of tents directly in front of the Temple stretched across to the far bank. Behind the tents, a ring of people watched a wrestling bout. A miniature ship on runners glided toward the bridge, towed by three men and bearing several others. A horse-drawn cart on the usual wheels crossed its path.

To one side, a ring of spectators watched a bull-baiting. Miranda averted her eyes hastily. "If they mean to kill the poor beast, they should just do it," she muttered.

"Yes. We'll stay away from there."

The wind shifted, bringing the sounds of flute and violin and the scent of roasting meat. And something noxiously smoky. Miranda covered her nose.

"Sea coal smoke from London's hearths," Richard said. "On such a cold day, it can't rise and hangs over the city worse than usual." Smiling, he added, "The wind will change in a moment."

A group of men in laborers' rough garments milled about the riverbank, carrying shovels and spades. "A penny," a man's coarse voice cried from the group. "A penny for them as is out o'work from the freeze?"

"That means a penny each," Richard murmured, "and I'd give you odds they're all beggars anyway." Yet he slid his arm free of her hold, pulled out his purse and gave them each a penny.

A sturdy, broad-shouldered man stood by the wide, shallow stairs down to the river. "Need any help climbing down, sir?" Gesturing to one of the boats clustered around the foot of the stone stairway, he added, "You can step into m'boat. Froze in place, she is."

"My thanks." With movements so swift she almost missed them, Richard took out his purse and slipped the man a coin. "Waterman," he explained quietly under the fellow's thanks. "He truly is out of work today, with no one needing a ride across. The watermen and the lightermen, the fellows who move goods across the river, organize the fairs, but what they charge tradesmen and punters to join in doesn't make up for all they lose."

The passage of so many feet had worn away the ice on the stone stairs, but Richard offered his arm again. "Watch your footing," he advised her.

She laid her hand on his wrist. He was so careful of her, as no one had been since her early childhood. Many men of his rank would've stood on ceremony. That he didn't made him that much more appealing. Yes, he was well favored and financially secure, but what mattered more was that he was also kind and determined and highly skilled. Any woman would be drawn to such a man.

There could be no harm in enjoying his attention for the time she had it.

Stepping carefully, she said, "It's like a city on the ice. Astounding."

"These fairs started in James I's reign, but I've heard Henry VIII once went to Greenwich by sleigh when the river froze and Queen Elizabeth walked on the ice."

They reached the bottom of the stairs. Peering through the crowd, he said, "We're to meet Lucius by the dancing, at the far bank. Let's stroll through the tents on our way."

"As we would if we'd come to enjoy the fair," she said.

"Yes." Richard's face went stony, and pain flashed in his eyes. He must be thinking of his friend. Miranda squeezed his arm briefly. He patted her hand but kept his gaze straight ahead.

The tents held a wonder of items. Books, ale, a skittles game. In one, a printer named Croom made cards with visitors' names on them for sixpence.

"Would you like one?" Richard asked Miranda.

She hesitated. Sixpence sounded rather dear to her, but she knew it wasn't to him. "Yes, if you please."

He gave the printer the money and her name. A few minutes later, the man passed over a card that read, "Printed by Croom for Miranda Willoughby on the frozen Thames, October 1674."

She thanked Richard and tucked it into the muff. "It's a memento I'll treasure."

"I hope we'll have other reasons to look back on this day with pleasure."

If they could make the Council confront Lord Wyndon, that might help undo the changes. Richard's friend would return.

And Miranda would never have met any of them. She swallowed hard but said nothing. There was nothing to say.

They wandered outside again. The city's recent edgy mood seemed not to reach the ice. A drum joined the flutes and violins in a lilting air that came from behind the tents.

Just beyond them, with London Bridge looming across the sky, a ring of dancers spun and bowed on a sheet of canvas laid over the ice.

Richard guided her toward the music. Its bright, infectious melody seemed to defy the dark events of recent days. But it brought him no cheer. His face remained grim as he watched the dancers.

"When this is over," he said, "if you care to learn to dance, I'd be happy to teach you. That's 'Peppers Black.' Do you recognize it?"

Miranda was about to answer when her foot slipped. She clutched his arm. He grabbed for her and slipped as well. Stumbling for footing, they slid into a draper's cart laden with bolts of bright fabric. He grabbed it with one arm and yanked her close with the other.

Breathing hard, she stared up at him. He looked relieved, but his eyes also held unexpected warmth. Her breath caught in her throat.

"Are you all right?" His eyes locked on hers.

She nodded. "Thanks to you." The words had a strained sound born of her awareness of his nearness and the warm concern in his eyes.

Abruptly, his expression closed over. His eyes became bland. "Let's see if we can find something to eat while we wait."

Turning away was probably for the best. She might regret that there could be nothing between them, but that wouldn't matter anyway if they succeeded in fixing the timeline.

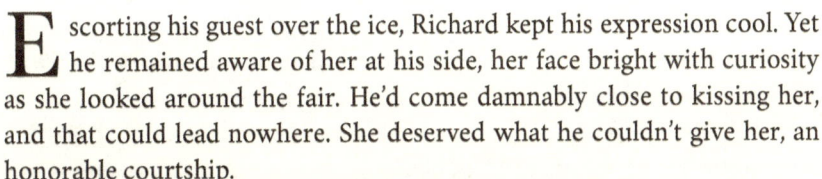

E scorting his guest over the ice, Richard kept his expression cool. Yet he remained aware of her at his side, her face bright with curiosity as she looked around the fair. He'd come damnably close to kissing her, and that could lead nowhere. She deserved what he couldn't give her, an honorable courtship.

"I hear Lord Trentford called this morning," he said.

"Yes, he was very kind."

"Do you like him?"

She hesitated. "Well enough, I suppose, but if we can undo the changes in history, that likely won't matter."

"Still, you shouldn't pass up a chance to build a better life. After all, the quest may not succeed."

His next words felt like ground glass in his throat, but he pushed them out. "Should you receive an offer you like, I will gladly dower you."

Her face paled. Staring straight ahead, she said, "That will not be necessary. Indeed, my lord, I cannot let you do such a thing."

"Richard, remember." He shouldn't sound so abrupt. His pointless attraction to her wasn't her fault.

"M'lord! Mistress," a friendly voice called.

Richard craned his neck toward the sound. Lucius picked his way over the ice toward them. A burgundy wool cloak shrouded his lean form, and the white plume on his wide-brimmed, black hat fluttered in the cold breeze.

"Good day, Lucius." Richard smiled and waved to him as though this were a chance encounter. He and Miranda met Lucius before he reached the crowd around the dancers. They could speak privately if they kept their voices down.

Richard said, "Lucius Balfour, meet our cousin, Miranda Willoughby. Miranda, Lucius heads the Gifted's Conclave Council."

Lucius touched his broad hat's brim. "Good day to you both, cousins."

"Good day," Miranda replied. Now that Lucius had arrived, all her attention was on him rather than the frivolous pursuits on the ice behind them.

Lucius glanced from her to Richard. "You wanted to speak with me, cousin?"

"I wanted to make you aware of Mistress Willoughby's visions," Richard told him. "I'm certain Wyndon knows more than he admits, and her visions tie him to some of the recent events."

Lucius turned to her. "You're a seer, then, cousin?"

"A fledgling one, yes." She described her dream about the bear following Richard and the one about him dueling Wyndon.

When she finished, Lucius shook his head. "It's not enough, not with the support Henry has on the Council."

"But the bear I saw—" she started.

"Not specific enough, I'm afraid," Lucius told her. He glanced at Richard. "Everyone knows of the enmity between you and Wyndon. We need something so definite as to be almost ironclad, or we'll never carry a vote to question him."

Richard answered, "He's studied necromancy." Choosing his words with care to avoid revealing Edmund's existence, he added, "My own studies imply that there's a realm between life and death that touches various times, as I said at the meeting. What if he has exploited it in some way?"

Lucius shook his head again. "I trust you, Richard, but suspicion alone isn't enough to sway most of the others. I wish we had more leeway." He shifted his cloak over his shoulder. Frowning, he looked down at the ice. "It seems to have grown warmer rather quickly."

"It does," Richard agreed. Intent on the conversation, he hadn't noticed. He glanced across the ice. A new, faint sheen, probably not visible to ordinary eyes, marked the surface of the ice.

Lucius's frown deepened. "It usually takes days for the ice to melt. Of course, it usually takes weeks to freeze, as well."

"We should go." Richard offered Miranda his arm. "We can continue this on firm ground."

"I believe you're right," Lucius said.

A loud crack, like the strike of lightning, split the air and stilled the music and voices. A moment later, screams followed. The three Gifted wheeled toward the sound. The ice was breaking.

People rushed toward the banks, slipping and falling and scrambling up again in a mad dash toward safety. A long crack in the ice caught the wheel of the passenger cart. The cart fell deeper into the ice, and the crack widened. The cart listed, spilling its passengers.

"We can help," Richard said to Lucius. "I'll return when I've seen Miranda to the bank." If she fell through—

"I can make it alone," she said despite the fear in her eyes. "You and Lucius can help others."

Lucius was already striding toward the cracking ice.

Richard shook his head. "I need to see you safe first."

With an arm around her waist to steady her, he hurried across the ice and up the Temple stairs to the bank.

More cracks appeared in the ice. One swallowed a tent. Richard turned and plunged into the fleeing crowd.

Miranda stood by the top of the stairs and huddled in her cloak. Watching Richard and Lucius, she barely noticed the people jostling her. Once they were off the ice, many turned to watch their fellows in peril.

The day's sudden warming probably portended something about the time changes, but she had no idea what.

Scanning the ice frantically, she spotted Richard. He and Lucius worked to help passengers of a cart caught in a crack in the ice while the driver frantically unhitched his team. Her Gifted eyes caught a faint hint of silver around Richard's and Lucius's hands when they bent to the ice. They were firming it.

Merchants scrambled to strike their tents. Already weakened by the warming day and stressed by the crowd's weight, the ice again cracked with another sharp report. Across Miranda's sight flashed a vision of the ice breaking into floes, spilling people and wares into the Thames.

She had to help, but how?

She didn't know weather magic, but she did know word magic. Could she use it now?

She walked a short distance from the crowded stairs and knelt by the water. Extending her hand over the ice would be too conspicuous, so she only pointed one finger as she whispered, "Cold. Be cold. Freeze." Nothing happened.

A channel opened in the cracking ice. The waterman on the stairs pushed his boat into the opening.

How had she felt when Arabella had pushed her power? She groped for the feeling. In a rush of magic that left her dizzy, she found it, but something seemed to hold it back. She pushed harder.

Another crack opened in the ice. The miniature ship on runners slid into it, passengers screaming.

Richard ran toward it, and the people tumbling out clutched at him, pulling him toward them as he tried to resist, to keep his arms free so he could help them. He broke away, only to have more people grab him. They were dragging him into the river.

The ice under his feet cracked, and Miranda had a sudden vision of him falling into the water, pushed down by people scrambling to escape.

CHAPTER 17

"No," Miranda gasped. Gathering her will, she pushed with all her being. "Freeze. Hold."

Magic roared through her like a flooding river. Power sang in her blood, surging from her finger to the ice. The chill of its firming echoed in her bones. Frost spread across it.

On the ice, Richard broke free of the grasping hands. The frost reached the widening crack where he worked. Frowning, he glanced at her. Their gazes met, and a flick of his hand, even as he pulled a drenched, shivering woman from the water, made the frost she'd created vanish.

Yet other cracks were forming all across the river. People stampeded for the banks. She couldn't stop all of the cracking, but mayhap she could help Richard and others near her.

Miranda repeated the incantation, pouring more into it, taking care this time to imagine the ice holding, not freezing anew. If it did that, people might look for the cause.

Abruptly, her power ran out. Spent and dazed, she swayed and had to steady herself with a hand on the ground. Where was Richard?

People still streamed past her, blocking her view.

Finally, she spotted him hurrying toward her among the last people on the ice. Miranda let out a relieved breath.

Full of concern, his eyes met hers. He rushed up the steps to the bank. "Are you well?"

She nodded, accepting his help to stand. They took a step, and the world spun.

He drew her close to peer into her face. "Miranda?"

"Just dizzy. It was difficult."

"It was astonishing," he corrected. "I was amazed when your magic joined with mine and Lucius's." He drew her against his side, and she leaned into his strength. The bay leaf scent of his clothes wafted into her nose, and his body felt strong and solid against hers. It felt good.

Too good.

"I can walk," she said, her voice weaker than she expected.

"Lean on me anyway. Such works take much of one's strength, even for those with more practice and experience than you have. After expending so much power, we both need food and rest. We've a major work of magic to face tonight. We must be ready for it."

The mantel clock ticked toward midnight, and someone tapped on Miranda's door. Her heartbeat quickened, and her hands felt suddenly cold. The time had come for the ritual. Thanks to resting through the evening, she no longer felt so weary, but she dreaded the rite she was about to undergo.

So much depended on it, and she had made so little progress controlling her power. Had gained so little experience. But Richard had much more. Perhaps that would suffice.

When she opened the door, his solemn eyes scanned her face. "Ready?"

Not by half. But Richard's friend had disappeared. Anyone night be next—Arabella, Miranda herself ... or even Richard.

"Yes," she answered, forcing determination into her voice. Fear chilled her veins and tightened her chest, but doing nothing, hiding from her power, would only make things worse.

Richard nodded. "Then let's go. We reach the pool through the library, and Morgan's handmaiden awaits us there."

They walked down the corridor in silence. Worried about what was to come, Miranda didn't feel inclined to conversation anyway.

The earl ushered her into the library, where a tall, solemn woman sat waiting for them with Arabella. The woman's thin face showed no great age, but silver threads glinted in her long, reddish braids. Instead of fashionable garb, she wore a straight, simple gown of silver velvet with green knotwork embroidery around its hem and its wide neck.

Richard introduced Miranda to the woman.

Ancient wisdom shone in the newcomer's dark eyes. "Well met, cousin. I'm Tessa, one of Morgan's handmaidens."

The idea of a woman as a guardian of anything still seemed strange, but there'd been too much strange happening in Miranda's life of late for her to blink at that. This gentle-looking woman must wield great power.

Arabella stood, her petticoats rustling. "Luck to you, my dears," she said. She kissed Richard's cheek and then, surprising her, Miranda's. "Richard, you'll let me know when it's done."

"Yes, Grandmère," he said, and she walked out of the room, closing the door behind her.

Tessa glanced at the mantel clock, which showed ten minutes until midnight. "This rite must begin at midnight," she said.

"Of course." Richard strode to the fireplace and touched the carved wooden shelving beside it. The shelf swung inward, revealing a narrow stone staircase descending behind the wall.

Miranda stared, amazed. What other secrets did this house hold?

"I'll go first," Richard said, "to avoid tripping the snares."

Miranda took a deep breath. "Snares?" she asked, looking from him to Tessa.

"Safeguards." He flashed her a quick smile. "You've nothing to fear so long as you've a family member in the lead."

Tessa nodded, apparently at ease. If this wise woman seemed confident, Miranda could at least pretend to be the same. Besides, she trusted Richard to help her if she needed it. She gathered her skirts and followed him into the darkness.

He summoned a glow around his hand to light their way. "Witchlight," he explained to Miranda. "You'll learn this, too."

"So you're a student," Tessa said as they wound downward into darkness. "You must be Richard's first."

"Grandmère has taught her much more than I." His voice echoed from the walls. "She has learned a great deal."

Mainly, she'd learned how terrifying such powers could be, but she put the thought aside. She'd longed to learn, and the only way out of this tangle was directly through it. Miranda kept a hand against the wall to steady herself and followed the winding stair in silence.

Long moments passed as they descended. Surely they'd passed the ground floor by now. How far down did this extend?

At last, Richard stopped before a rough stone wall. He pressed his palm to a spot that seemed like any other, and the wall swung back. The faint burble of falling water and a wave of moist, cool air came from the opening.

A tight band encircled Miranda's chest. Such secrecy implied great power and terrible knowledge. He'd said this was dangerous, but it seemed even more so now, in the darkness so far below the house.

They stopped in a chamber about twenty feet across. The light Richard held wasn't strong enough to show the ceiling, which was lost in darkness above.

He nodded to the far wall. "Should you ever need it, another tunnel lies there, by the basin."

"Behind the wall?"

"Grandmère can help you if I'm not here."

Tessa cocked an eyebrow at him. "Do you anticipate needing an escape soon, cousin?"

"Given the pace and tumult of these changes, who can say?" He snapped his forearm forward, as if tossing the light that surrounded his hand. The ball of light flew from one sconce to another, illuminating torches. It arrowed back to his hand, where it died.

The light revealed a vaulted ceiling. In the far corner a foot-wide waterfall tumbled four feet into a frothing basin and vanished.

Tessa nodded at the waterfall. "It will do."

She turned to Miranda, her gaze probing. "Morgan's pool at Pendragon has so much magic in the earth around it that its own power, which is greater than any it can give this fountain, lies contained. This place has no such safeguards. Once I add the water from Morgan's pool, its magic can flow between the two of you in unpredictable ways."

"You can change your mind," Richard said quietly.

But she couldn't. People who should live had died, including Richard's friend. Those who should be dead walked, and chaos ruled the weather. The changes to the past must be undone, the looming plague forestalled, or thousands could die. "If I can help, I must."

Behind her, Tessa said, "After I pour in the water I brought, you will each cut your left hand, for that one leads to the heart. The cut need not be large so long as it bleeds well. Then clasp your hands, cut to cut, and plunge them into the water at midnight."

Despite all she'd learned about healing, Miranda's stomach did a hard twist. But this was necessary.

She looked at Richard. In his dark blue eyes, she read steady resolve and no fear. She also read a question. She raised her chin in answer, and he nodded.

"We understand," he told Tessa.

"Very well, then." She walked to the basin with an uncorked flask in one hand. To Miranda, she said, "For you to See is not enough, for you've little knowledge. He has knowledge but cannot See. So you must do this together from beginning to end if you would find answers."

"Very well," Miranda said.

Tessa faced them again. "Let me warn you both that the pool's magic shows true, not only the vision within it but the hearts of those who use it."

She paused, as though to give her next words greater weight. "No one pays a fee for its use, but many have paid a price. We who guard it have seen betrothals and marriages, business dealings, and long friendships wither in its depths. I warn you, use it at your peril."

"Miranda?" Richard said quietly. His face had set in lines of grim determination.

If he could face this risk, so could she. After all, they had come here because they had no other ideas. "I'm willing."

"And I," he said.

Tessa told them, "When your blood enters the water, the mists will rise. When they do, summon the vision you seek."

"You'll need to do that," Richard told Miranda, "because the visions we want to explore are yours."

Tessa nodded. "You must remain intent on your goal, or the mists will turn to your own lives instead. I shall stand with you, of course, but I will not See what you do."

She emptied the flask into the frothing water, which churned silvery blue for half a dozen heartbeats before settling again. Eerie, ancient-feeling power whispered across Miranda's senses, and her stomach twisted.

"The pool's power cannot show you the future," Tessa told them. "It can show you the past. It can show you a dream or vision and any trails that lead to or from it. Within those limits, you can direct it."

Miranda's tight throat didn't allow words. She nodded.

"Our thanks, cousin," Richard said.

179

"I hope you can say that when you emerge. Luck to you." She walked to the foot of the stairs, then folded her hands. "I will tell you when midnight tolls."

Richard led Miranda to the water. "Are you ready?" he asked as they knelt by the bubbling basin.

She nodded, silently following. She could do this. She must do this. Too much depended on it.

"I'll go first," Richard said. He drew the dagger from the sheath at his waist. The blade flashed. Blood welled from a thin line that crossed his palm just below his fingers.

To her amazement, he smiled. "Ready?"

She managed a weak smile in return as she extended her hand. Again, he moved quickly. Not until she saw the blood welling did she feel the stinging pain it brought.

He held out his bloody palm, and she laid hers across it. Warm and sticky, their mingled blood oozed through her fingers as he wrapped his hand around hers. She took a deep breath, preparing herself. He did the same.

"Now," Tessa said, her voice suddenly ringing in the enclosed space.

Miranda and Richard plunged their joined hands into the icy basin below the waterfall.

Ripples spread outward from their hands. Beyond the ripples rose a silvery mist, shimmering like dew in a sunrise. It thickened into a cloud, and the shimmer became a surge that rushed toward them.

"Steady," Richard said. His grip tightened.

The mist surrounded them. It blotted out the sight of him, the feel of his hand on hers, the icy chill of the pool.

Alone in a ghost fog, Miranda fought panic. Nothing seemed real, and there was nothing to steady her. As a scream boiled into her throat, she sensed someone nearby.

Yearning poured from him, an aching loneliness that didn't conceal a resolute strength. Somehow, she realized that something set him apart from his fellows and created isolation he had learned to endure.

She knew that sense of being alone, just as she knew his determination not to let it lead him into temptation. And she knew him. They had met before, in a vision, and she needed him now. His presence steadied her.

With that, she could put a name to him. Richard.

The intense, beguiling awareness reminded her of Tessa's warning.

She forced her mind away from the emotions that swirled around her. This was no time to give them free rein.

The fog billowed. It spun aside and left her kneeling on dark, glassy nothingness where neither past nor future existed. Only the present mattered now. Drawing deep inside her, tapping her magic, she focused on the dragon vision.

~

Richard stood in purple-gray mists that stank of rotten eggs and hummed with power. A sense of purpose tugged at him, a need he had to answer. A call to arms.

With a crackle of purple power, the mists shimmering around him coalesced into silver armor etched with boars and sunburst roses. Wispy vapors hardened into a shield on his left arm—silver that bore a stripe of mulberry and one of blue, the center emblazoned with the white sunburst rose of York. A broadsword formed at his hip. As though he had willed them into being.

Another soul brushed his again, now tinged with panic. *Come. If you can hear, Sir Knight, come now. Oh, come!*

For that, he needed a horse. The mists between his legs solidified into a knight's high-pommeled saddle. Beneath it, a horse's powerful body formed, raising him. Its sleek, black head tossed. The transformation ended, and he sat atop an armored stallion that looked much like Zeus.

He touched his spurs to its sleek sides. The stallion surged into a gallop. Settling himself in the strange saddle, he turned his mount toward the beacon call.

The call grew steadily stronger. With no landmarks, he couldn't determine direction, but the summons drew him where he needed to go. Sounds came through the fog, thrashing noises such as a trapped animal might make. Slavering and snarling beasts. In his soul, a woman's desperation throbbed.

Miranda. In trouble and afraid and needing him. He spurred his mount to find her.

The fog thinned before him. There stood a red dragon, just as she had described. Between him and it, a bloody, rearing stag fought a half-score of smaller dragons. The stag fell.

Beyond it, on a carpet of mulberry bordered in blue, lay a white boar bleeding from gouges in its side.

Aware of what he did, yet apart from it, as though he watched through someone else's eyes, he drew his broadsword in a lightning arc. Bending low, he spurred his mount and charged.

The big dragon roared. Flame belched from its mouth.

Richard thrust his shield up, deflecting the fiery shaft. His attack caught the small dragons by surprise. Some fled. The horse's hooves smashed them into shadow that melted into the ground. Others attacked, but his blade slashed through them. Wounded, they also turned to shadow and melted.

He wheeled his mount to block the big dragon's way to Miranda and to the stag and the boar. Facing his foe, he sheathed his sword and flipped opened his visor.

The urge to speak filled him, and words burst forth. "Your time is done." His voice rang with power, startling him. "The untruths and evils you nurtured shall not prevail but pass away. They are but the shades of night, and I am the herald of day."

Stretching its full length upright, the dragon bellowed, the sound now hollow and impotent. The creature launched itself skyward and vanished into the gray clouds.

He frowned at it. Vanquishing such a beast couldn't be so easy. Why had it been?

∾

Miranda's body warmed, as though a shadow had passed away from the sun. She drew a shaky breath of relief and turned to the stag, which struggled to its feet. Its burns and wounds began, miraculously, to heal. When it glanced at her, the satisfaction in its dark eyes brought a smile to her lips.

She hurried forward as the knight—Richard—dropped his shield and dismounted.

The fog retreated. Sunlight pierced the dreamscape with color. Grass sprouting with lightning speed transformed the fog-wrapped realm into a bright meadow, and a warm, refreshing breeze wafted the scent of lavender through the air. The nightmare realm had become a place of peace and sanctuary.

She met Richard and the stag beside the wounded boar, now lying oddly still on a mulberry and blue carpet embroidered with white sunburst roses. Was it dead?

For all the heed he paid her or the stag, Richard might as well have been alone. He dropped to his knees and stripped off his helm and gauntlets. His sweat-dampened hair, cropped in a warrior's bowl cut, framed his strong features. Grief contorted his face.

He touched the boar's wounded side gently. "My liege. I am come too late." His low voice had lost its resonant power, and he frowned as though surprised at something.

Miranda's breath caught. She'd never seen a man touch an animal with such care.

Nay, you are come in time, Sir Knight. The stag's mental tone carried all the confidence the knight had lost. *Watch.*

The corpse glowed, softly and then more brightly. A shaft of sunlight touched it, and its battered hide became whole. The white coat took on a pure, silvery gleam. The boar rolled upright, facing them with its blue eyes solemn. *You three bring balm to a wounded soul. May you one day have the same.*

Richard set his jaw. Pain flared in his eyes before he masked it.

In a flash of brilliant light, the boar vanished. A rose bush laden with white blossoms stood in its place.

Hesitantly, Miranda reached toward a velvety flower.

Richard stood easily. "Allow me, my lady."

He used his dagger to cut a rose from the bush and to strip its thorns. Bowing slightly, he offered it to her. "For you."

She looked up at him, smiling, but the smile froze on her lips. The dark blue depths of his eyes held understanding of all the things she wanted but had stopped letting herself hope to have—home, companionship. Purpose. Longing such as her own lurked in his eyes, and pain.

"My thanks, Richard." She wrapped her fingers around the stem.

He cupped her cheek in his palm, and a vision flashed over her sight—of the two of them, naked, in a bed. As she gasped, the vision changed again, to one of him sitting in his library, gazing at nothing. An old man bereft of hope, he babbled aimlessly as he awaited a solitary death. The sight stabbed her heart.

"Miranda?" Richard drew her against his armored chest. Frowning, he tipped her chin up. "What's wrong, sweet? What did you See?"

"I don't know—it was ... sad." She swallowed hard. "Not part of this, I think."

It must not be, for nothing about him hinted that he'd shared those flashes, those visions within the larger vision realm. Besides, Tessa had said the pool's water couldn't reveal the future. The things she'd Seen but he hadn't must spring from her seer gift. What did they presage for him? For them?

Movement to one side caught her attention. He also turned to look. The stag pawed the ground. It tossed its great head as though in summons and bounded away.

Was it a signal that they should continue? Or a warning that they should stop? Feeling her way, she said, "I think we should follow."

"If you say so."

His mount pranced eagerly. He caught its reins, boosted her into the high saddle, and swung up behind her. They galloped after the bounding stag.

The meadow ended abruptly in shimmering fog. She clutched at his steel-clad arm, and he tightened his grip at her waist.

They stood atop a rise overlooking an open tract of land. In its center, reaching skyward like storm-blasted trees, stood the walls of a ruin. At one end stood a two-story wall, its arched openings empty and part of the upper story missing. A tall, pointed tower stood by the wall. Fallen stones lay here and there around the site. The overall pattern of the ruin formed a cross.

A leather folio lay at the ruin's center.

"The *Chronicle*," Richard said. "Somehow I know it even though I've never seen it. This must be Croyland. Perhaps this means we should go there."

Fog quickly obscured the scene. He slid his arm around Miranda's waist, drawing her closer, and the grip was comforting in the eerie, enshrouding vapors.

She shivered. "Richard, we should look for a way to undo these changes."

"That means we need to know who changed the past, and how."

Miranda concentrated on the means of the change, and the mists thinned.

A library came into view, books and scrolls jumbled on shelves and tables. "The library at Pendragon," Richard murmured.

By one shelf stood a stocky man with tawny hair. Wyndon.

The earl rolled a scroll with ornate ends that had a red dragon embossed on them, and Richard said, "I found one identical to that in his house."

"When you searched his house."

"Yes, the night you dreamed I was in danger. Let's watch."

Wyndon tucked the scroll into his coat, and the fog deepened.

Richard cursed softly. "The library is warded. How did he pass through the wards?" Edmund couldn't, or so he said. Why could Wyndon? Was it because he was still alive?

He winked out of sight, though the room remained visible. Fog again obscured everything but her. It shimmered faintly. The shimmer darkened, blotting out the eerie half-light of the scene. With it went all sense of time and place.

The disorientation lasted only a few moments. Then the darkness became eerie blue witchlight in the dank chill of the underground chamber, where she and Richard knelt together by the fountain, still hand in hand.

CHAPTER 18

Strange visions of experiences that seemed real, and yet not, swirled through Miranda's mind. Caught between slumber and awakening, hours after the vision ritual, she couldn't banish them.

When sleep at last claimed her, she fell deeper into the tide of images. They washed around and through her as though she looked at life through someone else's eyes.

Wearing armor, she knelt before the altar of a deserted chapel. In Yorkshire, she somehow knew. Moonlight streaming through holes in the roof mottled the floor with irregular patches of silver. She clasped her bare hands around the cross at a sword's hilt, the leather grip smooth under her fingers, and raised the sword, hilt upward, to the bare altar.

Hating the words but compelled by honor, she said, "By the blood of Morgan, on the sword of Hawkstowe, and into all the dawns to come, I swear."

Lightning flashed in the clear summer sky and flooded the room with blinding white brilliance. Thunder boomed.

When the light faded, the chapel wavered. The room vanished, leaving her under an open sky.

The stone floor became icy water that dragged at her already sodden clothes. The sword became a jagged plank she clutched to stay afloat. A wave surged over it and slapped her face. Coughing and spluttering, she knew, in the way of dreams, that she had struggled in the water, in the English Channel, for a long time.

She managed a rasping breath. The shore looked so very far away, a dark shadow against the starry sky. Weary from a long battle against the waves, she fought to stay afloat.

Her legs were so tired. Her arms ached.

She must reach the beach. Failure meant doom beyond death. She sagged against the plank, but every moment she rested let the outgoing tide carry her farther from the shore. It would be so easy to let go, to slip below the water and rest.

Except that, for her, death promised no rest.

She took another deep breath. It came out as a sob, but she found the strength to kick. Closing her eyes to avoid seeing how far away safety lay, she kicked again.

The water and the plank vanished. Sunlight warmed her face. She opened her eyes to a grassy hillside covered in the bright, fragrant blossoms of spring. A short distance past the base of the hill stood a manor with two towers inside crenellated walls, all of grey stone. The half-timbered upper stories on the end of the great hall and on the gatehouse stood out in contrast. The sight gave her a warm, pleasant sense of homecoming. She knew that castle. It was Hawkstowe, in Cumberland.

"There you are, dear," a woman said.

Turning, she saw Arabella, a much younger Arabella whose black hair bore only faint threads of silvery gray. The dowager countess sat in the grass.

Love swelled in Miranda's heart.

"I've been waiting," the dowager countess said. "Your ride ran overlong today, Richard."

Richard?

Miranda looked down at hands squarer and larger than her own. At legs encased in fine wool breeches and leather boots. But how? What was this?

Struggling to understand, she spun. The hillside wavered. Fog surrounded her. She tripped and shut her eyes against the impact.

She opened them and gasped. The hillside had vanished. She lay in a soft bed in a dark room. Her chamber at Hawkstowe House.

She raised one hand, a familiar hand. Her own. Blinking at it, she took a shuddering, relieved breath. What an odd dream, but was it only that?

From a ruined castle in the Yorkshire dales to a shipwreck in the

Channel and thence to Cumberland she had gone. All of it seemed so real. Surely it wasn't just a dream. It must be something more.

The idea made her shiver, but she dared not dismiss it. She pushed open the bedcurtains. The table by the bed held a candlestick with a beeswax taper, a ghostly blade in the dim light. She lit the candle magically, allowing herself a moment's satisfaction that she could, and swung her bare feet to the floor.

Sleep had fled for now, but perhaps she could read. Arabella had shown her the hidden part of the library, where the books on Gifted history and traditions were kept. Mayhap something there would help her understand. She could write down the things she'd seen, too. There would be paper and ink in the library desk.

She donned the dressing gown Arabella had given her and padded barefoot down the cold corridor. As Miranda walked, the mental images grew clearer. They were not dreams. But they were not like her visions of power, either. So what were they?

She set the lighted candle on the library's ornate mantel so she could stoke the banked fire. As the flames blazed anew, she sat back on her heels. Her mind drifted, and unbidden, the images appeared again.

Of course. Recognition stopped her breath. She sat upright in wonder.

Richard. In the dream, his grandmother had called her by his name. It had felt wrong, but Miranda had seen the weight of those memories in his eyes when he gave her the rose during their shared vision at the pool, and now she had dreamed his memories.

This must be a result of using the water from Morgan's pool. If so, Tessa's warnings made sense. Joining with Richard in the vision had felt ... intimate. And now she was privy to some of his memories.

He would hate that if he knew.

But how could he not? If she knew this about him, wouldn't he—oh, no, did he see her as deeply? If so, what had he seen?

The library door opened. Richard walked in carrying a tray that bore two silver plates and tankards, a crusty loaf of bread, a long knife, and a block of pale yellow cheese. In the firelight, his eyes were grave.

She rearranged her skirts to cover her feet. Unbound hair might strain the proprieties, but there was no one else awake to know.

"I saw the light under the door as I walked by," he said. "Although we ate after the rite, I'm hungry again. I thought you might want something too."

"Now that you mention it, I think I could eat a side of beef." Seeing him felt strange with these memories of his so fresh in her mind, especially as this was their first meeting since they'd parted after the rite.

He set the tray on the table by the hearth. "We've bread, cheese, and spiced cider." Slicing cheese and breaking off chunks of bread, he said, "Sit still. I'll bring it to you."

"I can help."

"It's done." He dropped a square of fine linen across her lap and handed her a plate of food.

"You do that very well. Of course, you have done it before. Not ... not only at the inns on our way here from Dover?" Bewildered by the strange certainty, she looked up at him.

Watching her intently, he said, "I have. At an inn in France, as a matter of fact. If you know that, the pool must have acted on you as it did on me."

So he did know things about her. At the thought of her lonely years laid bare to him, Miranda's face heated. *Please let him not see it in the dim light.*

Quietly, she said, "When you came in, I had just begun to realize that I knew things I couldn't know about you." How embarrassing, both to have such personal knowledge of him and to imagine what he might know of her. "I didn't do it apurpose."

"Of course not."

Uncertain what to say next, she watched him move around the room. He set a tankard of cider on the floor by her chair.

She did have questions about something not so personal. Discussing it might ease the tension. "You said Morgan's pool was named for the Morgan of legend? Was she as the old tales portray her?"

He served himself cheese. "Morgan le Fay? Yes and no. She had the power and strength of will but not the cruel nature ascribed to her in the tales."

"I've never heard much about her."

"We've books about her somewhere here, in the section on our history." He frowned at the shelves. "As I told you, Merlin and his twin sister, Morgan, with others of our kind, served the man legend calls King Arthur. As the Saxon push gained strength, the Britons withdrew into Wales, and the twins found themselves increasingly at odds."

"Over what?"

"The law of the Gifted, set down when we arrived here, forbids the use of magic for personal or tribal—national, if you will—gain. When matters grew desperate, Morgan advocated pulling back. Merlin believed England's future depended on more open use of magic. She swore to oppose him, and Arthur agreed with Merlin. Rather than battle those she loved, she withdrew into the south of England, to Avalon."

"Where is Avalon? I've often wondered."

"At Glastonbury, yet not." He smiled briefly. "That's a different tale. In due time, Morgan's fears came to pass. Arthur suffered a mortal wound, and the Britons lost all chance of retaking their lost realm."

"That was just as the stories say, then."

He nodded. "Both Merlin and Morgan had served their principles, so our people decided to honor them. Men of the line thus call themselves sons of Morgan, while our women style themselves daughters of Merlin. We do it in respect and gratitude and to remind ourselves of our kinship to one another."

He took a sip of ale. "What else would you like to know?"

She pondered while she chewed crusty bread and tangy, smooth cheese. "You said the Gifted 'arrived here.' From where? Who were they?"

He shook his head. "No one knows any longer, save that they came from a far distant land."

He didn't seem inclined to add more, and she had run out of questions about history. The silence grew heavy.

He looked thoughtfully at her. "This new ... awareness, if you will, is strange."

"Do you have questions to ask me, Richard?"

"Some." He glanced down at his plate and then up at her. "Have you always been alone? Or only since your parents died?"

"When Mother told me about my Gifts, I began to stay away from other children. I was five, I think. She told me over and over that I mustn't let anyone know what I could do, that discovery meant death, and I knew it would have. I couldn't stop learning. I didn't want to. So I avoided others instead."

"After your parents died, you naturally felt more alone than ever."

"I lived with my uncle and aunt for a few years. Once I was old enough, they tried to find a husband for me, but I couldn't bear the one man who offered. They had several children of their own, and their bakery couldn't support me, too, so they found me the place at the inn."

"It wasn't a home to you."

Miranda shook her head. "I had to keep my distance because of my magic. Besides, some of the other maids thought me haughty, especially for such a supposedly homely girl. I can see how they thought that. I had some education—I could read. And I came from London."

"There's more than you told me to your reasons for disguising yourself," he said, his gaze intent. "If you'll tell me, I'd rather hear the reasons from you than guess."

"Men were looking at me, even before I left London, and in a way that made me uneasy. As though I hadn't any clothes on."

Remembering it made her insides churn, and she caught a flash of anger that seemed, strangely, to be from him. Miranda took a deep breath and finished, "I changed my appearance a bit at a time, so no one who saw me every day would notice. And no one who didn't would look twice. I feared having anyone realize I was different from those around me."

"But you had a friend or two at the inn," he said.

"Oh, yes. Lucy always looked out for me. She looked out for everyone. Bess was my friend, too, but she married and moved away. I hoped to save enough money to someday leave the inn, perhaps find a position in a household. I know it must seem trivial to you, but—"

"Everyone needs a dream, some hope for the future." His mouth turned down at the corners, as though in self-derision. "At least you had the sense to hope for something you might attain."

She wanted to ask what he had not attained, but his stiff posture and shuttered features discouraged her. They ate in silence for a few minutes while she considered how to approach him.

At last, she said, "I find this awkward, Richard. I don't know everything about you, but the things I do know, the images I saw in your eyes in the vision, showed me a life very different from my own."

"A life sometimes not preferable to yours, I would imagine." He set his empty plate on the floor and gave her a wary look. "You needn't sit there searching for words. You answered my questions. I'll answer yours."

"How did you know I was trying to find words?"

His brow furrowed. "I can't explain it. Odd, isn't it?"

"Indeed." How strange. And faintly troubling.

Misgivings aside, though, she liked knowing more about him. She might've been disturbed to have him know how she'd lived, save that he wasn't speaking to her or looking at her any differently.

He shrugged. Spreading his hands, he said, "Tessa warned us. I suppose we'll grow accustomed to this awareness in time, or perhaps it will fade. What do you want to know?" Despite his words, his posture remained stiff and his eyes, averted.

"I saw you clinging to a board. In the Channel, I think. You were afraid, not of dying but of something worse than death. What did I see?"

His body tensed again. His mouth tightened, and an odd echo of discomfort quivered in her chest. Was she feeling what he did? She must be. What had that pool done?

"When I was sixteen, not long before the Restoration, I sailed across the Channel to bring King Charles money from Royalists in England. You may be too young to remember that Cromwell's soldiers, Roundheads to us, demanded elaborate signed permissions for moving through the countryside."

She nodded, and he continued, "To one with my Gifts, their rules presented no difficulty, so I volunteered for the task. On the return trip, I was caught in a storm. The boat sank, fortunately not too far from shore for me to swim. An ordinary man would have died. I managed to live."

He had explained the fear, but not the *worse than death.* Did his evasion have anything to do with the horrible vision she'd unwittingly scried in the fire? She sensed that he didn't want her to press further. Well, there were things she would prefer not to discuss, too.

"One day, near dawn, you went to the chapel of a deserted castle. In summer, I think. You didn't want to. It made you sad and angry. You knelt in a musty chapel with a sword in your hands. Will you tell me about that? Or have I trespassed on your good will?"

He took a deep breath. Fleeting sharpness like the ghost of pain flitted through her chest. The lines in his face deepened.

"I had to go there, to a place called Middleham, in Yorkshire, on Midsummer Night for my family's honor." His voice rasped, as though he dragged the words from somewhere deep inside him. "As generations have before me, I went there to honor our debt to Richard III. I'd promised my father I would."

"What debt? And why Yorkshire?"

"If you don't know what the debt is, I'd rather not go into it." When she nodded assent, not wanting to pry into something private, he added, "I went to Middleham because that was King Richard's favorite holding. No one has lived in the castle for some time, so I was able to use its chapel. My father used the village church."

His smile looked forced, and the echo of his difficulty producing it jabbed into her heart. He said, "Doing such a thing in London would be rather conspicuous."

Remembering that sudden flash of lightning, she nodded. An odd tangle of emotions coiled in her chest. Bitterness warred with sadness and a strange pride, none of them her own.

Taken together, her vision and this awareness of him signaled some dreadful doom awaiting him, a horrible fate he didn't believe he could escape and didn't want to discuss.

Despite it, he treated his servants kindly, risked his life for England, and offered her reassurance, even hope for a better life. If only she could comfort him, but his closed expression warned her not to try.

The silence suddenly seemed awkward. She bent to collect their dishes and cups.

"I'll do that," he said. "The servants are long since abed. As for the vision, it confirms our original interpretation of your dream, with the added details of the stag and the small dragons. The stag likely represents Sir George Buck, who wrote a defense of King Richard. That's the book that has been altered."

Trying to recall what he'd said a few days ago, she asked, "Because a monastic chronicle has gone missing?"

Richard nodded. "That chronicle contained material vital to the book's defense of the king. As for the dragons, they likely stand for all those who've gnawed away at the king's good name."

"I wonder why I never saw them in an earlier vision."

"Likely because you can't control the visions yet, so you receive only glimpses. Once you refine your skills, you'll be able to explore the images as we did this evening, but without needing the pool's water. At least the rite gave us a clue, sending us to Croyland, or Crowland, as the old name was, where the *Chronicle* was written."

"What do you think we can do there?"

"The *Chronicle* contained material, as we discussed, that undercuts the idea that King Richard had a motive for murdering his nephews. It also may have clues to traveling in time. Perhaps that's why the vision sends us to Croyland."

"Do you think whoever caused all this upheaval has the *Chronicle*?"

"It seems likely."

He gathered the crockery. Setting it on the tray, he said, "Perhaps the book we saw in the rite was the *Chronicle*. If not, perhaps the monks treasured it enough to make a copy. Someone may have hidden it at the Dissolution of the Monasteries, and someone in Croyland may have that secret copy."

"That seems like a very thin hope."

"It does, and I don't see what use finding a copy would be, unless we can somehow substitute it for the original. Or if it contains other information we need, of course. Regardless, I think we are summoned to Croyland."

"I agree. Where is Croyland, anyway?"

"In Lincolnshire. Assuming a secret copy of the *Chronicle* exists, someone of Catholic sympathies, if not the Catholic faith, probably has it. Persuading anyone to admit to either the faith or the copy will take some doing. Anyone whose family has kept the thing this long probably treasures it, besides not wanting to risk imprisonment for nonconforming religious practices."

"Of course."

"The queen is Catholic and may be able to help. I'll request an audience. But now you should try to rest. Dealing with magic as strong as the pool tires even those with more experience than you have in working with such power."

"I am rather weary now," she admitted.

They walked to the doorway together. In the opening, he turned. The blue of his eyes darkened into an intent stare.

He set the tray on the corridor floor and took her hands in his. The contact now seemed disturbingly familiar. A tingle of warmth brushed her heart.

"You won't have to struggle anymore," he assured her. "Whatever happens, I'll see that you have a safe place to go, a comfortable place that you like. I swear it."

Then she would never see him again. Her stomach felt suddenly cold and hollow, but she smiled. "I know you will, Richard. I thank you for that."

"I couldn't do otherwise."

Yet his loneliness still echoed in her heart. As though of its own volition, her right hand slowly rose. Did she dare? He didn't draw away, so she brushed her fingertips over the lines of care around his eyes. "You are very kind, and quite amazing. I only wish I could repay you in some way."

He clasped her hands in his and raised them to his mouth. His warm breath brushed over her knuckles before he kissed them. Awareness of him, of his touch, his dark hair soft against her wrist, and the warmth in his eyes rippled through her.

"If I were an ordinary wizard," he said, "or even an ordinary man, I would court you, Miranda. But I am not. My family carries a curse I've sworn not to continue. Marriage is thus not for me, and anything less is not for you."

The pool had given her no knowledge of what that curse was, and he clearly didn't mean to tell her. Searching his gaze, she said, "Sometimes a man tries to protect a woman from things she doesn't fear."

"That's a man's duty, to protect the women around him."

Still holding her hands, he gave her a wry smile. "Use your Gifts well and be happy, and you will repay me in full."

It was a generous answer, so why did she feel so hollow inside?

CHAPTER 19

Richard woke abruptly. Edmund sat in the chair by the hearth. "Good morrow, grandson."

Sitting up in bed, Richard scrubbed a hand over his face. The mantel clock softly chimed five, and he sighed. Frequent practice might help him reach the shadowland sooner, but he also needed to sleep.

He climbed out of the bed he'd scarcely had time to warm. "I'll fetch my pebble."

"I'd hoped you would reconsider this mad scheme," Edmund said, scowling, as Richard walked to his desk.

"I can't." Richard plucked the stone from the desk's top drawer. "I've had enough of debating this, Edmund. It's necessary, and if I'm willing to bear the risks involved, the man who dragged his family into an apparently unending mire is in no position to argue. Besides, for all any of us knows, I might be the next to vanish."

Edmund's eyes flashed. His gaze locked with Richard's. Richard set his jaw. Enough was, by God's feet, enough. This was important in a way that far transcended any one family's troubles.

At last, Edmund looked down. "So be it."

He squared his shoulders and stared at Richard. "Hold the stone in your hand. Now, think of how this feels, talking to me. Form a portal and reach for me."

Richard tried, rimming his dressing room door in magic.

"Are you reaching, lad?"

"Aye."

Richard walked. Kept walking. A cold current pushed against him. He crossed the dressing room threshold and halted, swallowing a frustrated *'Od's fish.*

Edmund shook his head. "Are you keeping your mind on me?"

"As best I can. I did feel the cold again."

"That's a good sign. Try again."

They spent the next hour and a bit more on fruitless attempts. At last, Richard conceded defeat for the night and climbed back into the bed. "We can try again tonight."

"Why not now?"

"I'm to meet Jeremy at Lambeth Palace and go through the archbishop's archives again." If they were lucky, they'd find a point of change to help narrow their search for the pivotal event. Or else references to a fifteenth-century heresy trial involving claims of time travel.

"Before you go," Richard said, "I've a question." He told Edmund about the vision of Wyndon stealing the scroll from Pendragon's library.

Frowning, Edmund rubbed his jaw. "Despite all the time I've spent here, there's much I don't know about this place. I do know, however, that there are differing levels of power. The wraiths are mad, almost mindless. They're trapped here, and I can command them, perhaps because I'm not condemned to remain here. Yet I cannot leave. If Wyndon did as you say, he's able to travel here freely. That may mean he has abilities I do not, as I have those the wraiths do not."

Edmund hesitated for a moment. "You know, Richard, that Willoughby lass has much to recommend her. There is an old saying, *A seer need not scry to See what is, what was, and what will be.* She could help you determine which events should be happening and which should not. And she possesses not only magical Gifts but strength of heart. A man wants that strength in a wife."

"Don't tread that path." Richard swallowed against a surge of frustration. Miranda would help straighten things out no matter what happened between them. If he wanted more, that was his problem. It wasn't going to be hers. "You trapped all your direct heirs with your guilt, Edmund. I won't allow you to drag her into it as well."

"Marriage, a good marriage, can help stave off the curse-spawned madness, Richard. It's obvious you care for her."

"I do," Richard said evenly. "Too much to inflict our family troubles on her, so stop pushing."

Edmund's shoulders drooped. "I do regret all this, lad."

Softly, Richard said, "I know, but unfortunately that doesn't mend much. Take yourself off, Edmund. I must dress and head to Lambeth."

While he searched the archives with Jeremy and Cabot this morning, he would try not to think about how much Kit enjoyed any kind of puzzle. This afternoon, he and Miranda had an audience with Queen Catherine to request her help with the Catholics of Croyland.

Nodding, the ghost said, "Farewell, grandson."

Edmund's image wavered and disappeared. Richard rubbed eyes. A moment later, the clock on his mantel struck six.

He hadn't told his valet to attend him. As he stoked the fire and then dressed, he considered his actions of the night before. Perhaps he shouldn't have told Miranda so much. Better to say too much, though, to a woman who believed herself insignificant, than to leave her ignorant of her value.

The pool had done something to them both. Created a ... sympathy of some sort. Yes, he'd been drawn to her from the time they met, but this increased wanting, this tenderness, was an effect of the bespelled water. It would surely fade in time.

He knotted his cravat, a plain linen one instead of the ornate, lacy ones he wore when he went to court. Now he knew why Miranda had adopted such a homely disguise. She hadn't done it, as he'd originally assumed, so she could exercise discretion in choosing her swains. She had done it so she would have no swains. She had chosen loneliness over a loveless marriage.

He'd made the same choice for different reasons.

Yet after all his care around women, fate did this to him. It threw into his protection a woman he could love.

The image of her rose in his mind, her fingers warm and gentle on his face as she sought to ease his pain. Richard shuddered.

No. Not a woman he could love. A woman he did love.

The thought went through him like a hammer stroke. It froze his arm as he grasped a shoe.

He couldn't love her. He wouldn't.

That way lay disaster.

The flames danced in the hearth. As they would one day for George— still his heir, no matter how unfit. There was no helping that, though.

Richard had a duty to the generations to come, even if he could save them only by stopping their coming.

Yet Kit's reminder echoed in his ears. He also had a duty to the folk of Hawkstowe.

Richard shook his head. He would tend to his people by fixing the sequence of time so George never became betrothed to the Wyndon girl. Then he would shake some sense into George.

But he wouldn't ruin Miranda's life for the sake of his duty.

Women always admired Sir Lancelot, he thought, buckling his shoes. They saw his noble strengths and his hopeless love. Lacking the armor of legend, no real man could measure up to that.

A man could do better in one way, though. Lancelot's mythical piety and strength dazzled women so that they overlooked his great failing. That lay not in loving Guinevere. No man could choose where he loved, as Richard now knew beyond doubt. No, Lancelot failed in that he allowed his love to bring Guinevere to ruin.

Richard would see that nothing of the sort happened to Miranda.

~

Queen Catherine received Richard and Miranda in her closet, a small, private chamber in her suite of rooms. Two windows in the paneled walls looked out on the Thames, and a painting of a large church hung on the wall by the door. One lady in waiting stood behind the queen, who sat in an ornate chair by one window. A tapestry of a pastoral scene hung beside her chair.

Being private with royalty was even more intimidating than being presented at a large gathering. Miranda's throat felt tight, and her breath seemed short. *Please don't let me have to say anything.*

Queen Catherine smiled. With a nod at the painting, she said, "The Cathedral and monastery of St. Jeronimo in Belém, near my home in Lisbon." Gesturing to the three less ornate chairs grouped near hers, she added, "You may be seated, if you wish."

Miranda's throat eased. The queen must've seen her looking at the painting, but her casual manner made the occasion less frighteningly formal.

Holding his plumed hat in one hand, Richard said, "We thank Your Majesty. For the boon we mean to ask, however, we prefer to stand."

"Intriguing." Queen Catherine's glance sharpened. "What say you, then, my lord?"

"We come on a quest, Majesty." He glanced at Miranda. "It's a matter of ancestry."

"Your lovely companion's ancestry, perhaps?" The queen directed a warm glance at Miranda. "Is this, perchance, regarding a possible marriage?"

Miranda's cheeks heated, but Richard's expression didn't change. She couldn't sense what he felt.

"One never knows," he said gravely. "The monks at Croyland created a chronicle that contains information we need. We hope someone in the town may have kept a copy when the abbey was dissolved, and we need Your Majesty's help."

The queen's expression hardened. "What sort of help?"

Understanding that reaction too well, Miranda found the courage to speak. "As Your Majesty doubtless knows, those of your faith have little reason to trust strangers these days. Coming from a family of Dissenters, I understand this."

The queen's eyes flashed. "England has treated us shamefully," she said in a low, tight voice.

"I can only, with regret, concur," Richard said. "Those of your faith in Croyland will have no reason to confide in us or even to acknowledge their faith. Why should they risk fines or harassment on our behalf? Unless I have a reference from someone on whose word they know they can rely."

"You do, indeed, ask a great boon." The queen stared over their heads, considering.

At last, she glanced from one to the other of them. "We can promise you naught, my lord, save that we will consider your request. Either way, we will notify you of our decision."

The tension in his shoulders eased. Bowing, he said, "Your Majesty has our deepest gratitude."

"Save your thanks until you know whether we can help you. You may withdraw."

They thanked her and backed from the room. In the anteroom, a stout, middle-aged man stood as they passed. He headed for the queen's door, and the usher announced him as Master Withers from the Worshipful Company of Bowyers.

Richard leaned over to Miranda. "Her Majesty is patroness of the

Archers' Company of the Honorable Artillery Company," he explained. "Since the bowyers make the bows, she takes an interest in their charitable pursuits."

A queen interested in archery? Who would've guessed?

An usher opened the corridor door, and they stepped into the hallway. "We'll go home and practice," Richard said. "After what you did at the frost fair, I suspect your control is much improved."

As they reached the stairs, a cheerful voice behind them called, "Ah, there you are, Richard."

He shot her a warning look as they turned.

King Charles's long legs carried him down the corridor at a pace that made his chest-length, curly black wig fly out at the sides and left his less fit courtiers several paces behind. Half a dozen of them trailed him, their faces red with the effort of keeping up.

Miranda swallowed a gasp and curtsied to the floor.

"A good day to Your Majesty," Richard said, bowing deeply.

"The same to you, my friend, and to you—Mistress Willoughby, is it? The queen told us you were coming today. You are just in time to see our new experiment." The king didn't break stride.

Richard smiled at Miranda and tugged her upright. The king's party turned a corridor. She and the earl joined the small group behind him. They turned another corner and plunged down a staircase.

"We're headed for the privy garden," Richard said.

They would be cold, but perhaps the king was too excited to care. For that matter, she didn't either. She and Richard accompanied the king by his personal invitation, a privilege she'd never thought to have.

A fortnight ago, she would've tried to avoid this because she feared she couldn't fit in. Now, thanks to Richard and his grandmother, she had learned to move through these circles as though she belonged. This day would be another memory to cherish. If she remembered anything of this once they fixed the timeline.

"What experiment is this, Your Majesty?" Richard asked.

"For a more powerful telescope. Has to do with the size of the mirrors, or so we are told. Very promising." The king smiled in anticipation.

"How marvelous," Miranda whispered to Richard.

"The king loves such things," he said as they burst into the winter sunshine. "He has a laboratory in his private apartments."

The walled garden spread south toward Westminster, filling the space between the street, which was simply called The Street, and the Thames with wide, square plots of grass. They were brown now, but each held a statue. Men, women, children, birds, and even monsters graced the various squares.

The path before them led to a large pillar with odd-looking, circular inserts at the corners. As they walked past it, she noticed that there were four such faces, as well as one each facing north, south, east, and west.

"Sundial," Richard murmured. At her blank look, he added, "A way to tell the hour using the sun."

"How clever!"

"Yes. The king loves it."

Miranda had never seen a sundial. If only she could examine it further, but the king's rapid pace gave her no chance. That was all right, though, with so much to look at.

She glanced up at the palace walls. At the corridor window above the garden, near the banqueting house, George Mainwaring stood glaring down at them. He would hurt Richard if he could.

Richard didn't seem to notice, but Miranda glared back before moving closer to the earl.

Alas that she could do little to protect him from George's treachery. Richard deserved better from a kinsman. He was loyal, brave, and selfless.

No wonder she loved him.

Stunned, she stared across the garden and took a shuddering breath.

"Are you cold?" Richard asked, shifting so that his body blocked the wind from the river.

"I'm all right," she managed.

She'd felt this for days, but she'd told herself it was fondness or gratitude or friendship. Anything but what it was. But now, standing here beside him with his cousin looking so menacingly at him, she couldn't deny her feelings.

Unfortunately, there was nothing to be done about them. Nothing save enjoying what time she had with him. That time was fleeting anyway, and fixing the timeline might mean they didn't even remember each other.

As though sensing her distress, he clasped her hand. The folds of their cloaks concealed the grip, so no one would notice, but the contact and the affection that came with it were a comfort.

The king's words flowed around her like the babble of a distant brook. She couldn't love Richard. Not a man who stood so far above her. A man whose blood carried a curse.

But she did.

~

"I don't know which would be worse," Richard said to Cabot that evening, "plague or a sickness such as the one ripping through the livestock." The two men waited for Jeremy in a narrow alley south of the old artillery ground in Spitalfields.

"I don't want the opportunity to know." Cabot glanced at the guarded doorway Jeremy had entered.

"Nor do I," Richard told him, "but they wouldn't have sent to the archbishop for a mere ague."

He and Cabot paced back and forth to stay warm. This situation brought to mind the plague vision of Miranda's that Grandmère had described to him. Alas that it hadn't been more detailed.

"Horrible as plague is," Richard said, "it would be more manageable than the mysterious ailment killing livestock."

"True enough," Cabot muttered.

The Gifted could sometimes cure early cases of plague. They couldn't cure whatever ailed the animals because they couldn't identify it.

If that spread to people ...

It was bad enough to have people disappearing, he thought with a pang of loss for Kit, to have them not even remembered by anyone unGifted who loved them. Now this.

Word had reached Lambeth Palace this afternoon. The archbishop had sent Jeremy, who was dining with Richard and Cabot at a tavern near Lambeth Palace when word reached him, to investigate.

Cabot blew out an explosive breath. "What the devil's keeping Jeremy?"

Richard smiled. "Jeremy's patient. Unlike either of us. He'll take his time."

No one had yet painted the red *X* denoting plague on the door of the afflicted house, despite the guard outside. Only invoking the archbishop's authority had gained Jeremy admittance.

"We'll need healers," Richard said quietly, stamping his feet against the chill. "As with the outbreak in 'sixty-five."

The Gifted healers had saved many, but even their strength had limits. More than sixty-eight thousand people had died despite Gifted healers who worked themselves into exhaustion.

Richard paced along the alley. "I need to go, Cabot, to Croyland. Whatever the answer to this time problem, it doesn't lie in London."

"You trust her vision that much, then?"

"Absolutely," Richard said, surprised to find that he meant it.

"No word from the queen?" Cabot asked.

"Not so far." Richard stared down the alleyway. "In truth, I'm tempted not to wait for Her Majesty's response. I feel as though time is slipping away and we must act soon or else fail."

"Yet you're taking Miranda. Didn't you say traveling by coach makes her ill?"

Richard nodded. "She needs Grandmère's posset to endure any long journey. But Wyndon has taken an interest in her, and she's safer with me than here with Grandmère. I don't trust the house wards to keep Wyndon out if he's truly determined. Besides, I don't want to risk her having another significant dream in my absence."

Nor did he want to leave her for days. Parting would come soon enough.

"After what she did at the frost fair," Richard mused, "I thought her control had improved. Then the ritual with the water carried it to new levels." Ones that were embarrassing for them both. "She now can light or snuff candles and has made a good start at learning defensive magic. While she can't yet control a visionary scrying, she can handle a basic one."

After a moment, Cabot said, "Have you thought what to do about her when you conclude this quest?"

"She told Grandmère she likes to sew. I thought I might set her up with her own shop somewhere—perhaps in Havelock, if Kit knew of a place."

If they set history to rights, Kit would return, but Miranda would likely disappear into a past where she and Richard had never met. Hating the idea, he forced his voice level. "A woman alone would be safer in a village than in a place like London or Dover."

"So she would." Looking up at the cloudy sky, Cabot noted, "Of course, the only true security for a woman lies in marriage."

Richard's gut tightened, but he kept his voice even. A few more exchanges, and he could broach the subject his conscience had been spurring him to raise. "Perhaps she'll meet someone once she finds a home."

Cabot shook his head. "Unlikely, though I would hope she might. She's too refined."

Richard couldn't argue with that. Her educated speech and her stubborn ways and her personal fastidiousness would render most of the men she would likely meet in a small village unappealing to her. Unless, of course, she grew lonely enough to settle for one of them.

After a moment, Cabot said, "You obviously care for her. Why don't you marry her?"

"You know why." It was just like Cabot to twist a plan that way. "And before you remind me what Kit said, I assure you I haven't forgotten, but I've a duty to her as well as to the folk on my lands." And the doomed heirs he'd resolved not to sire.

Richard gazed at the narrow doorway across the alley without seeing it. Here was the chance he'd sought, an opportunity to suggest that Cabot marry Miranda. There was no one Richard would trust with her more. Yet the words stuck in his throat.

Jeremy stepped out into the moonlight, his presence a welcome excuse to delay the unhappy topic. Jeremy spoke quietly to the guard, who nodded.

Turning to Richard and Cabot, Jeremy shrugged. "This is as Miranda foresaw, but it's not plague."

They walked a little way down the street. "It looks like plague," he continued, "with swelling and red blotches in the groin and armpits. The stench of the afflicted person's breath is similar, but it has a different feel to it."

"What do you mean?" Richard asked.

"When I touch someone afflicted with plague," Jeremy said, "I know that's what it is. You would, too, if you'd spent a lot of time on healing. I recognize it. This isn't it."

They walked several paces in silence. The streets were always less crowded after dark, but now, with only a few people scurrying about their business, they seemed eerily empty.

Jeremy said, "I don't know what's sickening people. I pray it's not a reaction to unnatural forces in the world, such as the animals have had."

He shoved his hair out of his face and sighed. "I only know what isn't doing it, and I wasn't able to give that man much ease, perhaps because I can't stop whatever's making him ill. Meanwhile, I must think of something to tell the archbishop."

Richard didn't envy him. Archbishop Sheldon was no one's fool, and dealing with unGifted people about such matters posed delicate questions of truth. "I'll go home, then," Richard said, "and send word to Lucius, though I won't wait for another infernal, tedious debate in the Council. Do you have a recommendation?"

"Considering how quickly this seems to be spreading—five houses on this street already, with two dead—and how fast the animals died … " Jeremy hesitated. "Fix the blasted timeline, or we'll have a situation that makes the plague of '65 look like a small inconvenience."

CHAPTER 20

William sauntered into the Wyndon House library. "I've news, Father."

"Did you arrange for plague relief, as I instructed you? We must keep up appearances while we await the final changes." Henry set his book, the Earl of Rochester's poems, on the table beside his chair.

The future he intended to carve for England was worth a few deaths, but aid would convince the other Gifted to continue ignoring Hawkstowe's suspicions. "Once the changes overtake the present, all should be well, but we must appear concerned until then."

"Of course I made the contributions. Told Lucius I'd volunteer for the Conclave's healers, though I'm not that good at it. Then I had coffee with George Mainwaring."

Grinning, William plopped into a chair. "George bribed a kitchen maid he used to bed. With money I gave him. A royal messenger came to Hawkstowe House this morning. Not an hour later, Hawkstowe and the girl set out in his carriage with a maid and baggage."

Henry acknowledged the maneuver with a nod. "That's reliable, then. They're away from their friends. Vulnerable."

"Are you going after them?"

"Of course. Where did they go?"

"Lincolnshire," William said. "Crow-something."

Croyland, it must be. Perfect. That was far enough from London to make travel between the two slow and torturous, especially with the roads so battered and mired from the weather.

Henry smiled. "Every man has his weakness, my son. Hawkstowe's is that he cares."

If Henry could isolate the wench, he could force her to tell him whatever she knew. She was stubborn about questions, but perhaps she could be tricked into revelations.

He could also eliminate her if need be. Nothing could stand in the way of the changes now rolling forward. If the girl had Seen some way to undo them, she had to die.

CHAPTER 21

P*lease*, Miranda thought, watching the priest, *let this man have what we need*. Though the day was fading, she and Richard had come directly here upon reaching Croyland, pausing only to take rooms at the inn.

Father Gregory read the queen's brief message slowly. He looked to be in his mid-forties, with gray hair at his temples and strands of gray in his tidy, brown beard. Deep lines of care marked his face and fanned from the corners of his eyes. Considering the increasing persecution of Catholics, Miranda supposed the priest had ample worries to age a man early, even without the food shortages and plague-like disease spreading in London.

Richard's expression showed only polite interest, but she knew how much this meant to him.

The cottage's plank floors and tiny hearth fire provided little comfort to offset those cares. The room bore no ornamentation except a dark wooden crucifix on the wall by the hearth. Hung with worn, brown wool curtains, the poorly leaded windows provided little defense against the drafts.

While their host examined the royal seal, Miranda resisted the urge to slide her chair closer to the fire. Her fur muff's comfort felt decadent in such barren surroundings.

Father Gregory's brown eyes rose, studying them. "An impressive recommendation." He folded the paper and handed it to Richard, who slipped it into his coat pocket. "What help do you seek, my lord?"

"Have you heard, Father, of the *Croyland Chronicle?*"

"I can't say that I have. I assume there's some connection with the old monastery here?"

"For several hundred years, the Croyland monks kept a record of the events in the realm. It may hold information important to my family. I hope someone may have kept a copy when the monastery was dissolved. Someone who might have entrusted it to a Catholic family here in Croyland."

"You want my help in finding that copy, if it exists."

Richard nodded. "Your parishioners have no reason to trust me, a nobleman not of their faith. Without your help, I cannot hope that they would disclose anything to me. Even locating them is a problem. Asking everyone I meet who his Catholic neighbors are would hardly earn me anyone's trust."

"No, it wouldn't." The priest shrugged. "I'll ask about the book, but I think I would know if anyone in my parish had such a thing. It would be greatly treasured."

"We appreciate whatever help you can give us, Father, even if it leads to naught."

"It well may. My inquiries will take a few days. How can I reach you, milord, mistress?"

Richard rose. Miranda and their host also stood.

"We're at the Royal Oak in the High Street. Ask for Richard Mainwaring." When the priest raised his eyebrows, Richard explained, "I consider this business private. People tend to pay attention to Lord Anybody, but no one will give an untitled gentleman a second glance."

"Very well, my lord. I hope to have news for you soon, but I must again caution you not to hope for much."

With a wry smile, Richard said, "Nor do I, Father, but I cannot overlook any possibility."

Miranda dropped the priest a curtsey. "Good day, Father."

The priest's eyebrows rose, but he didn't comment. Still, he deserved that mark of respect, the only one she could offer.

Richard gestured for her to precede him. When they reached the door, he paused. "For the poor box, with our thanks for your help." He drew a fat purse from his coat pocket and set it on the table by the door.

A flush of gratitude stained the priest's thin cheeks. "Thank you for that, milord. Our parish has many needs."

"In the current political climate, I imagine so, but not everyone agrees with the extremists in Parliament. I'm glad to be of help." He bowed and ushered Miranda out.

As the door closed, she heard coins clink. Softly, she said, "That was well done of you, Richard."

"'Tis only fair. I put enough gold in that purse to support a small household for a year. It won't make up for jobs lost to the Test Act, but it will feed a few people."

Again, he displayed his generous nature. As he'd taken her in, clothed her, and treated her well, he was offering aid to those the king and Parliament would see shunned.

The Test Act barred Catholics and anyone else refusing to profess allegiance to the Church of England from holding public office. Many had lost their positions because of it, falling into poverty and desperation.

A swineherd and his three snuffling, muddy charges rambled down the street. The pigs looked pitifully thin.

"Not much of a herd." Richard nudged Miranda sideways, against the wall of a house, and stood between her and the beasts. Their passage churned the damp soil into a muddy bog.

"Thus far, Croyland has little to recommend it," he noted.

"I can't dispute that." Save that it gave them time, however fleeting, together. Perhaps she should feel guilty about taking pleasure in something that came of such tragedy, but she couldn't regret any time spent with him.

Even the High Street in Croyland was dirt. If not for the thick wooden pattens, or undersoles, she wore with her shoes, she'd be ankle-deep in the mire.

Most of the houses stood close together, as those in London had before the fire, with overhanging upper stories that blocked the sunlight. Puddles of slop dumped from upper windows added to the general stench. She and Richard stayed close to the walls to avoid any that were dumped as they passed. Despite the pattens, his arm provided welcome support as they slid through the mud.

"I feel as though we're running out of time," she said. "I haven't Seen anything, but I have a strong feeling of urgency."

"As do I. Even the weather returning to the usual doesn't seem right. It's like the calm before the storm. Although I'm needed in London, I feel as though I should go to Hawkstowe. My scrying shows my steward is coping well, but I should be with my people."

The crowds still in town for market day only added to the general muck and mess. Richard had been lucky to find rooms at a good inn. Crowds also brought the danger of sickness, but there was nothing to be done about that. People had business to transact.

The Royal Oak's faded sign came into view, a tree with a man, supposedly King Charles, in its branches. With the sun almost set, the image was harder to make out.

"At last," Richard said. "I'm ready for a hot meal."

They entered the inn. "Go on upstairs," he said. "I'll order food sent up."

With narrow windows in the front and none elsewhere, the long, low-ceilinged taproom was dim. Dingy, once-white plaster walls reflected lantern light poorly. Pipe smoke mixed an acrid stench into the food aromas and clouded the view of the room.

Miranda gave him a wry smile. "Considering the mud, Patience will be doubly grateful that we had her wait here." Richard hadn't wanted to make the maid privy to the discussion, and that had worked to Patience's advantage, letting her stay snug and warm in the hotel today.

"M'lord!" The cry came from across the tap room.

They swung toward it, Richard frowning. "Perhaps that call isn't for me," he murmured.

A sturdy figure pushed through the gloom and the crowd. "M'lord—that is, master!"

"Robin!" Richard stepped forward, then halted abruptly.

Miranda also stopped. What was the stable lad doing here? His pale face and worried frown boded ill.

"Master. I've news from London. Dire news, mil—sir."

The earl shot him a warning look. "We'll talk upstairs, Robin. You might have waited there with Patience."

"I wanted to see you as soon as you came in, master."

"I'll order the food," Miranda said. "Go on."

Richard thanked her with a nod. "Come, Robin." He mounted the stairs two at a time with the boy behind him.

When Miranda reached their private parlor, Richard greeted her with a tense expression. "Grandmère's ill. Has been since the day after we left."

"Oh, no—not that mysterious sickness?" She sank into a chair, the food she'd ordered forgotten. His worry tightened her chest and knotted her stomach, doubling the effect of her own concern.

"No, mistress," Robin said. "Quite sick to her stomach, she was, Jane said. But not this new plague or whatever 'tis."

Richard nodded at the reference to his grandmother's maid. "Go on, Robin."

"She wouldn't let nobody bleed her. When she stopped sickin' up and fell to sleep, Jane, she thought that was a good sign. Next morn, though, milady woke up a bit but wouldn't open her eyes. Mumbled about not t'bleed her and to send fer Reverend Winfield on account of him being good with herbs."

"What happened next?" Richard asked, his voice flint.

Miranda folded her hands in her lap, her grip tightening, as his impatience thrummed in her body.

"She fell back asleep. They couldn't rouse her, and the reverend was gone to Canterbury the day before she fell ill, and the cap'n with him, so Enderby, he said I was to come tell you. Sent me on Zeus, he did, figurin' as how you'd come in your coach and so would need a fast horse to ride back. He thought you wouldn't want no hired horse what might go lame on you."

The lad paused for breath, his face anxious. "I hope I done right, milord."

"Yes, Robin." Richard spoke calmly, gripping Robin's shoulder, but the fear jabbing him echoed Miranda's. "Go down to the kitchen and ask for food and a bed." He frowned at Miranda. "Did we order food?"

"It should arrive soon," she said.

Questions screamed in Robin's uneasy look, but he left the room as bidden.

Richard rubbed a hand over his face, finally letting his worry show. "Poison could have the effect Robin described, but how would she have taken poison? Not that it matters now. I've no time to waste."

"You must go at once, of course."

No hint of his feelings now leaked through his tight control, but his set face and stony eyes betrayed his anxiety. "They should have sent to

Lucius or even to Jeremy in Canterbury, but it's too late for that now. I can reach home faster than I can send word telling them who else could help." He walked to the hearth with his hands extended toward the fire.

After a moment, he said, "Have Patience pack your things. It's too late to set out now, so we'll leave at first light."

"We?" She frowned at him. "Enderby sent Robin on Zeus so you could make the best possible speed back to London, which you agree is critical. He made it here in a bit more than three days. Now you want to wait for the coach, which took five days? You could travel faster alone. I could wait here for news."

"Out of the question."

"Or follow you at a slower pace."

"Absolutely not." He scowled at her. "I won't leave you unprotected."

"Someone should wait to hear from Father Gregory."

"Grandmère's illness stinks of coincidence. I'll take no unnecessary risks with your safety."

"You risk your grandmother's life if you delay."

Pain flashed through his eyes. "She expects me to protect you, and I will."

Miranda glared at him. "What about what I expect?"

"You can't want me to leave you here. Grandmère may be genuinely ill, or she may have been poisoned. If the latter, it was done either to bring me out of Croyland or to separate me from you. I would rather risk Croyland."

His answer warmed her, but she forged ahead. "You can't know that. What about the time shift? The dreadful weather, the crop failures? The people disappearing?"

A flash of pain in his eyes told her that shot had gone home.

Though she shouldn't discount the possibility that Wyndon wanted to isolate her, she couldn't let Arabella die. Or give up a chance to find the *Chronicle* and put everything right again.

His face set in an expression she could only call dogged. "I have a responsibility to keep you safe."

Even if that meant sacrificing his grandmother? Miranda couldn't let him do that. "If Lord Wyndon harmed me, what would you do?"

His face hardened. "I'd kill him."

Around a rush of selfish pleasure, she said, "Surely he knows that. I'm safe from him, wherever I am."

"Unless he wants to provoke me into a duel."

"He must have any number of other ways to do that."

"He could provoke me in many ways," Richard said slowly, as though the words escaped against his will, "but none that would matter more to me. Not even the one he may already have chosen." Raw passion turned his eyes a dark, stormy blue.

Fierce joy pounded through her heart as desire crackled between them, but she made herself speak calmly. "The king, I assume, would also want an explanation, and so might the Conclave. So Wyndon has reason to avoid angering you. If he caused your grandmother's illness, he did it to draw you away from here, which bodes well for the results of our inquiries."

His shoulders relaxed. His eyes lost their intent stare, as though he considered what she had said.

He shook his head. "I won't risk it."

"Instead, you would risk your grandmother, who has done so much for me. No. I'll walk out of here first."

"You wouldn't. You've nowhere to go."

"I've worked all my life. I'll find a job." Her gaze locked with his. "I mean it, Richard. I do."

His eyes flashed. His jaw tightened. After a long moment, he ground out, "So be it, then, my lady, and may neither of us come to rue this day."

Weak pre-dawn light filtered through the parlor window, where Miranda stood watching the inn yard. An ostler brought Zeus into view. The stallion pranced as though he couldn't wait to depart. She saw no sign of Richard. Would he come to her, or had she angered him so much that he would ride away without a word?

She had presented a brave front to him out of necessity, but now that he was going, doubts clamored in her head.

Surely she would wait alone only for a few days, perhaps a sennight at most. Then she would be safe in London again.

She forced her chin up. Until Richard left, she would show no trace of concern. After that, she would do whatever necessity demanded of her.

In the hallway, a board creaked. Her pulse kicked, and Richard walked into the room. He was dressed for travel, in sturdy wool clothes and high leather boots.

He tossed his hat and his oiled leather cloak onto a chair and set a small, fat purse on the table beside it. "I don't know how I let you talk me into this."

"It's the right thing to do, and you know it."

"I wish I did."

He paced to the window. Staring down into the yard, he said, "I've paid the bill for the next ten days. That should suffice. That purse is for you, for any further expenses."

She nodded, and he continued, "It should be enough for any need that might arise. When I reach London, I'll send the Hawkstowe outriders, most of whom are Gifted, to escort you. Don't start home without them. Robin knows them. If he has any doubts, wait here for me. I'll return as soon as I can."

Even Gifted outriders would do only so much good against a wizard who could travel time, but they ought to deter any bandits. Although she hated to think of Richard riding back and forth so hastily, it seemed the wisest course. "As you wish, Richard."

"I'll be off, then." His glance caught hers. The shadow of her pain darkened his eyes. He, too, saw their final parting ahead. "Miranda ... "

She couldn't have said which of them moved first, but they met in the center of the room. As she reached up to him, Richard caught her close and lowered his head. Open and demanding, his mouth locked with hers. Her lips parted in instinctive welcome. Heat rushed through her veins and pooled in her lower body. Aching to be close to him, she lost awareness of everything else.

His mouth left hers to press hot, hard kisses down her throat and over the swell of her breasts. Gasping, she rocked against him, and he claimed her mouth again with a wordless, impatient sound.

Lost in a haze of pleasure and need and longing, she clung to him. An indeterminate time later, her head began to clear.

Outside, a horse whinnied.

I must go.

She heard him say it but couldn't understand how. He couldn't have spoken, not while he was kissing her.

Breathing hard, he raised his head. The depths of his eyes burned with the same fiery, frustrated desire that sizzled through her veins and ached in the depths of her body. She longed for the right to voice it, but he had made it clear that there could be no future for them, regardless of whether they could set history right. Instead, she touched his cheek gently.

He caught her hands, kissed them, and pressed them against his heart. "Don't leave the inn, Miranda. Promise me. Aside from other concerns, I don't want you to risk this sickness."

"The Gifted are immune, aren't we?"

"Thus far, but that may not last. Nor will it protect Patience or Robin."

With his departure looming, his worries returned. She felt them in his tight grip and read them in his intense stare. "I promise. I'll pray for your grandmother."

"I'll see you soon." He kissed her hands again and left.

She hurried to the window. A few moments later, wearing his hat and cloak, he emerged from the inn. With the ease of a natural horseman, he swung onto Zeus's back. He looked up at the window and raised a gloved hand to the brim of his hat in salute. Before she could return the gesture, he wheeled the stallion toward the gate.

Then they were gone. She took a slow, deep breath. Despite her insistence that he go, she had a niggling fear that he was right, that someone had intended to separate them.

Yet she had done what was right. She believed that with all her heart. But if trouble came, she would have to face it alone.

CHAPTER 22

T wo days and a bit more of idleness, coupled with worry for Arabella, took a toll on Miranda's patience. Richard had left the day before yesterday. With luck, he would reach London today. She hoped so. His grandmother needed his help.

Meanwhile, Miranda was heartily weary of the inn's parlor. Not even the warming glow of afternoon sunlight could make its dull, cream-colored walls interesting.

Across the hearth, Patience shifted in her seat. She didn't have to stay in the inn but had steadfastly refused to leave.

Miranda tied off her thread. In the center of the blue silk square, a nearly completed white boar stood. When she finished it, she would join a mulberry silk square to the blue one and make the two into a purse.

If only Arabella lived to use it.

In the meantime, a little solitude would be welcome. "Patience, would you fetch us ale?" Everything cost more now, so she was careful not to indulge too much, but at least the inn still had ale. The bread and meat were running low.

"Yes, of course, mistress!" The maid jumped up. She bobbed a quick curtsey and hurried for the door.

Miranda smiled as the door closed. She would probably never take for granted the luxury of having someone do for her.

"Here, now, you can't go in there!" Patience's muffled voice penetrated the closed door.

Miranda looked up. Someone else said something. Louder and closer, Patience spoke again. "My mistress don't want visitors. 'Specially not strangers. Here now!"

The door swung open. On the threshold, with Patience behind him looking furious, stood Lord Wyndon.

Shock like frigid water poured through Miranda's veins. On its heels came a thread of fear, but she squared her shoulders. "We have nothing to say to each other, my lord."

He strolled into the room, stripping off his gloves. With a cool smile, he settled himself in the chair Patience had used.

"Mistress, I tried," Patience began.

"Never mind, Patience. The ale, if you please." Miranda spoke firmly. Much as she longed for company, she couldn't involve Patience in magical business.

The maid looked mutinous but said, "Yes, mistress." She stalked out, pointedly leaving the door open.

Miranda adopted Arabella's poised, aloof manner and hoped Wyndon didn't sense her pounding heart. "Well?"

"The time changes will overtake us soon, as I believe the return of late October's usual weather portends. I cannot have Hawkstowe interfering while I forge a new England, a better one, for our people and the unGifted alike. An England where the use of our Gifts will no longer be a crime. Instead, it will offer greater social standing and wealth."

He paused, studying her. Softly, he said, "There will be no more need to hide. No more witchcraft trials such as the one that cost you your mother."

That was tempting. So tempting. Miranda swallowed hard. This man was not trustworthy. She couldn't forget that.

He eyed her appraisingly. "Keep Hawkstowe out of my way, and I'll make it worth your while. I can save your family."

The room blurred, giving way to a vision. Wyndon stood at the center of a spacious chamber with paneled walls. "They will serve us, or they die," he said. "Make that plain to them."

The scene shifted. Soldiers herded men and women—the unGifted—into the streets, forced them along with cudgels. One woman screamed and fell to the ground. The troop leader kicked her, then lifted his hand.

Flame shot forth. Shrieking, she writhed, and the stench seared Miranda's nostrils. She gasped.

The vision faded. The room snapped back into being, and Miranda shuddered. She mustn't let him know what she'd Seen, that he was lying to her about a *better* England.

Richard was right. Lord Wyndon must've caused Arabella's illness, drawn Richard away, and now wanted Miranda to betray their trust.

He watched her with hawk-like intensity. "Is something amiss, cousin?"

"No, of course not." She stiffened her spine. "You paint a pretty picture, my lord."

"It can come to pass. Join me, and you'll never empty another slop jar. You'll want for nothing, not food nor clothing nor comfort. I'll establish you in a place of honor and esteem far beyond anything you might dream."

An image flashed across her sight, vanishing in an instant, but lasting long enough for her to know all he said was a lie. He would give her to his son or to some friend of his to breed Gifted children. Bile threatened to choke her.

"No," she gasped.

He lunged across the space between them. Grabbing her chin in an iron grip, he demanded, "What did you See?"

"Nothing! Let go." She yanked at his wrist, to no avail.

Wyndon grabbed her arm and twisted it behind her, jerking her up and out of the chair. "You're a poor liar."

"I don't know what you mean," she cried, struggling against his hold. Fear tasted coppery in her mouth.

With a wave of his hand, he shut the door. He forced both her wrists behind her and held them with one hand while his other tightened on her throat. Magic crackled over her skin, and she could scarcely get her breath.

"If you cry out, you're dead," he warned. "You had a vision."

"No, you're wrong." She had to convince him, make him leave so she could somehow warn Richard of his plans.

He grabbed the top of her sleeve and shift at the neckline and yanked downward. The fabric tore, baring her breasts above her corset.

She gasped, and his magic pressed into her throat. Her breath came in quick, shallow bursts.

She still needed words to use the defensive techniques Arabella had taught her. Lighting a candle was one thing. Doing serious damage required far more control. Did she dare try it?

Better to try and die than be preyed upon and die anyway.

"Fire," she choked, pushing the power at the lacy stock frothing below his chin.

He shot back a wave of power that extinguished the sparks. He shook her, and only his hold kept her from falling.

"Alas for you, I must put you and your visions out of my way. I'd hoped to keep you, but you are more powerful than I suspected. I cannot risk your discovering the way to meddle with my plans."

Heart pounding, knees trembling, she fought for composure. If only she could free one hand, but his vise-like grip on her wrists gave her no room to move.

He yanked the bindings from her hair so the bunches of curls fell into cascades around her shoulders. He fingered a strand idly. "Very nice." He smirked into her face as though savoring her fear.

He pressed into her. Licking her neck, he whispered, "Lie with me as a sign of cooperation, and I won't kill you."

Bile choked her. She yanked hard and freed one hand. She raked her nails down his face.

He recoiled, his grip loosening.

Miranda snapped, "Away," magically pushing with all her might. Wyndon stumbled backwards. Screaming, she jerked free and ran for the door.

Inches from it, he caught her again. His fingers bit into the skin on her neck. "Be silent," he snapped. Ice stabbing into her throat cut off her scream. He smiled, and his eyes held vicious satisfaction.

Sudden insight chilled her. Somehow, she'd done exactly what he wanted.

In the corridor, men's voices rang. "This way!"

"Came from over here! Hurry!"

Wyndon smiled. "You've shaped your own doom, witch."

He flung her against the wall. Her head struck first. She slid to the floor, and the world went dark.

～

The world returned with a roar that pounded in the back of Miranda's head where she'd struck the wall. Several men had arrived. Two of them pulled her upright and held her. A third, after making the sign against the evil eye, jerked her gaping clothes together. She turned to him. Surely he would help her.

She opened her mouth, but no words came out. But how?

Lord Wyndon had squeezed her throat. Now she couldn't talk. Couldn't tell them what had happened.

Desperate to explain, she struggled against the men who held her. Their grip tightened.

"Better tie her hands," one of them said.

No, she screamed, but the plea made no sound. God's feet, if she couldn't talk, she couldn't tell them what had happened.

Holding a handkerchief to his cheek, Lord Wyndon spoke to the fourth man. "Thank God you arrived so quickly. I came to visit her, as a courtesy to my friend, her cousin. She sent the maid for ale and then tried to seduce me. Ripped her clothes open. When I resisted her, she shrieked out curses, calling on the dark powers."

The men shuddered.

Patience pushed into the room, white-faced. "It's not true. I tell you, milady's a good person."

The innkeeper rounded on her with a gesture that swept from Miranda's head to her feet. "A good person? Look at the wench. She fooled us all, she did."

Miranda shook her head. She tried with all her strength to deny that charge, but she had no voice.

If she couldn't talk, she couldn't use any magical tactic that could free her. She dared not anyway as long as they held her, but they would lock her up somewhere eventually. She could conceal herself with glamours, but doing so would only confirm the charge, and Wyndon would tie that to Richard. And to Patience and Robin.

The men wrenched her hands behind her and bound them. Lord Wyndon said, "I called out to God to save me, and He did. She fell silent and collapsed, just as you found her."

"That's a lie." Patience stamped her foot.

One of the men pushed her aside. "You're deluded, girl. She's bewitched you." He glared at her. "Or are you of her coven?"

Patience paled. Miranda shook her head at the maid. Patience pressed her lips together but held her ground.

"Mayhap she's the reason the crops have failed and the stock've sickened," the fourth man said. He grabbed Miranda's arm. Trying to talk, she gave him a pleading look.

Fear and hatred lit his eyes. "We'll lock her up, my lord. I expect the magistrate'll start the trial on the morrow. No sense in waiting months for the assizes on something like this."

"My thanks. I confess, I'd not rest easy with this woman roaming free. Perhaps you'd best lock up her stable lad and maid lest they try to aid her."

The glint in his eyes told Miranda Richard's servants would be hostages. If she used magic to escape, she would expose herself as a witch. Worse, Robin and Patience would suffer for associating with her.

Wyndon shook his head. "My poor friend, to be so deceived. Considering all the damage she's likely done, waiting for the assizes could be fatal."

"The magistrate'll likely think the same, milord. Given what you've told us, and the hand o'God in the matter, I reckon she'll hang."

∾

Stopping at night fed the impatience and worry gnawing at Richard, but it was unavoidable. The roads were drying but still boggy in places, slowing his progress and exhausting both him and Zeus. He followed the inn's landlord up the narrow steps. The man's lantern cast faint light, most of which his bulky girth blocked, over the rough, plank walls.

Even with Gifted sight, Richard could barely see the edges of the risers. Three long, tense days in the saddle, riding through countryside where the crops had failed, had drained him more than he expected.

He stumbled over an uneven step. Caught himself with a hand on the unpainted wall.

"You want to watch that, m'lord," the man said. "A bit high, that one." They turned and started down a narrow corridor. "We wasn't expecting nobody else, not so late and on such a night. We was about to go to bed."

"I apologize for disturbing you. I should have stopped at dark, but I have urgent business in London."

Richard had decided to use his title. He needed every advantage in this race to London, and landlords forgave noblemen for awakening them much more readily than they forgave their own sort.

"Well, you ought to be there tomorrow if the rain lets up. Hope it's worth the risks of ridin' so late. O'course, I reckon robbers don't get out much in such weather."

"I suppose not. Fortunately, I made good time before the rain hit." It turned the roads to muck that slowed his pace, and its chill had seeped into his bones. He'd expected to be in London today. Still, he'd made faster progress than the coach would've.

At the top of the stairs, the landlord pushed open a door. The lantern cast enough light to show that the plank walls were clean and the floor, swept. The signs boded well for clean sheets.

Bustling into the room and lighting the candles, the man said, "You can have the chamber to yourself, as you asked, and no extra charge this late at night. Just throw the bolt on the door when you retire."

"That's very kind of you."

"Happy to be of service, m'lord."

Around a yawn Richard said, "I plan to leave as early as I can, so I'll pay you now." He pulled his purse from his coat pocket and counted out the agreed-upon five pence, plus an extra penny for good will. Paying for an extended stay before leaving Croyland had left him low on funds.

The landlord's round, seamed face crinkled in a smile. "Thankee, milord, thankee kindly." He hesitated. "If you'd like a bite—we've not much, but—"

"Thank you, no." He'd eaten thin stew at an inn a few miles back. Even though he'd pushed Zeus magically, expending power he could ill afford, the fatigue weighting his limbs made food unappealing. "Good night to you, Master ... "

The man's name wouldn't come, though he'd heard it minutes ago.

Fortunately, the landlord didn't notice. He bade Richard a good night and left, closing the door behind him.

The room boasted a single window and a rickety-looking bedstead with slightly frayed, patched curtains of green wool. Rain plopped against the glass. The leading between the panes allowed cold air to seep in.

The place was nothing to boast about, but it was clean.

Richard drew the curtains. They promised little protection from the chill but better than none.

Against one wall stood a wooden settle, its seat worn by a procession of bodies. A rush mat covered the center of the floor. On each end of the plain mantel stood a wooden candlestick with a tallow candle, and by the hearth sat a plain, straight-backed chair.

He draped his wet cloak over the chair and stretched his aching shoulders. He had pushed both himself and Zeus too hard today. Even with magic augmenting the horse's strength, he could travel only so fast. They should have stopped at dark.

At least they would reach London tomorrow evening. Zeus could have a long rest, even if his master couldn't.

The idea of repeating this journey in reverse made Richard's stiff neck throb. He shrugged the thought aside, but it also brought back the uneasiness that had plagued him for hours, growing steadily stronger.

A wave of his hand, a flicker of power, and the fire caught. Although the flames soon danced around seasoned wood, they did little to banish the room's dank chill. He drew the chair close to the hearth. Surely he was imagining things, prey to worry born of fear for Grandmère.

But perhaps not.

He directed a tendril of power at the fire. Tired as he was, expending the energy felt like a mighty task, but the flames took on a bluish tint. At their heart, an image formed. He could scry through the wards at home because he'd set them himself, but they gave the fiery image an unsteady cast.

Grandmère's bedchamber looked as it always did, except that she liked it bright. Only one candle on the mantel burned, screened from the bed by the mantel clock. On a truckle bed next to the big bed, Jane, his grandmother's maid, slept.

If Grandmère had taken a turn for the worse, Jane wouldn't sleep. He might still reach home in time.

Grandmère also slept. Her body raised only a slight hump in the covers. He thought of her as indomitable and seldom remembered how frail age had made her.

She had to survive this. He couldn't lose her yet.

At least for now, she seemed as well as he could reasonably expect.

But if his unease didn't come from her, what created it? Fatigue and worry? Or Miranda? He turned the scrying to her.

The tiny image flickered, dissolved, and became a dark room with a dirt floor and no furnishings. Miranda huddled in a corner, trembling, with her hair wildly disheveled. What in Hell's bailey—?

Fury and fear brought Richard to his feet, leaning over the hearth,

225

before he remembered he couldn't reach her. He gripped the wooden mantel with both hands.

When she raised her head, tear tracks shone on her face. She held the gaping edges of her bodice together with one hand.

What the devil had happened? She should've been able to talk her way out of any problem, especially with magic behind her words and his name to shield her.

Except that he hadn't told her to reveal his status, nor had he done so himself. He'd been too preoccupied, too worried over leaving her and afraid for Grandmère.

Idiot. How could he have been so thoughtless?

Fighting his rage, he forced himself to sit, to focus. He set his jaw and looked back into time to the afternoon. At least he could still scry that far back. Two women held her down, naked, on a table in a room with rough stone walls—likely a gaol—while a third peered closely at her body. She thrashed between them like mad creature caught in a trap.

God's blood, no! On his feet again, he couldn't breathe, and his hands clenched into fists. Scrying didn't carry sound, only vision, but only one crime led to that sort of a search. The woman was seeking a flaw that would indicate an alliance with evil powers—a witch's teat.

Miranda was in prison, and he was three days away, even if he magically pushed Zeus to a dangerous extent. Meanwhile, Grandmère lay gravely ill, perhaps dying.

God's wounds!

He rubbed a hand over his eyes. Did Miranda face immediate trial? Had she already been tried? Desperate to know, he turned back to the flames.

Bit by bit, he traced her day back to the afternoon and watched, riveted to the vision, while Wyndon interrogated and then assaulted her. Wyndon gripped her throat, then flung her against the wall, stunning her. Men burst into the room. She spoke to them, growing increasingly frantic, as they seemed not to listen.

It all made sense now. Wyndon must have accused her of witchcraft, and that accusation, especially coming from a titled lord, would outweigh almost anything except intervention by someone with greater rank. With the crops failing and livestock sickening, he would be able to convince the magistrate not to wait for the quarterly assizes, the courts that usually tried witchcraft cases.

The flame vision faded. Tongues of gold and orange licked the wood.

Richard drew a slow breath against bone-chilling rage. He would kill that son of a mangy cur. After he saved Miranda.

Except, how could he? What about Grandmère? He couldn't abandon either of them.

He straightened abruptly. There was a way, perhaps a chance to save them both. If he lived through the attempt.

CHAPTER 23

"You're drunk or mad, Richard." Seated in the chair by the hearth, Edmund crossed his translucent arms and scowled.

"I drank only at dinner, and not much." With fury pounding through his heart and worry gnawing at him, Richard waved the comment away. "I need your help. I must reach London and then Croyland before dawn."

"You are certainly drunk. I knew it." Glaring at Richard, Edmund bounded from his chair.

Richard glared back. "If you say that once more—"

"As you've seen, lad, you can't learn that sort of thing in a moment. You need a deal more practice."

"You said one could travel across vast distances in that realm at great speed. Grandmère's gravely ill in London, and Miranda's in prison, apparently charged with witchcraft, in Croyland. This time, I must succeed. If I fail, they'll both die."

"Witchcraft? She seemed too clever to reveal herself."

"She walked into a snare set by Wyndon."

The ghostly eyes gleamed with martial light. "That vile knave." Edmund shook his head. "Still, Richard, after such a day as you've had, trying such a strenuous feat, you'd likely kill yourself."

"I must help them, no matter what the cost to me." Richard clenched his fists. "God's blood, Edmund, your mad curse got us all into this.

Either you help us, or I bloody well will be the last damned Mainwaring."

"What do you mean?"

"I never entirely gave up hope, no matter how poor the odds of lifting the curse. If Miranda dies on the gallows, I'll never wed. All the Mainwaring holdings will pass into Wyndon's control through George, and I'll stir not a step toward lifting your curse. You can rot there."

If a ghost's face could pale, Edmund's had. He retreated a step. "And you with me," he said. "And your father."

A painful shot, that. Robert Mainwaring's only error had been thinking, when his son was born, that honor forced him to continue the quest to clear a king's name.

Richard narrowed his eyes at Edmund. "If she dies, it will be because she's involved with us. Help me save her or suffer the consequences."

Edmund sighed. At last, he shook his head. "You've the right of one thing. I started this mess, so I'll help you and pray you don't kill yourself in the doing."

"My thanks, Edmund."

"Don't thank me until you live through it. How do you mean to save her, assuming you can breach the barrier? Whisking her magically out of the gaol won't clear the charges against her."

In his haste to rescue her, Richard hadn't thought about that. He couldn't let the charge of witchcraft hang over her head, and even he couldn't blot out people's memories, as he'd told her on a day that seemed so very long ago.

He couldn't stop the coming farce of a trial either. But Jeremy could. "I'll go to Canterbury first and from there to London."

"Have you not harkened to me? We're not talking about a mere conjuring. You can't pop in and out of the realm like a soap bubble. All the scrolls talked about how much power this would take. It will likely drain you to the core. You'll need luck to make one transit, let alone two, and 'tis madness to attempt three."

"I'm mad, then. Walk me through this once more."

Scowling, the ghost said, "Try to remember how this feels, talking to me. You need to reach beyond the visible, and may God forgive us both this folly."

~

229

The fear on Miranda's face haunted Richard as he led Zeus from the inn's stable. If not for him, she wouldn't be caught up in all this. Now, considering Wyndon's involvement and all a nobleman's influence meant, along with her muteness, she faced certain conviction. He couldn't reach her in time unless he somehow managed to enter the shadowland despite all his prior failures.

The little sleep he'd snatched did nothing to banish his weariness. His eyes felt as though they had dirt in them, and the sour taste of old wine lay heavy on his tongue. Still, he had no choice. He was Miranda's only chance, and she was ... his life's blood.

Death on the gallows tree—

A mailed fist squeezed his heart.

No. Not Miranda. Not while he could still fight for her.

He drew in a breath like daggers piercing his chest. He should have left her in London, behind the house's wards, but berating himself about that now wouldn't help.

Besides, the wards hadn't kept Grandmère safe.

At least the rain had stopped. He scooped up a twig from the inn yard. Tucked into his left glove, it would anchor him and, through him, Zeus to the living world so they could leave the realm of the dead when they reached Canterbury.

His gut knotted. For most of his life, he had dreaded the shadowland. Now he had no hope without it.

He rode Zeus down the muddy lane at a walk, Edmund a ghostly presence beside them. A brisk wind pushed the clouds east, here and there revealing a lone star or a shaft of moonlight. Frost formed on the bushes and trees and in the ruts of the road. His breath and the stallion's made tiny clouds of white in the clear air.

It was a beautiful night, but his mind kept replaying the image of Miranda in that cell. He set his jaw and clamped down on the fear. For this to succeed, to have any chance of saving her, he needed a clear head.

Richard extended his senses. As expected, only night birds and small animals stirred in the forest around them. It was time.

Trees ahead arched their branches above the road. "That shape should do for a portal," he said, nodding toward it.

"Aye." Edmund strode ahead. "I'll wait for you on the other side. Come and meet me, lad. This way."

Deep in his mind, Richard blocked Edmund's words and concentrated on the feeling of connection across the gap between the worlds of the living and the dead. Still reaching for it, he summoned power. He caught the memory of Miranda's afterworld vision. Gave the memory and the connection magical strength.

Reaching still farther, beyond the memory, he drew power from within him and focused on the arch shape between the trees. The space glowed faint silver.

The air thickened. Its chill deepened. When Zeus whinnied and balked, Richard forced him on.

Suddenly, the air cleared. The road lay before him.

Biting back a curse, he turned Zeus. The trees arching over the road still glowed argent. He'd been so close. But that wasn't good enough.

He kneed Zeus forward and tried again, reaching for the memory of Edmund in his chamber.

And failed again.

"Damnation," he muttered, turning Zeus. He cleared his mind of fear, of Edmund, of everything but Miranda, and kneed his mount forward.

This time, the chill led into air that felt thick, as though he and Zeus moved through an icy pond, except that there was no water. They stepped into a wave of even more intense cold. Richard shuddered and blinked.

When he opened his eyes, the world had disappeared. Around him churned dank, stinking fog. The mud underfoot had turned to solid shadow. The cold air crackled with power.

Hastily, as Edmund had warned him to do, Richard pulled magic from the mist to blanket himself and the horse. He had reached the place he'd seen in Miranda's vision, the site of his future non-rest. A realm of eternal damnation. A shiver ran over his flesh.

A gray shape swooped toward them, skeletal and ghastly. It shrieked with shrill, bone-rattling force. More shapes shot out of the mist. A man's spectral form appeared in front of him, a gaping wound in his brow. The wraith screamed, and Richard's flesh prickled.

Zeus reared. With a wild neigh, he tried to bolt. Richard tightened his grip on the reins and pulled the horse's head down.

"Begone," Edmund's voice said, and the wraiths retreated.

Sliding back in the saddle, Richard tightened his calves around Zeus's heaving sides. The stallion tried to buck. Richard stayed on but gritted his teeth and sent a tendril of power into the horse's mind.

Trembling, Zeus stopped fighting. He also stopped moving, but that was better than bucking and rearing.

The wraiths hovered nearby, watching. Anticipating, to judge by the chills rippling down his back.

"I told you not to bring him," Edmund said, his voice no longer rusty but deep and strong.

Panting, Richard turned his head. Knee-deep in mist, no longer translucent, Edmund stood a few feet off to his left.

"I told you I wouldn't leave him in an unfamiliar inn. We're here. What next?"

Edmund waved at the skeletal wraiths. "Off with you. There's naught for you here."

Frowning, he studied Richard. "You look near done in already. I don't think you've the power for this."

"Don't think. Talk." God's feet, the ghosts were leaving. "Do you have power over them?"

"We temporarily damned outrank the perpetually damned." Edmund's voice sounded wry. "You can't help anyone if you kill yourself trying. Rest a bit. Draw on the magic in the fog for strength."

"I haven't time to rest."

Edmund raised an eyebrow. "You'd best take it if this mad enterprise has any hope of success. This business may be like any other and grow easier with practice. But it may not. You must guard your strength."

Richard closed his eyes and breathed deeply, pulling power from the stinking fog though it burned his nostrils.

After a while, Edmund spoke again. "Remember to hold power around you at all times to fend off the damned, but reach into the world. Picture yourself moving across England, heading south toward Canterbury. Take magic from the mists if need be."

"Should I walk Zeus?"

"If you like, but you needn't."

Richard tightened his fist around the twig in his glove. As he drew power from the magic around him, he caught an odd sense of land rushing by, of scenery changing under the night sky. He couldn't see it. It felt more like something glimpsed from the corner of an internal eye. If he looked directly at it, it would vanish.

A moment or an hour might have passed when Edmund said, "Where are you?"

"I think, London."

Should he go to Grandmère? No. Only if he followed his plan could he help both her and Miranda.

Softly, Edmund said, "Keep going."

Time ceased to exist. The barely glimpsed scenery moved in a place apart from him, a place growing brighter.

"Now ... Canterbury. I can almost see it."

"Right, then. Take a deep breath. Reach for the world but pick a secluded spot. We don't need a second witchcraft trial. Now walk toward it."

The alley off Mercery Lane, near the cathedral close, would do. Jeremy lived near there, in St. George's Street. An enclosed bridge spanned the alley, joining two sides of a merchant's home. The area below the bridge would serve for a portal. Richard reached.

Glimpsing the alley, he pulled magic from the mists. The effort throbbed in his bones. He flung the power outward to form the portal. It formed more easily than the one he'd used to enter, but holding it took the dregs of his waning power. When he kneed Zeus, the stallion walked forward on unsteady legs.

The cold intensified, but the air gave no resistance. He urged Zeus onward.

Again, he shuddered and blinked. When he opened his eyes, the cathedral's spires towered over the half-timbered, two-story buildings ahead. He'd done it.

But the sky already paled with dawn's approach. This had taken too long. Under him, Zeus's sides heaved as though he had run a long race. Richard's chest felt tight and hot. His head pounded.

"Just a little way," he urged Zeus, his voice a hoarse croak. "Come on, lad. Then you can rest."

They emerged from the alley and turned left, then left again into St. George's Street. Jeremy's house stood a short distance away, but Zeus was wobbling. To spare him, Richard slid to the ground, only to find his own legs unsteady.

The world turned black at the edges. Jeremy's front steps seemed to leap away from him.

"Just a little farther." He forced himself upright, grabbed the reins, and staggered forward.

The city was rousing. A woman sweeping the steps of the house next to Jeremy's stopped to watch him. A passing carter gave him an odd look.

Probably thought he was drunk. But who ever heard of a drunk horse? Richard would have laughed if he'd had the strength.

Just a little farther.

The world spun. Jeremy's steps rolled away from him. Impossible. He lurched toward them.

The woman called out. Voices came toward him.

In front of Jeremy's house, he dropped the reins. He stumbled up the two steps to the door. It somehow had two knockers, neither of which he could grasp.

Hell with that. He pounded on the door. As the blackness crept into his vision again and the voices behind him grew louder, footsteps sounded inside, approaching.

Henning, Jeremy's gaunt, disapproving porter, opened the door. "Lord Hawkstowe, what—?"

Richard staggered past him, into the spinning entry. He fell against the newel post. Clutching it for balance, he called, "Jeremy!"

Henning said something he couldn't understand. Someone else said, "Richard? Good Lord!"

Richard shook his head hard. The fading world stopped whirling long enough for him to recognize Cabot rushing from the back of the house. Thank God. He took a step toward Cabot.

"Miranda—Grandmère—help." The world reeled. The floor jumped into his face, and blackness obliterated everything.

M iranda kept her chin level and her eyes on the jury, but they refused to look at her. Did they fear her? Or had they already made up their minds?

Our kind can charm our way out of such fixes, Richard had once said. Perhaps she could, if she were able to speak.

But she hadn't learned to affect people's minds as Richard had charmed Flora, the cook at the Golden Swan. All her practice with glamours and candles and scrying had been for naught. She didn't have the magical skills she most needed.

If the jury believed Patience, there might still be hope. But the jurors all frowned at the girl.

The townsfolk were jammed into the tiny guildhall. A makeshift arrangement of ropes and posts kept them back from the proceedings. Despite all the bodies in the chamber, the autumn chill pervaded the air. Drafts seeping around the high windows kept the air from warming, but her hands would've been icy anyway, from the dread that roiled through her.

At an ornate table in the front of the great room, the magistrate sat. A short, rotund man, he wore a long wig, a dark suit, and a perpetual scowl. The jurors on their two benches and the clerk taking notes at a small table flanked him.

Several feet from the jury, Miranda stood with her back to the crowd. Pikemen from the watch guarded her, but their hatred and the crowd's washed over her magical senses.

Patience sat on a stool by the magistrate's desk, her face furious despite the risk of drawing the crowd's hatred to her, too. She'd been brought in by armed guards, and Robin was nowhere in sight. Her loyalty was the only consolation Miranda had.

Patience jerked her chin up. "That Lord Wyndon is not my lord Hawkstowe's friend. I've overheard my lord call him a scoundrel. He pushed in to see my mistress though I told him she didn't want him there."

"That will do." The magistrate shot her an angry glance. "Did you see any indications that Lord Hawkstowe curried favor with Mistress Willoughby?"

"Sir? I mean, your honor? What'd you ask me?"

The magistrate sighed. "Did Lord Hawkstowe stay close to the accused? Did he seek to please her?"

"Why, no, my lord. Lord Hawkstowe, he's a friend o' the king, he is—"

Guffaws from the watchers interrupted her. She glared at the crowd. "He is," she shouted, stamping her foot, "and he'll show the lot of you, right enough!"

The magistrate banged a gavel for order, then turned to Patience. "Let me be more specific, girl. Does your master take the accused to his bed?"

Miranda's cheeks blazed with sudden heat, as though her longing had become public. If these people killed her, she'd die wishing she and Richard had shared more than longing.

Patience's jaw dropped. "Angels above, no, sir! She sleeps alone! Except for me on the truckle bed some nights." She threw a venomous glance at Lord Wyndon.

The magistrate banged his gavel to still the buzz rising in the room. "Just one more question, my girl, and I shall gladly let you go. Have you ever, on your oath, seen any sign that Mistress Willoughby bewitched

Lord Hawkstowe? Any strange behavior by him since she came into the household?"

Silence fell. The crowd held its collective breath.

Outrage blazed in Patience's eyes. "I have not, and anyone what says she did is a wicked liar."

"Mmm, yes." The magistrate excused Patience, who gave Miranda an apologetic look.

"Yes, well," the magistrate said. "Being unable to testify in her own behalf, the accused has written a statement, which I shall read: 'Lord Wyndon called upon me at the inn under the guise of friendship but spoke ill of Lord Hawkstowe and, for reasons he did not reveal, damaged my clothing, threatened me, and handled me foully.'"

A murmur rose from the crowd. The magistrate banged his gavel without looking up. "'I broke away from him, raking his face with my nails, and screamed. He caught me around the throat and hurled me against a wall. I struck my head. When I came to myself again, I could no longer talk. I swear I am innocent of any evil deed.' So ends the statement of the accused."

The magistrate briefly explained the law to the jurors. Without looking at Miranda, they left the room.

They were going to convict her. How could they not, after what they'd heard here and the way she'd looked when those men burst in?

With her voice silenced and Robin and Patience hostages, she had no hope. These people were not only ready but eager to believe the worst of her.

Thanks to her clumsily repaired bodice and her hair in tangled disarray, she must look like some wild creature. Using glamours to appear tidy, however, after everyone had seen her so disheveled and no one had helped her, would only encourage them to condemn her.

The fear settled into her heart with the harsh, heavy certainty of foreknowledge. She would die, and Richard would never know she loved him. Never know a woman could care for him despite his mysterious curse.

Tears welled in her eyes. Her throat closed. She blinked back the tears and the terror. She wouldn't quail before this mockery of justice. Death was but a passage. No matter how dreadful, only a passage.

The jurors filed back into the room. The clerk conferred with one of them and turned to the magistrate.

The magistrate looked at Miranda. "Face the jury," he said, and death shone bleak in his eyes.

~

R ichard struggled toward alertness. The foggy arms of sleep held tight, resisting. Something important buzzed in the back of his mind. It pulled him away, toward waking.

A fire crackled nearby. The air held scents of oak and apple.

He opened his eyes to the warm glow of firelight. He lay on his back, still dressed except for his boots, and propped on fat pillows. Above him hung a bed canopy of green velvet.

But whose bed? Where?

"Richard?" A man sat in a chair by the bed—Cabot—Miranda!

Richard bolted upright, and the room swayed around him.

"Easy." Cabot lunged from his chair and gripped Richard's shoulder, pressing him back on the bed. "Take it easy, Richard. Jeremy!"

Richard shrugged off his hand. The sky outside the casement window was dark. "What time is it? We must hurry."

The door opened. Jeremy rushed in. "Lie back, Richard. You're not going anywhere just yet."

Flinging Cabot's hand aside again, Richard snapped, "Miranda's in danger."

"We scried her. We know all about it." Cabot's eyes were the gray of a stormy sea.

Richard's heart contracted. "We're too late? No. We can't be." After all his struggles, too damned late? No, surely ...

"No," Jeremy told him firmly. "We've time, but you need rest if you're to be of any use."

Richard looked from one to the other of them. "Then you know all that's happened? Miranda and Grandmère?"

"We've deduced most of it from your mumblings and several scryings. Save how you came here," Cabot answered.

"What happened while I slept? Why didn't you wake me?"

Jeremy's voice cracked across his. "Lie down, Richard, or so help me, I'll tie you down."

Jeremy wouldn't urge rest if they needed haste. Richard lay back on the high pillows. "Rather overbearing for a cleric, aren't you?"

"Not for one who works with the archbishop." Jeremy took a cup from the table by the bed. "I've sent an aide posthaste to London with a message for Lucius. He's as good with herbs as I am. If anyone can help Arabella, he can."

Richard nodded acknowledgement. Grandmère was in good hands. "And Miranda?"

"She was tried today and convicted, but too late, fortunately, for an execution. Darkness had fallen by the time they concluded, and we like to conduct our hangings in daylight. The better people can see, the better the warning delivered."

"So we have until dawn," Richard said. "Not much time but enough. They moved quickly."

"No doubt, spurred by Lord Wyndon."

"That bastard." Richard looked up at Jeremy. "I'll kill him for this, Jeremy. Don't preach to me about forgiveness this time."

"Do you hear me arguing? Here, drink this. Slowly."

"What is it?" He sniffed, and the rich aroma of beef tickled his nostrils. His stomach rumbled, and he was suddenly ravenous from the magical work he'd done.

"Oxtail soup," Cabot said. "When it settles, you can have some cheese and bread."

Cabot brought a laden platter and set it on the mattress at Richard's side, then perched on the foot of the bed. Leaning against the carved post, he stretched one long leg out on the bed. Jeremy sat on the other side of the bed, also leaning against a post.

They looked so different and yet so alike, both friends beyond measure. Richard had always known they would follow him to the gates of Hell, as he would either of them. He'd never expected to ask exactly that of them, though.

Richard shrugged aside a chill at the thought and took another sip. The soup's heat felt doubly good against the dread the afterworld stirred in him. Half fearing the answer, he asked, "How is Miranda?"

"Enduring like a queen." Cabot tore the round loaf of bread into chunks. "She held her head high and never cringed. Magnificent."

"So long as she doesn't become a magnificent martyr." To cover his emotion, Richard took another sip. *Hold on, love. Whatever it takes, I'll save you.*

As Richard drank the thick broth, Cabot said, "Jeremy and I have been busy while you slept the day away. We've deduced you somehow traveled here from north Hertfordshire in a few hours. Can you do it again and take us along? Or will we all end up flat on the floor if you try?"

"I don't know." Richard handed the cup over. Cabot passed him a thick chunk of fresh bread and took one for himself.

Richard explained how he had passed through the afterworld. The brothers heard him in silence, but the growing tension in their faces said they grasped the implications of what he had done.

"Edmund warned me that being tired made the business even more dangerous. I'd like to think that's why I arrived here in such bad shape. I had pushed myself and Zeus all day, not knowing I had a major work of magic yet to face. By the way, how is he?"

"He's in the stable. He'll be fine." Jeremy's face settled into a faraway, thoughtful expression.

"My thanks."

Rising from the bed, Cabot said, "Given Edmund's warnings and the state you were in when you arrived, Richard, we'd be mad to try more than one transit in such a short time. London or Croyland but not both. I'm sorry."

Jeremy said, "He's right, I fear. If you want to save Miranda, you must trust your grandmother to Lucius."

Cabot added, "In Croyland, we'll be three against, possibly, an entire town. Folk don't like to be cheated out of a hanging."

"No. They don't." Reluctantly, wishing he didn't have to, Richard chose. "Croyland, then." *Keep that girl safe*, Grandmère had said, and so he would. But he couldn't lose his grandmother either.

Jeremy shifted against the bedpost. "This afterworld has staggering theological implications. I'd like to meet some of the souls who dwell there."

"Edmund says they're the *perpetually damned*. He warned me to guard myself at all times."

"Still, they might welcome the chance for salvation."

"Later," Cabot said. "We have someone living to save first. So can you take us back to Croyland that way?"

"If you're certain you're ready for this. You see how dangerous it is."

"Stow it," Cabot replied, "and tell us how we can help."

Their loyalty warmed him no less because he'd anticipated it. He chose a piece of cheese and leaned back.

"I need you, Jeremy, to take the lead and brandish the archbishop's authority like a sword. Are you willing?"

"More than willing. Then what do we do?"

CHAPTER 24

D awn approached, bringing death. Outside, the din of voices signaled a growing crowd eager to watch Miranda die.

She stared out the cell's high, narrow window at the lightening sky. She'd tried all night to break the silence Wyndon had imposed on her, but with no luck. Success likely wouldn't have made a difference anyway. After all, the jurors had ignored her written statement completely.

She ran her cold, shaking hands over her arms but couldn't seem to get warm. Somehow, she had to hold her head up. Hide her fear. When Richard heard of this, as Wyndon would surely see that he did, he wouldn't hear that she died cringing and pleading.

He would blame himself. He shouldn't, but he would.

I absolve you, she thought to him, hoping he could somehow sense her thought. *I love you. More than anyone, more than anything. I will love you forever.*

If only she'd had had the courage to tell him how she felt, how important he was to her.

If only she could have said good-bye.

A key rattled in the lock. The cell door opened to admit three burly, scowling men.

One of them held a pistol trained on her while another put a rough hemp noose around her neck. The third jerked her hands behind her back to bind them. Panic threatened to collapse her knees, but she forced them to lock.

If she'd been certain she could use the cloaking glamour to hide herself, she might've escaped when they opened the cell door. But then what would she do? Such an escape would confirm her guilt and leave Patience and Robin, who were held under guard somewhere, to face the town's wrath. She couldn't do that to them.

The guards led her outside and boosted her into the small cart there. A crowd of people massed behind it, many carrying torches against the predawn darkness. The driver clucked to his horse. The wagon lurched forward, but she managed not to fall.

The crowd surged toward the wagon.

"Witch!" a man shouted.

"Devil's whore!" a woman shrieked as she flung a dirt clod. It struck Miranda in the shoulder, and she flinched. Mistress Smith had gone through this same ordeal.

Doubtless, Mother also had.

There was worse to come.

Miranda shuddered. If she thought of what lay ahead, she wouldn't be able to control the terror clawing at her throat.

Similar taunts came from all sides. The words hurt less than she would have thought. Soon, they wouldn't matter. More dirt clods flew toward her. One hit her cheek with a hard, stinging blow. Gasping, she stumbled backward but again stayed on her feet.

For Richard.

The cart creaked through town, heading east toward the edge of the village. Still shouting, the crowd fell in behind it.

The driver passed the last house and turned aside, toward an elm with spreading branches. A stout ladder stood propped against the trunk. The driver pulled up beside it, below a thick branch about four feet above Miranda's head.

Her heart pounded so hard that she thought it might burst. If only it would.

Arabella had been right. A quick death would've been a mercy for Mistress Smith.

A burly, plainly dressed man who wore a black hood over his face removed the end gate of the cart. He hauled her from the wagon to stand on the ladder propped against the tree trunk.

When she was in place, on the fifth rung, high enough for all the crowd to see, he climbed into the wagon and tied the noose to the branch above her head.

The rough hemp dug into her throat. The rope gave her little room to move, not that moving would help. All too soon—

Oh, Richard, if only I could hold you just once more.

They'd touched each other so rarely, but each time had been precious. She called on the memories, savoring every look, every touch.

The sheriff, a short, stocky man, stepped forward. He raised his hands, and the crowd fell silent. He began to read the charges against her.

Pale pink and gold streaked the sky with the approach of dawn. Those with torches extinguished them in the dirt.

She turned her head to see the cross on the distant church tower. It was familiar, though she'd never been here before.

Except in a dream. One that had been a foretelling after all. But that didn't matter now.

Out of the corner of her eye, she saw Lord Wyndon's coach, but he no longer mattered either. Only her love, her faith and the promise of salvation still had any importance.

Whosoever believeth in Him shall not perish but have everlasting life. She swallowed hard against tears. *Good-bye, my love. I hope you break your curse and find happiness.*

Oh, Lord, I beg you, let it be quick.

The sheriff stopped reading. He turned to the executioner, who stepped behind the ladder. The crowd fell silent, waiting. Miranda's heart pounded wildly. She closed her eyes to hide her fear and block out the avid faces below.

A faint breeze brushed over her face with the scents of autumn leaves and damp earth. The last things she'd ever smell.

Richard ...

"Hold!" A deep, clear voice rolled over the silent throng. "In the name of His Grace The Archbishop of Canterbury, and by his authority, I command you, hold!"

Miranda's eyes flew open. Richard thundered down the road with the Winfield brothers, all on horseback, Jeremy standing in his stirrups. He wore a suit and cloak, as did Richard and Cabot, but Jeremy's were all in black. His white preaching bands, a white circle around his neck with two tabs hanging down, contrasted sharply with the black.

This couldn't be happening. She must have died, must be hallucinating.

Filled with love and fury, Richard's eyes met hers. His rage blasted into her chest.

This was real. He was real.

She gasped in relief and blinked back joyous, blinding tears.

The horsemen reached the crowd. Jeremy forced his way through to the sheriff. Miranda kept her eyes locked on Richard's stony face as he rode behind the wagon, his horse pushing through the startled townsfolk. He stopped beside the ladder and gripped it, holding it steady not only with his hand but with magic.

Suddenly, her view shifted. She almost lost her footing.

She saw herself, the dirt splotches on her clothes and face from the clods thrown by the crowd. Boiling fury—Richard's—came with the sight. She blinked, scarcely daring to believe he was truly here.

Somehow, she needed to let him know she was all right, now that he was with her.

His frown deepened. *Miranda? Did you say—or think—to tell me you were all right?*

Yes, but—you can hear me, as I hear you?

The ladder put her above him even though he sat astride that big horse. She stared down into his grim eyes. *I thought I heard you in my mind when you left Croyland, but I decided I must've been wrong. But just now, I heard you as though you had spoken.*

We can discuss that later, he sent to her. *Jeremy and Cabot and I have a plan to save you.*

His eyes were hard. *No matter what, you're leaving here with me.*

Cabot circled the crowd and stopped his mount directly behind the ladder.

Jeremy had dismounted and was talking to the magistrate in a voice she couldn't hear.

" ... entirely irregular," the magistrate blustered.

"No more irregular, I daresay, than interviewing witnesses, holding a trial, concluding it, and passing sentence, all in a single day," Jeremy answered, loudly enough for everyone to hear. "No doubt, at the urging of the most noble accuser."

You're safe, Richard's voice said in her mind. *Don't fear.*

I'm not afraid, not now that you're here. Richard, I love you.

Fierce joy flowed from him to her. *I love you,* he thought. *I'm a fool for thinking I could deny it. For not telling you.*

That doesn't matter. You're telling me now. When I saw you ride in, I didn't believe you were real. How did this happen?

It's a long story. Tenderness brushed her soul. *Later.*

Your grandmother?

Still holding on. Jeremy sent a message to Lucius, who's good with herbs ... Wait. The words *Privy Council* had caught his ear. Straining, she heard the magistrate.

"Yes, Reverend, but the verdict is entered. If the accused wishes to appeal, or the archbishop, that's a matter for the Privy Council. As I said."

"Did you give her the chance?" Jeremy asked.

"She didn't ask for it." As though he realized what he had said about the mute prisoner, the man's face turned red. "Now, see here, Reverend, if she wants to appeal, she can."

"She wants to appeal," Richard stated in a voice of flint. "You will enter a stay of execution, and I will speak to my friends on the Council and my very good friend King Charles, who will doubtless want to know why you placed haste above justice in this matter. They may have questions about your fitness for the office you hold. Especially since witchcraft charges are usually tried at the assizes."

The magistrate's jaw dropped. Jeremy shook his head at Richard, who thought, *God's wounds* and set his jaw.

The spectators muttered among themselves. Several crowded close to hear the conversation. One man, tall and gangly, moved toward the ladder.

Cabot fingered the hilt of the cutlass at his waist and stared down at the man. The fellow stopped in his tracks. Slowly, he backed away. The muttering grew quieter.

"Surely you would agree, sir, that the Church has a unique perspective on the forces of darkness." Jeremy sounded conciliatory. "If I might examine the prisoner, you might obtain important evidence."

The sheriff growled, "Or might not."

"We might not," Jeremy said, "but ensuring a just result must be worth hearing additional evidence."

"But the girl was struck dumb, she was." The magistrate mopped his face with a linen handkerchief. "She claimed Lord Wyndon grabbed her throat, but she had no bruises."

"As it happens, I'm skilled at treating injuries," Jeremy said. "Pressure on the throat can, in rare cases, stop the voice without leaving a mark."

In magical cases, Richard thought.

Jeremy continued, "If you prefer explaining to both the archbishop and the king why you decided the Church's judgment had no value, we will appeal the verdict now."

The magistrate mopped his brow harder. He and the sheriff exchanged a look. "I suppose 'twouldn't hurt to have the reverend examine the wench," the magistrate conceded.

Miranda glanced over the crowd. Lord Wyndon's coach stood at the back. Strange, that he hadn't tried to intervene.

Richard followed her glance. *He knows he's outmanned*, he told her. *He won't risk offending the king or the archbishop. This round is ours.*

This "round." As though it were a game. She shuddered.

The magistrate and the sheriff exchanged another look. The sheriff cleared his throat. "I've no men to manage the crowd. Wasn't counting on stopping no hanging, I wasn't."

Miranda's heart fluttered in new fear, but Jeremy merely raised an eyebrow. "If the folk of Croyland care more for blood than for justice, my comrades and I will undertake to manage. Take that noose off her, and let's go."

"Here, now," the magistrate said. "We ought to consult Lord Wyndon, him what brought the charges."

"Even he must defer to the archbishop," Jeremy said, "and to the king."

The sheriff turned toward the wagon. "I'll see he's told to meet us."

Jeremy mounted again. He guided his horse to a position between the crowd and the sheriff's cart.

Richard tweaked his sword hilt, as though making sure the blade was loose in the scabbard, then drew a pistol from under his cloak. He watched the crowd as the sheriff moved toward the wagon. His longing to cut the rope himself and have it done, his frustration that he couldn't, and his anger boiled into Miranda through the strange connection they shared.

The mutters from the crowd became shouts of indignation. As the sheriff climbed into the wagon and reached for the rope, several people hissed. When he untied the noose from the branch, the crowd surged forward.

Pistol in hand, Richard urged his mount in front of her. Cabot rode to his side, facing the mob with his cutlass at the ready.

Richard fired into the air. His horse startled but instantly came under control. The cart's driver struggled to control the horse in the traces.

In the instant of silence that followed, Richard switched his pistol to his left hand and drew his smallsword. His voice rang. "I'll skewer the next man who moves. If you so wish to see a hanging that you've no care for justice, let one of you take her place."

Letting power and rage seep out of him, he looked ready to slay them all single-handed. The muttering faded into uneasy whispers, and Miranda drew a relieved breath.

Jeremy raised his hands for silence, shouting, "Good people, I'm the Reverend Dr. Jeremy Winfield. I heard of this matter and so have come under the authority of His Grace, Archbishop Sheldon, to see that justice is done. Let the jurors stand forth."

Eddies of movement in the crowd disgorged several uneasy-looking men. They shuffled their feet and stared at the ground.

"We'll go to the church," Jeremy announced, "and I'll inquire of the prisoner before God's altar."

No one raised an objection. Cabot angled his horse to ride by the wagon. Richard turned to brush dirt off Miranda's face. *I can't ride with you, love, can't hold you. Not yet. That would undercut Jeremy's argument. Hellfire, look what they've done to you.*

It doesn't matter. Nothing matters except that you're here. You must find Robin and Patience. They're being held hostage to keep me from using my magic.

I'll make certain they're safe.

He dismounted and helped her take a seat in the cart, his grip steady and reassuring. Miranda's shaky legs welcomed the rest.

When he mounted again, he brought his horse to the cart's side.

The sheriff climbed into the cart, and their cavalcade set out.

Riding beside her, Richard thought, *If you don't know the answers, ask me. Grandmère hammered the catechism into me at an early age.*

As my grandmother, who didn't hold with Father's notions, hammered it into me. I'll clear myself, Richard, never fear.

I have faith that you will, but if all else fails, I'll save you myself and damn the consequences.

Henry watched from his coach as the crowd trailed after the sheriff's wagon. Let Hawkstowe think he'd won this round. He'd arrived in time to save his precious wench, but the time he'd spent on that had been a useful diversion. Soon it would be too late to change England's fate.

Any claims the wench made at this point would vanish in the wave of new history rolling forward.

In a few days, four or five at the most, the new past would overtake and reshape the present. Even if the Conclave arrested him, they wouldn't have time to stop it. Then Henry would have his vengeance. He could force the wench to serve him any way he chose, and Hawkstowe wouldn't be able to do a thing to stop it.

Hawkstowe's timely arrival was unsettling, however. He could only have come via the shadowland. Henry frowned. If the whelp discovered a way to travel there, could he undo the time changes?

He would still bear watching. Nothing must be allowed to stop the changes now surging toward the present.

God's blood. Henry rapped on the roof trap with his cane.

His coachman opened it. "Yes, my lord?"

"Back to London, Charles."

"Aye, milord." The trap dropped shut.

Hawkstowe and his friends likely wouldn't risk traveling the spectral realm again today. Henry could beat him to London. And to the Protectorate of England.

~

The sheriff kept a tight grip on Miranda's arm as he led her into the little stone church. His anger at having the hanging interrupted vibrated in the air around him. It would've frightened her if Richard and his friends hadn't been there.

They followed Miranda and the sheriff. Richard's anger at the treatment she'd received still boiled within him.

Just a little longer, and she could go to him.

The jurors stood under one of the rounded archways at the side of the chancel. The clerk perched on a bench by the pulpit. The magistrate glanced at the pulpit, shrugged as though thinking better of it, and sat next to the clerk. Hastily summoned, the parish rector lit candles.

Jeremy strode to the front of the sanctuary. Alone of them all, he looked completely at home.

"Take those ropes off her," he said to the sheriff. "Even if she had the blackest heart in England, she could do no evil here."

The sheriff silently cut the rope that had bound her hands, and she rubbed her aching wrists.

Jeremy had found a stool somewhere. He placed it at the front of the chancel, directly in line with the altar. Seating her there, he knelt in front of her. Gentle pressure from his fingers turned her head up and to the side. He touched her neck lightly.

"Wait," the sheriff said. "What about Lord Wyndon, him what brought the charge?"

One of the jurors, a short, thin man with a weathered face, stepped forward. "I seen his carriage headin' out o' town. When we come this way, it went t'other."

Jeremy glanced at the magistrate. "Then we needn't delay." He turned back to Miranda. "Don't try to speak yet."

Lines at the corners of his eyes and mouth spoke of both self-denial and self-control. A plain silver cross hung from a silver chain around his neck and down to his chest. She kept her gaze on it as he touched her throat.

Warmth seeped from his fingers into her skin. She had a sudden urge to clear her throat. With his back to the watchers, he glanced at her in warning. Instead, she swallowed hard.

"Ah, yes," he said. "Here it is, a slight swelling just where it would create pressure inside her throat."

"But she had no bruises," the magistrate said again.

"Sometimes one doesn't." Jeremy drew a clay pot from his coat pocket. When he removed the cork stopper, the sharp scent of thyme rose from the greenish salve within. He dabbed some of the salve on Miranda's neck. Rubbing the ointment in gently, he said, "See if you can manage a whisper."

She felt as though she could speak, but his choice of words advised her not to. She whispered, "I think—yes, Reverend, I can. Oh, thank you."

Shock rippled through the people in the church. He took the cross from around his neck and handed it to her. When she wrapped her fingers around it, one of the jurors gasped.

A few quick strides brought him to the pulpit. He picked up the heavy Bible there and brought it to lay in her lap. "Place your left hand on the holy book and hold the cross in your right."

He strode to stand beside the jury before he turned to face her. When she answered him, she would also be facing them.

"Can you recite our Lord's prayer?" He asked.

"Our Father which art in Heaven ... " As she spoke, her confidence rose. So did her voice.

The room was deathly silent.

When she finished, Jeremy nodded. "Now, Miranda Willoughby, on peril of your soul, have you any converse with Satan, his demons, or any of the minions of darkness?"

"No, Reverend. I have not."

He had phrased the question so she wouldn't have to lie about magic. Given his own powers, she should've expected that.

"Tell us what happened two days ago," he said.

She took a deep breath and began to talk. The jurors watched her attentively.

When she finished, Reverend Winfield turned to the magistrate. "Do you have any questions, sir?"

The man mopped his brow again. "Let us move to the Guildhall. So folk can hear for themselves, you know."

As Miranda stood, her glance fell on the tomb marker at her feet.

Josiah Pritchett, born 23 June 1610, died 7 November 1660, during the second year of our gracious Lord Protector Henry de Vere.

Henry de Vere? Lord Protector? Heaven help them all if that came to pass. *Richard, look at the stone.*

The sheriff led her forward, more gently this time, as Richard strolled casually toward the spot she'd occupied. His expression hardened. *So that was his endgame. But how in blazes did he make it happen?*

CHAPTER 25

"What shall I do with your old gown, mistress?" Patience frowned at the torn wool in her hands. She and Miranda were in their chamber at the inn in Croyland, where the landlord had surrendered their belongings.

Burn it hovered on Miranda's lips, but that would be a waste of good, warm fabric. "Do as you think best, Patience."

A short time ago, in the Guildhall, she'd again answered Jeremy's questions and repeated the catechism before the town. She'd been formally acquitted and released. Some people would still refuse to touch the cloth because of the witchcraft accusation, but others wouldn't be so particular.

"I'll pack it," Patience said. "We'll find a use for it in London."

Patience stuffed the discarded garments into Miranda's chest for the journey home. Miranda leaned over the basin in the corner, splashing cold water on her face.

Clean clothes and neatly braided hair were a relief, but she wouldn't feel truly clean again until she'd bathed. Preferably somewhere far from this town. And she couldn't seem to feel warm.

"Are you ready, mistress?" Patience asked.

When Miranda nodded, the maid opened the door. Richard waited in the corridor with Cabot, Jeremy, and Robin. The stable lad hurried in to grab Miranda's chest.

"The horses are put to." Richard spoke with his gaze fixed on Miranda's face. While he sounded calm, his face looked drawn with weariness. The emotions churning in his eyes echoed deep within her and made her heart pound.

Standing a foot away from her, he said, "We've reclaimed all our belongings. We'll leave as soon as you're ready."

"I'm more than ready," she told him. *You need rest, though. I can feel how tired you are.*

I'll rest when you do, when we're away from here.

I won't argue with that.

"I want a word with you before we depart," he said quietly, his gaze holding hers.

Everyone else filed out of the chamber. When the door closed behind Jeremy, Richard's mask of composure cracked. The strain of the day and the fear he'd felt were naked on his face as he opened his arms and stepped toward her.

Miranda rushed to him. He caught her tightly as she locked her arms around him. On blind instinct, she turned her face upward in time to meet his kiss.

It was deep and searing and unrestrained. The love he'd confessed burned in his kiss, and she returned it full measure.

When the kiss ended, he pressed his face into her neck. "Sweetheart," he groaned. With the word came a rush of guilt and relief and love that threatened to break her heart.

"It's all right now," she choked, fighting back tears. "Everything's all right."

He kissed her again, then held her even closer. In his arms, she felt truly safe at last, even warm, almost. She burrowed closer.

After a few minutes he straightened and kissed her forehead. "We should go," he said, "and travel as far as we can before dark."

"How is your grandmother?" she asked as they walked out of the chamber.

"Holding her own, but I want to reach her as soon as I can. And we must get word of Wyndon's endgame to Lucius as soon as we can."

Being glad Richard hadn't ridden for London with the Winfield brothers was selfish, Miranda knew, but she couldn't help it. Cabot and Jeremy could carry the news to London, but only

Richard's nearness kept her nightmare memories of the last few days at bay.

With Edmund standing by to help the Winfields travel, Richard had opened a portal in the woods off a deserted stretch of road. Edmund had promised to coach them on leaving the afterworld, which was easier than entering it.

Richard felt guilty about not going, Miranda knew, but didn't want to leave her unprotected, and his disappearance would be awkward to explain to Robin and Patience. So he rode back in the coach with her, though Edmund would notify him if his friends needed his aid to emerge in London.

Using their strange mental connection so Patience and Robin wouldn't overhear, Richard had told her how he'd come to her rescue and about the ancestor who'd helped him.

Held close by his arm around her shoulders, she asked, *Richard, what happened? How can we hear each other's thoughts, feel what each other feels?*

He ran his fingers idly along her arm. *I've never heard of such a thing, so I can only guess. You said you thought you heard me speak while I kissed you goodbye in Croyland?*

I decided I must have imagined it.

As I rode south that last day, I felt more and more uneasy. As your day went from frightening to terrifying.

And so he had come to save her. She still had difficulty believing he'd actually managed it. *Do you think you picked up my emotions?*

I might have. It's logical, that I can hear your thoughts when I'm near you but sense only your mood otherwise.

But how? She shifted to look at him.

He brushed her hair gently off her temple. *I suspect it's a combination of our different gifts and the awareness that started after we used the water from Morgan's pool. I didn't want to leave you. I was worried. So were you, I think, though you wouldn't admit it. I could see the day ahead when I would leave you forever, and I wanted to hold onto you somehow, even though I knew I couldn't. If you felt the same way—*

I did. She squeezed his free hand.

Then I think we somehow reached through that awareness the pool gave us and made a tie. His fingers caressed her shoulder.

It's a strange sort of sharing, but I like it. She hesitated. *Do you mind?*

Never. Fierce possessiveness roared through him and into her, but they couldn't do anything about it with Patience dozing on the opposite seat.

"Jeremy's posset should take effect soon," he said, gathering her closer. "Rest for a while, sweet. You need it."

So did he, but knowing what Wyndon intended would make true rest difficult to obtain for them both.

～

They stopped at dusk, well south of Croyland at a small inn on the Peterborough road. Miranda's modest chamber felt like a sanctuary, but she still couldn't seem to feel warm. Or to think of anything except that she had a second chance.

Richard loved her. She loved him. That much was beyond doubt. But he'd closed himself off, as though acknowledging what lay between them was as far as he meant to go.

She rubbed her hands along her arms. The place smelled clean enough though a steady draft crept around the single window. A bed curtained with blue hangings stood against one wall. Beneath it, the edge of a truckle bed showed.

Twin wooden armchairs, their seats worn smooth by long use, flanked the hearth. Most important of all, this place was not in Croyland. The sooner she could forget that town, the better.

Richard knelt by the hearth. Rippling from his extended hand, silver magic ignited the logs.

The silence weighed heavily on the air. She caught no sense of his locked-down emotions, but his face was drawn and pale with fatigue, and the tense line of his shoulders betrayed the effort he made to hold them straight.

Somehow, she had to save him from whatever his family curse portended. "I'm sorry you had nothing but trouble from Croyland," she said. "If I had gained more control over my power—"

"You're not at fault, Miranda. Besides, coming here let us find that tombstone. Cabot and Jeremy should reach London anytime now and alert the Conclave. For all the good that may do. As for the *Chronicle*, it was a slim hope."

Father Gregory had sent them a message saying he hadn't been able to locate a copy. Given the current hatred of Catholics and Miranda's witchcraft trial, it had taken courage for him to send word at all.

Richard's statement required no reply and so closed the conversation. Why would he not unbend, just a little?

Flames crackled around the logs. He stared at them, and Miranda saw that he'd scried his grandmother. Arabella's color seemed better.

Richard said, "Grandmère is rallying. Still, I'm anxious to see her." Scowling, he added, "And there's the matter of Wyndon's usurpation of power. We should prepare a full report for Lucius, including all that you Saw."

He rose, his gaze on the fire. "The room should warm soon."

Why wouldn't he look at her? He seemed to have withdrawn into himself again.

Patience had left to fetch supper. This might be their last private moment before they reached London.

"Richard, I don't care about your family curse, whatever it is. I love you. I will love you always."

Elation surged in their connection, quickly tamped. "Don't." He stared at the hearth.

"Don't feel it or don't say it?"

With a groan, he took one long stride to reach her. He caught her hands. "I can't inflict this curse on anyone else, especially you."

She gripped his warm, callused palms. "I don't fear it. I truly don't care about it."

He freed his hands, his expression hardening. "You should care." Pain flared in his eyes and in their bond. "Miranda—"

Out in the hall, Patience's cheerful voice said, "Right this way, lad. This chamber, down at the end."

Richard stepped away. When the door opened, he was jabbing at the fire with the poker. Miranda sighed. There had to be a way to ease the emotions that jabbed at him.

A young man carried a laden tray into the room. Patience transferred food from it to the table. When she finished, she asked, "Shall I stay?"

"No, Patience, thank you," Richard said. "I have the chamber across the hall and can help your mistress if she needs anything tonight. You've had a bad few days, so go and rest."

"Yes, milord. My thanks." Patience curtsied and left the room after the young man.

The chamber across the hall. Of course he'd booked that. Doing so was proper, even thoughtful. Except that without him there would be naught to keep nightmare memories at bay.

He tugged her against him, his arms tight, sheltering her. She clung to him and tried to memorize the way he felt in her arms.

Richard dropped a kiss on her hair. "I booked that chamber for propriety's sake. I will be wherever you need me to be, for as long as you need me there." He released her, and they took their seats at the table.

"I will always need you," she said quietly. As regret darkened his eyes, she added, "I realize that isn't what you meant, but I wanted you to know."

Still looking uneasy, he said, "We should eat."

Patience had brought a feast—oxtail soup, mutton collops, and thick, chewy bread with a plate of Stilton cheese to finish the meal. The food smelled wonderful, but Miranda had little appetite.

Richard, too, picked at his meal. "I failed you," he said abruptly, laying down his fork. In his eyes and in the awareness they shared, his self-doubt and guilt churned. "Seeing you about to hang—I'll never forget it. Or forgive myself. I can't believe you forgive me so easily."

"You did as I asked. There's nothing to forgive."

"Miranda—"

"No. Hush. No more." She cupped his stubbled cheek. "You and your friends rode through Hell for me. What more could any man do?"

A man could keep you safe. The words rustled in her mind. He drew her hand to his mouth. His eyes blazed. Through her rush of pleasure when he pressed his lips against her palm, she caught a raw surge of his love and regret and frustration.

She gripped his fingers. "Do you not understand that I would do anything, dare anything, for you?"

He stood in a swift, jerky motion, and released her hand.

"You deserve a husband and family."

"I want you, no matter what that means and for however much or little time we have."

"You shouldn't." A bitter smile twisted his lips. Staring into the fire, he said, "I didn't tell you the details of the family curse. When I die, I can't pass through the portal of judgment and learn my final fate."

He laid out an astonishing tale of magic misused, murder centuries past, and a king wrongly blamed. She wouldn't believe this if anyone else had described it, but she could feel that he was in deadly earnest.

He concluded, "I'll be trapped in the shadowland Cabot and Jeremy and I crossed to reach Croyland. In the same place we saw in your vision. The land of the damned. Until the end of time."

The frustration in his soul welled into the connection they shared. "Edmund cursed us all, and my mother never forgave my father for begetting a doomed son."

No wonder he called such a dreadful burden a curse. How could anyone pass such a thing along? Yet one night's work had destroyed two young lives and a king's good name. Some recompense was owed.

In a quiet voice his hard eyes belied, Richard said, "I won't do that to my son or, through him, to you. I won't give you cause to despise me."

"How could I despise you if my own failure to find the proof you need leaves you thus burdened?"

"My mother came to hate my father for the task he laid on me. She died of a winter fever when I was ten. When I was twelve, Grandmère gave me her last letter. In it, she railed against my father for dooming me."

"Did your father not tell her before they wed?"

"Yes, but they didn't think it mattered. She was a widow, childless, of a man who had five children by his first wife."

"She thought she was barren," Miranda breathed.

"As though that weren't enough, some men of our line become so obsessed with being unable to end the curse that they go mad. My grandfather shot himself, and my father … I've always wondered whether his death on the battlefield was truly a matter of happenstance."

That sounded horrible, but it didn't change her feelings for him. "I'll take my chances," she said.

Richard shook his head. "My parents followed their hearts to misery. I can't let that happen to you. To us."

"But it need not be the same."

Frowning, he paced to the hearth. He braced one hand against the mantel and stared into the flames. "Ah, but it must. The sins of the fathers, you know."

"I don't believe that." To keep from holding out her hands to him, she clasped them together. "Somewhere, someday, the scales will balance. It may take the right Mainwaring at the right time and in the right place, but they will. Unless you end the line."

His eyes narrowed. "Do you See that?"

"No." If only she did. "But I feel it."

"You wouldn't risk your son's soul," he said slowly.

"Not his soul. A part of his future, perhaps, but not his soul. His would stand in no more danger of eternal condemnation than yours. And he might save all the rest of you—unless we do it first. I promise you, I will never stop trying."

Softly, she said, "If we're able to restore the true course of events, what we feel may not matter anyway. But if it does, what right have we, if we should be blessed with a son, to decide he would rather not be born?"

Richard's eyes suddenly blazed, and an answering fire ignited deep within her. She held out her hand to him.

He came to her swiftly. Clasping her hand in both of his, he drew her to her feet and held her fingers to his lips. His eyes hot and intent on hers, he said, "If you're willing to risk all that, I can't turn away. For whatever time we have together, I want you as my wife. Will you marry me, Miranda? Marry me and leave the question of children to fate?"

Her heart leaped, and her throat tightened. "Are you certain you want a servant for your countess?"

"Not just any servant." He pressed a passionate kiss into her palm. "Will you wed me, curse and all?"

A bubble of joy burst inside her. "I will even wed you in the Church of England. Or in a barn, or in a ditch beside the road."

Laughing, he swept her into his arms for a deep, intoxicating kiss. He carried her to the bed and fell onto it with her, then rolled above her to rain kisses on her face until she laughed and begged him to stop.

The sweet weight of his body pressed down on her. Tender laughter sparkled in his eyes.

She slid her fingers into the thick hair that framed his face and drew his head down for a kiss.

It started gently but soon became hot and eager and deep. His tongue probing inside her mouth sent waves of excitement through her. She stroked his tongue with her own. They rolled onto their sides, and his fingers at her back unlaced her bodice.

He raised his head, his eyes intent. "Let me take this off, love. Let me see you. Touch you."

"Yes," she whispered, heart hammering. "If you'll allow me the same."

Nervous excitement simmered in her stomach as they peeled away each other's garments. At last only her shift and his breeches remained. The touches and kisses they exchanged and the fire they roused made undressing a delight she'd never imagined.

In the firelight, his skin turned bronze. The flickering light cast shadows over the planes of his face and body and the curved muscles of his arms as he picked her up and tucked her into the bed.

Sliding in beside her, he said, "Are you nervous, sweet? Thousands of men and women before us have done this, and all lived to tell the tale. We can wait, though, if you'd rather."

"I wouldn't." She ran her palm over his shoulder, down his muscular chest with its mat of soft, dark hair. "I trust you, Richard." Besides, everything could change by morning.

His eyes heated, and he cupped her breast, thumbing the nipple. Miranda gasped as her body arched. Imitating him, she rubbed her thumb over his nipple. The muscles in his chest tensed. His eyes closed. He groaned, and his pleasure flashed into her.

He tugged her hand down to the buttons on his breeches. When she fumbled with them, he helped her. His shaft sprang free, and she touched it tentatively with one finger.

Richard made a choked sound as he placed his hand over hers and showed her what he liked. His pleasure spread through her like fire in a tinder box and kindled a matching flame deep within her. She kissed the center of his chest. *Is this good?*

He gasped. *Sublime.*

He rolled above her, breaking her grip. His weight pressed her into the bed. Through her linen shift, he covered her nipple with his mouth. His warm breath teased the peak.

Gasping with pleasure, wanting more of him, she arched against him. He jerked open the neck of her shift. She had no time to feel shy before his head came down again, toward her other breast. His tongue stroked her like hot, wet velvet. The fire within her became a hollow ache.

As she tangled her fingers in his hair, he touched her between her legs. Shock clamped them together on his hand.

Passion glowed in his eyes. "You're so soft there, sweetheart. Let me touch you."

His fingers moved, and wildfire leaped within her. Her thighs relaxed, allowing him a firmer touch. Slowly, he traced the folds of too-sensitive skin, and she quivered in response.

Awash on a flood of shared pleasure, she couldn't think. He was touching her, and she was touching him, and she needed more. Kissing his shoulders, she caressed his warm, sleek back. "Richard ... "

"Yes, love." His shaft pressed against her. Some of the fear came back, but the need was stronger. Slowly, he sank into her. Their joining felt strange—tight, but with a wonderful, growing urgency.

He drew back his hips and thrust. Within her, something tore free. A choked cry escaped her as pain flashed down to her toes.

Richard lay still. His shoulders had gone hard under her hands, and lines of strain etched his face.

"I'm sorry," he gasped.

"It's better now," she assured him. As the pain faded, a restless need to move rose in her. She lifted her hips, experimenting, and whimpered at the pleasure as he sank deeper.

Richard groaned, thrusting slowly, then faster. Joining her in body and spirit. Soon she was twisting under him. The world narrowed to driving, fiery pleasure. Clutching him, she hovered on the lip of a wave. "Richard," she gasped.

"I love you." He thrust hard, then shuddered.

Deep within her, the wave crashed into a wall of rushing light.

When the light faded and the world returned, she and Richard were still joined. His head rested on the pillow by hers, and his thudding heartbeat pounded against her chest. She lay beneath him in a contented, wondering daze.

At last, he raised his head and kissed her. "All right?"

"Oh, indeed." Miranda smiled at him. His hair had fallen into his eyes. She brushed it back, exulting in her new right to touch him whenever she pleased.

He withdrew from her, leaving her with a strange, bereft feeling as he settled her against his side. She kissed his chest. A thin veil of sweat on his skin shone in the firelight.

They rested together, dozing. Miranda awoke first and so had a chance to look her fill. He was all solid muscle, strength he used to serve what was right. And he was hers.

Tentatively, she stroked his chest. Richard sighed and covered her hand with his.

"More," he murmured, smiling.

Exploring him with her hands and mouth, she gloried in his eager response.

I want you, he thought. *I will always want you.*

You have me, she promised as he sank into her warmth. Moving with him, she wrapped her legs around his waist. *Always.*

Perhaps not, they both knew. The shadowland waited just beyond the horizon. The specter of Wyndon still hovered near them, and they had history yet to put right, a deed that might erase all they had been to each other.

Pushing those worries aside, Miranda arched beneath him. Licked the side of his neck.

Thought vanished. They lost themselves in now.

CHAPTER 26

T he roads had dried, so the coach turned into the gate at Hawkstowe House three days later instead of four. Snuggled against Richard's side, Miranda said, "I hope your grandmother is up and about by now." Because Patience sat across from them, she silently added, *I hope she won't mind that we want to marry.*

Our *grandmother*, he corrected, *will be delighted. She was sitting up when I scried her this morning.* He dropped a kiss on Miranda's hair. "I'm eager to see her."

I hope you're right, on both points.

She gripped his hand more tightly as the coach cleared the entry arch. The courtyard walls gleamed in the setting sun. This was home now. She belonged in this lovely house, in this family with its history and traditions. At Richard's side, for as long as they might have.

The coach stopped, and a footman opened the door. Richard climbed out, then offered her his hand. Gathering her skirts, she glanced toward the portico. Enderby stood there, his face solemn and his garments black.

Black? Oh, no!

"Miranda?" Richard frowned. "What is it?"

She jumped to the ground. "Oh, pray, let me be wrong." Skirts in hand, she ran for the steps.

A strangled sound came from Richard. He raced past her. Taking the stairs three at a time, he reached the door in moments. Red-eyed,

Enderby looked solemnly up at him, and Miranda's heart ripped in twain.

~

An hour later, Miranda sat with Richard and Lucius in the library while Lucius told him of his grandmother's illness. Richard seemed stunned that his grandmother, the bulwark of his childhood, could be gone.

"She was better this morning," he repeated.

"Aye, cousin." Weariness lined Lucius's thin face. "She broke her fast with a hearty meal and called for her maid to dress her. The maid said she collapsed in mid-sentence."

He paused, his eyes sad. "I couldn't rouse her. I did my best."

"I know you did. I'm grateful."

Richard should have been here. Miranda bit her lip. He'd never say it, never blame her, but part of him would always wonder if he could have brought about a different outcome.

He caught her hand in a warm grip. *Don't tread that path. If I had it to do over, I would do the same. As she wanted.*

"It may be," Lucius said, "that her heart failed. She had fought for days against the poison. She must've been weary."

"You're certain it was poison?" Miranda asked.

"The curative herbs took far longer, in much greater doses, than would have been required if she'd merely eaten spoiled food. Jane said she fell ill after eating a sweet cake sent by Lady Vale, but the lady vows she sent no cake." He shook his head. "Her message sounded distraught."

"Of course." Richard slumped in his chair. "Lucius, I thank you for all your care. Where should I send a purse?"

"There's a baker's widow and family, name of Tate, in East Cheap who could use it."

"It will go tonight."

His eyes solemn, Lucius said, "The Winfield brothers came to me with grave charges against Henry de Vere."

"The charges are accurate."

"That's as may be, but Miranda's inexperience works against belief in her visions. Henry has many allies, as you know. They'll argue that the Croyland gravestone shows him doing only what he has advocated, turning these changes to our advantage."

"That can't excuse his assault on her."

Lucius frowned. "Only Miranda may bring that charge."

"I gladly will," she said. "He means to shape an England no decent person could want."

"I believe you," Lucius said, "and your charge against him is enough for a hearing. After much wrangling on the Council, I've had one set for the day after tomorrow. But we cannot scry far enough into the past to see what he changed, nor can we divine his intentions by scrying. On those, it will be your word against his."

Richard leaned forward. "Everyone present will know who's telling the truth."

"That doesn't mean they'll accept it. Truth isn't always the primary choice among us, as it isn't among the unGifted. Write a statement of your charges, Miranda, and I'll present it."

Lucius stood. "I can do no more."

I can, and I will. Richard's silent vow echoed in Miranda's mind. He also rose, and his hand caught hers as she stood.

Lucius glanced from one to the other of them. "If I may be so bold, cousins, am I to offer good wishes?"

Richard slid his arm around her waist. "You've keen perceptions, Lucius. Miranda has consented to wed me."

The older man favored her with a solemn nod. "That's a very good thing. Something joyous in a time of shared loss. May the Great Mother bless you."

"Thank you," Miranda said. *The Great Mother?*

Lucius worships the old powers. "I'll see you out," Richard offered.

"I can find my way." With a slight bow, Lucius left the room.

When the door closed, Richard stalked to the hearth. "Wyndon murdered her, just as he tried to murder you."

"You can't know that."

"I do know. I haven't had a chance to tell you, but the girl who served the cake has disappeared. Cook thinks George was bedding her." Richard snorted. "So much for his vaunted betrothal."

"Surely he wouldn't do that to your grandmother." But Miranda didn't feel certain at all.

Anger crackled through their bond. "I'd like to think he didn't know what he was doing. If he did, he'll rue it."

"What will you do?"

"What I would've done back in Croyland if you'd already been safely home. What must be done." Pain flashed between them, and he turned solemn eyes to her. "When I do, Miranda ... " Shaking his head, he caught her against him.

He would try to fix the timeline. If he succeeded, they would lose each other. Her throat tight with unshed tears, she locked her arms around his waist. *It's too soon, Richard.*

It will always be too soon. He tipped her chin up.

A footman knocked as he entered. "Captain Winfield and Reverend Winfield," he said solemnly, then stepped aside.

Richard kissed her quickly. *Later, heart of mine.*

Cabot and Jeremy hurried into the room. "Richard, Miranda," Cabot said, "I cannot tell you how sorry I am. She was a grand lady."

"Wyndon will be sorrier yet," Richard said. "What have you found about that tombstone?"

"The records are changing," Jeremy said as they all took seats. "Oliver Cromwell's son and successor, Richard Cromwell, apparently died of food poisoning in 1655 instead of becoming Lord Protector and ruling England when his father died three years after that."

"It was his bungling as protector that opened the way for King Charles's restoration." Jeremy shook his head. "Food poisoning."

Like Richard's grandmother. If not for the poison, her heart would not have failed.

"If there's no Richard Cromwell to bungle the protectorate, if history changes so that someone competent becomes—became, hellfire!—Lord Protector when Oliver Cromwell died, then there is no Restoration," Richard said, lacing his fingers through Miranda's.

"Exactly." Jeremy poured a glass of sack from the bottle on the table. "I checked the annals for the years around the date on that tombstone. The changes are moving forward in time. The new record contains preliminary moves toward abolishing the laws against witchcraft in 1661."

Richard's brows rose. "That would require either lunacy from Parliament or iron control of it."

"He prorogued Parliament, taking a lesson from Charles I. He does as he will," Jeremy said. "Or he did, thirteen years ago."

"Prorogued?" Miranda asked.

"A fancy term for sending them home," Richard explained. "I would wager he consolidated his power before making open moves. He may have done so for years."

"We must somehow stop that bastard," Cabot said. "Begging your pardon, Miranda. The sooner, the better."

"I think I know how." Richard's eyes looked bleak, like a stormy winter night. "Edmund once told me the afterworld touches all times. If I go there, perhaps I can figure out how Wyndon gained the ability to travel time, to make these changes, and then undo it."

"I'll help you," Cabot and Miranda said together. They glanced at each other, startled, then smiled.

"No," Richard said. "Tripling our risk makes no sense. Three can't move faster than one at this, and opening a portal for three is vastly more difficult than doing it for one."

Miranda frowned. "You shouldn't go there alone."

"I won't be alone. I'll have Edmund."

"A ghost doesn't seem like much aid," she replied.

"All will be well, love." Before she or the brothers could protest further, he continued, "We've something else to do first."

Putting his arm around her, he said, "Jeremy, tell us the fastest way to marry."

Jeremy and Cabot grinned at each other. "First," Jeremy said, "congratulations. As to the legalities, under the old law, if a betrothed couple anticipates the wedding, so to speak, they're as good as wed, but the Church officially disapproves of relying on that. You should have a formal ceremony. I don't suppose you would wait long enough to post the banns?"

Richard and Miranda smiled sadly at each other, then at him. Time was the thing they had least.

Jeremy nodded. "I'll help you obtain a special license, then. We've a busy day tomorrow."

Staring at the images in his parlor fire, Henry frowned. A wedding. Quite a step up, from serving wench to countess.

Hawkstowe looked besotted as they left the church, but would his new bride keep him occupied until the time changes overtook the present? Or would he use the shadow realm to track, and possibly undo in the real world, those changes? Did he even know he could? If he knew how, why hadn't he already done so?

A wise man would have, and Hawkstowe had to have traversed the shadowland to reach Croyland so quickly. But had he taken the time to explore it? Learning its ways had taken Henry weeks of travel there and a month of study at Pendragon.

In a rush to save his intended, Hawkstowe likely hadn't taken that time, so he couldn't have learned much about the place. Such as how to hide there. Or how to command the wraiths without actually speaking. Or how to use the magic there to become an immensely more powerful being.

Henry rubbed his chin. If Hawkstowe entered the afterworld again, he couldn't be allowed to leave it.

~

A scant hour after their wedding, Miranda sat in Richard's chamber —their chamber now, for a little while—and watched him button his leather jerkin. "I wish you would let me come," she said. "Or Cabot. I hate to think of you in that place alone."

He shook his head. "The afterworld is woven into my destiny, love, not yours." He shoved his foot into a boot and grabbed its mate. "Somewhere there, I've kinsmen, and Edmund will help me. He knows how its magic works."

She ran her left thumb over her gold and emerald wedding band. Arabella's—Grandmère's, it had been. Miranda would cherish it all the more for that reason.

Glancing at her hand, he smiled. "She would be glad to have you wear it."

"I hope so. I feel a little disloyal, wearing it so soon." Perhaps it was fitting, though. She had chosen his grandmother's path, embracing a doomed man's cause rather than blaming him.

"She had grown fond of you. I know she would want you to have it." His smile faded. "If we can restore the timeline, perhaps she can dance at our next wedding."

"I hope so." If they were still together when the timeline was restored. "Remember that vision I had of you in trouble in a mist-shrouded place. I'm terrified that it could come true."

"I'll be careful."

He had his boots on now. His gloves lay on the bed beside her. He tucked them into his belt, then drew her to her feet, his eyes intent. "I love you, my lady wife."

Cupping her cheek in his hand, he paused. His eyes searched hers, willing her to believe him. "Even if I succeed, sweeting, the correction may take time, as the changes did. I'm selfish enough to hope it does. I promise I'll return for our wedding supper."

"You'd better." Sudden fear threatened to choke her. "Richard, be wary."

"I will be. I have too much to live for."

Their lips met with soul-searing intensity. Too soon, he raised his head.

"Hold that thought." He brushed her hair back from her face. "You're the lady of the house now. The servants will mind you, and gladly, since they're so pleased about our marriage. Cabot and Jeremy will stay with you, and Jeremy will help you pass the time with more lessons in basic healing. With time travel, I can likely return an instant after I leave."

She nodded. "Do you have your anchor?" He had explained about needing one to return to reality.

"In my pocket, a stone from the garden. I'll be back before you have time to miss me."

"I already do, and I love you. Godspeed."

"I love you." He kissed her quickly, then turned his back, took three quick strides toward the suddenly glowing doorway, and disappeared.

R ichard stepped through the barrier, magical shields up, and the shrieking wraiths whirled around him. Their cries sent ice rolling down his spine, but he couldn't do anything about that.

He started walking. Calling for Edmund in this not-place didn't feel wise. Perhaps thinking of him would summon him.

Richard hadn't told Miranda everything. Putting history right had to come first, but he would also kill Wyndon for what he had done to her and to Grandmère. If he had to, he'd find a way to prove he acted within the rules of engagement.

One by one, the wraiths seemed to tire of their futile assault and dropped away. Still no sign of Edmund, though. Richard walked alone in the stinking fog.

Suddenly, the wraiths rushed back, surrounding him. The nape of his neck twitched, as though from a presence. Miranda's warning flashed back to him. He wheeled, too late. Someone's fist struck with enough magical force to pierce his shield and slam into his temple.

Head spinning, he staggered and caught a glancing blow from something hard. His vision turned black at the edges. His shield dropped, and wraiths dived at him. Desperately, he clung to consciousness. Had to focus—shield.

Something ripped down his back, piercing his jerkin and scraping his skin. Icicles of pain jabbed into his brain. Blind, he fell to his knees. Shields—couldn't—

Something yanked at his side. Ripped into his garments. Cold, fetid air rushed over him.

Battling the throbbing pain and cold, he gathered himself. Felt the power. Shields. Almost there.

The icicles lanced through his head, destroying his focus. Frigid, stinging hands grabbed his arms. Pinned them behind his back. Icy talons jabbed into his ballocks, and he choked on the pain.

When he pressed his thighs together, the talons tore open his back. Sharp, chilling claws flayed stripes across his chest, back, legs, and arms. Agony ripped a cry from him as hot, wet blood dripped from the wounds and stung his nose with its coppery scent. Pain flashed through him in a searing wave that stopped his breath as oblivion claimed him.

CHAPTER 27

An ugly death, being torn to bits by wraiths, but suitable for one of Hawkstowe's cursed destiny.

Re-emerging in his parlor doorway, Henry smiled. He'd done it. By lurking in the afterworld near Hawkstowe House, he'd seen the young fool enter the afterworld, then lain in wait in the mists. When the wraiths attacked, he'd used them for cover to strike his foe in the head. Once Hawkstowe lost focus, and thus dropped his shields, he was doomed.

Stumbling to a chair, Henry opened his fist and glanced at the pebble he held. Such an ordinary thing, yet so important. He tossed it into the basket by the hearth. Perhaps Hawkstowe's trapped, frustrated ghost would see him do it.

Too bad he hadn't been able to stay until the idealistic fool's last tortured breath, but he couldn't risk being out of reality when the time changes hit. He didn't know what would happen if he were, and he'd dared too much to jeopardize his chance at the protectorate.

Remembering the jagged, bloody wounds all over Hawkstowe's body, Henry smiled. The de Veres had beaten the Mainwarings at last. Soon, he would rule all England.

"Something has gone wrong." Pacing in front of the library hearth, Miranda glanced at the mantel clock. "Richard should have returned by now."

Seated at the table, Cabot and Jeremy exchanged a glance. "I'll see if I can figure out how to breach the barrier," Cabot said, "but I can concentrate better if no one's watching me."

"Use Richard's—our—chamber," Miranda suggested. "I believe you know where it is."

Cabot nodded, rising. On the way to the door, he squeezed her arm. "I'm sure he's all right." He left the room, closing the door behind him.

Miranda resumed pacing. "I'd just like to *do* something. Anything." Sewing wasn't nearly active enough, and she'd reached the limits of practicing the simple healing skills she'd learned.

"I pray for his success and safety." Jeremy looked down at his hands. "At times like this, I rue forswearing my powers."

Forswearing? "You healed my throat."

He shrugged. "Healing is the only one I use, as it serves others. The rest too easily become selfish. In the afterworld, Richard and Cabot had to shield me."

"Can you or Cabot teach me to do that? Shield, I mean."

"He can't manage it here. The shield seems to need something in the afterworld. Cabot and Richard both tried, in case they ever needed to travel there again."

Footsteps approached in the hallway, loud and fast. Cabot burst into the room. "We must go. Hurry."

"Go where?" Miranda demanded. "Did you find Richard?"

"No time. The protector's men—Wyndon's—are at the gate. With that scurvy rat, George. Morton refused to open up, so they're breaking down the gate. One of your footmen came running up the stairs to warn us."

"The time changes have caught us, then." Suddenly cold with fear, she hurried to the door. "If we're leaving, I'll need less conspicuous clothes. Wait here."

The Countess of Hawkstowe would stand out. The serving maid would not.

Morton hadn't opened the gate. Was Morton waiting for an order from her, Richard's wife? Were they even wed in the new reality? Or did Morton simply not like George? Whatever his reason, the gatekeeper had bought them valuable time.

Miranda ran down to her bedchamber and threw open the chest that held her old clothes. Even a small chest would be too much to carry, but she could bundle a few things in her spare cloak. She grabbed it and chose an old gown. Despite her new wardrobe, she'd kept her old garments as a hedge against whatever the future brought.

Miranda ran back to the library. As she entered it, shots sounded in the courtyard. She threw a startled glance at Cabot.

He sprang to the window to look. "The protector's men are through the gate. Miranda, Richard has a secret stair."

"I know. This way." Holding her skirts up, she ran for the library. She was Richard's wife, but would the stair open for her? Or only for him?

They raced into the room and to the hearth. Where had Richard tapped? She ran her finger along the edge of the carving. One spot tingled. She stopped. Tapped. Pressed.

The bookcase swung back, and she blew out a relieved breath. "I'll go first," she said. If the wall opened for her, surely the traps would stay their power. At least, she hoped so. "But I can't make witchlight."

Blue light flared around Cabot's hand, casting a ghostly glow downward, as Jeremy tugged the library door shut. They followed the winding stair to the bottom without incident. She slammed her palm against the wall, and it, too, fell back.

The magic had accepted her, so she was a Mainwaring now for certain. But for how long?

"The way out is there, by the water." Miranda hurried to it. That door, too, opened at her touch.

"There are no traps past the first turn," Cabot said. "Once we're there, let me lead. Richard and I used to play in the secret tunnels."

"If you know them, does Wyndon?"

"I doubt the Mainwarings shared the information, but that doesn't ensure anything when magic is involved."

Regardless, they were committed now. She touched the door, and it closed behind them. With Cabot's light revealing the way, they stepped into the narrow, low passage.

They wandered in darkness, sometimes splashing in puddles, sometimes stumbling over loose stones.

"Who built these tunnels?" Miranda asked, her voice low to avoid echoes.

"Each family built its own escape route." Cabot's soft tone didn't carry far. He glanced at his brother. "Our house is only half a mile away, and our tunnels connect with these. We should veer into ours in case Wyndon somehow discovered Richard's secret."

"If he discovered Richard's," Miranda asked quietly, "could he have discovered yours?"

"We don't know he learned of either. I recommend the change as a precaution, but it's up to you. We've a passage that emerges in a tavern cellar."

The idea made sense. "Lead on," she said.

They picked their way through the semi-darkness for another long interval. The uneven footing slowed their progress, and time seemed to drag. As they trudged through the tunnel, Miranda listened for sounds of pursuit.

At last, Cabot stopped. He touched a section of wall, and it swung inward. He ducked through the low opening. Miranda and Jeremy followed him up a narrow wooden staircase.

He paused at the top. "Let me see what's out there." His eyes lost focus. He must be extending his senses.

One day, she would have to refine her use of that trick. Except that she'd lost her teachers. And her love.

Her throat closed. She swallowed hard. Surely she would know if he died. Surely she would.

"All clear," Cabot whispered. He quenched his witchlight and tapped the wall. It swung inward to reveal a dim cellar. "Let me look around first." He slipped through the opening.

Cabot vanished. The world twisted around itself.

R ichard opened his eyes. He lay on a pallet in a tent of some blue fabric with Edmund seated on the ground at his side. The pain was gone.

Of course, dead men probably didn't feel pain.

The realization stabbed through him. Gone. All hope for England, for him and Miranda, was gone. There was no one other than Wyndon who could travel this realm now.

"How do you feel?" Edmund asked.

"Tired. For a dead man, I suppose," he said bitterly.

"You're not dead, no thanks to your folly."

"Not dead?" Truly? Was there still a chance to put everything right?

"Not," Edmund confirmed.

Richard laughed in relief, and Edmund added, scowling, "The next time you mean to try such a thing, let me know. I'll stand guard while you enter. At least my healing powers haven't grown rusty. Repaired your garments, too. Your clothes were in shreds."

The memory roared back, and Richard flinched. "My thanks. How long have I been here?"

"A couple of days, as time passes in the living world."

Days! Miranda would be frantic.

Richard sat up and felt for his pocket. It was gone, torn completely away. "My anchor, a stone—it was in this pocket. Did you take it?"

"No." Edmund's expression turned grim. "I heard a cry, came toward it, and saw wraiths assailing you. Mayhap they took it."

"I can't imagine why. Someone attacked me." Someone who'd used the wraiths for cover. "It must've been Wyndon. He must've taken the stone."

"You can't return to the living world unless someone anchored to it comes for you." Edmund paused. "I've seen them scry for you without success. They may think you're dead."

"I must let Miranda know I live." Richard pushed himself upright. Still no pain. Good.

Edmund rose, too. "You can reach only your blood kin—descendants, not that fool, George. Your friend Cabot tried to come for you, but he couldn't. Now he's disappeared, probably in a time shift."

Richard swallowed against a rush of grief. "Perhaps there's another way. Miranda and I have a unique bond."

"We'll see whether that can serve. Meanwhile, we've a more immediate problem. I've no food for you, nor water. I've sustained you by drawing power from the fog and transferring it to you, as with a healing spell. Now that you're recovering, you can draw power for yourself, but no magic can sustain you indefinitely. You've few days more—not even a sennight, I'd guess, before you become ill."

So he'd gained only a reprieve. He'd better not waste it, then.

"I must find Miranda. Then I need to learn how to set history right. Once I manage to escape from here."

Edmund looked gravely at him. "When we step outside, draw power to protect yourself, as you did before. I'll help if you need it."

They walked out of the tent and into the gray, foggy twilight. The wraiths dived at them. Richard ducked, reaching for power. It came in such a rush that his skin crawled with it and his gut churned. Hell's feet, why couldn't he have fought through the pain and shielded that way earlier?

The wraiths shrieked, clawing at him.

"Oh, begone." A wave of Edmund's hand banished them.

"Nice trick."

Edmund shrugged. "Think of your wife, and you'll find her."

Richard tried. As he and Edmund walked through the sulphurous mists, his confidence slowly grew. He'd formed armor in the vision he and Miranda had shared. Formed it with a mere thought. If he thought of a dagger, envisioned it in his hand ...

With a crackle of purple power, the mists formed into a slender, narrow-hilted dagger. "Useful," he commented.

"Not against wraiths," Edmund said dryly.

"Why can I do that, form something from nothing?"

"I've puzzled on that. Those who die pass through here, shedding the last of life's power as they move to the portal. The power stays here. As power from faith suffuses the Green Bull because of the old temple to Mithras."

Richard nodded. "Churches, I think, have some of the same. Power from centuries of magical working has also soaked into the earth and the air at Pendragon."

"Precisely. As with any power, we can tap it, but this source has accumulated for eons. We can therefore do astounding things with it." Edmund stopped, pointing ahead. "Richard, look. What do you see?"

"Only mist. I—wait. A chamber." He rushed toward it.

Edmund caught his arm. "You cannot reach it."

The scene had a foggy quality, as though he viewed it through gauze. Stifling his impatience, he said, "I see Miranda and Jeremy." So close, but impossible to touch. Yet his hand rose toward her anyway. "They look terrible."

"They've been in hiding since your wedding day. My congratulations on that, by the way."

A low hatch under the eaves appeared to be the room's entrance. Seated on pallets on the floor of a cramped chamber, Miranda and Jeremy shared a meal of bread and cheese. In a garret, to judge by the rafters that barely left them room to sit. They could likely stand only at the far side of the space, where the roof sloped upward. Both wore cloaks, so the room must be cold.

A narrow window overlooked the street. The pallets, an unlit brazier in the corner, and a chamber pot provided the only furnishings.

Gathering power, Richard flung it at the hatch. Nothing happened.

"I warned you," Edmund said. "Without an anchor, you've no link to that world."

But he did. He had Miranda and their strange bond. *Miranda, my own. I'm here.*

But he couldn't feel her presence, only see her, and no response came. His fists balled, and frustration tangled with fear in his gut. He had to reach her, or more than their love was doomed.

"We must do something," Miranda said, her eyes hard. "We cannot lurk here forever."

"We must know how matters stand, whom we can trust, before we can plan." Jeremy rubbed his hand over his face. "In any case, Richard would want you out of danger. You should stay here."

"Richard isn't here to have an opinion," she snapped.

Her pain tore at Richard's heart. *I'm here. Damnation!*

Willing her to feel his presence, he walked through the gauzy scene and knelt beside her. She didn't so much as glance his way, not even when he put an arm around her. It passed through her, and he bit back a curse. Foolish, this stinging feeling that she'd rebuffed him. Irrational. She didn't know he was there.

Biting her lip, she muttered, "I beg pardon, Jeremy. I don't forget we've lost Cabot and Kit, but I won't believe Richard is also gone."

Miranda continued, "If he were dead, I'd know it. I'm sure I would." She huddled deeper into her cloak, her old, faded blue one.

Where was the new one, green velvet lined with sable?

Yes, my lady, Richard thought to her. *I'm here.* He reached out to her. Again his hand sliced through her form as it would through air.

God's blood, so close, and yet so out of reach. Miranda, sweetheart.

She showed no reaction. *Hellfire!*

Edmund said, "Try again while she sleeps. The mind has lower defenses then. That's why I first visited you when you slept, not that you ever made that easy."

Although Richard couldn't touch her, he traced the line of her back with his hand. Somehow, he would return to her. "Tell me about this place so I can restore the timeline and go home."

~

"Richard," Miranda whispered. For a moment, she had almost thought ... But that was mad. She glanced at Jeremy.

He didn't seem to have noticed anything. He must fear for Cabot as much as she did for Richard. The changes in history had overtaken them as they left the warded tunnels. She and Jeremy had found themselves in the middle of King Edward Street, near the Fleet River. Now a former Winfield retainer hid them in a warded nook above his tavern in Fleet Street.

Despite Jeremy's reluctance to use his magic, they'd both tried to scry for Cabot, for Lucius, for anyone they knew, but failed. Those people were either dead or magically hidden too well.

"We should try again to enter the shadow world," Jeremy said, rubbing his hands over his face. "If we can manage that, we can meet up with Richard or this Edmund and try to put matters right."

"We've tried for the past two days, Jeremy. Unless you know some other approach, doing the same thing again and again likely won't succeed. If we can't reach anyone there, Richard said, we can't pass through."

He scowled. "We must try something. We can't just sit—"

Loud voices cut through the din below. Shouting. Shrieks.

She and Jeremy exchanged worried glances. He peered through a knothole in a floorboard. "Soldiers," he murmured.

"You, you, and you," a rough voice barked. "Lord Withersby needs servants. You'll do, and honored for it."

"But I've a family to care for," a woman's voice protested.

"No one refuses," the rough voice said.

"But—no! No, please! I'll come, I'll do whatever you say." Her voice rose in a shriek. The stench of burning wool filled the room.

The slice of Jeremy's face Miranda could see turned ashen. His lips moved as though in silent prayer.

She peered between the floorboards. The narrow crack gave her a limited view, but enough to see a brown skirt blazing below. Did the soldiers mean to burn that woman alive?

Coup de grâce, Arabella's voice in her memory said. Miranda shuddered. Could she kill this woman to spare her pain? If she did, would the Gifted with the soldiers sense—

The rough voice said, "That's better. Don't give us any more trouble." A pause. "Any o'you lot. Now let's go."

Jeremy glanced up and whispered, "Fire's out."

"Can we help?" she murmured

He shook his head. "Not against a wizard and soldiers."

She peered through a crack in the floor. Men wearing breastplates and helmets pushed half a dozen people into a line. One woman had a large, charred hole in her skirt and petticoats. The blistered flesh of her legs showed through.

Miranda ached to do something, anything, but Jeremy was right.

She slumped against the wall. "The Gifted never terrorized others. Why now?"

"It happened, and more often than we'd like to admit. Why do you think the fear of witchcraft persists? Some folk, Gifted and not, will do anything for power, but they're few enough that the rest of us keep them in check. Somehow, we must find others like us."

She had Seen something much like this, and now it had come to pass. What worse horrors lay in store?

～

"Again," Richard said to Edmund. "Tell me again how you talk to the others." He swept his gaze around the tent. What wouldn't he give for a single drink of cool, fresh spring water?

"I think of them, but I don't actually go to them, nor do they come to me." Frowning, Edmund shook his head. "I'll ask the others if they know anything about splicing time, though I wouldn't hold out much hope. Meanwhile, practice traveling."

"While Wyndon grinds England under his boot. Damnation, Edmund. There must be something you're forgetting to mention."

Edmund raised an eyebrow. "How many times did you have to practice glamours before you could hold one steady?"

When Richard's jaw tightened, the ghost nodded. "Precisely," Edmund said. "Traveling. One bit at a time, Richard."

Perhaps he had a point. "Traveling, then. To Plymouth. I like one of the taverns." He'd often been there with Cabot, who could talk for hours about the English fleet sailing from there to defeat the mighty Spanish Armada.

"All right, then. Off with you."

"You're not coming?"

"I rather thought you wanted to be alone."

The memory of Miranda's grief-stricken face still burned in him. "I do," Richard agreed. "Edmund, do you sleep?"

"Sometimes, but I don't need to. I exist in the middle of a waking dream, you see. I created the tent to protect you. I don't need it, either."

"I see."

"No, you don't," Edmund replied, "but I'm sorry to say, you will one day." He sighed heavily. "Richard—truly, I am sorry."

"I know. Forget it. You saved my life, after all." The help Edmund had given him since their meeting in Dover had bled away the last of Richard's resentment. Behind it lay only a soft, silvery regret.

Edmund looked down at his toes. "Go on with you. I've things to do."

"How will I find you again?"

"Look for me, as you do for the places you want to see. Then you'll find me."

"Very well, then. I'll see you later." Richard gathered power to shield himself and stepped out into the mist. Peering through it, as he had earlier, he sensed the world moving by.

Could he make it move faster?

Wraiths swirled around him. He ignored them, and they gradually drifted away. As he walked through the stinking fog, the world moved at its same pace, as Edmund had told him it would. Scowling, he slowed his steps.

He hadn't visited Plymouth in a couple of years. Then, he'd met a Dutch double agent in a tavern near the docks. Was the coffee house opposite it still open? Legend had it that Drake had dined there the day before he faced the Armada.

What a day that must have been, with ships anchored in the harbor and long boats docked at the wharves, waiting to take the captains to their crews. Had those legendary captains really played at bowls that day?

I sound like Cabot, he realized, grinning. The grin faded as he also realized he had lost track of the real world.

Ah, there lay Yelverton. Only a little farther.

Time moved so strangely here. He had to reach London again while Miranda slept.

There was Plymouth. He concentrated on the coffeehouse, as he had done with the alley in Canterbury, and found himself standing opposite the old tavern, in front of the coffee house. Save that the coffee house and tavern signboards were gone. Had they fallen in a storm?

People were hurrying toward the wharves. Again watching through gauzy haze, he fell in with the crowd.

They were talking about a battle. Had the Dutch taken arms again? The people's clothes—

"Who are you?" someone asked behind him.

Wheeling, he tightened his defenses. The man staring at him had dark hair and gray eyes. His square-jawed, aristocratic face had passed its first youth but not yet reached great age. It bore a curious expression.

In all, the man looked much like the portrait of Miles Mainwaring, right down to his clothing, the doublet, puffy breeches, hose, and high boots of an Elizabethan captain. Richard's heart beat faster.

But the man didn't look gauzy. He seemed as real as Edmund, so did he belong here? Was he as sane as he appeared, or was he a wraith in disguise?

"First, tell me who you are," Richard said.

The man raised one eyebrow. "Sir Miles Mainwaring. Now, who are you?"

Richard rocked back on his heels. Miles Mainwaring had commanded the *Queen's Honor* against the Armada. How had the old seadog gotten here? Assuming he was who he claimed to be.

"Richard Mainwaring. Lord Hawkstowe, thanks to you."

Miles shrugged. "We'd had that title since Arthur's day. It seemed little enough for the Queen to give back what her sire had taken."

A woman walked through Richard. He glanced over himself. Although he found no damage, his stomach did a slow roll.

Miles drew Richard into the shadow of a building. Frowning, he demanded, "If you're real and not a shade, where were you born, that I don't know you?"

"At Hawkstowe in June 1642."

Miles blinked, then raised an eyebrow again. "Good God, man, how did you come to 1588?"

"1588?" Richard stared at him. "This is 1674."

Miles snorted. "The devil, you say." He nodded at the crowd. "Where d'you think they're going? Off to the wharves to see the captains set out, is where."

"Set out? You mean—?"

"To meet the Armada, lad."

"God's blood." Richard forgot the Armada. He had breached time. Had discovered the means Wyndon had used to change history. He could change it back.

If he could escape this place.

CHAPTER 28

"If you've figured out the time currents, Richard, why come back here before trying to see when Wyndon stole the scroll on necromancy?" Edmund frowned. "Why not tend to everything in one effort?"

"I don't want to miss Miranda's dreams." When a pitying look swept over Edmund's face, Richard shot him a warning scowl. "I had no way to know the hour in London. Since she hasn't retired, I'm going to Pendragon—and Wyndon and the scroll, I hope—now."

"Good luck, then." Edmund rubbed his jaw as a distant, thoughtful expression stole over his face. "You know, Richard, once you're free ... "

"What?"

"Nothing. It can wait." With a brisk, shooing motion, Edmund herded him toward the opening. "Soonest done, and all that. Off with you."

That was an odd change of mood, but Richard shrugged. Edmund would tell him, or not, eventually. Now, he had other matters to attend to.

At the tent opening, he paused. "I wish I could see my father."

"He cannot come forward in time to you." Edmund studied the fog shrouding his boots. "Even if he weren't trapped in his own time, he couldn't face you. The madness fades when they arrive here, but the guilt over not lifting the curse does not."

Edmund sighed. "I think you can travel time, where I cannot, because you yet live. If so, you might be able to go to your father, but I wouldn't. Not yet."

Richard had come to trust Edmund, so he nodded. "Father should know—that is, I understand, Edmund. I've been happy despite it all. Tell him."

"Of course." Edmund hesitated. "Be careful, grandson."

"I will." With a nod, Richard strode into the mist.

Reaching for the world let him sense it moving past. Miranda's presence in London lured him like a beacon, but he had a job to do now. At least learning time travel moved him a step closer to fixing the problem.

And losing her forever.

Jaw set, he banished the thought. Somehow, they would be together again, even if not for long.

As he drew farther from Edmund, the wraiths swirled around him. Their screeches stabbed into his spine, and the skeletal claws swiped at him, bouncing off his magical shield.

Emulating Edmund, he snapped, "Begone" and sent a flare of magic at them. They wheeled away.

Richard gave a grim nod. Good to know he could do that.

Wyndon and the scroll. Pendragon. He kept his mind on that image. He had to know when Wyndon stole the scroll so he could put it back. Or, better yet, take it before Wyndon did. Anyone living who could reach this place could wreak havoc on the world. It would be better if no one figured out how to do that.

Something in the living world tugged at him. He followed its pull. The mists thinned, revealing Pendragon Manor, secret haven of the Gifted. The late afternoon sun cast slanting, golden light over the long, low, stone building and brightened its roof thatching.

The tug continued, drawing Richard into the building. He passed through walls as though they weren't there. The library was warded to prevent anyone from removing anything. That obviously hadn't stopped Wyndon, but why?

He obeyed the compulsion and found himself in the library. As usual, jumbled stacks of scrolls and books littered the long walnut table and spilled from the ceiling-high shelves. The doorway glowed silver, and Wyndon suddenly appeared in the room. Not in the shadowland but actually in the chamber. He could only have come from the afterworld. How, without Richard's seeing him there?

Was the fact that this had occurred in the past creating a rift of some kind? Something that kept Richard from encountering the man he watched, even though they both reached this place via the shadow realm?

Even more important, how had he breached the library wards? Any wards other than Mainwaring ones would stop Edmund. Was this another difference between what the living could do in the shadowland and what the dead could?

Wyndon hurried to the corner shelf. Stretching up, he reached behind a stack of big, leather-bound books. He drew back a thick scroll like the one Richard had seen in his house. He unrolled it quickly, scanning its contents.

Richard slid behind him to read over his shoulder. One word leaped off the page, *Necromancy*. This was the scroll Richard had seen in Wyndon's house. As he'd guessed, Wyndon must've learned to travel here the same way Richard had, by speaking with one already trapped in the shadowland. From that, all else flowed.

But that must've already happened, if he'd come through the after-world to steal the thing.

Tucking the scroll under his arm, Wyndon hurried to the door, which glowed soft argent. He strode toward it and vanished. Richard braced himself, but apparently the past in the real world didn't coincide with the past here. It seemed always to be "present" here, with a view of whatever time or place one chose. No future, no past.

No hope.

Richard grimaced. Fatigue weighted his limbs, and his stomach growled with hunger, reminders that he couldn't sustain himself on the mists for long. He'd found the key to fixing everything. If he went back in time and stole that necromancy scroll before Wyndon ever saw it, Wyndon would never learn how to change history. All would be as it had been before.

He and Miranda would never have met.

The thought stabbed his soul. What would be, would be, but if he could hold her just once more ... He drew in a sharp, painful breath and set his jaw. First things first.

To change anything, he had to reach the living world, which meant someone anchored to it had to come and free him. The shadowland was the last place he wanted Miranda to see, but she was the only person he might be able to reach. Could he let her risk coming here?

This was what came of power assuming its rightful place. Standing at the window of what would once have been the king's apartments in Whitehall Palace, Lord Protector Henry de Vere, formerly the mere Earl of Wyndon, savored the view.

Moonlight shone on the river, a silvery path broken by the black shadows of ships riding at anchor. Under his heel, London lay at peace. The time plague outbreak was ebbing, and stern allocation of resources, backed by the power of Henry's Gifted allies, had protected the capital from the food shortages the time changes had caused.

Now that the time stream had settled, the weather had calmed. Agriculture should return to its usual production levels, as would trade.

Seated at the table behind him, William said, "There's an excellent cheese course, Father."

"Of course there is. The Lord Protector of England dines only upon the best." Henry strolled back to the table and took the seat across from William's.

William raised his wine goblet, fine Venetian glass rimmed in gold, in salute. "No more skulking in the shadows and pretending to live ordinary, unGifted lives. We can be seen for what we truly are, masters of all we survey."

"Not quite." Henry seated himself and selected a wedge of Stilton. "But very nearly. France appears likely to stop rattling her sword, and Spain cowers before us. As for the Low Countries, profitable trade will pacify them."

"Destroying the Ile de France would convince Louis to turn Charles Stuart over to you."

The French king still harbored the fugitive prince, proclaimed but not crowned as Charles II in the new reality. "Stuart has little money and fewer followers. Let's not borrow trouble, William."

Now that Henry had averted the Restoration, *proclaimed* was as close to the throne as Stuart would come. "As for the French Gifted, if they prefer to remain hidden, that's their choice. Stupid but theirs."

"And so typically French." Smirking, William selected a piece of cheese. "We've a new crop of Gifted breeding wenches in custody. A couple of them required some persuasion but ultimately saw reason."

"They'll see the benefits eventually." Such as sturdy roofs over their heads and fine food. Their common lives couldn't ensure that. They wouldn't even have to raise the brats they whelped. The Gifted fathers would see to that.

"Some of them love their husbands," William pointed out. "Some have religious scruples about fornication and adultery, but in the end, they preferred breeding Gifted heirs for their betters to the deaths of their families and friends. When the Gifted lords come for Parliament, they'll have a wide choice."

"They'll welcome that choice after tomorrow's decree."

It would order that all peerages descended to the eldest Gifted son, legitimate or not, or else lapsed. Any titles not currently held by a Gifted peer would also instantly lapse. The protectorate could then bestow them on its Gifted allies.

Since the chance of producing a Gifted heir rose if both parents were Gifted, the lords would benefit from having breeders in addition to, or instead of, their unGifted wives. "Within a generation, Gifted nobles will wed only our own kind."

"Possibly sooner. I hear Lady Benton had an unfortunate accident. Or so Lord Benton says." William sipped wine. "Ah, well. Benton can choose a breeder or else wed a Gifted lady."

Henry grunted. "Speaking of breeders, have you found the Hawkstowe wench?"

"As you predicted, the reward offer bought information. She's hiding in a Fleet Street tavern. The guards are on their way to seize her and her male companion, who could be Jeremy Winfield. He's no threat, of course." William shook his head. "What a fool, eschewing the full use of his power."

"He's religious." Henry shrugged. "I want that woman. If she's with child, we must know. Our victory isn't complete while that wretched line endures."

"I assume we'll kill any brat she whelps."

"If it's male." Pausing, Henry eyed William. How far ahead could the boy think? "If it's a daughter, what do you suggest?"

After a moment, William's eyes lit. "A de Vere heir out of the last Mainwaring would subjugate their line to ours forever."

"Very good." He was a bright lad. A worthy successor but too ambitious to be allowed to know that. "I want Hawkstowe's widow. Breaking her will be a pleasure, and if she bears a girl, you can have the child."

William smiled. "Think of Hawkstowe's ghost watching her moan and thrash under you when you ride her. Or seeing her bear your son."

"I will enjoy that. Unless she holds dangerous knowledge."

Such as how to travel the afterworld, which Hawkstowe and the Winfield brothers, at least, had done. She must be aware of its existence, but she might not know how to enter it. Admiralty records of the new history showed Cabot Winfield killed in the abortive rebellion of 1669. Hawkstowe's other close friend, the Earl of Havelock, had also died in the new timeline.

"If she does have dangerous knowledge?" William asked.

"We'll kill her, of course. And Winfield for certain."

R*ichard*, Miranda thought. *If you're there, give me some sign. Anything. I can't believe you're dead. I won't.*

She could almost feel him near. Almost. What a wretched word.

Believing he lived grew harder with each passing hour. Had he become trapped in the afterworld, or had her horrible vision of him under attack there come true?

At last, her body's weariness overcame her fear. She fell into an uneasy doze ....

And met Richard on a hillside bright with summer flowers. He smiled at the swaddled infant in his arms. "He has your eyes."

She took the baby, its small, bundled frame a sweet weight in her arms. Eyes the same light blue as her own stared back at her. "He's so tiny."

Richard put his arm around her. "I'm glad he was born at Hawkstowe. I've always loved this place."

Smiling at him, she noticed the manor beyond him. Morning sunlight washed over the gray stone of the hall, tower, and crenellated walls and gave the half-timbered upper stories of the great hall and the gatehouse a faint glow. Smoke rose from the kitchen. With it came a faint scent of roasting mutton.

What a beautiful day.

"I love Hawkstowe, but I love you more," he said, his voice low and soft.

She turned to him. The blue of his eyes warmed as he cupped her cheek. Beyond him, the manor and the hillside and the forest wavered. This was a dream. "No—Richard!"

She clutched at his fading shape. As her hand went through him, the baby disappeared. Everything turned gray. Tears welled in her eyes, and Miranda fell to her knees.

"Richard—Richard, oh, pray, don't go."

"I haven't gone."

Mist swirled everywhere. Scrubbing at her eyes with the back of one hand, she said, "Richard?"

"Here, beside you." His voice came from over her right shoulder.

Although she felt his presence, she saw nothing. "Where?"

The mists faded into the secret room. "No—"

"I'm in the afterworld, and you're with Jeremy. Just don't awaken." He stood before her, looking real and solid despite sulphurous mists wafting around him.

"Then—I'm dreaming?" Could this possibly be happening? Was he really there? Or a figment of desperate love?

"You still sleep, but I'm no dream. I'm alive, love. Edmund saved me."

The words struck her like a hammer in her chest. New hope constricted her lungs until she could scarcely breathe. She drew in a shuddering, gasping breath. Holding it, she fought to control herself.

"Listen, sweet, because I don't know how long I can hold this link. I've found out how Wyndon went back in time. I can fix the timeline if I can leave here. Unfortunately, I don't have an anchor. He stole it."

"Then you're trapped," she said slowly as her heart plummeted. "Oh, Richard. Cabot already tried to come look for you. He couldn't breach the barrier—he thought, because he hadn't talked from this side to someone on the other side. Jeremy and I both tried today. And Richard—I'm so sorry, but now Cabot's gone."

"I know. I overheard you earlier. That's another reason to put all this right."

There just might be a way. "I'm talking to you, connected to you," she realized. "Mayhap I could—"

"Perhaps, but if you do, Miranda, I don't want you coming here. If you and Jeremy can open a portal, let him come fetch me. This place is vile and dangerous."

"I don't care. I told you, I would dare anything for you."

"I care," he said, his face grim. "Besides, the transition requires channeling pure, raw power and sustaining it. You haven't enough experience doing that. Jeremy has more training than you do, has even been here, and still couldn't form a portal. Frankly, the odds that either of you can do it are slim, and even worse for the possibility that you can learn to do so quickly. But we must try."

"Tell me what to do." She had to see him, touch him. Know he was no dream. "Whatever it's like there, it can't be worse than the England Wyndon has made. His soldiers set a woman on fire for refusing to serve one of his friends."

"Evil bastard." His lips tightened.

After a long moment, he said, "You'll need an anchor, a stone or a fallen twig, not something anyone has broken or shaped. Something easy to carry."

"I've nothing like that, but I can find a stone in the street. And one for you as well."

"Jeremy and I can share one if we travel together." He paused, frowning. "A bigger problem is that you can't use your magic while you sleep. Edmund talked me through coming here while I was awake. When you awaken, mayhap I can reach you, now that you know I'm near."

"Oh, I hope so." Despite his firm tones, she felt something in their connection. He seemed weary. "Richard, are you all right?"

He smiled, and she could almost feel his hand on her cheek.

Almost. That a horrid word again.

"There's a limit," he said, "to the time I can sustain myself here, with no food or water, so haste is vital."

The words struck at her heart. "Richard—"

"I love you, Miranda. I—"

Something scraped nearby, yanking her from sleep. From him. No ...

I'll stay near you. Try to reach me, said Richard's voice in her head, fading as she came fully awake.

The scratching came again, and she awoke with a jolt.

With a glance at Jeremy, who rubbed a hand through his rumpled hair, she pushed herself upright. Blue witchlight showed around the door.

The bolt shot back magically. Vergil, the tavern owner, opened the hatch and poked his head inside. The blue glow gave his worried face a spectral cast. "You must go. We've had word from spies in the palace. Soldiers are coming for you." He scrambled back down the ladder.

Miranda and Jeremy gathered their things and climbed down the ladder. Across the dark common room, Vergil waited by the alley door. Expecting soldiers to burst in at any moment, she and Jeremy rushed across the room and out the door.

The alley behind the tavern lay in deep shadow. A chill wind blew off the Thames, sending clouds scudding across the sliver of moon. She turned to Vergil, who stood silhouetted in the dark doorway. "Are you certain you won't come with us?"

"We'll do well enough. We've plans laid. Hurry." He shut the door, and a *thunk* signaled the bolt sliding home.

She glanced at Jeremy, his features barely visible in the dimness, even to her Gifted eyes. "Do you have any idea where we should go?" Too many of the Gifted knew about the tunnels, so he'd said using them was dangerous. Above ground, at least they had room to run if they needed to.

"Listen." He tensed, his head cocked.

Distant thumps, growing louder. Rhythmic. Marching men.

"Not that way." She hurried toward the alley's other end. There, too, came the sound of marching feet.

"This way," he whispered. "We'll circle behind them."

"What way? There's no other alley."

He stepped into heavy shadow. "Yes, there is," he said. His hand reached for her, ghostly pale in the moonlight. She took it, and he drew her into a low, cramped space. He stooped under its low overhang.

"Magic will hide us from men's sight and from scrying," he said. "But anyone Gifted who's nearby will feel it, and we know Wyndon has Gifted in his army. Your choice."

"Once they know we've left the tavern, they'll hunt for us. Let's hide magically. If you can do that."

"In the interest of protecting you, I can."

She invoked power, summoning an image of the alley empty. That should conceal her. Jeremy winked out of sight. He groped for her hand, then folded his warm, invisible one around it.

The contact whispered over her senses like fine silk on flesh as his power brushed hers. Their glamours merged, and she could see him.

"This passage is left from before the Great Fire," he said softly. "It ends near Pudding Lane."

Where her father and brother had died. *Please let that not be an omen.*

As they walked, she caught no hint of Richard's presence. He must not be able to reach her when she was awake, and that meant he couldn't teach her to open a portal. But she had to. If she couldn't, he would starve to death. His soul would be trapped in the shadowland forever, and nothing could set history to rights.

∼

The sky was growing light when Jeremy stopped. "The alleys end here. We need help. The rector of All Hallows Barking, by the Tower, dislikes seeing people hunted. He sheltered Royalists during the Protectorate and Dissenters after. If he's still alive in this new time, we can trust him."

Of course, he might not be alive, but if Jeremy had a better suggestion, he'd make it. Miranda had nothing to offer. "Lead on, then, Jeremy."

With their concealing glamours overlapping, they plodded onward. Weariness from sustaining the invisibility glamour dogged her. It drew more power than the old disguise she'd used in Dover.

They crossed St. Botolph's Lane, then swung north, away from the river, on a street she didn't know, while the city slept around them.

The buildings looked wrong, though. Wooden instead of the brick or stone used since the Great Fire. Old, with upper stories overhanging the street. As though the fire had never happened. Which might be the case.

She mentioned her observation about the buildings to Jeremy. He glanced around. "You could be right. If so, there are all sorts of alleys where we could hide. Or our enemies could. If we meet trouble, Miranda, run. I'll try to gain time for you, but I don't fight magically." He paused at a corner.

"Even against such evil?"

"I beat my sword into a ploughshare long ago, but I'll do what I can to defend you."

"As I will you." She couldn't abandon him.

"No. If it comes to that, run. You're a greater threat to Wyndon than I am."

Across the street, a shopkeeper opened his shutters. His tired-looking wife swept the doorstep. The city was awakening.

Jeremy pressed a finger to his lips for silence before he stepped into the street.

Even though the sun was rising, she counted only three shops opening. Was London so dangerous now that folk waited until the morning arrived in full before unbolting their doors?

They followed a narrow lane past a churchyard, and Jeremy frowned. "Someone's blocked up the alley I wanted to use," he whispered. "We'll have to go up to East Cheap and cut over."

As they passed a narrow alley, a voice within it cried, "Halt!"

Her breath caught, then her heart roared to a furious beat. A score of men raced out of the alley, halberds at the ready. "You there!" The lead guardsman pointed directly at them. "Halt in the name of the Lord Protector."

But she and Jeremy were invisible. She glanced to the side. Jeremy had a shadow. So did she. How?

"Run," he snapped. He pushed her toward the river and charged, bare-handed, toward the guardsmen.

She couldn't leave him. "Fire," she shouted, and willed it. A wall of flame sprang up in front of the guardsmen. Through it, she saw them stop. "Jeremy!"

Even as he backpedaled, the fire died. The guards' leader strode forward. They followed.

"Ice," she cried, pouring her soul into the word. With a broad, sweeping gesture, she spread her power across the ground ahead of the whole troop. They lost their footing, but she couldn't hope the wizard wouldn't counter her. If only she had more training.

"Fire," she yelled again. Her heart was racing, her breath coming in gasps. This took so much power. She gestured to their breastplates and they heated to glowing orange. Struggling to doff them, the men shrieked and squirmed.

Jeremy grabbed her hand. "Run," he panted.

They wheeled. Could she put the guards to sleep? Could she ... kill them?

Searing pain struck her back and slammed her forward. She and Jeremy tumbled to the ground. Agony roared through her mind. Blackness danced across her vision. Breathing hurt.

Beside her, Jeremy writhed. Sounds came toward them. Boots on cobblestones. She and Jeremy had to stand up, run. But she couldn't.

A man seized her arms. When he rolled her over, torment shot through her back. She cried out as it hit the cobblestones. Panting, she bit her lip against further protest.

Darkness swelled behind her eyes. She couldn't pass out now. Mustn't.

A sandy-haired, bearded man looked down at her. His eyes hard in a weathered face, he hooked a chain that bore a plain onyx disc around her neck. The chain pulsed against her throat.

"She's secure," he said. His words seemed to come from a great distance.

Another man, tall and grizzled and impassive, knelt at her side. He gripped her hand, and energy flowed into her from him. Up her arm, across her shoulders, and down her back it rolled. The pain eased, then died. Dazed, she stared at him.

His mouth moved. Gradually, the words made sense " … netted a couple more Gifted. The reward'll be welcome, even split amongst us. Stand them up, and let's turn them in so we can collect it."

The soldiers pulled her to her feet and bound her hands behind her. Her bodice sagged off her right shoulder, revealing her breast down to the corset edge. Her cheeks blazed with embarrassment.

The magical strike to her back must have damaged the bodice. She couldn't straighten it with her hands bound. The corset's whalebone held it upright, but rough edges jabbed into her back. A subtle hum from the amulet buzzed in her ears.

The leader fingered it. "Don't try your magic."

They shoved her toward Jeremy, who wore similar bindings. Blood trailed from cuts at the corner of his mouth and over his left eye. If she could use her magic, she could heal that.

"How did you find us?" he demanded.

"Felt your magic as you came near. The pair of you have a great lot of power. Too bad you decided to use it."

So these men weren't sent for them. The encounter was pure bad luck. Worse luck, that they had a Gifted leader.

The guards formed around them. "You can march," the leader said, "or we'll drag you. Move out." He kept a hard, painful grip on her arm, hurrying her along.

They walked east, toward the Tower, not toward Whitehall. "Where are we going?" she asked.

The leader turned a stony look on her and touched her amulet. Orange light flared at his fingertip. The chain suddenly blazed hot against her neck, pain shooting into her chest. Down her limbs. Her legs collapsed.

"Miranda!" Jeremy's voice sounded far away.

The leader caught her, his finger steady against the stone. Weight compressed her chest. Struggling to breathe, she writhed in his grasp as he edges of her vision turned black.

"You mean to give me trouble?" he asked.

She shook her head.

He removed his finger, and her chest expanded in a great *whoof* of inhaled air. "See that you don't." He jerked her upright and onward, his hold like a band of iron.

Stumbling, she gasped for breath. Her chest burned, and her arms and legs ached, but she battled her fear. Giving in to it would paralyze her.

"We're going to the Tower," he said casually, "where you'll learn what trouble really is."

The Tower. Site of beheadings and torture. If she and Jeremy went in there, they'd never escape.

CHAPTER 29

P lodding along amid the guards as the day brightened, Miranda fought the mental haze the amulet generated. She couldn't even think clearly, let alone try to find a way to escape.

A middle-aged woman opened a house door and began sweeping the stoop. The city was coming to life, as it hadn't during their battle in the street. Any commotion usually drew a crowd, but not in Wyndon's England. Now people feared being noticed. No one made eye contact with her or, apparently, anyone else.

Another detachment of guardsmen stalked down the street. They veered toward the group holding Miranda and Jeremy.

The newcomers stopped before the guards, blocking the way. "We've an assignment for you," a man's harsh voice said. "Captain Bartlett's orders."

Miranda's captor tightened his grip until she gasped in pain. "We've Gifted prisoners to deliver and a reward to claim."

"You can claim your reward at the Tower later," the newcomers' leader said. "Now you're to make for Wapping Stairs and break up a cabal of Gifted rebels. If you catch them, it'll more than double your prize."

"You go, then."

"The captain wants you to handle it." The man paused, then shrugged. "Your funeral. Move out, lads."

"Wait." Miranda's captor yanked her forward as his men parted ranks. "Take them, but I'll have my reward, if it comes out o' your skin."

"You'll have it, all right." The other leader gripped her arm, not as hard as his comrade had. The helmet's steel brim cast his eyes into shadow, but she knew him. Lucius. The head of the Gifted Conclave. Had he sided with Wyndon? Or was this a rescue?

One of his men took custody of Jeremy. The other troop marched east, toward the Tower and, beyond it, Wapping.

Heading back up Tower Street the way they had come, Lucius murmured, "Take heart, cousin, but show no sign."

Not a turncoat, then. Miranda bit back a smile.

More shops were open, and more people stood on their front steps. No one looked at the passing group.

The guard detachment turned toward the river on Harp Lane, then ducked into a narrow alley between a house and a tavern. Still in good order, they marched down a narrow set of stairs and into the tavern's cellar.

The last man slammed the door. "Locked and warded, Lucius."

Miranda and Jeremy grinned at each other.

"Mere thanks aren't enough," Miranda noted, "but I'm grateful."

Jeremy bowed to Lucius. "Indeed, and my thanks as well."

"Thwarting the Lord Protector," Lucius assured him, "is a pleasure. We'll have someone see to your back, Jeremy."

Lucius raised his hand, and lanterns on the wall flared into brilliance, revealing meat hanging from rafters and casks of beer or wine around the walls. He smiled at Miranda, then at Jeremy. "I imagine you'd like to have those amulets off. We'll find a serviceable bodice for you, Miranda, don't fear."

One of the other men untied her hands and unhooked the pendant she wore. He passed it to Lucius, who regarded it with icy eyes.

Turning it in his hands, Lucius commented, "Simple to use but a nasty piece of work." He gave it to one of the other men. "Take one to Callista. We'll need the other." To Miranda he said, "Callista's trying to discover how to defeat them."

The man who'd removed her amulet doffed his cloak and laid it around her shoulders. She smiled her thanks.

With a comforting pat on her arm, he walked over to Jeremy. "Let me look at your burns, cousin."

Accepting a tankard of ale, Miranda asked, "How did you find us?"

"You and Jeremy are special targets for Wyndon. I've been scrying for you. I saw you leave the tavern, saw you captured."

One of the men handed her a plate of bread and cheese as Lucius said, "We came as soon as we could. Then it was a simple matter of showing the guards something they expected to see."

"I'm grateful, of course, but won't those men report catching us?"

Lucius smiled, his eyes bright with enjoyment. "Our man at the Tower will record that two unnamed Gifted were brought in and will pay those guardsmen their reward. Once paid, the men won't care what became of you."

"Have you been in hiding all this time?" She adjusted the cloak around her shoulders for more coverage.

"I move from place to place, bolt holes I prepared long ago. The head of the Conclave must be ready for trouble. I'm fortunate to have these few of my blood kindred and a score of others I know I can trust."

She glanced around at the grim-faced men in guard leather and steel. "Thank you," she told them. "All of you. I thank you with all my heart."

They nodded acknowledgment, and Lucius's eyes twinkled. "Making trouble for the protector is their favorite sport."

The twinkle faded as he added, "We've a plan to stop him. It's dangerous, a single roll of the dice on which all depends, but we cannot wait for ideal conditions. Too many people are suffering. Having you and Jeremy in hand gives us a way to draw Wyndon out. Are you interested?"

"Extremely," Miranda said.

"The guard unit we sent to Wapping Stairs won't find a cabal there. While they may assume their quarry had moved on, they might complain about upstarts sending them out of their way. We cannot afford to have our man at the Tower draw too much scrutiny. We must act tonight if we can."

So there was no time to sleep and thus none for Richard to try to instruct her in reaching the afterworld. Not that he'd thought the chances of success were very good.

As Lucius detailed his plan to capture Wyndon, one thought kept running through Miranda's mind. If Wyndon had manipulated history through the afterworld, he knew how to travel there. He could release Richard. But he wouldn't do so voluntarily.

Could he be tricked into doing so? Was his need for revenge strong enough to draw him into a fatal mistake?

"What is it?" Lucius asked.

Miranda glanced around them. He and she were alone in a corner. Softly, she said, "Richard is trapped in the realm between life and death, the one he mentioned to you, but he yet lives."

Lucius frowned, and she added, "It's how Wyndon changed the past, by traveling through there."

Lucius studied her, eyes narrowing. "Go on."

"Richard has discovered the way to restore the true sequence of events, but he cannot leave that place to do it without help. He meant to try to teach me, before Jeremy and I had to flee, but he wasn't optimistic about our chances of succeeding."

Lucius studied her. At last, he said, "For the moment, let's say I believe you. If you could help Richard, he would be free already. Whose help do you need?"

"That's the tricky part. Richard cannot last much longer without true food and water, but the only other person who knows how to enter that realm is Lord Wyndon. If your plan succeeds, there may be a way to convince him."

Moonlight tipped the ripples from the barge's oars with silver and shadowed the passengers' faces. With rhythmic, swishing strokes, the small band of Gifted traveled toward Whitehall and a confrontation that could determine England's fate.

And Richard's.

Miranda had never sought a fight. Never wanted one. But she couldn't shrink from this one. The man at the Tower, who turned out to be the Lord Lieutenant, its commander, had sent word to Whitehall that she and Jeremy had broken under interrogation, revealing themselves as two of the protector's most sought-after fugitives. Wyndon had ordered them brought to him.

So much depended on so few, but Lucius had insisted some of their group stay in reserve, to continue the resistance if this plan failed.

Close to the bank, the barge drifted downriver. The city stood silent around it. With midnight drawing nigh, most Londoners had long since gone to bed. Miranda and Jeremy sat in the barge's center with the absence of bindings concealed by their cloaks.

Lucius and his band, seventeen men and three women, including Anne Wilfleet, the fishmonger's daughter, had magically disguised their features lest the palace guards recognize any of them before they reached Wyndon. Fighting their way out of the palace would be difficult enough without also fighting their way in.

"There won't be hangers-on about Whitehall this late," Lucius said quietly, "and the guard will be light."

"I wish I had more practice using magic as a weapon," Miranda admitted.

"Starting fires provides a distraction at minimum," Lucius said. "If you use that skill judiciously, it can also kill. Just do what you can." Turning to Jeremy, he added, "You could have remained behind. Your prayers would mean much to some of us."

"I, too, will do what I can," he said.

Ahead, a fish jumped. Ships at anchor loomed like dark hulks in the moonlight. The waves lapped against their hulls with soft, slapping sounds. On another barge near Whitehall's garden stairs, upriver from the main stairs for the palace, three of Lucius's wizards waited to carry the group to safety.

Moonlight shone white against the sprawling palace's stone walls. With the tide out, Whitehall Stairs rested against the muddy bank. The oarsmen beached the barge.

"Halt," ordered a man at the top of the stairway. "Who goes there?"

The man in the front of the boat replied, "Important prisoners, Lady Hawkstowe and Jeremy Winfield. The Lord Protector wants to question them himself."

The guard raised a lantern, peering into the darkness. Lucius thrust Miranda forward so the light struck her face. The guard chuckled. "I reckon you'll eat well tomorrow. Take them to the banqueting house. I'll send word to his lordship."

Miranda's and Jeremy's companions hustled them up the creaky stairs, then down a corridor. Several armed men in the red and blue of palace guards fell in with them.

Miranda's stomach churned. She'd never dreamed of a struggle with such high stakes. She took a slow breath in and let it out, then drew another. Her stomach didn't settle.

All the while they walked farther from the river, making their escape route longer and more complicated.

Ahead of them, the banqueting house jutted from the palace's bulk. Candlelight glowed faintly in its windows. To its left lay the privy garden. It could be reached from the banqueting house by descending a staircase in the corridor on that side of the building. To avoid the palace's many residents and guards, their group would exit into the garden and race through it to the river stairs between the garden and the bowling green.

If Wyndon chose to see his supposed prisoners somewhere else, they would still make for the garden stairs.

Their escort led them inside, up a staircase, and into a long, high-ceilinged room. The few candles left most of the painted ceiling in shadow. Flanked by two doors, a dais bearing a single chair stood at the far end. They marched toward it.

"Prisoners to their knees," the palace guard said.

Lucius and his men pushed Miranda and Jeremy forward and down, then stood behind them. There they stayed for long minutes.

At last, two more uniformed guards entered from the left doorway behind the dais. After them came Wyndon. He stalked in and seated himself.

Miranda's mouth went dry. Although she swallowed hard, fear still tasted coppery on her tongue, but she was supposed to appear afraid.

Wyndon's lips curved in a tight, hard smile. "Lady Hawkstowe. Reverend Winfield. We meet again at last." He glanced at Lucius. "You commanded this unit."

"I did." Lucius dropped his disguise and stepped forward. "Henry de Vere, I arrest you in the name of the Gifted Conclave."

Wyndon stared at him, then laughed. "You senile fool. I've scoured London for you, and now you deliver not only two of my prize quarry but yourself." On that last word, golden light erupted around his hands and roared toward Lucius, whose green blast blocked it.

With a deafening boom, the power bursts exploded, shattering windows. One of Lucius's men fired another blast toward Wyndon. His two guards dropped, clutching their throats.

Two burly men and Anne Wilfleet flung magical bolts at Wyndon, backing Lucius. The combined blasts blew their target off his feet.

Behind Miranda, something exploded and knocked her to her knees. Small stones and other bits of debris rained down her, and she covered her head. Her ears rang from the noise. Surely it would draw the entire garrison here.

Jeremy helped her up. "Keep your head low."

Nodding, she coughed from the dust in the air. Her heart pounded, and her ears rang, but her mind felt oddly clear. She looked around for Lucius.

He and another man had Wyndon in their grasp, dragging him from the dais. One of the amulets hung around his neck.

"To the river," Lucius shouted.

As their group hurried toward the door Wyndon had entered, Miranda glanced back. The front wall of the banqueting house was a gaping hole that showed the palace yard and the dark night beyond.

One of the men ran to peer through it. "Guards coming that way."

"Hurry," Lucius said. "Will, Edgar, Anne, covering fire."

The fishmonger's daughter and two men dropped back, hands glowing with magic. In the middle of the pack, Miranda and Jeremy rushed past the dais, into the corridor, and down the stairs. Miranda's heart pounded wildly as they bolted into the privy garden. In the moonlight, the statues in each of the square plots looked like ghostly sentinels.

Soldiers rushed into the garden from the royal apartments, near the river wall. No escape that way.

The soldiers opened fire. Gunshots echoed in the night, and clouds of gunpowder smoke quickly obscured the guardsmen. From the corridor window behind the Banqueting House, bolts of magic whizzed out at the fleeing group in a rainbow of colors that heated the air but flew wide.

At her side, Jeremy said, "They won't risk hitting Wyndon. Come on, we're heading for the street."

Hustling her along, he added, "Stay close to the building. It makes the angle of fire more difficult."

When she blinked at him, stunned that a man who'd foresworn battle knew that, he said, "My brother's a naval officer, remember?"

From a window above the garden, a burst of blue power crashed into the fleeing group.

Three men fell, screaming in agony. The air stank of smoke and burned flesh. Miranda clenched her teeth against nausea.

A tall man near the front stopped. Feet braced, he blasted the garden wall by the street. It collapsed as another blast from the corridor above struck the ground, spewing shrubbery, turf, and shattered marble into the air.

Miranda, Jeremy, and several others reeled from the blast and fell. Dust hung in the air around the rubble, a pile at least five feet high. She coughed again as dust clogged her nose and mouth.

She and Jeremy pulled themselves up and rushed on. They scrambled over the wreckage of the garden wall and found themselves in the street with the ornate, checkerboard gate on their right. To the left, a plainer one with round towers some distance away marked the end of the palace.

The rear guard, now reduced to Anne and one of the men, clambered over the wreckage. The group bolted toward the old palace and Westminster Abbey.

"We must be heading for Westminster Stairs," Jeremy muttered.

With Jeremy at her side, she pounded after the leaders. Someone at the front of the group loosed a blast of magic, and then the leaders were racing through the gate.

Corsets weren't made for running. Her breath came in short, harsh gasps, but she kept pace. Death would be better than captivity at the hands of Wyndon's men.

"If we had a secure place to hide," Jeremy panted as they cleared the gate, "Wyndon would make a good hostage." He gulped air.

Miranda flinched as she passed the gate's fallen guard.

A booming sound came from behind them, then a cry. Over her shoulder, she saw the man in the rear fall, writhing.

Their party raced along the road, passing darkened houses. Behind them, the lone survivor of the rear guard, Anne, blew out the gateway's ceiling in a deafening blast of green light.

Rubble crashed down, its impact shaking the ground so they all staggered. The old palace of Westminster loomed ahead, most of its windows dark above its stone outer walls.

Miranda had lost sight of Wyndon. If he'd escaped, would she even know? She glanced back at Whitehall Palace. Men on horseback clambered cautiously over the ruined gate.

"Horses," she screamed toward those at the front of their group. Moonlight glinted off an onyx amulet, and she spotted Wyndon before the men hauling him along blocked her view.

The horsemen would have to take care crossing the rubble, but once they cleared the pile, they'd overtake the fleeing group in no time.

Jeremy caught her arm. New strength flowed into her. Her steps gathered speed. Her breathing eased. He must've shared his power with her.

Running full out, they veered right, heading for the Collegiate Church of Saint Peter, better known as Westminster Abbey. Why were they not heading for the river stairs?

The group dashed for the massive, stone structure that gleamed in the moonlight. The smaller, paler shape of St. Margaret's church stood nearer, but the leaders ran past it.

Miranda and Jeremy passed stragglers from their group.

"No," Jeremy said. "They're running into the Abbey."

Blue light burst against his back. He staggered. Making a choked sound, he fell.

"Jeremy?" She ran back for him. His shirt and jerkin had been seared through, and red blisters covered his back.

"Go," he choked.

"I won't leave you."

The stragglers, four men and Anne, slowed. Behind them, horsemen galloped, closing the distance much too fast.

"Take her," Jeremy urged, his voice rough with pain.

"No." She couldn't leave him. He was her companion and Richard's friend. The last one left alive, possibly.

"No choice," one of the men said. He and Anne caught Miranda's arms and carried her forward.

"He wouldn't want you to die with him," Anne panted.

Two other men grabbed Jeremy, hoisting him to his feet.

"Leave me," he gasped.

"If we must," one promised.

They ran headlong past St. Margaret's, toward the double doors in the towering wall beyond it. The doors flew open ahead of them, and they raced into Westminster Abbey's sheltering darkness. The men carrying Jeremy plunged through behind them.

Anne slammed the doors shut. She waved her hands. The doors glowed, the light slowly fading. As she sagged against the doorframe, the remaining wizards raced toward other doors.

The dim glow of witchlight lit the aisles. Miranda ran to Jeremy. He lay still, with his eyes closed, near the steps to the high altar. Someone's cloak covered him. His breathing rasped. She touched his cheek gently.

He glanced up at her, his eyes dark with pain. "We are profaning ... this place," he whispered.

"We have no choice," she said gently. "Once I catch my breath, I'll see if I can heal you."

Such a positive use of her magic wouldn't balance the destruction this night had seen, but at least she wouldn't feel conflicted about it.

Jeremy shook his head. "Save ... your strength. You'll need it."

If the next part of their plan succeeded, he meant.

She glanced around and saw Lucius on the steps to the choir enclosure. He looked weary. Her own hands shook with reaction and fatigue. She clasped them together.

Their comrades, reduced to eight from the score who'd gone to Whitehall, stumbled wearily toward Lucius. To their right stretched the long nave, its roof supported by stone pillars, its walls towering above the floor. Without sunlight behind them, the stained glass windows looked like dark markers on the walls.

Far above, lost in gloom too high for their faint light to reach, was the arched, vaulted ceiling. Only Gifted eyes could have seen it at all.

Despite the darkness and the danger, the magnificence of the church took her breath away. Power hung in the air, strength accumulated through centuries of the faithful worshipping here. Jeremy was right. Their conflict profaned this place.

"The horsemen were closing too quickly," Lucius said. "We couldn't have held them off long enough for our barge to retrieve us. We're all weary, I know, but before we rest, we must ward the sanctuary. Quickly."

Then what? How could they escape if Wyndon's men surrounded the church?

One of the men stayed with the prisoner. One walked over to kneel by Jeremy, and the rest of the group scattered for the walls, each placing their palms flat against the stone.

"Now," Lucius said.

A rainbow of colors flowed out of the wizards' hands. Slowly, irregularly, as though the weary Gifted struggled with the task, the colors inched up the walls, brought the stained glass windows to vibrant life in a dazzling kaleidoscope of emerald and scarlet and azure and gold, and spread across the ceiling. Every inch of the church sparkled with magical power that sent prickles down Miranda's neck and along her arms.

The group, some swaying on their feet with fatigue, returned to Lucius's side. "Why here?" a man who looked to be about forty asked.

Lucius said, "If we'd made for the river, we would've been trapped. At least this place has power we can draw to hold our wards."

"And then what?" someone called out. "We can't hold this indefinitely."

"So we negotiate," Lucius answered, but his gaze flicked to Miranda. If their admittedly desperate plan succeeded, the group would never have been here at all.

Wyndon's lip curled. "There aren't enough of you to hold the wards more than a day or so. You're trapped. Beg for mercy, and I may spare you."

"The abbey itself is a place of great power," Lucius said. "Power we can tap in a righteous cause. A day is long enough for you to undo what you've done."

Jeremy groaned softly. The sturdy, thirtyish man kneeling by him gripped his shoulder. "Easy, cousin. Give me a moment, and we'll begin."

Miranda squeezed Jeremy's arm, the only comfort she had to offer, before she stood and walked toward the group around Wyndon. Their plan had called for Jeremy to help her with Wyndon. What if he couldn't?

"I won't undo anything," Wyndon said flatly. "You fools, England is almost what she should have been, a land ruled by those with the power to hold what we have. A land where we needn't hide. Where we enjoy the privileges our power deserves. You'd give that up to the unGifted?"

"There are more of them than of us," Lucius said.

"More chickens, too," Wyndon said, "but I don't see you turning the realm over to them. Think of it, man. No one need ever hang for witchcraft again."

Miranda clenched her fists. "You dare invoke that after what you did to me?"

He shrugged. "One uses the tools at hand. Most who hang for witchcraft are innocent, and those few of the Gifted who hang rarely consort with the dark powers. If you care so much for the innocent, think on that."

Miranda shook her head. "Pretty words count for little when backed by evil deeds."

"You've tampered with time itself and broken nature's law," Lucius said, "and you will put it right."

"Not even if you kill me for it," Wyndon said quietly. "But you won't, because that isn't what you do."

"Don't be too sure of that." Lucius beckoned to several of his men. They drew a little apart, leaving Miranda with Wyndon. Their low voices didn't carry far enough to be understood. Others of the group were sitting or lying on the floor to let their magic recover from the running battle.

Wyndon quirked an eyebrow at her. "Reconsidering my offer? You should. You're trapped like rats in a cage here."

"Do you know what happened to Richard?" Her voice shook, but maybe that was all right. Wyndon had to believe she was worried.

"Your husband, you mean? You've risen far in the world, serving wench."

She clenched her fists in her skirts. "Do you know where he is or not?"

Jeremy walked toward her. He was already recovered?

"Are you sure you should be up?" she asked.

"I'm the new guard." He patted her shoulder. "After the healing energy I just received, I'm in better shape than anyone here, at least until the others have rested."

"I'm surprised you're considered a fit guard," Wyndon said, "since you won't fight magically."

Jeremy's lip curled in an uncharacteristic sneer. "I don't need magic to knock you down."

"Jeremy, please." Lowering her voice, Miranda added, "Richard went into that place, the one where people go when they die, and didn't return. He told me you know how to go there. So you're the only one who can find him."

Wyndon shrugged. "Perhaps he's left you."

Miranda flinched and hoped it looked genuine. "He wouldn't."

"If he lost his way there," Wyndon said, "he's dead unless he knew to shield himself from the wraiths, the damned souls who're trapped there. Even if he could do so, he'll starve to death eventually. If he doesn't first let his shield lapse and fall prey to the wraiths. They'll tear him apart."

Jeremy snapped, "Stop it, Wyndon."

"She asked," Wyndon pointed out.

"Is there a way to save him?" Miranda asked. "Doing so would help your cause with the Conclave."

Wyndon raised an eyebrow. "Come now, your common ladyship. You can't expect me to believe that."

Jeremy took a step nearer, his fists clenched. "Is there a way to free him?"

"I'll tell her," the prisoner said, jerking his head toward Miranda, "but not with you hovering. I make no promises, but it may not be too late to save him."

Softly, her eyes begging him, Miranda said, "Please, Jeremy. Where can he go, anyway, without his magic?"

Scowling, Jeremy backed off about twenty feet.

"You said we could save Richard." Keeping her voice low, Miranda let a pleading note creep into it. "How?"

"The answer for my freedom—and your services as my seer," Wyndon replied, his voice soft so it wouldn't carry.

With a loud, crackling noise, something struck the building. The floor trembled, and the rainbow warding flickered.

"I can't let you go," Miranda protested softly. She cast a nervous glance at the group around Lucius.

"Then your husband will certainly die." Wyndon shrugged. "Horribly."

Miranda gnawed her lip. "If I let you go—if ... would you drop your feud with Richard?"

"That was of his making more than mine. I'll drop it if he does."

The building shook again. The wards flickered and blurred. Gifted ran to reinforce them.

"If my men break through before you decide," Wyndon said coolly, "I'll have no reason to bargain."

A voice from the group of men around Lucius said, "We should kill him. That would stop this."

"Only for a moment," someone else said. "Until someone takes his place."

Jeremy stood with his arms crossed and his feet planted. His narrow-eyed stare at Wyndon didn't waver.

"You'll save Richard from the wraiths? You'll protect us both?" Miranda asked.

"If he still lives, I will. If he doesn't, you've no obligation to me."

Except, of course, that the man lied as easily as he breathed.

Miranda frowned at him. "If you stop the wraiths from killing Richard," she began, knowing that was already done, "and do nothing to harm him, I'll serve as your seer for one year."

"Two," he said smoothly.

Of course, he had no intention of limiting her service, but she had no intention of making a promise that would bind her. *Richard, you'd better be there.*

"Done," Miranda said. She snatched the amulet from around Wyndon's neck. He magically burst the ropes at his wrists. She threw herself against him, knocking him sideways so the bolt he aimed at Jeremy flew wide.

As the other wizards shouted and rushed toward them, Wyndon grabbed her hair and dragged her a single step to her right. In a blast of freezing cold, the world wrenched out of being.

CHAPTER 30

Wyndon's grip loosened. Miranda leaped to her left, away from him. Purple-gray fog surrounded her with the stench of rotten eggs. Gaunt, wasted faces rushed toward her. With a gasp, she ducked. Taloned hands ripped at her clothes. She fell to her knees.

Her skin tingled, power shrouding her in protection, and the hands no longer assailed her, though they still pushed against whatever shielded her. She raised her head, peering past the screaming, darting shapes.

Richard and Wyndon stood a few feet to her right, Wyndon stumbling backward as the skeletal shapes raged around them. The glow around the two men must be magical shielding.

Richard closed the distance and slammed a fist into Wyndon's face. Wyndon lost his footing and fell.

A broadsword formed in Richard's hand, its point at Wyndon's throat.

"Don't move," Richard said in a voice that could've frozen the Thames in summer. Keeping his attention on Wyndon, he held out an arm to Miranda. "Are you hurt, love?"

She ran to him, and he drew her close. Until this moment, she hadn't realized how much she feared he'd died, that she'd imagined their conversation. She buried her face in his neck. He smelled the same, of bay leaves. Felt the same, sturdy and warm, though with fatigue dragging at him. This was real, not some desperate dream she'd conjured.

Whatever happened next, at least they were together.

I hated this plan while you were hatching it, he told her, *but you've done well. Even if you did it by coming here.*

Where he hadn't wanted her. *Richard—*

"Good work, lad." A man strode out of the fog. Not quite so tall as Richard, he had the same coloring, though silver streaked his shoulder-length, black hair. He was narrower of frame and squarer of jaw, but he had the same nose and eyes. He wore a green velvet tunic, matching hose, and low boots of dark leather. At his side dangled an empty scabbard.

Noting her glance, he said, "It belonged to the sword of Hawkstowe. Edmund Mainwaring, at your service, Lady Hawkstowe."

"I'm honored to meet you, my lord."

Wyndon snorted. "This isn't the banqueting house at Whitehall."

"Nor shall you ever see it again," Richard said. "You attacked Miranda and murdered my grandmother. Now you're going to pay for that. Stand up."

Wyndon flung himself backward. His shielding aura flickered out. The wraiths swooped in, only to meet renewed shielding. Richard slashed at them, but his blade had no effect. The bastard was hiding behind them.

"Stay behind me," he told Miranda. His magic still encased her in a protective aura. *Feel what I'm doing to shield you and do the same. Draw power around you from the fog.*

With his mind guiding hers, she did as he said. Power crackled purple around her and sizzled through her with dizzying force.

"Steady." He tightened his hold until the dizziness faded.

Now her own power protected her. She caressed his cheek and found it thin, the cheekbone sharp under his new, scruffy beard. In his arms, she could feel the weariness he fought. *Richard?*

One can't live on magic forever, or so Edmund tells me. He smiled in her mind. *I'll be fine as soon as I have food and water, and some true rest. Pray, tell me you brought an anchor.*

A pebble tucked into my bodice.

Excellent.

The wraiths wheeled away from Wyndon. He stood alone, magically shielded, clad in black armor, and holding a broadsword and a black shield.

"I suppose it's useless trying to bargain with you," he said, "but if you join me, I'll lift your family curse."

Richard smiled. "I already know how to do that."

"You may think you do, but all you can manage is to create more time-related problems." He stalked toward Richard and Miranda.

Backpedaling, Richard kept Miranda behind him. His magic drawing on the pervasive vapors raised goose bumps on her flesh. The fog swirled around his body, hardening until he, too, wore plate armor and held a shield. that matched the ones in Miranda's visions.

As Edmund drew her aside, she said, "Richard, no. Don't fight him." *Remember my dream. If he kills you, there's no hope for fixing the timeline.*

Richard raised his sword in a guard position. *Your dream doesn't fit these circumstances. If I kill him here, he can't stop us from fixing history, and then none of this will have happened. If we take him back, Lucius will insist on a trial, and all the while, innocent people are dying.*

Richard's lips curved in a grim smile. "To the death. And may right prevail." He dropped the face plate on his helm.

Wyndon laughed. "Morality has no power here, stripling. Lay on." He dropped his own face plate and swung.

Richard caught the blow on his shield. He cut low, trying to slip under his adversary's guard. The black shield turned the blade. Wyndon's sword struck Richard's shield with a loud crack.

Miranda winced, but Richard didn't falter. He sliced toward his foe's side. Dodging, Wyndon swung backhanded for Richard's neck.

Richard ducked. Leaped back and jerked his shield up. Twisted clear of a shortened thrust toward his face. His blade glanced off the vambrace on his foe's left forearm.

The men exchanged a wild flurry of blows. They stepped back, panting, a hollow sound when filtered through their helms.

"You've more skill than I thought." Wyndon's face plate muffled his voice. "More, but not enough."

He backed off. The swirling mists obscured his outline, then turned purple and concealed him utterly.

Frowning, Richard flipped up his face plate. Sweat trickled down the side of his face and beaded on his upper lip. "Edmund?" he said.

"I know not, lad, but there's a wicked feel to the mist."

Miranda shivered at the energy crackling in the fog. "Can we stop what he's doing?"

"Not without knowing what that is," Edmund said.

The swirling mists expanded, stretching upward to a height three times that of a man. The swirl tightened into a shape, and a black dragon trumpeted into the mists. When it looked back at them, its purple eyes glinted with malevolence.

"Christ's bones." Edmund thrust her behind him. "Feel the power he's drawing—seems the bastard mastered a skill we all thought only a legend."

"Edmund, send Miranda home." Richard dropped his face plate.

"Not unless you come, too," she insisted.

I can't. We may never have as good a chance to stop him.

Would killing him here even do that? They couldn't leave him here alive, either, to work more mischief.

Flame belched from the dragon's mouth. Richard raised his shield in time to deflect the flare, but he staggered backward. He turned to Edmund. "Go!"

Richard raised the shield against another flare. Edmund tugged at Miranda's arm.

"I won't leave him," she insisted. "Can't you help him?"

Richard leaned forward, into the fire. Behind the shield, he held his sword up. He took a step, and then another. The sharp forward angle of his body revealed his strain as he pressed toward his foe.

Grimly, Edmund said, "I *am* helping him, by protecting you."

Pain flared in her bond with Richard. With it came suffocating heat. Every breath burned in Richard's chest. This hadn't happened in the dream.

Somehow, she had to help. She lunged toward him.

Edmund caught her arm. "No, child. If that beast puts a claw on you, Richard will surrender."

The truth in his words hit her like a blow from a cudgel. Having Edmund guard her deprived Richard of aid that might save his life.

She pressed a fist to her mouth. Should she leave? Could she, without knowing he was safe? If she did, he would be trapped here. She had a single anchor stone, and she didn't know how to come back for him.

Richard had almost reached the dragon. He drew back his sword arm. The beast let out a rumble that sounded like laughter. As Richard thrust, its great tail whipped around its body. The tail hit Richard's shield and knocked him into the air.

Pain screamed through the bond, down his limbs and hers. Miranda shuddered with its force.

His sword dropped from his hand. The shield fell away. With a great, clanking thud, he landed. He rolled twice, ending face-down, and lay still. The armor vanished.

Miranda stifled a cry. His pain still racked her, so he must live, but he lay so still.

The dragon trumpeted again. Fire curled around its snout as it turned toward its helpless prey.

Gaunt shapes swirled from the mist, heading for Richard. From Edmund's hand, argent power flared to beat them back.

Miranda shivered. Richard's pain shuddered in her bones and screamed over her limbs. "I'll distract it. You help Richard."

"While the beast slaughters you. No, lass. I'll draw the creature off while you help Richard. I think I can still protect you from the wraiths." Armor formed around Edmund's body.

"I can protect myself," she said.

The dragon looked at them in triumph. Its lips drew back in a gesture that might have been a smile. It took another step toward Richard.

She'd had little practice with healing, but she would find a way. "Tell me when."

"Go." With surprising lightness for a man so heavily armored, Edmund sprang away from her. "For God, England, and King Richard," he shouted, charging forward.

Purple sparks sizzled from his hand. The mists around the dragon sparked with purple, as though catching fire.

The creature recoiled. Although the sparks died, they had caught its attention. It turned toward Edmund. Flame blazed from its snout.

Miranda ran to Richard and dropped to her knees beside him. Red blisters from the fire's heat mottled his waxen skin. This close, his searing agony washed over her face. She gritted her teeth as tears of shared pain oozed from the corners of her eyes.

The dragon roared. She looked up.

Some thirty yards away, Edmund stood between them and the beast. His sword had become the great weapon of English yeomanry, a longbow. He let fly a shaft and then, so quickly that she blinked, another. The arrows seemed to form already nocked on the string.

Flame belched from the dragon's mouth. The arrows blazed in the air and fell, but others were already in flight.

She turned back to her husband and gripped his hand. *Richard!*

He stirred faintly but didn't rouse.

She had to hurry. Setting her fingertips beside the worst of the burns on his face, she traced their shapes and envisioned them fading. Magic tingled in her fingers. Nothing else changed.

Desperate, she flung a mental deluge of power at him. It flared down her arm and into her hand, then washed over him, across his face and body, like an amber wave.

Agony blazed in their bond. His eyes jerked open. They clenched shut, and he choked back a cry. Miranda gasped but kept her grip on him. Suddenly, as though a dam of healing power had burst, the pain washed away.

His face relaxed. The blisters shrank, fading into his normal skin color. The pain in the bond became a dull ache. He sat up slowly.

The dragon swatted Edmund. His feet left the ground, and his form turned green. In a flash of sparks, he disappeared.

Shrieking wraiths rushed out of the mist. As Richard spun magic into a shielding cocoon, he said, "Feed power to me, love, as you do when you heal."

Channeling magic down her arm, she felt it merge with his, a tingling in her hand like the one she'd felt at her nape when Arabella joined their magic to scry.

The lunging, clawing wraiths surrounded them, but their cocoon gleamed with power.

Richard smiled grimly. A wave of his hand sent the wraiths wheeling away. He sprang to his feet. Armor formed around him again as he drew her upright. "Stay shielded and run a few paces away. Draw its attention." A sword formed in his right hand. "Go."

Pulling power from the reeking fog to strengthen her shield, she picked up her skirts and ran. The wraiths screamed around her. She couldn't help hunching her shoulders beneath her protective aura.

Behind her, the dragon roared. A glance over her shoulder showed her that it had turned toward her.

She stopped and dropped to her knees, pretending to cower from it, but kept her right hand at her side.

Thought seemed to become reality here, at least when it came to objects. Mayhap she could use that.

"Thought to being, fog to stone, strike that dragon's big jawbone," she muttered quickly, imagining a large boulder flying toward the dragon's breast. She poured magic at the image.

A current of air shot toward the dragon and punched through the wraiths. It solidified. Became a flying rock the size of her torso. The dragon roared, flame searing her missile.

"So there," she muttered, exultant.

She had distracted the creature, and with a new skill. How else could she use it?

Richard leaped through the wraiths screaming around him. He landed astride the base of the dragon's tail and caught a spiny scale to hold on. The dragon roared again. The tail whipped back and forth but not enough to dislodge him. The beast's forepaws couldn't reach him.

Miranda hurled another stone, then fought fatigue to make herself a triangular, blue shield. If Richard used one in addition to a shielding aura, she also should.

Cautiously, she walked forward. The flitting wraiths' screams jarred her ears and spiked into her soul, but she couldn't let them distract her. At her command, flames danced along her shield. Good. Dividing the beast's attention would help Richard.

He reversed his sword and drove the blade between the spine scales. Purple blood spurted over his hands and thighs. The beast shrieked, a sound sharp with agony. It shifted as though to roll, but Richard wrenched the hilt over and down. A loud crack sounded, and the dragon screeched. Its tail stopped moving.

The wraiths dived for it, and Richard leaped clear with the broken sword dissolving in his hand. He formed another in an instant.

Very good, he sent to her, *but stay back now.*

He needed to slay the dragon, not protect her. She crouched where she was.

The dragon's head swung back and forth. The fog at its tail turned bright purple. It roared. The tail whipped toward Richard, who leaped over it just in time.

Miranda stifled a cry. The dragon must have used the mists to heal itself. If it could repair the damage so easily, how could he kill the beast?

CHAPTER 31

The dragon's chest expanded in a great, rasping indrawn breath. Invisible currents of power rushed past Miranda, streaming toward it like an icy wave.

She flung power in front of Richard to form a magical wall that glowed silver. Flame cascaded from the dragon and poured around her wall, leaving him untouched. But his weariness and discouragement throbbed in the bond they shared.

He hurried to her, drawing power from the fog and expanding the barrier to cover them both. "I don't know how to counter this."

"I have an idea. Say the words from the vision."

His momentary doubt flicked her, but he drew more power until he glowed a brilliant argent. When she reached for him, he clasped her hand. "Together, we're more," he said. "Feed power to me again."

She tried, and shared power flowing through her surged, singing in her blood and filling her with light until she felt like living silver. It rippled outward from her and Richard, forcing the wraiths back from it like a battering ram.

Richard glanced at her. "Far more," he said with a smile.

Flame boiled around their magic barrier but left them unscathed. The dragon roared. It took one stride toward them, and then another.

Richard released her. He stepped clear of their wall with his sword raised, his shield high, and their joined power humming in the bond they shared.

"Your time is done," he said, his voice ringing with power. "The untruths and evils you nurtured shall not prevail but pass away. They are but the shades of night, and we are the heralds of day."

"We?" Miranda asked.

"You're here for a reason. I can't destroy him with my power alone." Richard planted his feet. With both hands locked around the hilt, he pointed his sword at Wyndon, and that same argent power shot from it, spinning a brilliant cocoon around the dragon.

She drew magic from the fog, and he pulled it along their bond, into him, and then funneled it to join the cocoon until it glowed sun-bright. Miranda squinted against the light. Abruptly, the cocoon dropped. Wyndon stood alone, unarmored and staggering.

Richard charged. Wyndon formed a sword in time to slash at him. Richard ducked, then stabbed him through the heart.

Wyndon collapsed, his body shimmering. It thinned until Miranda could see fog through it, and then it disappeared.

"Gone," Richard said. "To whatever hell awaits him."

His sword and bloodied armor melted away, and he turned toward her. Deep lines of fatigue marked his face, but his eyes held satisfaction and relief.

She ran to him. He lowered his head for a long, deep, hard kiss. When he raised his head again, he smiled. "You, my lady, never cease to amaze me."

Laughter rolled out of the fog, and Edmund followed it. "She saved your life, lad. She's a worthy countess, indeed."

Frowning, Richard said, "Headstrong, too," but his eyes twinkled in his weary face. "What happened, Edmund? I feared he'd destroyed you."

Edmund shrugged. "As I have power over the perpetually damned, the living must have power over me. He banished me but couldn't destroy me. After all, I'm already dead."

Richard released her. Solemnly, he offered his right hand to Edmund. "You've now saved my life twice, helped me here, and guarded my lady. I forgive you."

Edmund blinked. His mouth opened and closed. Finally, he managed, "Thank you, lad."

Ignoring the outstretched hand, he embraced his grandson. Richard returned the embrace.

The two men stood locked together for a long moment before Edmund stepped back. "Now be off with you," he said. "The living don't belong here."

"I hate to be the sour in the cream," Miranda said, "but did killing Wyndon here truly solve the problem?"

Richard and Edmund frowned, looking so similar that she ached for their long estrangement. Shadowed with regret, Richard's eyes sought hers. "I saw him in the Pendragon library, taking the scroll I found at his house. From it, he learned to contact the dead and to come here."

"So taking it before he can will fix the timeline?" she asked.

"If we go back in time and take it before he does, or better yet, before he first sees it," Richard said, "everything should go back the way it was." He swayed and shook his head as though to clear it.

"You need food and rest, lad," Edmund stated, frowning.

"Soon enough," Richard muttered. "First we've a job to do."

Putting the past to rights, he meant. The coming loss of him weighed on Miranda's heart like a boulder.

With a look that said he knew the words were inadequate, he added, "I'm sorry."

Everything would go back. Everything.

There would be no need for a warning vision of a dragon and a boar, no ill wind. No summons that brought him to her.

She and Richard would never have met.

Miranda drew a slow, painful breath. At last, she said, "We have no choice."

Richard drew her close, and she held him tightly. His breath made his chest rise and fall against her cheek. His heartbeat thumped faintly by her ear. At least he was alive.

"I'm sorry, love," he repeated.

"I know. So am I." She kissed his shoulder. "We need to find some food, for us both but especially for you. I can feel how weary you are."

"I'm not completely spent," Richard insisted.

If he could see how drawn and tired he looked, he would agree with her.

He kissed the top of her head, and his hand caressed her back. *A little longer*, he thought to her, his heart heavy. *We'll have a little more time together.*

Yes, my heart. Swallowing against grief to come, she asked, "Having died here, will Wyndon exist in the restored timeline? If he doesn't, wouldn't that change history, too?"

He shrugged. "So far as I know, no living person ever died here before. But if we put everything back the way it should've been, he will never have been here at all, never had the chance to die here."

Miranda shook her head. All these possibilities threatened to make her eyes cross.

"We'll just have to see," Richard said. "I found that I could pass through the wards on the protector's chambers and eavesdrop." With a glance at Edmund, he added, "Must be one of those things the living can do but the dead cannot. Anyway, I learned he didn't tell his son how to breach the barrier. Wyndon probably feared being overthrown."

"What a treacherous family," Miranda muttered.

Richard nodded. "Too true, love. As near as I can tell, Wyndon always disliked Richard Cromwell—held him in contempt for being so inept. He once said the Gifted should have seized power in the confusion and disorganization after Oliver died. Young Wyndon ingratiated himself with Oliver after his son's death, so that he was named Oliver's heir. His older self probably counted on that when he went back to kill Richard Cromwell."

Edmund's face brightened. "While you're fixing things, you could save the lads in the Tower. Avoid the curse altogether. Free everyone."

She and Richard glanced at each other. As though she'd confirmed his doubts, the brief flash of hope in his heart flickered out.

Grim-faced, he turned to Edmund. "Having the boys live instead of die would create more changes. Lead to more chaos. We have no right."

"Richard," Edmund began. "For the sake of justice—"

"No. Chaos has prevailed these past weeks. Any change ripples ever wider. If we do as you ask, some people will live who didn't before. Others will die. Who should or shouldn't live has nothing to do with it. Who are we to decide that?"

Edmund scowled. "We are men with a duty to right the wrong I committed."

Richard's arm tightened around Miranda, almost as though he needed her belief in him for support. "By saving the boys in the Tower, we injure other innocents, perhaps thousands. That doesn't balance the scale. It's wrong. I won't do it."

"I can't intervene," Edmund said. "Only you can go back to save King

Richard's nephews and free us all. Free the children you hope to have, Richard."

Richard held Edmund's gaze. After a moment, he spoke in an even voice. "If their mother can bear the risk to them, so can I."

"She may not be their mother," Edmund snapped.

"If she isn't, no one will be."

Her hand rested against his chest. Beneath the linen, his heart beat steadily with a pain that racked both their souls. Suddenly, hope flashed through him, resonating in the bond.

"Your confession," he said to Edmund. "It burned in the early 1600s. Saving it wouldn't change anything, especially if we don't produce it until the present time. It'll end the curse, but that won't affect anyone living."

"An excellent notion." Edmund beamed at him. "You'll find it in a leather case beneath the hearthstone in the Hawkstowe muniments room."

"Muniments?" Miranda asked.

Richard replied, "Important family documents. Other valuables tend to wind up there, too." He slid an arm around her. "We've mischief to undo, my lady."

"I've been thinking about that missing book," she said. "Where could you put something so no one could ever return it to its rightful owner?"

"You'd need a place no one knew about. Or could reach if they did." His eyes lit. "Edmund, pray excuse us."

Richard held out his hand to her. When she grasped it, the grip felt warm and firm and alive. She smiled at him. At least they had each other for a little longer, even though they were in this nasty place.

They walked together into the mists. "Where are we going?" Miranda asked.

"I hope, to the *Chronicle*. Once the dead arrive here, they don't care about anything in the world behind, and the living, in theory, can't enter this realm. If they did, they'd have no reason to find the place I seek."

"You were destined to come here, and Wyndon knew it."

"I couldn't leave if I were dead, and he thought no one else living could come. Once I arrived, I'd hardly seek out the place that symbolizes what the curse denies me."

Miranda raised an eyebrow. "That portal of judgment you mentioned? The one the curse blocks you from entering?"

"Yes. It's the passage from this world to the last. If reaching it's like seeking anything else here, we have only to think of it and we'll find ourselves heading toward it. If Wyndon put the *Chronicle* there, the portal is a landmark that would help him find it faster."

He walked a few steps in silence. "Besides, it's time I faced all of this fully. I need to see the portal."

Through the mists ahead, something glowed. The portal? They hurried forward.

The glow brightened. The sulphurous vapors dispersed, revealing a tall, pointed arch three times the thickness of her body. Twice Richard's height, the plain golden structure cast a sunny light on their faces. Golden mist shimmering within it obscured any view beyond the arch. The dank, purple-gray vapors of the afterworld wafted around and above it.

Richard stopped, staring at it. Disappointment shadowed his eyes and whispered in their bond. "I hoped to see past it," he said, "even if I can never go."

"One day, you will," she insisted. "Once we retrieve that confession, there's nothing to stop you."

He brushed his fingers against the shimmering surface, but they didn't pass through. "I hear a bell. I feel it ... in my soul. And a voice, saying, 'For you, not yet.'"

"That might mean we'll succeed, the 'yet' part."

"It may say that because I'm not dead yet. Touch it, love. It won't hurt."

She poked carefully. The fog in the archway looked misty but felt deceptively firm. How strange, but the words resonating in her heart brought no comfort. "It said, 'For you, not yet.' Mayhap that doesn't mean anything except that we're alive."

"Ah, well. As you say, perhaps that's a good sign." He turned away, and she felt the effort he made to keep his spirits up. "Let's see if there's a 'behind' to it."

He tripped over something and knelt, groping in the fog. "Something leathery. A big book. Ah-ha."

Standing, he held the object clear of the fog. The reeking vapors had spotted the leather folio but otherwise not hurt it. He unbuckled the straps and opened it. Ornate script covered the parchment within.

He leafed through the pages, then stopped abruptly. "It's a listing of the Croyland abbots. Then it picks up with events of 1453." When he raised his head, triumph shone in his eyes. "This is the missing volume of the *Chronicle*. Let's see if it holds the clues Kit mentioned."

Miranda peered over his shoulder, but the cramped, ornate writing was difficult to read.

"Here it is," he said, "Sixteenth February, 1463, the date Wyndon had jotted down, and the heresy trial of one Brother Ignatius of Croyland."

His eyes skimmed over the page. "Interesting. Listen to this. *When past and future are rent in twain, you cannot weave them whole again. To restore the future that should be true, you must rend the fabric of time anew.* Or so poor Ignatius claimed."

"That seems to confirm that we're right to take the scroll before Wyndon finds it. That's making another change, rending time again."

"Indeed." Glancing over the page, Richard said, "Looks like some of them were trying to say he was insane, but he claimed to have walked the path of death with a foot in life on either side. That's the same description I saw in an old scroll about theories of traveling time at Pendragon."

"Do you think this monk actually traveled time?"

"I don't know. He certainly seems to think he did, looking at this."

"Is there anything else useful?"

"Let's see. There's a bit about making a gateway, but it doesn't explain how." He skimmed further. "Hmm. This is strange, another excerpt from his heretical writings. *If one alive twice in a time should meet himself, only one surviveth. The one belonging in that time absorbeth the other as a cloth doth draw water.*"

"So if we go to past eras to fix things, we'd best not meet ourselves?" Miranda guessed.

"It seems so. If Wyndon went back to kill Richard Cromwell, he must not have encountered his younger self."

"Is there anything about necromancy or wraiths?"

He read further before answering. "There doesn't seem to be anything here that explains how to cross the barrier or trap a wraith. Nothing on necromancy. So the *Chronicle* won't lead anyone here without that scroll on necromancy. It's safe to put the *Chronicle* back."

Richard ran a hand through his hair. "Let's see how Jeremy and the others are doing."

They walked through the sulphurous fog until the sanctuary of the abbey appeared. Its walls still glowed with warding.

Miranda said, "Our friends are still trapped, but now without Wyndon as a hostage."

"Their enemies don't know that. Still, we'd best hurry to put things

319

right," Richard said. "I don't want to risk their deaths, even deaths that will soon come undone."

"Nor do I," Miranda agreed. Even though that meant bringing their precious time together to an end that much faster.

Richard kissed her. The arm not holding the book whipped around her and drew her close. Miranda slid her arms around his waist and tightened her hold. When he raised his head, he cupped her cheek gently.

"Some part of me," he said quietly, "will always belong to you."

"As I will to you," she promised, brushing his hair off his face.

"We don't need to put this book back," he said quietly. "Taking the necromancy scroll will do that. Until then, it'll be safe here."

When she nodded, he set the leather volume down beside the portal and grasped her hand. They took one step together before he stumbled.

Miranda pulled him to a stop. The burst of energy he'd gotten from discovering the *Chronicle* had faded. His face looked drawn with fatigue.

"How many times will you need to enter and leave this place to put things right? Once out and back in to take that scroll, and the same for Edmund's confession? Can you do all that?"

He hesitated. Grudgingly, he said, "I doubt it. Not without food and rest. I also need to find an anchor, since we'll eventually have to leave here separately, step into the world and let our other selves absorb us, I suppose. Unless the time changes rolling forward take care of that for us. If they do, we'll simply disappear from here."

Perhaps never to meet again. Or know they ever had met. Fighting despair, she leaned into him.

Miranda had never realized the sound of another person's breathing could be painful. She lay in the darkness of a curtained bed and the warmth of Richard's embrace. They were safe. For now. But every breath he drew reminded her that those she would hear him draw were numbered.

They had no money to pay for food or a place to stay in the living world, so Richard had brought her to a place where he owned everything, Hawkstowe Manor. Because he wasn't in residence, there were few servants in the house, all of them asleep in the gatehouse.

His time in the shadowland and the effort of returning from it had left him weary and almost dazed. They had raided the larder, sharing the makeshift meal of meat, cheese, bread, and wine in his chamber, and then he'd brought her to his bed.

"This is where the Earl and Countess of Hawkstowe belong," he'd said sleepily.

It was also, she realized, the bed she'd Seen them share in the vision. Did that mean they'd share it again? Or was this the only time?

She lifted her head to peer through the bed curtains, and Richard's arms tightened possessively in his sleep.

Nestling into his side again, she tried to memorize the way his bare body felt, the bay scent of his skin with faint hints of sweat, and the rhythm of his breathing. If only she could keep the memory of this closeness, even if she didn't remember him, it would comfort her.

Surely she would have that. The two of them deserved that much.

But what people deserved usually had little to do with what they got.

Richard sighed. His hand moved down her arm, and his growing awareness prickled across their bond. "Mmm, you're so warm," he murmured.

"So are you," she whispered. She kissed his chest.

With a groan, he rolled above her and claimed her mouth in a deep, passionate kiss. She ran her hands over his broad shoulders, down his back to his taut buttocks. The thought of losing him hurt so that she couldn't breathe.

"Don't," he said softly against her neck. Pain that matched hers vibrated between them. "Don't think of it now, wife. For now, just know how much I love you."

Tears welled in her eyes, but she held him closer. "And how much I love you. How right you feel above me. How complete I feel when you join with me."

He raised his head to wipe her tears away, and his eyes were suspiciously bright in the dim light. His lips brushed gently over hers. "We must go, sweet. Much as I'd rather stay here with you, people are suffering. We've a duty to perform."

"I know." She kissed him quickly and made herself climb out of bed. Together, they dressed in silence.

~

A short time later, Miranda and Richard stepped into the afterworld, heading for Pendragon Manor. The wraiths attacked but couldn't even begin to penetrate the magical shielding she and Richard created together. The creatures soon gave up and sought easier prey.

First, Richard guided her to the day Wyndon stole the necromancy scroll. Going back from there to the day he first found it, then to the day before, was simple.

Richard slipped into the library and brought the scroll back to the shadowland. "Such an innocent-looking thing," he said, "to be the source of so much trouble."

"I hate to destroy any source of magical knowledge," Miranda said, "but that scroll is simply too dangerous."

"I agree." In a burst of purple-tinted, magical flame, he destroyed the scroll. Flecks of ash drifted into the knee-high fog that hid the shadowy ground.

"It's odd," Richard said, "that Wyndon and Edmund were both watching the Golden Swan's yard from the afterworld but Edmund didn't see Wyndon. Nor did Wyndon and I see each other in the afterworld when I watched him take the scroll. But he entered the library from here."

"Maybe it's something to do with traveling time. But that wouldn't explain the inn yard."

"We'll ask Edmund," Richard said. "I wonder, though, if it has to do with something Kit mentioned, about traveling currents in time."

Miranda nodded, "Let's go find Edmund."

"There is a chance," Richard said, clasping her hand as they walked. "If we're outside time when the change ripples through, we might remember."

"But won't staying here longer change things, too?"

"Not if we make certain we return to the world before we met. I hope." He kissed her brow.

"I hope so, too."

"Will Edmund forgive you—or me—for not saving the boys in the Tower?" she asked.

"In time, perhaps he'll realize one wrong cannot make up for another. At least Kit and Cabot and Grandmère should be alive. If we successfully undid everything, Wyndon should be alive, too."

Miranda nodded. There was no way to be certain what would happen. They'd done what they believed was right, at least.

Richard said, "Now let's see to the confession. It burned in a fire on November second, 1605, at Hawkstowe. We'll go to the fire and then the day before it."

They walked through the stinking fog until he said, "This should be it."

They emerged in a round room with walls of plastered stone and a narrow window. Wooden chests of various sizes, gold and silver plate and goblets, and miscellaneous axes, daggers and swords lay around the room.

Richard grabbed a dagger from a nearby table to pry up the hearth-stone. He set the stone aside and raised stricken eyes to her. The space underneath it was empty.

~

Unfortunately, Edmund knew nothing about why his confession had vanished. Miranda and Richard looked back in time for it but found no trace. As though it had never been written.

"Perhaps someone screened magically stole it," Richard said, "even before you ever placed it there. Would that block your sight?"

"It could. But I wrote it. I know I did."

Quietly, Richard said, "Yet we cannot find it. Perhaps you only meant to write it, Edmund, or even thought you did. But if all else failed, we should be able to find it on the day you wrote it. Yet even that is beyond us."

"Hellfire," Edmund muttered. He scrubbed a hand over his face.

Richard asked, "Do you know how you or I could be in the shadow-land, in the same place as Wyndon, and not see him, nor he, us?"

Edmund shook his head. "I watched you talk by the welling Dover. If Wyndon was in the yard, mayhap if he traveled time, he and I would not have been ... in the same current of time. Nor he and you when you went back to see the results of his earlier trip back to the library because you started from different places, as men may travel two smaller rivers to reach the Thames."

Richard frowned. "That's all confusing."

"I'm only guessing," Edmund said. "We may never know for certain."

"I can live with that," Richard replied. He turned to Miranda. "Based on what the *Chronicle* said, if we step into the real world and meet ourselves, the versions of us who belong at that point in time will absorb us. With our memories of what's happened, if we're fortunate."

Edmund embraced each of them and kissed Miranda's forehead. "I hope you find each other again."

They bade him farewell and turned away.

"I want to see if the *Chronicle* is gone," Richard said.

He refused to admit to any hope of a change in the portal's message, but that had to be his reason for going again. That was fine with her. She too wanted to hear something different.

"I don't understand," Miranda admitted as they walked to the judgment portal. "How can something like the confession be gone, and we can't find it? Edmund can't? This place touches all times and places."

"There's much about it we don't know."

The portal glowed in the darkness, drawing them. When they reached it, Richard knelt beside it and felt in the fog. "No *Chronicle*. We'll check on it to be sure, but I believe it must be where it belongs. If I think of it, the magic here will lead me to it, no matter which realm it's in."

"So the corrections are rolling forward."

Sadness vibrated between them. Richard said, "But you've given me hope. As Jeremy tried to. I wonder ... "

He turned from her and ran a hand slowly down the portal. And froze. His eyes widened.

Miranda reached for him. Wild-eyed, he caught her to him.

"Richard? What—"

"Miranda—oh, love—touch it." Disbelief covered his face, but he tugged her hand, leading her toward the glowing arch.

A vision flashed through her mind—of Richard, older but recognizable, standing before the portal. The mists inside the archway parted before him, and she stood within its frame.

She brushed her fingertips over the golden surface. *Choose your fate* said a voice in her head.

Stunned, she turned to him. "Richard?"

"It said I could choose," he told her, looking dazed. "I saw that I could pass through. Not be trapped here. But no one else could." Their gazes met, and his firmed. "I can't—if I—we have sons, I can't abandon them."

"Nor can I." She swallowed hard. "Richard, it said I could choose, too. At least, I think that's what it meant." Looking up at him, she said, "I'll help you, before death or after, if I can—if I can only remember—"

The odds against that threatened to choke her. She buried her face in his shoulder, and his heartache rippled into her.

But they'd both been in the vision she'd Seen during the rite at his house. And in her dream with the baby. Was there hope? Or did those visions depend on the altered timeline?

"If we're outside time when the change ripples through," he said again, "we might remember. I hope." He kissed her brow.

"So do I."

"Everything related to Wyndon's plan was wrong history, so all that should go away and leave what should have been."

Together, they followed the pull of Richard's intention to the Cottonian library. The stolen volume of the *Croyland Chronicle* rested with its fellows on a large shelf. So that, too, was done. And their time was running out.

They watched time flow past in Dover. Miranda's real-world self carried trays and made beds and cleaned fireplaces. "I feel like a ghost," she said, "watching this."

"It's strange," he agreed. "You know, in your visions, I was the herald of day, but the title rightly belongs to you."

"My vision didn't lead us to the *Chronicle*, only to trouble."

"That trouble forced me to learn to travel the afterworld. Without that, we'd never have restored the timeline. Because of you, we saved England from Wyndon's darkness. You helped to defeat him and, if we're reading the portal right, as I think we are, brought me salvation."

He kissed her temple lightly. "That's the same as a new day, and we did it together."

"Together," she murmured, savoring the word.

They watched events flow past. "One day blends into the next," Miranda observed. "It's difficult to tell what day this is, but I think we're almost to the day of the hanging."

She drew his head down to kiss him. "I love you. No matter what happens, some part of me always will."

Long and deep and powerful, the kiss rolled through her. The strength of his body, the security of his arms, the passion in his kiss seared her heart. Somehow, she would imprint them on her soul.

Richard broke the kiss but held her tightly. "Remember Edmund's saying about seers, *A seer need not scry to See what is, what was, and what will be.* If that's true, your seer gift may help you remember."

His lips brushed her hair, and he added, "Surely one of us will remember something about all this."

"I hope so."

Her real-world self sat in a cart that rolled toward the hanging tree. "It's almost time," she said.

His eyes reflected her pain. If he kissed her again, she wouldn't have the strength to leave him.

She raised a hand to his face, only to have her fingers pass through him. His eyes widened as black spots danced in front of her eyes. The spots whirled into unrelieved blackness.

"I love you," he cried, his voice sounding desperate but far away, and then there was nothing.

CHAPTER 32

Miranda stumbled backward. She fell against the inn's cart. The driver, Elijah, leaned over her, his weathered face creased. "Miranda, are you ill?"

"No, just ... dizzy for a moment." She clung to the cart's side and shook her head to clear it. The world steadied, but strange images swirled through her mind. Men and dragons. Explosions. Knights.

Had she run mad?

The crowd was dispersing. Poor Mistress Smith's body hung limply from the tree. At least her torment was over.

"You're pale. Climb in and sit." Elijah offered her a hand to climb into the cart. "We'd best get you back to the inn."

"That sounds good."

He clucked to the horse, and the cart lurched into motion. Miranda stared at the familiar countryside without truly seeing it. All during the drive, the face of a man ran through her mind. He had dark hair and deep blue eyes that changed from stern to happy to pained to loving. Lying between her thighs, he kissed her naked breasts.

Her cheeks warmed. Heat pooled in her lower body, and she pushed the image aside. Best to tend to her work and worry about dreams later.

They arrived at the inn during supper service. Customers flooded the common room. She and the other maids carried trays and fetched drinks and answered questions. She didn't have time to worry about illusions.

As the meal service wound down, Miranda went out to the well for water. She had her hand on the windlass with the bucket nearly to the top when a man's deep voice said, "Allow me."

The voice was familiar. Miranda wheeled toward it. The tall, dark-haired man she'd daydreamed about stood in the twilight. But then he was gone.

She must've imagined him. Miranda rubbed her eyes, untied the bucket, and took the water into the inn.

Yet the man's face haunted her. She seemed to remember him from somewhere, remembered talking to him. In the inn yard. By the old Roman lighthouse at Dover Castle.

But she'd never been to the castle. How could she recognize the lighthouse?

Later, as she climbed to the garret with Lucy, the images swirled through her mind. She rubbed her brow. She was probably tired, confusing Grandmother's stories with life. Or distressed about the hanging today and dreaming up things that might've saved Agnes Smith.

Or saved Mother.

She undressed and climbed into her narrow bed. Sleep claimed her, and the mystery man walked in her dreams.

Rubbing her eyes, Miranda climbed out of bed. There was no use sleeping when dreams kept her from resting well, as they had for the past five nights. Last night's had been particularly intense, of the mystery man wearing armor and battling a black dragon while she and another man helped him.

To put time to rights sprang into her mind as she dressed.

What did that mean?

Mother had said she possessed the seer gift but hadn't been able to teach her much about it. Yet Miranda felt certain she could use a fire to scry—and where had she learned that word? Mother had never used it. The dreams a couple of nights ago, though, they'd been about learning to scry, learning from an older woman who was firm but kind.

All these dreams felt true, and her instincts had never steered her falsely. Then there was Mother's advice never to ignore a dream of power.

Faint light showed in the garret window, but the sky outside was mostly dark. The other maids slept.

Miranda started toward the kitchen, feeling her way down the back stairs in the darkness. The inn was silent around her, the guests still abed.

As she neared the bottom, light and the sounds of voices spilled from the kitchen. The scents of roasting beef and fresh, yeasty bread wafted upward.

When she stepped into the big, warm room, Owen, the brown-haired scullery lad, sat at the long table, eating porridge. Around him, cooks kneaded dough and roasted meat and stewed vegetables to start the day.

Miranda dished up a bowl of porridge for herself and took it to the corner near the hearth, where she would be both warm and out of the way. Perched on a low stool, she studied the fire. Could she scry with all the activity around her? Even more important, could she truly do it at all, or had the strange dream been only that?

Slowly, drawing on a feeling that might've been instinct or memory, she fed power to the flames under the meat jack. When each flicker of the flame, each sizzle of grease dropping onto the logs, resonated in her head, she envisioned the face of the woman who'd been in last night's dream.

A sixtyish woman with silvery hair in curls on either side of her face, sharp cheekbones, and keen, intelligent green eyes appeared in the flame. Wearing an oddly familiar, green dressing gown, she sat beside a hearth faced with beautiful blue-and-white tiles and ate a simple meal of meat, bread, and an oatcake.

This could be an illusion, but Miranda knew, as Mother had said she would, that it was real. This was happening now.

She swallowed a shout of exultation, and a name sprang to her mind, Arabella. Grandmère. Grandmother, but whose?

A face appeared in the flames, the mystery man's, with deep blue eyes and chiseled features. Familiar.

Richard.

Miranda's throat closed. Blinking back tears, fighting a strange mix of joy and uncertainty, she bowed her head over the porridge.

He was riding a black horse down a country lane, but where?

Flora, the cook, called, "You all right, Miranda? Somethin' wrong with the porridge?"

"Everything's quite all right," Miranda said, beaming up at the cook. "It's wonderful, really."

Flora blinked, probably not expecting such enthusiasm, but turned back to the bread she was kneading.

Spooning up porridge, Miranda looked again at the fire. Richard's image had vanished while she was distracted, but summoning it again was simple. Trying for a wider view, she saw the tall man riding beside him, a man whose sun-lightened hair and gray eyes also evoked a name, Cabot.

Memories came like a flood—London, Whitehall, Jeremy and Patience and Robin—and she almost dropped the bowl. Reeling with the force of the memories, she steadied herself against the stone fireplace.

The more she saw in the flames, the more her confidence grew. These people were her kindred.

Then she saw herself in bed, making love to the dark-haired man, to Richard. To her husband.

The world seemed to shift out from under her. The room seemed to close in on her.

She set her bowl on the hearth and bolted, rushing into the corridor and out the back door into the cold, foggy morning. The chilly air felt sharp and clean after the crowded kitchen.

Another vision flashed over her sight, herself standing high above a crowd, a noose around her neck. *Croyland* echoed in her brain, and she pushed it aside.

What was happening? Whatever these visions were, they rang with the power of being real.

Richard's face rose in her mind again, and love welled in her heart. She had to find him. He might know what was happening.

In one of her dreams, he'd said he was on the road from Portsmouth with Cabot when her dragon—whatever that meant—found him. Mayhap he was there now. Mayhap that was what she'd seen in her scrying this morning.

Wherever he was, he would return to London eventually. She'd Seen where he lived and knew how to find him there. While she didn't have enough money for the London coach, even if she rode on top, she could probably buy cheaper passage with one of the wagoners who regularly stopped here. Master Warren would help her choose someone trustworthy, and her instincts would surely guide her.

In the meantime, she would see what had happened to their friends— and to the author of all that trouble, Lord Wyndon.

More memories rushed in, intimate and detailed. Richard touching her. Herself glorying in that.

Miranda swallowed hard and locked her shaking hands together. No man had ever touched her that way, but she knew those feelings. She remembered them.

What she had shared with Richard was real, and now she ached to see him again.

Yet the prospect made her hands cold and her stomach fluttery. Only a fool would assume that would go well. Her seer gift had aided her in remembering all that had happened, but as best she could determine, he wasn't a seer.

What if he didn't still love her? Worse, what if he didn't even remember her?

~

"I don't see why you want to come to Dover," Cabot said as he and Richard walked their mounts down the Folkestone road. "If you're trying to delay our return to London so you can miss the White Rose banquet, just say so. I'll back you."

"I haven't been here in quite a while. I want to see it." To find the explanation for his strange dreams and the eerie, inner compulsion that led him here. "You can go ahead and report to the Admiralty about your refit."

"The Admiralty can wait a few days."

The conversation seemed familiar, but it was unlike Cabot to make the Admiralty wait. "You're unusually curious."

"You're unusually mercurial. I'd best come along in case you lose your wits altogether."

The half-timbered building by the lane ahead also seemed familiar, though Richard had no memory of coming here before. *The Golden Swan Inn*, the sign hanging out front read. Richard nodded to it. "Let's water the horses and eat."

"Might as well," Cabot said, and he turned Neptune to follow Zeus.

They rode through a short passage and into a wide inn yard. Galleries ran along the sides of the upper floor.

Four large wagons stood in the sunlit yard, their teams still hitched but wearing feed bags.

Opposite the entry, an open doorway spilled light and voices into the yard. That must be the public room.

Beside it, another passage led to a rear yard and a stable. They looked familiar. So did the well visible in the rear yard. Frowning, Richard dismounted.

"Richard?" Cabot leaned down from Neptune's back.

A dark-haired, pox-scarred woman walked across the rear yard in the afternoon light. He knew her, but who was she?

For a closer look, he summoned power. Her homely disguise turned translucent, like a reflection in a window pane.

And he had done this before. With her. His mouth went dry.

Richard thrust his reins at Cabot. "Hold these." Without waiting for a reply, he strode toward the far passage.

The woman knelt and patted a calico cat. With a last, smiling word to the animal, she rose and turned to the well.

Her eyes flicked toward him ... but not away. She froze in place, her face pale.

A name sprang into his head. "Miranda?"

Her cheeks flushed. With a gasp, she ran toward him.

He started to reach for her, but a flood of memories came with her, a jumble. Standing still, he tried to sort it. God's feet, who was she?

She halted before him, the joy dying out of her eyes. Her disappointment echoed somewhere inside him.

What in blazes?

"You don't remember," she said quietly.

"I ... don't know. I remember something, just ... It's confusing."

"Yes, it is." She bit her lip, hands clenching in her skirt. "Did you dream of me?"

When he nodded, some of the wariness faded from her expression. She said, "You once told me, *A seer need not scry to See what is, what was, and what will be.* Do you remember that?"

"I ... almost," he ground out. The memories were surging now. Rushing forward. "You're a seer? You are. You're ... "

His wife?

How was that possible?

"Yes." Cautiously, she reached a hand toward his face. She touched him, and awareness flooded from her into him, the rush of memories sorting themselves. They were things that had happened but should not have.

Yet here he was, with her.

Richard grinned. *Yes,* he thought. *Oh, yes.*

Yes, indeed, came back to him on exultant wings.

She flung herself into his arms and rained kisses over his face until he caught her mouth in a long, deep celebration.

This time, forever, he promised her silently.

Beaming, she pulled her head back to look up at him. "I love you. Always." She laid her palm against his cheek.

"I love you, too." He laughed down at her. "We'll need to marry again. This time, we'll do it in fine style."

"I don't care how it's done, so long as we wed." She locked her arms around his waist, and all the confusion of the past days fell away.

The slow *clip-clop* of hooves sounded behind Richard, and Cabot rode through the passageway on Neptune, leading Zeus.

With a bemused smile, Cabot said, "There must be a good tale to explain this."

Miranda flashed Richard a mischievous look. "Good day, Captain Winfield. I cannot tell you how glad I am to see you again."

"Again?" he repeated, frowning.

A man in rough work clothes hurried from the stable. "I can take your mounts, sirs."

He must be an ostler. As Cabot dismounted and passed him the reins, the man asked, "Are ye staying the night, sirs?"

"We're not sure yet," Richard said, eyeing Miranda and feeling her happiness resonate between them.

"As ye like." The ostler tugged his forelock and departed with the horses.

Keeping one arm around Miranda, Richard smiled at his perplexed friend. "Cabot, meet Mistress Miranda Willoughby, my once and future wife."

EPILOGUE

Hawkstowe Manor, Cumberland
One year later

Miranda carefully lifted Robert Edmund Mainwaring, Viscount Ambleside, from his cradle. Smoothing her sleeping babe's christening gown with one hand, she smiled up at Richard.

"A big day for our lad," she told him.

"Yes." He gently stroked the babe's round cheek with one finger. "I want to protect him from everything. I hope we've done as we should, love."

By having him at all, Richard meant. Miranda leaned into her husband's side. "My Sight gives me no guidance on the future of the curse, but I have faith that all will be well. We'll give him and any other babes we have a good life."

She dropped her forehead to his shoulder for a moment. "What will be, will be. We must make the best of it."

"As you've always done." He squeezed her waist. What the portal had told them that last time had deepened his hope. It would have to be enough.

"I checked on Wyndon," Richard said, lowering his voice. "Still no sign of his traveling the afterworld. Edmund is keeping an eye on him, too."

The step-thump rhythm on the rush matting out in the hall signaled Grandmère's approach. She walked with a cane now but was as energetic and interested in everything as ever.

And she was alive, a fact both Miranda and Richard cherished daily.

"Your guests are here," Grandmère told them as she walked into the room. She smiled at the sleeping baby. "I sent them into the chapel, where they're all waiting for the honored guest. Don't be long. Jeremy should be ready for us by now. He seems very excited about performing the baptism." She turned and made her way out of the room.

"We should go down," Richard said. He offered Miranda his arm.

"Is Edmund here?" she asked.

"He was but left for the chapel." Richard grinned. "He still hasn't gotten over his delight at having our Robin bear his name, too."

"It seemed only fitting," Miranda said.

She and Richard walked together down the stairs and into the old Great Hall, where one of the four long tables was set with fine linen. They'd decided to keep the christening celebration small so they could have it here, in the place they both loved.

George had come, too. Richard's marriage had made him realize he shouldn't count on being the heir, that he would have to make a place for himself on his own. He'd stopped drinking, though it hadn't been easy, and now managed one of Richard's manors in Devonshire.

Kit had come from Northumberland with his new bride, and Cabot was home from the West Indies for the winter. Having everyone here made this day doubly special.

Richard held the heavy oak door for her and their son. Across the dirt-packed courtyard lay the ancient chapel. Jeremy stood in the doorway in a black cassock with a white surplice over it and prayer bands around his neck. A long, narrow black scarf lay across his shoulders with its ends hanging down in front. He smiled at them.

"Let's give our son his official start in life," Richard said.

The baby sighed, as though he heard, and Miranda chuckled. "He couldn't have a better gathering on this day."

Together, she and Richard walked into the sunlight with their boy.

The End

The Boar King's Honor Trilogy will continue with The Steel Rose, coming in 2020 from Falstaff Books!

MORE ABOUT RICHARD III AND THE MAINWARING CURSE

I've been interested in the controversy surrounding Richard III most of my adult life. A college classmate gave me a copy of Josephine Tey's *The Daughter of Time*, and that book reminded me that getting one's history from a playwright, even one so well known as Master Shakespeare, isn't always wise.

Since then, I've read widely about King Richard and his nephews. Turning over what I read, playing "what if," one of my favorite games, led me to write this book and its siblings in the trilogy.

I don't think the historical evidence supports the traditional view of Richard III as a power-mad, murderous hunchback. While I would never say that it's impossible for him to have murdered his nephews, I haven't seen anything that convinces me unequivocally that he did, and without that proof, I believe he's entitled to the benefit of the doubt.

No one knows for sure what happened to Edward IV's sons. I chose the Duke of Buckingham as the culprit in the murders because he fit my story scenario. He was also one of the earliest alternative suspects to cross my horizon. He rebelled against Richard III in 1483, around the time the two boys disappeared from the Tower, and there was no parliamentary act declaring that the duke should sit on the throne. He arguably had more of a motive to do away with them than King Richard did.

The *Titulus Regius* was a real act of parliament declaring that Richard III was the rightful king. Henry VII really did order all copies burned unread. The *Croyland Chronicle* did set forth the text. Two sets of bones were found under a staircase at the Tower of London in 1674. Those bones are now interred in Henry VII's beautiful chapel in Westminster Abbey.

Whether the bones actually are the remains of Edward IV's sons, however, is open to debate. Modern scientists have taken issue with the forensic examination of the 1930s, and the Crown refuses permission for an examination with modern DNA techniques.

The theory I've always liked was that Richard III had the boys spirited out of the country as the threat of Henry Tudor's invasion loomed. I first read this in *The Mystery of the Princes* by Audrey Williamson, but there are many books proposing other theories. Matthew Lewis's *The Survival of the Princes in the Tower* examines a wide range of theories about the boys' fates, and his biography of Richard III, *Loyalty Binds Me*, explores the king's life, particularly the early years, in a way that does not cast him in the most villainous possible light.

Modern historians range all along the spectrum of opinion from those who think Shakespeare had it pretty much right to those who think pretty much every wrong laid at Richard III's feet is bogus. That's part of the fun of reading about this and weighing the different arguments.

For more information, check the websites of the various Richard III Society branches around the world. You can also find an essay on my website, https://www.nancynorthcott.com/me-and-richard-iii/.

Meanwhile, in the world of fiction, the Mainwarings' quest to lift their family curse continues in *The Steel Rose*, which is set during the Napoleonic Wars. You can find more information here: http://www. nancynorthcott.com/the-steel-rose/

AFTERWORD

Thank you for reading *The Herald of Day*. I hope you enjoyed it. If you're inclined to leave a review on an online vendor site, I would appreciate it. Just be aware that any pop-up review option at the end of the book will not show up on the site.

There's information on my website (http://www.nancynorthcott.com) about how to obtain signed cards showing the covers of my books and short stories. I don't keep addresses, so asking for a cover card won't get you on any mailing list. If you're interested, here is the URL http://www.nancynorthcott.com/for-e-book-readers/.

If you'd like me to keep you posted about new releases, you can sign up for my newsletter on the right-hand sidebar of my homepage. Just go to www.nancynorthcott.com. I never share your email. Newsletters come out only when I have a new release or other important news, so you'll hear from me just a few times a year.

Thanks again!

ACKNOWLEDGMENTS

This book is one I've had in my head and played around with for a long time. I had encouragement and help, which ranged from brainstorming to research assistance to feedback from a number of people. The Mystery Mavens, Paula Connolly, Dawn Cotter, Terry Hoover, Susan Luck, Cathy Pickens, Mary Tribble, and Ann Wicker, were part of the early development of this project.

Nancy Knight and Patricia Rice were among the first people to like this story. Along with the late A.C. Crispin, they encouraged me to get it out into the world. The DC2K Writers also urged me not to forget this book, which was my introduction to them in A.C. Crispin's Advanced Writing Workshop at Dragon Con. Debbie Yutko provided invaluable feedback.

The Brinker Group, Paul Barrett, Dennis Carrigan, Sandy Hill, and Ed McKeown, also helped refine the concepts for this book and its world.

The authors of Avocat Noir, Jeanne Adams, Donna MacMeans, and Cassondra Murray, were always willing to kick ideas around, and I had essential feedback from Linda Ayers, Jeanne Adams, Wendy Felker, Van Garrison, Rae Latte, Cassondra Murray, Berta Platas, Michele Roper, Gerri Russell, Susan Sey, and Ann Wicker.

The members' library of the Richard III Society, American Branch, was a wonderful resource in this book's early days.

The Romance Bandits are an indispensable source of supportive comments and/or kicks in the pants, whichever is needed at the moment. Anna Sugden and her husband, a/k/a Doc Cambridge, fed my Richard III interest by toting me to various sites, all of which are way cooler than they were when I first visited them more than a decade ago.

Sherri Smith graciously shared her M.A. thesis on witchcraft trials in seventeenth-century England along with her research materials.

PJ Ausdenmore stepped in to help on short notice and gave me important advice. Even though I didn't use any actual Portuguese phrases, Eilis Flynn was generous with her knowledge of the language.

Andrew Nunn helped with my research in London. Jules Langley went with me to Dover to scope out locations for this book and one of its sequels. Rob Rundle wandered London with me looking at various locations.

I always appreciate the help of my agent, Beth Miller, who supports my writing in all its forms. I'm also grateful to John Hartness, Melissa McArthur, and the team at Falstaff Books for giving *The Herald of Day* and its siblings a home.

Lyndsey Lewellen created this gorgeous cover.

I'm a history and fantasy geek and a research nerd, among other things, and my husband freely admits he knew this when he married me. He has tramped through castles and battlefields, carried home suitcases full of books, and remained ready to consult on anything I might be mulling over, all without complaint. He and our son always wanted me to put this book out in the world. *The Herald of Day* would still be a "someday" project without their ongoing support and encouragement. Thanks, guys!

FALSTAFF BOOKS

Want to know what's new & coming soon from
Falstaff Books?

Join our Newsletter List
& Get this Free Ebook Sampler
with work from:
John G. Hartness
A.G. Carpenter
Bobby Nash
Emily Lavin Leverett
Jaym Gates
Darin Kennedy
Natania Barron
Edmund R. Schubert
& More!

http://www.subscribepage.com/q0j0p3

ABOUT THE AUTHOR

Nancy Northcott's childhood ambition was to grow up and become Wonder Woman. Around fourth grade, she realized it was too late to acquire Amazon genes, but she still loved comic books, science fiction, fantasy, history and YA romance. A sucker for fast action and wrenching emotion, she combines the magic and high stakes she loves in the books she writes.

A highlight of Nancy's college years was the summer she spent studying Tudor and Stuart Britain at the University of Oxford. She has written freelance articles and taught at the college level. Her most popular course was on science fiction, fantasy, and society. She has given presentations on Richard III and the Wars of the Roses to college classes studying Shakespeare's *Richard III*.

Married since 1987, Nancy and her husband have one son, a bossy dog, and a house full of books.

For more information about Nancy and her books, check out http://www.nancynorthcott.com.

You can also connect with Nancy on social media:
Facebook: https://www.facebook.com/nancynorthcottauthor
Twitter: https://twitter.com/NancyNorthcott
Goodreads: https://www.goodreads.com/Nancy_Northcott
Pinterest: http://www.pinterest.com/nancynorthcott/

ALSO BY NANCY NORTHCOTT

Fantasy

The Boar King's Honor Trilogy:

The Herald of Day

The Steel Rose (forthcoming)

The King's Champion (forthcoming)

Science Fiction

The New Badge in the *Welcome to Outcast Station* anthology

Scorpions for Christmas in the *Christmas on Outcast Station* anthology

Romantic Spy Adventure

The Deathbrew Affair

Romantic Suspense

Danger's Edge, an Arachnid Files novella in the anthology *Capitol Danger*

www.ingramcontent.com/pod-product-compliance
Lightning Source LLC
Chambersburg PA
CBHW031611100726

47898CB00006B/1745